EMPIRE OF SILVER

Also by Conn Iggulden

The Emperor Series

The Gates of Rome
The Death of Kings
The Field of Swords
The Gods of War

The Conqueror Series

*Wolf of the Plains**
Lords of the Bow
Bones of the Hills

Blackwater

By Conn Iggulden and Hal Iggulden

The Dangerous Book for Boys
The Dangerous Book for Boys Yearbook

By Conn Iggulden and David Iggulden

The Dangerous Book of Heroes

*Published in the USA as *Genghis: Birth of an Empire*

THE CONQUEROR SERIES

EMPIRE OF SILVER

Conn Iggulden

HarperCollins*Publishers*

HarperCollins*Publishers*
77–85 Fulham Palace Road,
Hammersmith, London W6 8JB
www.harpercollins.co.uk

Published by HarperCollins*Publishers* 2010

1

A catalogue record for this book
is available from the British Library

ISBN: 978 000 728800 7

This novel is entirely a work of fiction.
The names, characters and incidents portrayed in it are
the work of the author's imagination. Any resemblance to
actual persons, living or dead, events or localities is
entirely coincidental.

Typeset in Minion by Palimpsest Book Production Limited,
Grangemouth, Stirlingshire

Printed and bound in Great Britain by
Clays Ltd, St Ives plc

Mixed Sources
Product group from well-managed
forests and other controlled sources
www.fsc.org Cert no. SW-COC-001806
© 1996 Forest Stewardship Council

FSC is a non-profit international organisation established
to promote the responsible management of the world's forests.
Products carrying the FSC label are independently certified
to assure consumers that they come from forests that are managed
to meet the social, economic and ecological needs
of present and future generations.

Find out more about HarperCollins and the environment at
www.harpercollins.co.uk/green

To Katie Espiner

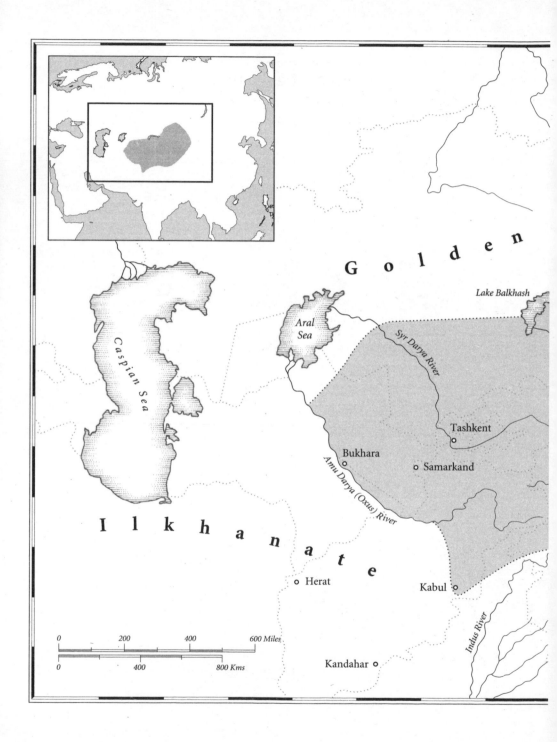

Golden

Lake Balkhash

Aral
Sea

Syr Darya River

Caspian Sea

Tashkent

Bukhara

Samarkand

Amu Darya (Oxus) River

Ilkhanate

Herat

Kabul

Indus River

0   200   400   600 Miles

0   400   800 Kms

Kandahar

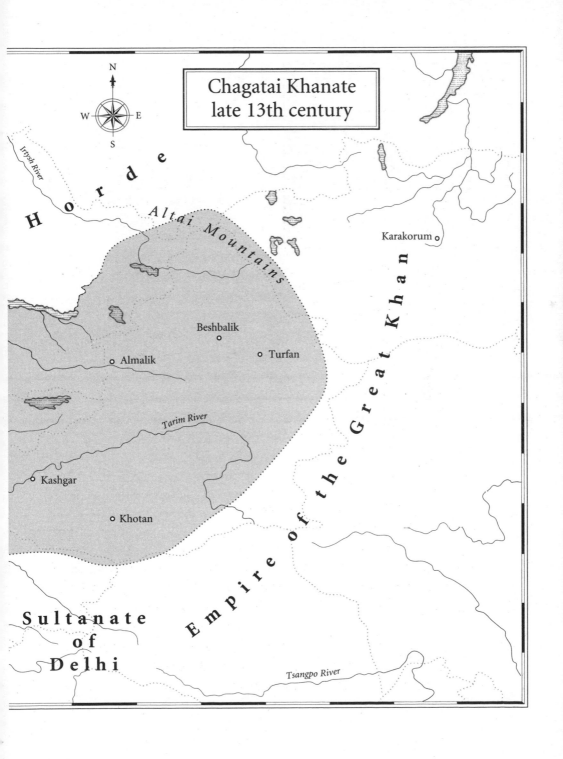

Chagatai Khanate
late 13th century

PROLOGUE

He trudged through a landscape of gers, like grubby shells on the shore of some ancient sea. Poverty was all around him: in the yellowing felt, patched and repaired endlessly over generations. Scrawny kid goats and sheep ran bleating around his feet as he approached his home. Batu stumbled over the animals, cursing as water slopped from the heavy buckets. He could smell pungent urine in the air, a sourness that had been missing from the breeze over the river. Batu frowned to himself at the thought of the day he had spent digging a toilet pit for his mother. He had been as excited as a child when he showed the results of his labour. She had merely shrugged, saying she was too old to go so far in the night, when good ground was all around her.

She was thirty-six years old, already broken by sickness and the years passing. Her teeth had rotted in her lower jaw and she walked like a woman twice her age, bent over and limping. Yet she was still strong enough to slap him on the rare occasions

1

Batu mentioned his father. The last time had been just that morning, before he began the trek to the river.

At the door of her ger, he eased the buckets down and rubbed his sore hands, listening. Inside, he could hear her humming some old song from her youth and he smiled. Her anger would have vanished as quickly as always.

He was not afraid of her. In the last year, he had grown in height and strength to the point where he could have stopped every blow, but he did not. He bore them without understanding her bitterness. He knew he could have held her hands, but he did not want to see her weep, or worse to see her beg or barter a skin of airag to ease her misery. He hated those times, when she used the drink to hammer herself into oblivion. She told him then that he had his father's face and that she could not bear to look at him. There had been many days when he had cleaned her himself, her arms flopping over his back, her flat breasts against his chest as he used a cloth and bucket to scrub the filth from her skin. He had sworn many times he would never touch airag himself. Her example made even the smell of it hard on his stomach. When its sweetness was combined with vomit, sweat and urine, it made him retch.

Batu looked up when he heard the horses, grateful for anything that would keep him outside a little longer. The group of riders was small by the standards of a tuman, barely twenty horsemen. To a boy brought up on the edges of the camp, it was a glorious sight for a morning, a different world.

The warriors rode with very straight backs and, from a distance, they seemed to radiate strength and authority. Batu envied them, even as he ached to be one of their number. Like any other boy of the gers, he knew that their red and black armour meant they were Ogedai's own Guard, the elite warriors of the tumans. Stories of their battles were sung or chanted on feast days, as well as darker tales of betrayal and blood. Batu winced at the thought. His father featured in some of those,

2

which prompted sidelong glances at his mother and her bastard son.

Batu hawked and spat on the ground at his feet. He could still remember when his mother's ger had been of the finest white felt and gifts had arrived almost daily. He supposed she had once been beautiful, her skin fresh with youth, where now it was seamed and coarse. Those had been different days, before his father had betrayed the khan and been butchered for it like a lamb in the snow. Jochi. He spat again at the word, the name. If his father had bent to the will of the great khan, Batu thought he might have been one of the warriors in red and black, riding tall among the filthy gers. Instead, he was forgotten and his mother wept whenever he talked of joining a tuman.

Almost all the young men of his age had joined, except for those with injuries or defects of birth. His friend Zan was one, a mix-blood Chin who had been born with a sightless white eye. No one-eyed man could ever be an archer and the warriors had turned him away with kicks and laughter, telling him to tend his flocks. Batu had drunk airag for the first time with him that night and been sick for two days. The recruiters had not come for him either, not with the betrayer's blood running in his veins. Batu had seen them out looking for strong lads, but when their gaze passed over him, they shrugged and turned away. He was as tall and strong as his father had been, but they did not want him.

With a shock, Batu realised the riders were not passing through. He watched as they stopped to speak to one of his mother's neighbours and he took a sharp breath in amazement as the old man pointed in Batu's direction. The horsemen trotted towards him and he stood rooted, watching as they came closer. He found he did not know what to do with his hands and folded them over his chest twice before letting them dangle. From inside the ger, he heard his mother calling some question, but he did not reply. He could not. He had seen the man riding at the head of the group.

There were no pictures in the poor gers, though one or two Chin paintings had found their way into the homes of the wealthiest families. Yet Batu had seen his father's brother once. On a feast day years before, he had crept up close, peering between warriors for a sight of the great khan. Ogedai and Jochi had been with Genghis then and time had not faded the bright memory, among the most bitter-sweet in all his young years. It had been a glimpse of the life he might have had, before his father threw it all away for some petty squabble Batu did not even understand.

Ogedai rode bareheaded, in armour lacquered shining black. He wore his hair in the Chin style, as a heavy rope falling from a topknot on a bare, shaved scalp. Batu drank in every detail of the man as his mother's voice called plaintively again from inside. He could see that the great khan's son was looking directly at him and speaking, but Batu was tongue-tied, dumb. The yellow eyes were bright up close and he was lost in the realisation that he was staring at his uncle by blood.

'Is he slow-witted?' one of the warriors said. Batu shut his open mouth. 'My lord Ogedai is speaking to you, boy. Are you deaf?'

Batu found himself flushing with great heat. He shook his head, suddenly irritated to have such men ride up to his mother's ger. What would they think of the patched walls, the smell, the flies in the air? It was humiliating and his shock turned quickly to anger. Even then, he did not reply. Men like these had killed his father, his mother said. The life of a ragged son would mean little to them.

'Have you no voice at all?' Ogedai said. He was smiling at something and Batu responded crookedly.

'I have,' he said. He saw one of the warriors reach down,

but he did not expect a blow and he staggered a step as a mailed glove connected with the side of his head.

'I have, *my lord*,' the warrior said without heat.

Batu shrugged as he straightened up. His ear was burning, but he'd known worse.

'I have a voice, my lord,' he said, doing his best to remember the warrior's face.

Ogedai discussed him as if he wasn't present. 'It wasn't just a story then. I can see my brother in his face and he's already as tall as my father. How old are you, boy?'

Batu stood very still, trying to collect himself. Some part of him had always wondered if his mother had been exaggerating his father's position. To have it confirmed so casually was more than he could take in.

'Fifteen years,' he said. He saw the warrior begin to lean forward again and added 'my lord' quickly. The warrior leaned back in his saddle and nodded to him complacently.

Ogedai frowned. 'You're old to be starting out. Training should begin at seven or eight at the latest, if you're ever to draw a good bow.' He saw Batu's confusion and smiled, pleased to be able to do such a thing. 'Still, I will be watching you. Report to General Jebe tomorrow. He has his camp about a hundred miles to the north, near a village by a cliff. You can find it?'

'I have no horse, my lord,' Batu said.

Ogedai glanced at the warrior who had struck him and the man raised his eyes to heaven before dismounting. He passed the reins into Batu's hands.

'Can you ride at least?' the warrior said.

Batu was awed as he took the reins and patted the muscular neck. He had never touched an animal as fine.

'Yes. Yes, I can ride.'

'Good. This mare is not your horse, understand? She will carry you to your post, but then you will take some old sway-back and return her to me.'

'I don't know your name,' Batu said.

'Alkhun, boy. Ask anyone in Karakorum and they'll know me.'

'The city?' Batu asked. He had heard of the stone thing rising from the soil on the back of a million workers, but until then, he had not believed it.

'More a camp than a city at the moment, though that is changing,' Alkhun confirmed. 'You can send the horse by the way station riders, but tell them to go easy with her. I'll take any whip marks out of your hide. Oh, and welcome to the army, boy. My lord Ogedai has plans for you. Don't disappoint him.'

PART ONE

AD 1230

CHAPTER ONE

The air swirled with marble dust that glittered as it caught the evening sun. Ogedai's heart was full as he guided his horse down the main thoroughfare, taking in every sight and sound around him. There was a sense of urgency in the cacophony of hammer blows and shouted orders. The Mongol tumans had gathered outside the city. His generals, his people had been summoned there to see what two years of labour had created: a city in a wilderness, with the Orkhon river tamed and bent to his will.

Ogedai reined in for a moment to watch a group of workmen unload a cart. Nervous under his gaze, the labourers used ropes, pulleys and sheer numbers to manoeuvre blocks of white marble onto low sledges that could be dragged into the workshops. Each milky block was subtly veined in a light blue that pleased Ogedai. He owned the quarry that had birthed the stones, hundreds of miles to the east, just one of a thousand purchases he had made in the last years.

There was no doubt he had been extravagant, spending gold and silver as if it had no value. He smiled at the thought, wondering what his father would have made of the white city rising in the wilderness. Genghis had despised the anthills of humanity, but these were not the ancient stones and teeming streets of an enemy. This was new and it belonged to the nation.

There had never been a treasury like the one he had inherited, amassed from the wealth of China and Khwarezm, yet never spent by its khan. With the tribute from Yenking alone, Ogedai could have sheathed every new home in white marble or even jade if he had wanted. He had built a monument to his father on the plains, as well as a place where he himself could be khan. He had built a palace with a tower that rose above the city like a white sword, so that all men could see the nation had come far from simple gers and herds.

For his gold, a million men had come to work. They had crossed plains and deserts with just a few animals and tools, coming from as far off as Chin lands or the cities of Samarkand, Bukhara and Kabul. Masons and carpenters from Koryo had made the journey, called to the west by rumours of a new city being built on a river of coins. Bulgars brought stocks of rare clays, charcoal and hardwood in great caravans from their forests. The city filled with traders, builders, potters, food-sellers, thieves and scoundrels. Farmers scenting a profit brought their carts for days of travel, all for the strings of metal coins. Ogedai gave them gold and silver from the earth, melted and shaped. In return, they gave him a city, and he did not find it a bad bargain. For the present, they were the colourful crowds of his city, speaking a hundred tongues and cooking a thousand different foods and spices. Some of them would be allowed to stay, but he was not building it for them.

Ogedai saw green-handed dyers flatten themselves against the walls, their red turbans dipping in respect. His Guards cleared the way ahead, so the son of Genghis could ride almost in a dream. He had *made* this place from the camp of gers his father had known. He had made it real, in stone.

It still amazed him. He had not paid for women to travel with his workers, but they had come with their husbands and fathers. He had wondered for a time how he would establish the businesses every city needed to thrive, but traders had approached his chancellor, offering horses or more silver to lease new properties. The city was more than a simple collection of houses. Already it had a vitality of its own, far beyond his control.

Yet not completely. A quirk in the plans had created an area of small alleyways in the south of his city. Criminal gangs had begun to flourish there until Ogedai heard. He had ordered eight hundred buildings torn down, the whole area redesigned and rebuilt. His own Guard had supervised the hangings.

The street fell quiet as he passed, the labourers and their masters bowing their heads as they saw the man who held the power of life and death and gold over all of them. Ogedai took a deep breath of the dusty air, enjoying the taste of it on his tongue and the thought that he was literally breathing in his creation. Ahead, he could see the towers of his palace, crowned in a dome of gold beaten thinner than the paper of his scribes. It raised his spirits to see it, like sunlight trapped and held in his city.

The street widened as it grew before him, its stone gutters polished. That section had been finished months before and the bustling crowds of labourers fell behind. As Ogedai trotted on, he could not help glancing at the boundary walls that had so confused his Chin architects and labourers. Even from the low vantage point of a saddle, there were moments when he could see over them to the green plains beyond. The walls of Yenking had not saved that city from fire or siege, he knew. *His* walls were the warriors of the khan, the tribes who had brought a Chin emperor to his knees and razed a shah's cities.

Already, Ogedai loved his creation, from the vast expanse of the central training ground, to the red-tiled roofs, the paved gutters, the temples and churches and mosques and markets and homes by the thousand, most still empty and waiting for life. Scraps of blue cloth fluttered in the plains wind on every corner, a tribute to the sky father above them all. In the south, green foothills and mountains stretched far away and the air was warm with dust as Ogedai rejoiced in Karakorum.

The twilight was deepening into a soft gloom as Ogedai handed his reins to a servant and strode up the steps to his palace. Before he entered, he looked back once more at the city straining to be born. He could smell fresh-turned earth and, over it, the fried food of the workmen on the evening air. He had not planned the herds of livestock in corrals beyond the walls, or the squawking chickens sold on every corner. He thought of the wool market that had sprung up by the western gate. He should not have expected trade to halt simply because the city was unfinished. He had chosen a spot on an ancient traders' road to give it life – and life had begun pouring in while whole streets, whole districts, were still piles of lumber, tile and stone.

As he looked into the setting sun, he smiled at the cooking fires on the plains surrounding the city. His people waited there, for him. His armies would be fed on rich mutton, dripping fat from the summer grass. It reminded him of his own hunger and he moistened his lips as he passed through a stone gate the equal of anything in a Chin city.

In the echoing hall beyond, he paused for a moment at his most extravagant gesture. A tree of solid silver stretched gracefully up to the arched ceiling, the centre point open to the sky like the ger of any herdsman. It had taken the silversmiths of Samarkand almost a year to cast and polish, but it served his purpose. Whoever entered his palace would see it and be staggered at the wealth it represented. Some would see an emblem for the silver people, the Mongol tribes who had become a nation. Those with more wisdom would see that the Mongols cared so little for silver that they used it as a casting metal.

Ogedai let his hand slide down the bole of the tree, feeling the metal chill his fingers. The spreading branches reached out in a parody of life, gleaming like a white birch in moonlight. Ogedai nodded to himself. He stretched his back as lamps were lit by slaves and servants all around him, throwing black shadows and making the evening seem suddenly darker outside.

He heard hurrying footsteps and saw his manservant, Baras'aghur, approaching. Ogedai winced at the man's keen expression and the bundle of papers under his arm.

'After I have eaten, Baras. It has been a long day.'

'Very well, my lord, but you have a visitor: your uncle. Shall I tell him to wait on your pleasure?'

Ogedai paused in the act of unbuckling his sword belt. All three of his uncles had come to the plains around Karakorum at his order, gathering their tumans in great camps. He had forbidden them all from entering the city and he wondered who would have disobeyed him. He suspected it would be Khasar, who regarded orders and laws as tools for other men rather than himself.

'Who is it, Baras?' Ogedai asked quietly.

'Lord Temuge, master. I have sent servants to tend him, but he has been waiting now for a long time.'

Baras'aghur made a gesture to indicate a sweep of the sun in the sky and Ogedai pursed his lips in irritation. His father's brother would be well aware of the nuances of hospitality. Simply by arriving when Ogedai was not there to greet him, he had created an obligation. Ogedai assumed it was deliberate. A man like Temuge was too subtle not to grasp the slightest advantage. Yet the order had gone out for the generals and princes to remain on the plains.

Ogedai sighed. For two years, he had readied Karakorum to

13

be the jewel in an empire. His had been a splendid isolation and he had manoeuvred to keep it so, his enemies and friends always off balance. He had known it could not last for ever. He steeled himself as he walked after Baras'aghur to the first and most sumptuous of his audience rooms.

'Have wine brought to me immediately, Baras. And food – something simple, such as the warriors are eating on the plain.'

'Your will, my lord,' his servant said without listening, his thoughts on the meeting to come.

The footsteps of the two men were loud in the silent halls, clicking and echoing back to them. Ogedai did not glance at the painted scenes that usually gave him so much pleasure. He and Baras'aghur walked under the best work of Islamic artists and it was only towards the end that Ogedai looked up at a blaze of colour, smiling to himself at the image of Genghis leading a charge at the Badger's Mouth pass. The artist had asked a fortune for a year's work, but Ogedai had doubled his price when he saw it. His father still lived on those walls, as well as in his memory. There was no art of painting in the tribes he knew and such things could still make him gasp and stand in awe. With Temuge waiting, however, Ogedai barely nodded to his father's image before he was sweeping into the room.

The years had not been kind to his father's brother. Temuge had once been as fat as a feasting calf, but then lost the weight rapidly, so that his throat sagged into flaps of skin and he looked far older than his years. Ogedai looked at his uncle coldly as he rose from a silk-covered chair to greet him. It was an effort to be courteous to a man who represented the end of his time apart. He had no illusions. The nation waited impatiently for him and Temuge was just the first to breach his defences.

'You are looking well, Ogedai,' Temuge said.

He came forward as if he might embrace his nephew and

14

Ogedai struggled with a spasm of irritation. He turned away to Baras, letting his uncle drop his rising arms unseen.

'Wine and food, Baras. Will you stand there, staring like a sheep?'

'My lord,' Baras'aghur replied, bowing immediately. 'I will have a scribe sent to you to record the meeting.'

He left at a run and both men could hear the slave's sandals clattering into the distance. Temuge frowned delicately.

'This is not a formal visit, Ogedai, for scribes and records.'

'You are here as my uncle then? Not because the tribes have selected you to approach me? Not because my scholar uncle is the one man whom all the factions trust enough to speak to me?'

Temuge flushed at the tone and the accuracy of the remarks. He had to assume Ogedai had as many spies in the great camps as he had himself. That was one thing the nation had learned from the Chin. He tried to judge his nephew's mood, but it was no easy task. Ogedai had not even offered him salt tea. Temuge swallowed drily as he tried to interpret the level of censure and irritation in the younger man.

'You know the armies talk of nothing else, Ogedai.' Temuge took a deep breath to steady his nerves. Under Ogedai's pale yellow eyes, he could not shake the idea that he was reporting to some echo of Genghis. His nephew was softer in body than the great khan, but there was a coldness in him that unnerved Temuge. Sweat broke out on his forehead.

'For two years, you have ignored your father's empire,' Temuge began.

'Do you think that is what I have done?' Ogedai interrupted.

Temuge stared at him.

'What else am I to think? You left the families and tumans in the field, then built a city while they herded sheep. For two years, Ogedai!' He lowered his voice almost to a whisper. 'There are some who say your mind has broken with grief for your father.'

Ogedai smiled bitterly to himself. Even the mention of his father was like tearing the scab off a wound. He knew every one of the rumours. He had started some of them himself, to keep his enemies jumping at shadows. Yet he was the chosen heir of Genghis, the first khan of the nation. The warriors had almost deified his father and Ogedai was certain he had nothing to fear from mere gossip in the camps. His relatives were a different matter.

The door swung open to reveal Baras'aghur and a dozen Chin servants. In moments, they had surrounded the two men, placing bronze cups and food on crisp white cloth before them. Ogedai gestured for his uncle to sit cross-legged on the tiled floor, watching with interest as the older man's knees creaked and made him wince. Baras'aghur sent the servants away and then served tea to Temuge, who accepted the bowl in relief with his right hand, sipping as formally as he would have in any ger of the plains. Ogedai watched eagerly as red wine gurgled into his own cup. He emptied it quickly and held it out before Baras'aghur could move away.

Ogedai saw his uncle's gaze flicker over the scribe Baras'aghur had summoned, standing in a respectful attitude against the wall. He knew Temuge understood the power of the written word as well as anyone. It had been he who had collected the stories of Genghis and the founding of a nation. Ogedai owned one of the first volumes, copied carefully and bound in hard-wearing goatskin. It was among his most prized possessions. Yet there were times when a man preferred not to be recorded.

'Give us privacy, Baras,' Ogedai said. 'Leave the jug, but take your scribe with you.'

His manservant was too well trained to hesitate and it was but moments until the two men were alone once again. Ogedai drained his cup and belched.

'Why have you come to me tonight, uncle? In a month, you

16

can enter Karakorum freely with thousands of our people, for a feast and a festival they will talk of for years.'

Temuge studied the younger man before him. The unlined face looked weary and stern. Ogedai had chosen a strange burden for himself, with this city. Temuge knew there were only a handful of men in the camps who cared more than a bronze coin for Karakorum. To the Mongol generals who had known Genghis, it was a colossal conceit of white marble and Chin design. Temuge wished he could tell the young man how much he loved the creation without it seeming like greasy flattery. Yet he did love it. It was the city he had once dreamed of building, a place of wide streets and courtyards and even a library, with thousands of clean oak shelves lying empty for the treasures they would one day hold.

'You are not a fool, Ogedai,' Temuge said. 'It was not by chance that your father chose you over older brothers.' Ogedai looked up sharply and Temuge nodded to him. 'At times I wonder if you are a strategist like General Tsubodai. For two years, the nation has been without a leader, without a path, yet there has been no civil war, no struggle between princes.'

'Perhaps they saw my personal tuman riding among them, my scribes and spies,' Ogedai replied softly. 'There were always men in red and black watching them for treachery.'

Temuge snorted. 'It was not fear but confusion that held them. They could not see your plan, so they did nothing. You are your father's heir, but you did not call them to take the oath. No one understands it, so they wait and watch. They *still* wait to see what you will do next.'

Temuge saw Ogedai's mouth twitch as if he wanted to smile. He longed to know his nephew's mind, but with this new generation, who knew how they thought?

'You have built your city on the plains, Ogedai. The armies have gathered at your call, but now they are here and many of them have seen this glorious place for the first time. Do you expect them simply to bend the knee and give their oath? Because you are your father's son? He has other surviving sons, Ogedai. Have you considered them at all?'

Ogedai smiled at his uncle, amused at the way the man seemed to be trying to pierce his secrets with his gaze. There was one he would not find, no matter how closely he peered. He felt the wine spread its glow inside him, easing his pain like a caress.

'If that was my intention, uncle – to win two years of peace for myself and build a city – well, I have done it, have I not? Perhaps that is all I wanted.'

Temuge spread his hands. 'You do not trust me,' he said, genuine hurt in his voice.

Ogedai chuckled. 'As much as I trust anyone, I promise you.'

'A clever answer,' Temuge said coldly.

'Well, you are a clever man. It's what you deserve,' Ogedai snapped. All the lightness had gone from his manner as he leaned forward. Imperceptibly, his uncle eased himself back.

'At the new moon,' Ogedai went on, 'I will take the khan's oath of every officer and prince of the blood in the nation. I do not have to explain myself, uncle. They will bend the knee to me. Not because I am my father's son, but because I am my father's chosen *heir* and the leader of the nation.'

He caught himself, as if he was about to say too much, and Temuge watched a shutter drop over his emotions. Here was one son who had learned the cold face early.

'You did not tell me why you came to me tonight, uncle,' Ogedai went on.

Temuge let out a sigh, knowing the moment had slipped away.

'I came to make sure you understood the danger, Ogedai.'

'You are frightening me,' Ogedai said with a smile.

Temuge flushed. 'I am not threatening you.'

'Where can this terrible danger spring from then, in my city of cities?'

'You mock me, though I travelled here to help you and to see this thing you have built.'

'It is beautiful, is it not?' Ogedai said.

'It is wonderful,' Temuge said, with such transparent honesty that Ogedai looked more thoughtfully at his uncle.

'In truth,' Ogedai said, 'I have been considering the need for a man to oversee my library here, to collect scrolls from all corners of the world until men of learning everywhere know the name of Karakorum. It is a foolish dream, perhaps.'

Temuge hesitated. The idea was thrilling to him, but he was suspicious.

'Are you still mocking me?' he said softly.

Ogedai shrugged. 'Only when you blow like an old sheep with your warnings. Will you tell me to watch my food for poison, I wonder?' He saw Temuge's face grow mottled as his peevishness resurfaced and he smiled.

'It is a real offer. Any other man in the tribes can herd sheep and goats. Only you could herd scholars, I think. You will make Karakorum famous. I want it to be known from sea to sea.'

'If you set such a value on my wits then, Ogedai,' Temuge said, 'you will listen to me, this once.'

Ogedai sighed. 'Speak then, uncle, if you feel you must,' he said.

'For two years, the world has waited for you. No one has dared to move a soldier for fear they would be the first example you made. Even the Chin and the Sung have been quiet. They have been like deer who smell a tiger somewhere close. That has come to an end. You have summoned the armies of the nation, and a month from now, if you live, you will be khan.'

'If I live?' Ogedai said.

'Where are your Guards now, Ogedai? You have called them back and no one feels their suspicious eyes riding through the camps. Did you think it would be easy? If you fell from a roof tonight and broke your head on all this stone, who would be khan at the new moon?'

'My brother Chagatai has the best claim,' Ogedai said lightly. 'Unless my son Guyuk is allowed to live. Tolui too is in the line of my father. He has sons grown strong: Mongke and Kublai, Arik-Boke and Hulegu. In time, they could all be khans.' He smiled, amused at something Temuge could not see. 'The seed of Genghis is strong, it seems. We all have sons, but we still look to Tsubodai. Whoever has my father's unbeatable general will carry the army, don't you think? Without him, it would be civil war. Is that all those with power? I have not mentioned my grandmother. Her teeth and eyes are gone now, but she can still be fearsome when roused.'

Temuge stared at him.

'I hope your actions are not as careless as your words. Double your personal guard at least, Ogedai.'

Ogedai nodded. He didn't bother to mention that the ornate walls concealed watching men. Two different cross-bows were centred on Temuge's chest at that very moment. It would take only a particular gesture with Ogedai's hand for his uncle to be ripped from life.

'I have heard you. I will consider what you have said. Perhaps you should not take on the role in my library and university until the new moon has come and gone. If I do not survive it, my successor may not have such an interest in Karakorum.' He saw the words sink in and knew that at least one of the men of power would be working to keep him alive. All men had a price, but it was almost never gold.

'I must sleep now, uncle,' Ogedai said. 'Every day is full of plans and work.' He paused in the moment of rising and went on. 'I will tell you this much. I have not been deaf or blind these last years. My father's nation has ceased to conquer for a time, but what of that? The nation has been fed on milk and blood, ready to be sent out into the world with fresh strength. And I have built my city. Do not fear for me, uncle. I know everything I need to know of the generals and their loyalties.'

He came to his feet with the suppleness of youth, while his uncle had to accept his outstretched hand and winced as his knees cracked aloud.

'I think your father would be proud of you, Ogedai,' Temuge said.

To his surprise, Ogedai chuckled.

'I doubt it. I have taken Jochi's bastard son and made him a prince and a minghaan officer. I will raise Batu further still, to honour my brother's memory. Genghis would never forgive me for that.' He smiled at the thought. 'And he would not have loved my Karakorum, of that I am certain.'

He called for Baras'aghur to lead Temuge out of the dark city, back to the stifling air of treachery and suspicion that was so thick in the great camps.

Ogedai picked up his jug and cup, filling the goblet once again as he walked to a stone balcony and looked out at the moonlit streets. There was a breeze blowing, cooling his skin as he stood there with his eyes shut. His heart ached in his chest and he gripped his arm as the pain spread. He felt fresh sweat break out as his veins throbbed and pulsed at frightening speed, soaring for moments until he felt dizzy. He reached out blindly and held the stone sill, breathing slowly and deeply until the weakness left him and his heart beat slowly once again. A great pressure released in his head and the flashing lights dwindled to mere points, shadows that only he could see. He looked up at the cold stars, his expression bitter. Below his feet, another chamber had been cut from the stones. At times, when the pains came with a force that left him trembling and weak, he had not expected even to finish it. Yet he had. His tomb was ready and he still lived. Cup by cup he emptied the jug, until his senses swam.

'How long do I have left?' he whispered drunkenly to himself. 'Is it days now, or years?' He imagined he talked to the spirit of his father and waved the cup as he spoke, spilling some wine.

'I was at *peace*, father. At peace, when I thought my time was at an end. What did I care for your generals and their . . . petty struggles? Yet my city has risen and the nation has come, and I am *still* here. What do I do now?'

He listened for an answer in the darkness, but there was nothing.

CHAPTER TWO

Tolui stroked his wife's damp hair idly as he lay back and watched his four sons whoop and splash in the waters of the Orkhon. The sun was warm as they lay there and only the presence of his guards nearby prevented complete relaxation. Tolui grimaced at the thought. There was no peace to be had in the camp, with every man wondering whether he was a supporter of Chagatai or Ogedai or the generals – or perhaps one who would inform for any of them. At times, he wished his two older brothers would settle it somewhere quiet, so that he could enjoy being alive on such a day, with a beautiful woman in his arms and four healthy sons pleading to be allowed to swim over a waterfall. He had forbidden it once, but he saw that Kublai had dared Mongke once again and the two of them were creeping closer and closer to the bank, where a goat path led up to the source of the roaring river. Tolui watched from under half-closed lids as the two older boys glanced guiltily at their parents, hoping they were asleep in the warm sun. Arik-Boke and Hulegu were in on it, of course, their bony boy's frames almost shaking with excitement.

'Do you see them?' Sorhatani murmured.

Tolui smiled. 'I am half-tempted to let them try it. They swim like otters, both of them.'

It was still a new skill to tribes raised on grassy plains. For those who learned to ride before they could speak, the rivers were the source of life for the herds, or an obstacle when they were swollen in floods. Only recently had they become a source of pleasure to the children of the tribe.

'You won't be the one who has to soothe their wounds when they take the skin off their backs,' Sorhatani said, relaxing into him, 'or splint their bones.'

Yet she said nothing as Mongke suddenly darted for the track, his naked body gleaming. Kublai shot a last, sharp look at his parents, but neither moved, and in an instant, he was off as well.

Tolui and Sorhatani both sat up as soon as the boys were out of sight. They exchanged a private look of amusement as Arik-Boke and Hulegu craned to see the top of the plunging falls above.

'I don't know who is worse, Mongke or Kublai,' Sorhatani said, pulling a grass stalk and chewing the end. He chuckled and they both said 'Kublai' together.

'Mongke reminds me of my father,' Tolui said a little wistfully. 'He fears nothing.'

Sorhatani snorted softly. 'Then you will remember what your father once said when he had to choose between two men to lead a thousand.'

'I was there, woman,' Tolui said, his mind leaping to her point. 'He said Ussutai feared nothing and felt no hunger or thirst. That was why he was unfit to command.'

'Your father was wise. A man needs to feel a little fear, Tolui, if only to have the pride of conquering it.'

24

A wild shout made them both look up as Mongke came over the falls, yelling in excitement as he managed a crude dive and plunged into the pool at its foot. The drop was little more than ten feet, but to a boy of eleven, it must have been terrifying. Tolui relaxed and chuckled as he saw his oldest son surface, blowing and gasping, his teeth very white against his sun-browned skin. Arik-Boke and Hulegu cheered, their voices high as they looked up again for Kublai.

He came over backwards in a tumble of limbs, moving so fast that he left the torrent of water and fell through empty air. Tolui winced at the flat smack that carried clearly across the water. He watched as the other three looked for him, calling and pointing to each other. Sorhatani felt her husband's arms tense as he prepared to leap up, but then Kublai surfaced, roaring. His entire body was flushed red on one side and he limped as he climbed out, but they could see he was panting with exhilaration.

'I'll have to beat some sense into them,' Tolui said.

His wife shrugged. 'I'll get them dressed and send them to you.'

He nodded, only half-aware that he had waited for her approval to punish the boys. Sorhatani smiled at him as he walked away. He was a good man, she thought. Not perhaps the strongest of his brothers, nor the most ruthless, but in all other ways, the best of the sons of Genghis.

As she stood and gathered the clothes her sons had left on every bush around them, she recalled the one man who had made her afraid in her life. She cherished the memory of the time when Genghis had looked on her as a woman, rather than just the wife of one of his sons. It had been on the shore of a lake, thousands of miles away in a different land. She had seen the khan's eyes brighten at her youth and beauty, just for an instant. She had smiled at him then, terrified and awed.

'Now, there was a man,' she murmured to herself, shaking her head with a smile.

Khasar stood on the wooden base of the cart, leaning back against the white felt of the khan's ger. It was twice as wide and half as high again as the homes of their people, and Genghis had used it for meeting his generals. Ogedai had never claimed the enormous construction, so heavy that the cart had to be pulled by six oxen. After the death of the great khan, it had sat empty for months before Khasar made it his own. As yet, no one had dared to dispute his right to it.

Khasar smelled the fried marmot meat Kachiun had brought for the midday meal.

'Lets eat outside. It's too fine a day to sit in the gloom,' he said.

As well as the steaming platter, Kachiun carried a fat skin of airag which he tossed to his brother.

'Where are the others?' he said, placing the platter on the edge of the boards and sitting with his legs swinging.

Khasar shrugged. 'Jebe said he would be here. I sent a messenger to Jelme and Tsubodai. They'll come or they won't; it's up to them.'

Kachiun blew air from his lips in irritation. He should have passed on the messages himself, to be sure his brother didn't forget or use the wrong words. There was no point in berating the man who was digging his fingers into the pile of steaming scraps. Khasar didn't change and it was both infuriating and comforting at times.

'He's nearly finished that city of his,' Khasar said, chewing. 'Strange-looking place, with those low walls. I could ride right over them.'

'I think that is his point,' Kachiun replied. He took a pouch of unleavened bread from another pot, waving his hand to

26

clear the steam as he filled it with meat. Khasar looked baffled and Kachiun sighed.

'We are the walls, brother. He wants people to see that he does not have to hide behind stones like the Chin. Do you understand? The tumans of our army are the walls.'

'Clever,' Khasar said, munching. 'But he'll build walls eventually, you watch. Give him a year or two and he'll be adding stones. Cities make you afraid.'

Kachiun stared at his brother, wondering if he had managed a bit of real wisdom. Khasar noticed his sudden interest and grinned.

'You've seen it. If a man has gold, he lives with the terror that someone will take it away from him, so he builds walls around it. Then everyone knows where the gold is, so they come and take it. That's the way it always goes, brother. Fools and gold, together.'

'I never know if you think like a child or a very wise man,' Kachiun said, filling another pouch and chewing.

Khasar tried to say 'wise man' around a large mouthful and choked, so that Kachiun had to pound him on his back. They had been friends for a very long time.

Khasar wiped tears from his eyes and took a deep breath and a swig of airag from the bulging skin.

'He'll need walls at the new moon, I should think.'

Automatically, Kachiun looked to see if anyone could overhear them. They were surrounded by empty grass, with just their two ponies grazing nearby. Beyond them, warriors were busy in the sun, preparing for the great competition Ogedai had promised. There would be prizes of grey horses and armour for wrestlers and archers, even for those who won foot races across the plains. Everywhere they looked, men were training in groups, but there was no one loitering too close. Kachiun relaxed.

'You have heard something?'

'Nothing, but only a fool would expect the oath-taking to go without a hitch. Ogedai's not a fool and he's not a coward. He faced me when I was running wild after . . .' He hesitated and his eyes grew distant and cold for a moment. 'After Genghis died.' He took another swig of the harsh spirit. 'If he'd taken the oaths immediately, not a man in the tribes would have dared raise a hand to him; but now?'

Kachiun nodded grimly.

'Now Chagatai has come into his strength and half the nation wonders why he isn't going to be khan.'

'There will be blood, brother. One way or another,' Khasar replied. 'I just hope Ogedai knows when to be forgiving and when to cut throats.'

'He has us,' Kachiun said. 'That is why I wanted to meet here, to discuss our plans for seeing him safe as khan.'

'I haven't been summoned to his white city for my advice, Kachiun, have you? You don't know whether he trusts us more than anyone else. Why should he? You could be khan if you wanted. You were Genghis' heir while his sons grew.' Khasar saw his brother's irritation. The camp was full of such talk and both men were tired of it, but Khasar just shrugged.

'Better you than Chagatai, anyway. Have you seen him out running, with his bondsmen? So young, so *virile*.'

He leaned over the edge of the cart and spat deliberately on the ground. Kachiun smiled.

'Jealous, brother?'

'Not of him, though I do miss being young sometimes. Now some part of me is always aching. Old wounds, old knees, that time when you completely failed to stop me getting speared in my shoulder – it all hurts.'

'It is better than the alternative,' Kachiun said.

Khasar snorted.

They looked round as Jebe approached, with Tsubodai. Both of Genghis' generals were in their prime and Kachiun and

Khasar shared a glance of private humour at the way they came striding confidently across the summer grass.

'Tea in the pot, meat in the bowl,' Khasar said without ceremony as they climbed the steps up to the old khan's ger. 'We are discussing how to keep Ogedai alive long enough for him to carry the white tails.'

The symbol of the united tribes still fluttered above his head, horsetails that had once been a riot of tribal colours, until Genghis had bleached them pale and made them one. No one had dared to remove the symbol of power, any more than they had queried Khasar's use of the cart.

Tsubodai made himself comfortable on the wooden edge, his feet dangling as he dug into the meat and bread. He was aware that both Kachiun and Khasar were waiting for what he would say. He did not enjoy the attention and he ate slowly and cleared his throat with airag.

In the silence, Jebe leaned back against the felt wall and looked at the city in the distance, a white haze in the warm air. He could see the golden dome of Ogedai's palace and it struck him that it resembled a yellow eye staring out of the city.

'I have been approached,' Jebe said. Tsubodai stopped chewing and Khasar put down the skin of airag as he was about to drink. Jebe shrugged. 'We knew one of us would be, sooner or later. It was a stranger to me, wearing no marks of rank.'

'Sent by Chagatai?' Kachiun said.

Jebe nodded. 'Who else? But no names were mentioned. They do not trust me. It was just a light touch, to see which way I would jump.'

Tsubodai grimaced. 'You jumped here, in full view of the tribes. No doubt they are watching you now.'

'What of it?' Jebe said, bridling. 'I was loyal to Genghis. Do I demand to be known by my birth name, as Zurgadai? I carry the name Genghis gave me, and I am loyal to the son he named as heir. What do I care who sees me talking with his generals?'

29

Tsubodai sighed and put aside the final piece of his meal.

'We know who is most likely to disrupt the oath-taking. We do not know how they will do it, or how many men will support them. If you had come to me quietly, Jebe, I would have told you to agree to anything they say and learn their plans.'

'Who wants to go creeping about in the dark, Tsubodai?' Khasar said scornfully. He looked to his brother for support, but Kachiun shook his head.

'Tsubodai is right, brother. This isn't just a matter of showing we support Ogedai and all right-thinking men following us. I wish it was. There was never a khan of the nation before Genghis, so there are no laws for how he passes on his power.'

'The khan makes the laws,' Khasar replied. 'I didn't see anyone complaining when he made us all take an oath to Ogedai as heir. Even Chagatai got down on his knees for that.'

'Because his choice was to fall flat or die,' Tsubodai said. 'Now Genghis is gone and the men around Chagatai are whispering in his ear. They are saying the only reason he was not heir was his struggle with his brother, Jochi, but Jochi is dead.'

He paused for a moment, thinking of the blood that had splashed on snow. His face was utterly blank and they could not read him.

'There are no traditions to tell us how to act,' Tsubodai went on wearily. 'Yes, Genghis chose his heir, but his mind was clouded with anger over Jochi. It was not so many years ago that he favoured Chagatai over all his brothers. The nation talks of nothing else. At times, I think Chagatai could press his claim *openly* and become khan. He could walk right up to Ogedai with a sword and fully half the army would not stop him.'

'The other half would tear him to shreds,' Khasar said.

'And in a stroke, we would have a civil war that would break the nation in two. Everything Genghis built, all our strength, wasted on an internal struggle. How long would it be then before the Chin rose against us, or the Arabs? If that is the future, I would rather see Chagatai take the horsetail banner today.' Tsubodai held up his hand as they began to protest. 'That is not a traitor speaking, do not think it. Have I not shown that I followed Genghis, even when everything in me cried out that he was wrong? I will not fail his memory. I will see Ogedai as khan, on my word.'

Once again, he thought of a young man who had believed his promise of safe passage. Tsubodai knew his word was worthless, where it had once been iron. It was an old grief, but on some days he bled as if he had just been cut.

'You had me worried,' Khasar said.

Tsubodai did not smile. He was younger than both the brothers, but they waited patiently for him to speak. He was the great general, the master who could plan any attack on any terrain and somehow snatch victory. With Tsubodai, they knew Ogedai had a chance. Kachiun frowned at the thought.

'You should look to your own safety as well, Tsubodai. You are too valuable to lose.'

Tsubodai sighed. 'To hear such words while I sit by the ger of my khan. Yes, I will be careful. I am an obstacle to the one we all fear. You should be sure that your guards are men you trust with your life, who cannot be bribed or threatened without them coming to you. If a man's wife and children go missing, will you still trust him to watch you as you sleep?'

'That is an ugly thought,' Jebe said, with a wince. 'You truly think we are at that point? On such a day I can hardly believe in knives in every shadow.'

'If Ogedai becomes khan,' Tsubodai went on, 'he could have Chagatai killed, or simply rule well or badly for forty years. Chagatai will not wait, Jebe. He will try to arrange a death, an accident, or he will try to take it by force. I cannot see him sitting idly by while his life and ambition is decided by others. Not the man I know.'

31

Somehow the sun seemed less bright after such cold words. 'Where is Jelme?' Jebe asked. 'He told me he would be here.'

Tsubodai rubbed the back of his neck, making it crack. He had not slept well for many weeks, though he would not mention it to these men.

'Jelme is loyal; don't worry about him,' he muttered. Some of the other men frowned.

'Loyal to which son of Genghis?' Jebe said. 'There is no clear path in this, and if we do not find one, the nation could be torn apart.'

'Then we should kill Chagatai,' Khasar said. The others grew still and he grinned at them. 'I am too old to be guarding my words,' he said with a shrug. 'Why should he have it all his own way? Why should I check my personal guards, to be sure no one has turned them against me? We could end this today and Ogedai would be khan at the new moon with no threat of war.' He saw their cold expressions and spat once again. 'I won't dip my head at your disapproval, so don't expect it. If you prefer to watch your backs for a month and make secret, clever plans, that is up to you. I could cut right through it and see an end. What do you think Genghis would say, if he were one of us, here? He'd walk right in and cut Chagatai's throat.'

'He might,' Tsubodai admitted, who knew better than most how ruthless the khan had been. 'If Chagatai was a fool, I would agree with you. If there could be surprise, yes, it could work. I'd ask you to test it, but you'd get yourself killed. Instead, take my word on this – Chagatai is ready for such a move. Any group of armed men approaching his tuman is met with bristling weapons and warriors ready to charge. He plans murder every day, so he fears it as well.'

'Between us we command enough men to get to him,' Khasar said, though less confidently.

'Perhaps. If only his ten thousand responded, we could still reach him, but I think it has already gone further than that.

Whatever game Ogedai has been playing, he has given his brother two years to whisper and make promises. Without a khan's shadow, *all* of us were forced to rule the lands around us, to act as if we were the only voice that mattered. I found I enjoyed it. Did you not feel the same?' Tsubodai glanced around at the others and shook his head. 'The nation is falling apart into tribes of tumans, bound not by blood but by the generals who lead them. No, we will not attack Chagatai. My purpose is to prevent civil war, not to be the spark that sets it off.'

Khasar had lost his keen look as Tsubodai spoke, subsiding with an irritated expression.

'Then we are back to keeping Ogedai alive,' he said.

'More than that,' Tsubodai replied. 'We are back to keeping enough of a nation intact for him to have something to rule as khan. I hope you did not expect me to have an answer on a single day, Khasar. We could win here and see Ogedai with the horsetails, yet watch as Chagatai takes away half the army and half the nation. How long would it be then before *two* khans and their armies were facing each other on a field of war?'

'You have made it clear, Tsubodai,' Kachiun said, 'but we can't just sit and wait for disaster.'

'No,' Tsubodai said. 'Very well, I know enough to trust you. Jelme is not here because he is meeting two of the generals who may be loyal to Chagatai. I will know more when I have exchanged messages with him. I cannot meet him again – and yes, Khasar, this is the sort of secret game you despise. The stakes are too high to make a false step.'

'Perhaps you are right,' Khasar said thoughtfully.

Tsubodai shot a sharp glance at the older man.

'I will also need your word, Khasar,' he said.

'On what?'

'Your word not to act on your own. It is true that Chagatai runs every day, though he does not go far from his warriors. There is a small chance you could arrange archers in place to take him from cover, but if you failed, you would ruin everything your brother worked for, everything that cost the lives of so many of those you loved. The entire nation would go up in flames, Khasar.'

Khasar gaped at the general who seemed to be reading his very thoughts. His guilty expression was there for all to see as he forced the cold face. Before he could reply, Tsubodai spoke again.

'Your *word*, Khasar. We want the same thing, but I cannot plan around you, without knowing what you will do.'

'You have it,' Khasar said grimly.

Tsubodai nodded as if it was a minor point in a discussion.

'I will keep you all informed. We cannot meet often, with the number of spies in the camp, so we will send trusted messengers. Write nothing down and never use the name of Chagatai again, not after today. Call him the Broken Lance if you must speak of him. Know that we will find a way through.'

Tsubodai rose smoothly to his feet and thanked Khasar for his hospitality.

'I must leave now, to find out what they promised Jelme in return for his support.' He bowed his head and climbed lithely down the steps, making Khasar and Kachiun feel old just to watch.

'Be grateful for one thing,' Kachiun said softly, watching the general stride away. 'If *he* wanted to be khan, it would be even harder.'

CHAPTER THREE

Ogedai stood in shadows, at the base of the ramp that led to light and air above. The great oval was finished at last, the smell of wood, paint and varnish strong in the air around him. It was easy to imagine the athletes of his people walking out to the roar of thirty thousand men and women. Ogedai saw it all in his mind and he realised he was feeling better than he had for many days. The Chin healer had spoken much about the dangers of foxglove powder, but Ogedai only knew that it eased the constant ache in his chest. Two days before, a sharp pain had driven him to his knees in his private apartments. He grimaced at the remembered pressure, like being trapped in a small space and unable to open his lungs to air. A pinch of the dark powder mixed in red wine had brought release like ropes snapping around his chest. He walked with death, he was certain of it, but it was still two steps behind.

The builders were leaving the great stadium in their thousands, though Ogedai barely looked at the river of exhausted faces passing him. He knew they had worked all night so he would be satisfied, and that was only right. He wondered how they felt about the emperor of the Chin kneeling to his father. If Genghis had been forced to such a shame, Ogedai doubted he could be so calm, so accepting. Genghis had told him that the Chin had no concept of nation. Their ruling elite talked of empires and emperors, but the peasants could not stand high enough to see so far. Instead, they found smaller loyalties to cities and local men. Ogedai nodded to himself. It was not so long since the tribes of his people had done the same. His father had dragged them all into a new era and many of them still did not understand the breadth of his vision.

Most of the crowd stared at the ground as they walked past, terrified of attracting his notice. Ogedai's heart began to beat faster as he saw a different reaction in some of those approaching him. He felt the need to walk out of the shadows into light and had to strangle the urge. His chest ached, but there was none of the terrible weariness that usually dogged him no matter how much he slept. Instead, his senses were alive. He could smell and hear everything around him, from the garlic-laced food of the workmen, to the whispered voices.

The world seemed to strain and then burst, leaving him almost dazed. Ahead of him were men who stared and then deliberately turned away, their reaction marking them out like a raised flag. Ogedai saw no signal, but almost as one they drew knives from their clothing; short, hacking blades of the sort carpenters used to trim posts. The crowd began to swirl as more and more people realised what was happening. Voices cried out hoarsely, but Ogedai remained very still, the centre of the growing storm. He had locked eyes with the closest of the men as he shoved his way past others, his blade held high.

Ogedai watched the man approach. Slowly, he opened his arms wide, then wider, his outstretched hands buffeted by the fleeing crowd. The attacker shouted something, a wild sound lost in the clamour. Ogedai showed his teeth as the man was struck from the side, his body crumpling away from the armoured Guard who had hit him.

As his Guards trampled and slaughtered the men in the shadowy tunnel, Ogedai slowly lowered his arms, watching coldly. They left two alive, as he had ordered, clubbing them down with sword hilts until their faces were swollen masks. The rest were killed like goats.

In just moments, the first officer stood before him, his chest heaving and his pale face spattered with filth.

'Lord, are you well?' the man said, a study of confusion.

Ogedai turned his gaze away from the soldiers still thumping at the dead flesh of men who had dared to attack their master.

'Why would you think otherwise, Huran? I am unharmed. You have done your work.'

Huran bowed his head and almost turned away, but he could not.

'My lord, there was no need for this. We have followed these men for two days. I have searched their lodgings myself and there has never been a moment in Karakorum when I did not have eyes on them. We could have taken them without any risk to you.'

He was clearly struggling to find the right words, but Ogedai felt lighter and stronger than he had in too long. His mood was mellow as he replied.

'Say what you have to say, Huran. You will not offend me.' He had released the man from any need to guard his speech, and he watched the tension and stiffness vanish.

'I live, I work, to protect you, lord,' Huran said. 'On the day you die, I die, I have sworn it. But I cannot protect you if you are . . . if you are in love with death, lord, if you want to die . . .' Under Ogedai's cool gaze, Huran stumbled over the last words and fell silent.

'Put your fears to rest, Huran. You have served me since

I was a boy. I took risks then, did I not? Like any other lad who thinks he will live for ever?'

Huran nodded. 'You did, but you would not have stood with your arms wide then, not with a killer running at you. I saw it, lord, but I did not understand it.'

Ogedai smiled, as if instructing a child. Perhaps it was his closeness to eternity in those moments, but he felt almost light-headed.

'I do not want to die, I promise you, Huran. But I am not afraid of it, not at all. I held open my arms because, in that moment, I did not care. Can you understand that?'

'No, lord,' Huran said.

Ogedai sighed, wrinkling his nose at the smell of blood and excrement in the tunnel.

'The air is foul here,' he said. 'Walk out with me.'

He skirted the heaped bodies. Many had been killed by accident in the fray, simple workmen trying to get out of the darkness. He would have some payment made to their families, he thought.

Huran stayed at his side as the light brightened and Ogedai's gaze fell on the completed arena. His mood soared higher at the sight of the tiered seating, thousands upon thousands of benches stretching into the distance. After the bloodshed at the entrance, it had emptied at astonishing speed, so that Ogedai could hear the song of a bird in the distance, clear and sweet. He was tempted to call across the space to see if his voice would echo. Thirty thousand of his people could sit and watch races and wrestling and the archery wall. It would be glorious.

A spot on his face itched and he rubbed it, raising a reddened finger before his eyes. Someone else's blood.

'Here, Huran, in this place, I will be khan. I will take the oath from my people.'

Huran nodded stiffly and Ogedai smiled at him, knowing

his loyalty was absolute. Yet he did not mention the weakness of the heart that could take his life at any moment. He did not tell Huran that he woke each morning with sharp relief that he had survived the night to see one more dawn, nor how he stayed awake later and later each evening in case that day was his last. The wine and the foxglove powder had brought him relief, but he knew every day, every *breath*, was a blessing. How could he fear a killer when he was always in death's shadow? It was amusing and he chuckled until he felt the ache in his chest again. He considered taking a pinch of the powder under his tongue. Huran would not dare ask about it.

'There are three days until the new moon, Huran. You have kept me alive until now, have you not? How many attacks have you thwarted?'

'Seven, lord,' Huran said softly.

Ogedai looked sharply at him. 'I know of only five, including today. How do you make seven?'

'My man in the kitchens stopped a poisoning this morning, lord, and I had three warriors of your brother murdered in a brawl.'

'You were not certain that they were here to kill me?'

'No, lord, not certain,' Huran admitted. He had left one alive and worked on him for part of the morning, earning nothing but screaming and insults for his trouble.

'You have been rash, Huran,' Ogedai said, without regret. 'We have planned for such attacks. My food is tasted, my servants are hand-picked. My city is under siege from the sheer number of spies and warriors pretending to be simple painters and carpenters. Yet I have opened Karakorum and people are still flooding in. I have three Chin lords staying in my own palace and two Christian monks who have taken a vow of poverty, so bed down in the straw of my royal stables. The oath-taking will be . . . an interesting time, Huran.' He sighed at the soldier's grim worry. 'If all we have done is not enough,

39

perhaps I am not *meant* to survive. The sky father loves a good game, Huran. Perhaps I will be taken from you, despite all your efforts.'

'Not while I live, lord. I *will* call you khan.'

The man spoke with such assurance that Ogedai smiled and clapped him on the shoulder.

'Escort me back to the palace then, Huran. I must resume my duties, after this small amusement. I have kept Orlok Tsubodai waiting long enough, I think.'

Tsubodai had left his armour in the palace rooms he had been given. Every warrior in the tribes knew that Genghis had once approached an enemy without weapons, then used a scale of his armour to cut the man's throat. Instead, Tsubodai wore a light deel robe over leggings and sandals. They had been laid out for him, clean and new, of the best materials. Such luxury in those rooms! Ogedai had borrowed from every culture they had encountered in conquest. It made Tsubodai uncomfortable to see it, though he could not find words for his discomfort. Worse was the bustle and hurry of the palace corridors, packed with people, all intent on errands and work he did not understand. He had not realised there were so many involved in the oath-taking. There were Guards at every corner and alcove, but with so many strange faces, Tsubodai felt a constant itch of worry. He preferred open spaces.

The day had half gone when he grabbed a servant running past him, making the man yelp in surprise. It seemed Ogedai had been busy with some task in the city, but he knew Tsubodai was waiting.

Tsubodai could not leave without giving insult, so he stood in a silent audience room, his impatience growing harder to mask as the hours fled.

The room was empty, though Tsubodai still felt crawling

eyes on him as he strolled to a window and looked over the new city and beyond to the tumans on the plains. The sun was setting, throwing long lines of gold and shadow on the ground and streets below. Ogedai had chosen the site well, with the mountains to the south and the nearby river wide and strong. Tsubodai had ridden along part of the canal Ogedai had built to bring water into the city. It was astonishing, until you considered that a million men had worked for almost two years. With enough gold and silver, anything was possible. Tsubodai wondered if Ogedai would survive to enjoy it.

He had lost track of time when he heard voices approaching. Tsubodai watched closely as Ogedai's Guards entered and took positions. He felt their gaze pass over him and then settle, as the only possible threat in the room. Ogedai came last, his face puffier and far paler than Tsubodai remembered. It was hard not to remember Genghis in those yellow eyes, and Tsubodai bowed deeply.

Ogedai returned the bow, before taking a seat on a wooden bench under the window. The wood was polished and golden and he let his hands enjoy the feel of it as he glanced out at Karakorum. He closed his eyes for a moment as the setting sun cast a last glimpse of gold into the high room.

He had no love for Tsubodai, for all he needed him. If the general had refused Genghis' most brutal order, Ogedai's older brother Jochi would have been khan long since. If Tsubodai had stayed his hand, disobeyed just once, there would be no crisis of leadership heading towards them, threatening to destroy them all.

'Thank you for waiting. I hope my servants have made you comfortable?' he asked at last.

Tsubodai frowned at the question. He had expected the rituals of ger courtesy, but Ogedai's face was open and visibly weary.

'Of course, lord. I need very little.'

41

He paused as footsteps sounded outside the doors and Ogedai rose as new Guards entered, followed by Tolui and his wife Sorhatani.

'You are welcome in my home, brother,' Ogedai said, 'but I did not expect your beautiful wife to attend me.' He turned to Sorhatani smoothly. 'Your children are well?'

'They are, my lord. I brought only Mongke and Kublai. I do not doubt they are causing trouble for your men at this very moment.'

Ogedai frowned delicately. He had asked for Tolui to come to the palace for his own safety. He knew of at least two plots that sought to dispose of the younger brother, but he had expected to explain in private. He glanced at Tolui and saw his brother's gaze rise and drop for a moment. Sorhatani was hard to refuse in anything.

'Your other sons? They are not with you?' Ogedai said to his brother.

'I have sent them to a cousin. He is taking a fishing trip out west for a few months. They will miss the oath-taking, but I will have them make it good when they return.'

'Ah,' Ogedai said, understanding. One pair of sons would survive, no matter what happened. He wondered if it had been Sorhatani who had changed his order for the whole family to appear at the palace. Perhaps she was right to be less than trusting in such bleak times.

'I have no doubt General Tsubodai is bursting with news and dire warnings, brother,' Ogedai said. 'You may return to your rooms, Sorhatani. Thank you for taking a moment to visit me.'

The dismissal could not be refused and she bowed stiffly. Ogedai noticed the furious glance she shot at Tolui as she turned. The gates swung open again and the three men were left alone, with eight Guards along the walls.

Ogedai gestured to a table and they sat, all warier than he could once have believed possible. Losing patience with it all,

Ogedai clinked cups together and filled each one, pushing them towards his guests. They reached for them at the same time, knowing that to hesitate would show they feared poison. Ogedai did not give them long, emptying his own in three quick gulps.

'You two I trust,' he said bluntly, licking his lips. 'Tolui, I have stopped one attempt to kill you, or your sons.' Tolui narrowed his eyes a fraction, growing tense. 'My spies have heard of one other, but I do not know who it is and I am out of time. I can deal with those who seek my death, but I must ask that you stay in the palace. I cannot protect you otherwise, until I am khan.'

'Is it so bad then?' Tolui asked, astonished. He had known the camp was in turmoil, but to hear of open attacks had shaken him. He wished that Sorhatani were there to hear it. He would only have to repeat it all later.

Ogedai turned to Tsubodai. The general sat in simple clothes, but he radiated authority. Ogedai wondered for a moment if it was simply reputation. It was difficult not to look on Tsubodai with awe if you knew what he had achieved in his life. The army owed their success to him as much as to Genghis. Yet for Ogedai it was harder not to look on him with hatred. He locked it away, as he had for more than two years. He still needed this man.

'You are loyal, Tsubodai,' he said softly, 'to my father's will, at least. From your hand, I have word of this "Broken Lance" each day.' He hesitated, struggling for calm. Part of him wanted to leave Tsubodai outside Karakorum on the plains, to ignore the strategist his father had valued over all others. Yet only a fool would waste such a talent. Even then, challenged openly, Tsubodai had not confirmed he was the source of the messengers who appeared at the palace, though Ogedai was almost certain.

'I serve, lord,' Tsubodai said. 'You had my oath, as heir. I have not wavered in that.'

For an instant, Ogedai's anger rose in him like a white spike in his head. This was the man who had cut Jochi's throat in the snow, sitting there and talking of his oath. Ogedai took a deep breath. Tsubodai was too valuable to waste. He had to be managed, thrown off balance.

'My brother Jochi heard your promises, did he not?' he said softly. To his pleasure, the colour fled from the general's face.

Tsubodai remembered every detail of the meeting with Jochi in the northern snows. The son of Genghis had exchanged his life for his men and their families. Jochi had known he was going to die, but he had expected a chance to speak again to his father. Tsubodai was too much of a man to quibble over the rights and wrongs of it. It felt like a betrayal then and it still did. He nodded, jerkily.

'I killed him, lord. It was wrong and I live with it.'

'You broke your word, Tsubodai?' Ogedai pressed, leaning across the table.

His cup fell with a metallic clang and Tsubodai reached out and set it upright. He would not take less than his full share of blame; he could not.

'I did,' Tsubodai replied, his eyes blazing with anger or shame.

'Then redeem your honour!' Ogedai roared, slamming his fists into the table.

All three cups crashed over, spilling wine in a red flood. The Guards drew swords and Tsubodai came to his feet in a jerk, half expecting to be attacked. He found himself staring down at Ogedai, still seated. The general knelt as suddenly as he had risen.

Ogedai had not known how the death of his brother had troubled Tsubodai. The general and his father had kept all that between them. It was a revelation and he needed time to think about what it meant. He spoke instinctively, using the man's own chains to bind him.

'Redeem your word, general, by keeping another son of

Genghis alive long enough to be khan. My brother's spirit would not want to see his family torn and abandoned. My father's spirit would not. Make it so, Tsubodai, and find peace. After that, I do not care what happens, but you will be among the first to take the oath. That would be fitting.'

Ogedai's chest hurt and he could feel sour sweat under his arms and on his brow. A great lethargy settled across his shoulders as his heart thumped slower and slower, reducing him to dizzy exhaustion. He had not slept well for weeks and the constant fear of death was wearing him to a shadow, until only his will remained. He had shocked those present with his sudden rage, but at times he could barely control his temper. He had lived under a great weight for too long and sometimes he simply could not remain calm. He *would* be khan, if even for just a day. His voice was slurred as he spoke. Both Tsubodai and Tolui watched him with worried expressions.

'Stay here tonight, both of you,' Ogedai said. 'There is nowhere safer on the plains, or in the city.'

Tolui nodded immediately, already ensconced in his suite of rooms. Tsubodai hesitated, failing to understand this son of Genghis or what drove him. He could sense a subtle sadness in Ogedai, a loneliness, for all he was surrounded by a great host. Tsubodai knew he could serve better on the plains. Any real threat would come from there, from the tuman of Chagatai. Yet he bowed his head to the man who would be khan at sunset of the following day.

Ogedai rubbed his eyes for a moment, feeling the dizziness clear. He could not tell them that he expected Chagatai to be khan after him. Only the spirits knew how long he had left, but he had built his city. He had left a mark on the plains and he would be khan.

∗   ∗   ∗

45

In darkness, Ogedai awoke. He was sweating in the warm night and he turned over in bed, feeling his wife stir beside him. He was drifting back into sleep when he heard a rattle of running footsteps in the distance. He came alert instantly, raising his head and listening until his neck ached. Who would be running at such an hour – some servant? He closed his eyes again and then heard a faint knock at the outer door of his rooms. Ogedai swore softly and shook his wife by the shoulder.

'Get dressed, Torogene. Something is happening.' In recent days, Huran had begun the habit of sleeping outside the rooms, with his back to the outer door. The officer knew better than to disturb his master without good reason.

The knock sounded again as Ogedai belted a deel robe. He closed the double door on his wife and crossed the outer room, padding barefoot past the Chin tables and couches. There was no moon above the city and the rooms were dark. It was easy to imagine assassins in every shadow and Ogedai lifted a sword from where it hung on the wall. In silence, he removed the scabbard and listened at the door.

Somewhere far away, he heard a distant scream and he jerked back.

'Huran?' he said. Through the heavy oak, he heard the relief in the man's voice.

'My lord, it is safe to open the door,' Huran said.

Ogedai threw back a heavy bolt and lifted an iron bar that anchored the door to the stone wall. In his nervous state, he had not noticed that the corridor cast no threads of light through the cracks. It was darker out there than in his rooms, where dim starlight gleamed through the windows.

Huran came in quickly, stepping past Ogedai to check the rooms. Behind him, Tolui ushered in Sorhatani and his two eldest sons, wrapped in light robes over their sleeping clothes.

'What is happening here?' Ogedai hissed, using anger to cover his spreading panic.

'The guards on our door went away,' Tolui said grimly. 'If I hadn't heard them leave, I don't know what would have happened.'

Ogedai tightened his grip on the sword, taking comfort from the weight of it. He turned at a spill of light from the inner doorway, his wife silhouetted against the lamplight.

'Be still, Torogene, I will attend to this,' he said. To his irritation, she came out anyway, her night robe clutched around her.

'I went to the nearest guardroom,' Tolui went on. He glanced at his sons, who stood watching in open-mouthed excitement. 'They were all dead, brother.'

Huran grimaced as he peered out into the dark corridors.

'I hate to lock us in, my lord, but this is the strongest door in the palace. You will be safe here tonight.'

Ogedai was torn between outrage and caution. He knew every stone of the vast building around them. He had watched each one cut and shaped and polished and fitted into place. Yet all his halls, all his power and influence, would be reduced to just a few rooms when the door closed.

'Keep it open as long as you can,' he said. Surely there were more of his Guards on their way? How could such an attempt have slipped past him?

Somewhere nearby, they heard more running footsteps, the echoes clattering from all directions. Huran put his shoulder to the door. From the blackness, a figure loomed suddenly and Huran struck with his sword blade, grunting as it slid off scaled armour.

'Put that away, Huran,' a voice came, slipping into the room.

In the dim light, Ogedai breathed in relief. 'Tsubodai! What is happening outside?'

The general said nothing. He dropped his sword on the stone floor and helped Huran bar the door, before taking up the blade once again.

'The corridors are full of men; they're searching every room,' he said. 'If it were not for the fact that they have never been inside your palace before, they would be here already.'

'How did you get past?' Huran demanded.

Tsubodai scowled in angry memory. 'Some of them recognised me, but the common warriors have not yet been told to cut me down. For all they know, I am part of the plot.'

Ogedai sagged as he stared round at the small group who had run to his rooms.

'Where is my son Guyuk?' he said. 'My daughters?'

Tsubodai shook his head. 'I did not see them, lord, but there is every chance they are safe. You are the target tonight, no one else.'

Tolui winced as he understood. He turned to his wife. 'Then I have brought you and my sons to the most dangerous place.'

Sorhatani reached out to touch his cheek.

'Nowhere is safe tonight,' she said softly.

They could all hear voices and running feet coming closer. Outside the city, the tumans of the nation slept on, oblivious to the threat.

CHAPTER FOUR

Kachiun walked his pony across the churned grass of the encampment, listening to the sounds of the nation all around him. Despite the stillness of the night, he did not ride alone. Thirty of his personal bondsmen went with him, alert for any attack. No one travelled alone in the camps any more, not with the new moon almost upon them. Lamps and mutton fat torches spat and fluttered at every intersection of paths, revealing dark groups of warriors watching him as he passed.

He could hardly believe the current level of suspicion and tension in the camps. At three points, he was challenged by guards as he approached Khasar's ger. In the night breeze, two lamps cast writhing yellow shadows at his feet. Even as Khasar came yawning out onto the cart, Kachiun could see bows drawn and sighted on him.

'We need to talk, brother,' he said.

Khasar stretched, groaning. 'Tonight?'

'*Yes*, tonight,' Kachiun snapped.

He didn't want to say more, with so many listeners nearby. For once, Khasar sensed his mood and nodded without any more argument. Kachiun watched as his brother whistled softly. Men in full armour walked in from the outer darkness, hands near their swords. They ignored Kachiun and walked to their general, standing close by his feet and looking up at him for orders. Khasar crouched and murmured to them.

Kachiun mastered his impatience until the men bowed their heads and moved away. One of them brought Khasar's current mount, a gelding near black in colour that whickered and kicked out as they saddled it.

'Bring your bondsmen, brother,' Kachiun said to him.

Khasar peered at him in the dim light, seeing the strain in Kachiun's face. He shrugged and gestured to the officers nearby. Another forty warriors trotted to his side, long woken from sleep by the presence of armed men near their master. It seemed that even Khasar was taking no chances on those nights while they waited for the new moon.

Dawn was still hours away, but with the camp in such a state, the movement of so many men woke everyone they passed. Voices called out around them and somewhere a child began wailing. Grim-faced, Kachiun trotted his mount beside his brother, silent as they headed towards Karakorum.

Torches lit the gates in dim gold that night. The walls were pale grey shadows in the darkness, but the western gate gleamed, oak and iron, and clearly shut. Khasar frowned, leaning forward in his saddle to strain his eyes.

'I haven't seen it closed before,' he said over his shoulder. Without thought, he dug in his heels and increased his pace. The warriors around him matched him so smoothly it could have been a battlefield manoeuvre. The noises of the camp, the calling voices, all were lost in the thump of hooves, the breath of horses, the jingle of metal and harness. The western gate of Karakorum grew before them. Khasar could now see ranks of men, facing outwards as if challenging him.

'This is why I woke you,' Kachiun replied.

Both men were brothers to the great khan, uncles to the next. They were generals of proven authority, their names known to every warrior who fought for the nation. When they reached the gate, a visible ripple ran through the ranks of men there, vanishing into the darkness. The bondsmen halted around their masters, hands on sword hilts. On both sides, the men were strung as tightly as their bows. Kachiun and Khasar glanced at each other, then dismounted.

They stood on dusty ground, the grass long since worn away by traffic through the gate. Both men felt the sullen gaze of those who faced them. The men at the gate bore no marks of rank, no flags or banners to identify them. For Kachiun and Khasar, it was as if they looked upon the raiders of their youth, with no allegiance to the nation.

'You know me,' Khasar roared suddenly over their heads. 'Who dares to stand in my way?'

The closest men jerked under a voice that could carry across battlefields, but they did not respond, or move.

'I see no signs of tuman or minghaan in your ranks. I see no flags, just dog-meat wanderers with no master.' He paused and glared at them. 'I am General Khasar Borjigin, of the Wolves, of the *nation* under the great khan. You will answer to me tonight.'

Some of the men shuffled nervously in the lamplight, but they did not flinch from his gaze. Khasar guessed the best part of three hundred men had been sent to close the gate and no doubt it was the same on the other four walls of Karakorum. The bondsmen snarling at his back were outnumbered, but they were the best swordsmen and archers he and Kachiun could field. At a word from either of them, they would attack.

Khasar looked at Kachiun once again, controlling his anger

at the dumb insolence of the warriors facing them. His hand dropped to his sword hilt in unmistakable signal. Kachiun held his gaze for a moment and the warriors on both sides tensed for bloodshed. Almost imperceptibly, Kachiun moved his head a finger's width left and right. Khasar frowned, showing his teeth in frustration for an instant. He leaned in to the closest of those before the gate, breathing into his face.

'I say you are tribeless wanderers, without marks of rank or blood,' Khasar said. 'Don't leave your posts while I am gone. I am going to ride into the city over your bodies.'

The man was sweating and he blinked at the growling voice too close to his neck.

Khasar remounted and he and Kachiun swung away from the pools of light and the promise of death. As soon as they were clear, Kachiun edged his mare over and tapped a hand to his brother's shoulder.

'It has to be the Broken Lance. Ogedai is in the city and someone does not want us riding to his aid tonight.'

Khasar nodded, his heart still hammering. It had been years since he had seen such a show of rebellion from warriors of his people. He was raging, his face flushed.

'My ten thousand will answer the insult,' he snapped. 'Where is Tsubodai?'

'I have not seen him since he went to Ogedai today,' Kachiun replied.

'You are senior. Send runners to his tuman and to Jebe. With them or without them, I am going into that city, Kachiun.'

The brothers and their bondsmen split up, riding different paths that would bring forty thousand men back to the gates of Karakorum.

For a time, the noises on the other side of the door died almost to nothing. With silent gestures, Tsubodai and Tolui lifted a heavy couch, grunting with the effort. It took both of them to shove it across the entrance.

'Are there any other ways in?' Tsubodai murmured.

Ogedai shook his head, then hesitated.

'There are windows in my sleeping chamber, but they open onto a sheer wall.'

Tsubodai cursed under his breath. The first rule of battle was to choose the ground. The second was to know the ground. Both had been taken from him. He looked around at the shadowy gathering, judging their mood. Mongke and Kublai were wide-eyed and thrilled to be part of an adventure. Neither realised the danger they were in. Sorhatani returned his gaze steadily. Under that silent stare, he took a long knife from his boot and passed it into her hands.

'A wall won't stop them tonight,' he said to Ogedai, pressing his ear to the door.

They fell silent as he strained to hear, then jumped at a crash that made Tsubodai leap back. A thin trail of plaster dust curled down from the ceiling and Ogedai winced to see it.

'The corridor is narrow outside,' Ogedai muttered, almost to himself. 'They don't have room to run at it.'

'That is good. Are there weapons here?' Tsubodai asked.

Ogedai nodded. He was his father's son. 'I'll show you,' he said, beckoning.

Tsubodai turned to Huran and found the senior man ready at the door. Another crash sounded and voices rose in anger outside.

'Get a lamp lit,' Tsubodai ordered. 'We don't need to stay in the dark.'

Sorhatani set about the task as Tsubodai strode through to the inner rooms. He bowed formally to Ogedai's wife, Torogene. She had lost her sleepy look and smoothed down her hair with water from a shallow bowl, placed there ready for the morning.

Tsubodai was pleased that neither she nor Sorhatani seemed to be panicking.

'Through here,' Ogedai said ahead of him.

Tsubodai entered the sleeping chamber and nodded in appreciation. A small lamp still glowed there and he saw the wolf's-head sword of Genghis on the wall above the bed. A bow gleamed on the opposite side, each layer of horn and birch and sinew polished to a rich colour.

'Do you have arrows for it?' Tsubodai asked, bending the hooks open with his thumbs and hefting the weapon. Ogedai smiled at the general's evident pleasure.

'It is not a decoration, general. Of course I have arrows,' he replied. A chest produced a quiver of thirty shafts, each the product of a master fletcher and still bright with oil. He tossed it to Tsubodai.

Outside, the crashing went on. Whoever it was had brought up hammers for the task and even the floor trembled with the blows. Tsubodai crossed to the windows set high in the outer wall. Like the ones in the outer room, they were barred in iron. Tsubodai could not help thinking how he would break in, if he were attacking the rooms. Though they were solid enough, they had not been designed to withstand a determined enemy. That enemy was never meant to get close enough, or to have time to hammer out the bars before Ogedai's Guards cut them to pieces.

'Cover the lamp for a moment,' Tsubodai said. 'I do not want to be visible to an archer outside.' He pulled a wooden chest to the window and crouched on it, then rose suddenly to the barred space, ducking back just as quickly.

'There's no one in sight, lord, but the wall to the courtyard below is barely the height of two men. They will come here, if they can find it.'

'But first they'll try the door,' Ogedai said grimly.

Tsubodai nodded. 'Have your wife wait here, perhaps, ready

to call if she hears anything.' Tsubodai was trying to defer to Ogedai's authority, but his impatience showed with every thump from the corridor outside.

'Very well, general.'

Ogedai hesitated, fear and anger mingling, swelling in him. He had not built his city to be torn screaming from life. He had lived with death for so long that it was almost a shock to feel such a powerful desire to live, to avenge. He dared not ask Tsubodai if they could hold the rooms. He could see the answer in the man's eyes.

'It is strange that you are present for the death of another of Genghis' sons, don't you think?' he said.

Tsubodai stiffened. He turned back and Ogedai saw no weakness in his black stare.

'I carry many sins, lord,' Tsubodai said. 'But this is not the time to talk about old ones. If we survive, you may ask whatever you need to know.'

Ogedai began to reply, bitterness welling up in him. A new sound made them both whip round and run. An iron hinge had cracked and the wood of the outer door splintered, a panel yawning open. The lamplight from the room spilled out into the darker corridor, illuminating sweating faces. At the door, Huran speared his blade into them, so that one at least fell back with a cry of pain.

The stars had moved part-way across the sky by the time Khasar roused his tuman. He rode at the head in full armour, his sword drawn and held low by his right thigh. In formation behind him were ten groups of a thousand, each with their minghaan officers. Each thousand had its jaguns of a hundred men, led by officers bearing a silver plaque. Even they had their structures: ten groups of ten, with equipment to raise a ger between them and food and tools to survive and fight. Genghis and Tsubodai had created the system, and Khasar hadn't given it a thought when he issued just one order to his quiriltai, his quartermaster. The tuman of ten thousand had formed on the plain, men running to their horses in what looked like chaos before the ranks coalesced and they were ready. Ahead lay Karakorum.

Khasar's outriders reported other tumans on the move all around him. No one in the nation slept now. To the smallest child, they knew this was the night of crisis, so long feared.

Khasar had his naccara drummers sound a rhythm: dozens of unarmed boys on camels whose sole task was to inspire fear in an enemy with a rolling thunder. He heard it answered ahead and on the left, as other tumans took up a warning and a challenge. Khasar swallowed drily, looking for Kachiun's men ahead. He had the feeling that events were slipping from his control, but he could do nothing else. His path had been set when men at the gate had dared to refuse a general of the nation. He knew they were Chagatai's, but the arrogant prince had sent them out without his unit markings, to do his work like assassins in the night. Khasar could not ignore such a threat to his authority – to all the stages of authority that he represented, down to the youngest drummer on a sway-backed beast. He dared not think of his nephew Ogedai trapped in his own city. He could only react and force his way in, hoping there would be someone still alive to save.

Kachiun joined him, with Jebe's Bearskin tuman and Tsubodai's ten thousand. Khasar breathed in relief as he saw the banners stretching away into the dark, a sea of horses and flags. Tsubodai's warriors knew their general was in the city. They had not disputed Kachiun's right to order them in his place.

Like a mountain slowly falling, the vast array of four tumans drew close to the western gate of Karakorum. Khasar and Kachiun rode forward, hiding their impatience. There was no need for bloodshed, even then.

The men at the gate remained still, their weapons sheathed. Whatever their orders had been, they knew that to draw a blade was to invite instant destruction. No man wanted to be first.

The tableau held, with just the snorting of horses and fluttering banners. Then out of the darkness rode a new group of men, their passage lit with burning torches held by bannermen, so that in an instant, every man there knew that Chagatai had arrived.

Kachiun could have ordered Khasar to block Genghis' son and had his own tumans cut a way into the city. He felt the weight of the decision hang on him, time running slowly as his pulse raced. He was not a man to hesitate, but he was not at war. This was not the desert of Khwarezm or the walls of a Chin city. He let the moment pass, and as it went, he clutched at it desperately, almost throwing away his life when it was too late.

Chagatai rode in like a khan, his bondsmen surrounding him in square formation. Some of the men at the gate went sprawling as horses knocked them down, but he did not look round. His gaze was fixed firmly on the two older generals, his father's brothers, and the only men who mattered in the camp that night. He and his horse were armoured and the air was cold enough for Kachiun to see plumes of mist from man and beast alike. Chagatai wore an iron helmet, with a horse's-mane crest whipping through the air as he came in. He was no longer the boy they had known and both men tensed under his flat stare.

Khasar made a hissing sound under his breath, signalling his anger to his brother. They knew Chagatai was there to prevent them entering Karakorum. They were not yet sure how far he would go to keep them outside.

'It is late to be training your men, Chagatai,' Khasar snapped, his voice loud.

They were separated by less than fifty paces, closer than he

57

had been allowed to the man in a month. Khasar ached to reach for his bow, though the armour would likely save his target and then there would be a blood-letting on a scale unseen since they had destroyed the Xi Xia. The prince shrugged as he sat his horse, smiling with cold confidence.

'I am not training, uncle. I am riding to see who threatens the peace of the camp in darkness. I find it is my own uncles, moving armies in the night. What am I to make of it, eh?' He laughed and the men around him showed their teeth, though their hands never left the bows, swords and lances with which they fairly bristled.

'Be careful, Chagatai,' Khasar said.

The prince's expression went hard at the words. 'No, uncle. I will *not* be careful when armies ride through my land. Return to your ger, your wives and children. Tell your men to go back to theirs. You have no business here tonight.'

Khasar took a breath to roar an order and Kachiun shouted before he unleashed the tumans.

'You have no authority over us, Chagatai! Your men are outnumbered, but there is no need for blood to be spilled. We will enter the city tonight, now! Stand aside and there will be no strife between us.'

Chagatai's horse sensed his surging emotions and he had to turn it on the spot to stay in position, sawing its mouth with the reins. They could read the triumph on his face and, privately, both men despaired for Ogedai in the city.

'You misjudge me, uncle,' Chagatai shouted, making sure he was heard by as many ears as possible. '*You* are the ones trying to force your way into Karakorum! For all I know, you are planning bloody murder in the city, a coup, with my brother's head as the prize. I have come to stop you entering, to keep the peace.' He sneered at their surprise, his face savage as he waited for the arrows to fly.

Kachiun heard movement on his right and jerked in the

saddle to see vast ranks of men moving into position around him, their officers lit with torches. He could not judge the numbers in the starlight, but his heart sank as he saw the banners of those loyal to Chagatai. The two sides glowered at each other, roughly equal, but Chagatai had done enough and he knew it. Kachiun and Khasar could not begin a civil war in the shadow of Karakorum. Kachiun looked east for the first signs of dawn, but the sky was dark and Ogedai was on his own.

CHAPTER FIVE

'Down, Huran!' Tsubodai snapped.

He notched an arrow on the string as he ran. Huran dropped flat below the hole in the door and Tsubodai sent a shaft hissing through into the darkness beyond. He was rewarded by a choking cry as he drew and loosed again. The distance was no more than ten paces. Any warrior of the tribes could have hit the gap, even under pressure. As soon as Tsubodai shot the second arrow, he dropped to one knee and rolled out of the way. Before he had stopped moving, a shaft buzzed into the room, going almost too fast to see. It struck behind Tsubodai with a loud thump, quivering in the wooden floor.

Huran had taken up a position with his back flat to the door, his head turned towards the hole. He was rewarded as a hand darted through, fingers scrabbling for the locking bar below. Huran swung his sword horizontally, cutting through meat and bone and almost jamming the blade into the wood. The hand and part of the forearm dropped to the ground and an unearthly screaming sounded before it too was choked off. Perhaps those outside had led the man away to be tended, or killed him themselves.

Tsubodai nodded to Huran as their eyes met. Regardless of rank, they were the two most capable warriors in the room, able to remain calm and think, even when the smell of blood was thick.

Tsubodai turned to Ogedai. 'We need a second position, lord.'

The man who would be khan was standing with his father's wolf's-head sword drawn, breathing too shallowly and looking paler than Tsubodai had seen him before. Tsubodai frowned to himself as Ogedai didn't respond. He spoke louder, using his voice to snap the younger man out of his trance.

'If the door goes, they will rush us, Ogedai. You understand? We need a second place, a line of retreat. Huran and I will stay by this door, but you must get the boys and women back to the inner rooms and block the door as best you can.'

Ogedai turned his head slowly, dragging his eyes away from the dark hole that seemed to vomit forth the hatred of those behind it.

'You expect me to burrow myself away to gain a few more heartbeats of life? With my own children being hunted some-where out there? I would rather die here, on my feet and facing my enemies.'

He meant it, Tsubodai saw, but Ogedai's gaze drifted over Sorhatani and her two sons. For a moment, he locked eyes with his younger brother Tolui. Ogedai wilted under the stares of the family.

'Very well, Tsubodai, but I will return here. Tolui, bring your wife and sons and help me block up the inner door.'

'Take the bow with you,' Tsubodai said, yanking the quiver from his shoulders and tossing it to Ogedai.

The group of five moved back carefully, always aware of the

line of sight for an archer in the halls outside. They knew a bowman was waiting in the darkness and they knew the patience of their people, used to hunting marmots on the plains. The archer's field of vision formed a cone that crossed the outer room down the centre.

Without warning, Ogedai darted across the space and Sorhatani rolled, coming smoothly to her feet like a dancer. No arrow came as they reached a safe spot and turned.

Tolui stood on the other side. He had found a place in the shelter of a heavy beam with his sons, his face stiff with fear for them.

'I will go last, lads, understand?' he told them.

Mongke nodded immediately, but Kublai shook his head.

'You are the largest and the slowest,' he said, his voice quavering. 'Let me go last.'

Tolui considered. If the archer was waiting with an arrow on the string and the bow half bent, he could loose a shot in an eye-blink, almost without aiming. Any of the men there would have wagered on the archer over them. The crashing at the door had stopped, as if the men outside were waiting. Perhaps they were. Out of the corner of his eye, he saw Ogedai's wife Torogene beckoning to him.

It was just a few feet across a room, but it had become a chasm. Tolui took a deep, slow breath, calming himself and thinking of his father. Genghis had told him about breath, how men will hold theirs when they are frightened, or take a sudden breath before they launch an attack. It was a sign to watch for in an enemy. In yourself, it was a tool to manage fear. He took another slow breath and his hammering heart eased slightly in his chest. Tolui smiled at Kublai's nervous defiance.

'Do as you're told, boy. I'm quicker than you think.' He laid a hand on each son's shoulder and whispered. 'Go together. Ready? Now!'

Both boys sprinted across the innocent-looking space. An

arrow flashed through the gap, passing behind Kublai's back. He fell sprawling and Sorhatani dragged him clear, hugging him to her in desperate relief. She turned with her sons to look at Tolui, who nodded to them, sweat beading his brow. He had married a woman of aching beauty and he smiled at her fierce expression, like a mother wolf with her cubs. The archer was clearly ready and they had been lucky. He cursed himself for not following immediately, before the archer could notch another shaft. He had lost the moment and perhaps his life as a result. He looked around for some sort of shield – a table, or even a thick cloth to spoil the man's aim. The corridor was still silent as the attackers let their bowman work. Tolui took another slow breath, readying his muscles to spring across the gap and dreading the thought of a shaft tearing into him, smashing him off his feet in front of his family.

'Tsubodai!' Sorhatani called.

The general glanced back at her, catching her beseeching gaze and understanding. He had nothing to block the hole for the time they needed. His gaze fell on the single lamp. He hated the thought of plunging the room into darkness once again, but there was nothing else. He swept it up, flinging it through the hole from the side of the door. The crash sent Tolui safely across the gap to his family and Tsubodai heard the thump of an arrow released into the door itself, the aim ruined. Kublai cheered the act and Mongke joined him.

For a few moments, the room remained lit by the flaming oil on the other side, but the men there stamped the flames out and they were left in blackness once again, far deeper than before. There was still no sign of dawn. The furious crashing resumed and splinters flew as the door groaned in its frame.

Tolui worked quickly at the entrance to the inner room. The door there had none of the strength of the outer one. It would not delay the attackers beyond the first few moments. Instead, Tolui kicked out the delicate hinges and began to make a barricade across the doorway. As he worked, he gripped his sons by the neck in quick affection, then sent them scurrying into Ogedai's sleeping chamber to gather anything they could lift. He saw Torogene murmuring to them and they relaxed as she directed them. Both young men were used to their mother's commands and Torogene was a large woman, motherly and brisk in her manner.

There was another small lamp there. Torogene handed it out to Sorhatani, who placed it so that some of its light reached Tsubodai. It made huge shadows in the rooms, great dark figures that leapt and danced, dwarfing them all.

They worked in grim concentration. Tsubodai and Huran knew they would have just moments to retreat when the outer door gave way. The couch braced against it would be no more than a nuisance to the attackers as they poured in. Behind them, Sorhatani and Tolui built their barricade without speaking, jittery from fear and lack of sleep. The boys brought them wood panelling, bedclothes, even a heavy pedestal that had to be dragged over the floor, leaving a long scar. It would not hold against determined men. Even young Kublai understood that, or saw it in his parents' bleak expressions. When their pitiful collection of debris was in place, they stood behind it with Ogedai and Torogene, panting and waiting.

Sorhatani rested one hand on Kublai's shoulder, holding Tsubodai's long knife in the other. She wished desperately for more light, terrified of being killed in the gloom, overwhelmed by struggling, bloody bodies. She could not consider losing Kublai and Mongke. It was as if she stood on the edge of a high cliff and to look at them was to step off and drop. She heard Tolui's long, slow breaths and copied him, breathing through her nose. It helped a little, in the dark, as the outer door cracked suddenly down its length and the men outside grunted and howled in anticipation.

Tsubodai and Huran were both wary of the archer on the

other side of the door. Each man had to judge when the blows against the rapidly splintering wood would obstruct the hidden man, then strike a blow into the faces in the dark. The attackers were pressing, knowing they were near to getting in at last. More than one fell back with a cry from a sword blade, licking out like a fang and withdrawing before the archer could see through his own people. Someone out there was dying noisily and Huran was panting. He was in awe of the ice general fighting at his side. Tsubodai could have been at a training bout for all the emotion his face showed.

Yet they could not hold the door. Both men tensed as a low panel broke into splinters. Half the door remained, cracked and loose. Crouching men came struggling under the locking bar and both Huran and Tsubodai stood their ground, plunging their blades into exposed necks. Blood splashed them both as they refused to yield, though the archer had moved and sent a shaft that spun Huran around, winding him.

He knew his ribs had broken. Every breath was agony, as if his lungs inflated against a shard of glass, but he could not even check the wound to see if his armour had saved him. More men were kicking at the bar, loosening its bolts in the wall. When that finally gave way, the two warriors would be swallowed in the flood.

Huran gasped hoarsely as he continued to strike out, seeking bare necks and arms beyond the hole. He saw blades jabbing at him and felt blows on his shoulders and legs. He could taste iron bitterness in his mouth and his arms seemed slower as he swung and swung, each breath burning him with its sweetness and heat.

He fell then, thinking he must have slipped in someone's blood. Huran saw the iron bar spring out. The room seemed lighter somehow, as if the wolf's dawn had come at last. Huran gasped as someone trod on his outstretched hand, breaking bones, but the pain was fleeting. He was dead before Tsubodai had turned at bay to face the men who roared into that room, wild with release and hungry to do their work.

The stalemate at the gates had become Chagatai's triumph. He had enjoyed his uncles' expressions as Jelme brought a tuman up to his side. Tolui's tuman had matched him on the other side, its men straining at the leash with knowledge that their lord and his family were trapped in the city, perhaps already dead.

One by one, all the generals of the nation brought their men to the city walls, stretching away into the darkness. More than a hundred thousand warriors stood ready to fight if they had to, but there was no battle heat in them while their commanders sat and stared coldly at each other.

Jochi's son Batu had declared for Kachiun and Khasar. He was barely seventeen years old, but his thousand men followed his lead and he rode with his head high. He was a prince of the nation despite his youth and his father's fate. Ogedai had seen to that, promoting him as Genghis would never have done. Even so, Batu had chosen to stand against the most powerful man in the tribes. Kachiun sent a runner to him to thank him for the gesture.

In Tsubodai's absence, Kachiun's mind was running faster than his peaceful look suggested. He thought Jelme was still loyal to Ogedai, though Chagatai had accepted him. It was no small thing to have perhaps a sixth of an enemy's army ready to turn against him at a crucial point. Yet the sides were too evenly matched. Kachiun had a vision of the army falling in on itself until there were just hundreds left alive, then dozens, then just one or two. What then of the great dream Genghis had given them? He at least would never have countenanced such a waste of life and strength – not among their own people.

The wolf dawn showed in the east, the faint greying of the

land before the sun rose above the horizon. The light spread over the host gathered by Karakorum, illuminating the faces of the generals and their men so that there was no need for torches. Even then, they did not move and Chagatai sat and chatted with his bondsmen, barking out laughter as he enjoyed the new day and everything it would bring.

When the first thin line of gold appeared in the east, Chagatai's second in command clapped him on the back and the men around him cheered. The sound was quickly taken up by the other tumans on his side. Those with Khasar and Kachiun sat in sullen and thoughtful silence. It did not take a mind like Tsubodai's to interpret Chagatai's pleasure. Kachiun watched with narrow eyes as Chagatai's men began to dismount, so that they could kneel to him as khan. He pursed his mouth in rising fury. He had to stop it, before it became a wave across all the tumans and Chagatai was made khan on a wave of oaths, before Ogedai's fate was even known.

Kachiun moved his horse forward, holding up a hand to the men who would have followed him. Khasar too came forward, so that they rode alone through the ranks of men towards Chagatai.

Their nephew was ready from the first step they took in his direction, as he had been all night. Chagatai drew his sword in unmistakable threat, but he still smiled as he gestured to his bondsmen to let them through. The rising sun lit the host of warriors. Their armour glimmered like a sea of iron fish, scaled and dangerous.

'It is a new day, Chagatai,' Kachiun said. 'I will see your brother Ogedai now. You will open the city.'

Chagatai glanced once more at the dawn and nodded to himself.

'I have done my duty, uncle. I have protected his city from those who might have run riot inside on the eve of the oath-taking. Come, ride with me to my brother's palace. I must be certain he is safe.' He grinned as he spoke the last words and Kachiun looked away rather than see. He watched the gates begin to open, laying the empty streets of Karakorum bare before them.

Tsubodai was no longer a young man, but he wore full armour and he had been a soldier longer than most of the attackers had been alive. As they came in a welter of limbs and blades, he darted six steps away from the door. Without warning, he spun and lunged, taking the closest man to him through the throat. Two more brought their blades down in reaction, hacking wildly at his scaled armour and leaving bright marks in the tarnish. Tsubodai's mind was perfectly clear, faster than their movements. He had expected to retreat immediately, but the hurried blows showed him their weariness and desperation. He struck again, reversing his blade for a pull stroke that jerked the steel across a man's forehead, opening a flap so that he was blinded with blood. It was a mistake. Two men grabbed hold of Tsubodai's right arm. Another kicked his legs away and he fell with a crash.

On the ground, Tsubodai exploded into a frenzy. He lashed out in all directions, using his armour as a weapon and always moving, making himself harder to hit. The metal plates on his leg opened a gash in someone's thigh and then he heard roaring and still more men poured into the room, more than it could hold. Tsubodai struggled on desperately, knowing he had lost and Ogedai had lost. Chagatai would be khan. He tasted his own blood in the back of his throat, as bitter as his rage.

At the barricade, Ogedai and Tolui waited shoulder to shoulder. Sorhatani stood with the bow, unable to shoot while Tsubodai still lived. When he went down, she sent two shafts between her husband and his brother. Her arms were nowhere near strong enough for a full draw, but one of the arrows checked a man in his rush while the other ricocheted away into the ceiling. Ogedai stepped in front of her as she struggled to notch a third with shaking fingers. The view beyond the barricade was blocked with grasping hands and blades and bloody faces. She did not understand what was happening at first. She flinched at a roar as more men came into the outer room. Some of those struggling with Ogedai and Tolui turned at the sound and then they were yanked back. Sorhatani saw a sword appear through the throat of a man facing her, as if he had grown a long and bloody tongue. He fell jerking and the view was suddenly clear.

Ogedai and Tolui panted like dogs in the sun. In the other room, a group of armoured men were finishing off the attackers with quick, efficient blows.

Jebe stood there, and at first he ignored the survivors, even Ogedai. He had seen Tsubodai on the ground and knelt at his side just as the general struggled to his knees. Tsubodai was shaking his head; dazed and gashed, but alive.

Jebe rose and saluted Ogedai with his sword.

'I am pleased to see you well, my lord,' he said, smiling.

'How are you here?' Ogedai snapped, his blood still surging with anger and fear.

'Your uncles sent me, lord, with forty bondsmen. We had to kill a lot of men to reach you.'

Tolui clapped his brother on the back in delight before he turned and embraced Sorhatani. Kublai and Mongke punched each other on the shoulders and mock-scuffled until Kublai was in Mongke's headlock.

'Tsubodai? General?' Ogedai said.

He watched as Tsubodai's glazed eyes cleared. A warrior put out his hand to steady the general and Tsubodai batted it away irritably, still shaken by how close he had come to death at the feet of the attackers. When Tsubodai got to his feet, Jebe turned to him, as if reporting.

'The Broken Lance closed the gates of the city. All the tumans are outside, on the plain. It may be war yet.'

'How then did you get inside my city?' Ogedai demanded. He looked for Huran and remembered with a pang of loss that the man had given his life at the first door.

'We climbed the walls, my lord,' Jebe said. 'General Kachiun sent us before he rode to try and force his way in.' He saw Ogedai's look of surprise and shrugged. 'They are not so very high, my lord.'

The rooms were lighter, Ogedai realised. Dawn had come to Karakorum and the day promised to be fine. With a start, he remembered this was the day of the oath-taking. He blinked, trying to put his thoughts in some sort of order, to see a way through after such a night. That there even was an 'after' was more than he had expected in the last moments. He felt dazed, lost in events beyond his control.

In the corridor outside, running footsteps could be heard. A messenger came pelting into the room and skidded to a halt, shocked by the mass of dead flesh and the collection of blades levelled at him. The room stank of opened bowels and urine, thick and choking in the enclosed space.

'Report,' Jebe said, recognising the scout.

The young man steadied himself. 'The gates have reopened, general. I ran all the way, but there is an armed force coming.'

'Of course there is,' Tsubodai said, his deep voice startling everyone there. They all looked to him and Ogedai felt a surge of relief that he was there. 'Everyone who was outside the walls last night will be coming here to see who survives.' He turned to Ogedai then.

'My lord, we have just moments. You must be clean and changed when they see you. This room must be sealed. It will keep for today at least.'

Ogedai nodded gratefully and Tsubodai snapped quick orders. Jebe went first, leaving six men to form a guard for the one who would be khan. Ogedai and Torogene followed, with Tolui and his family close behind. As they hurried down a long corridor, Ogedai saw that Tolui's hand kept drifting to his wife or his sons as he strode, still hardly able to believe they were all safe.

'The children, Ogedai,' Torogene said.

He glanced at her and saw that her face was pale and drawn with worry. He put his arm around her shoulders and both of them took comfort from the other. Looking over her head, Ogedai could see no one who knew the palace well. Where was his servant, Baras'aghur? He addressed Jebe, as the closest man.

'General, I must know if my son Guyuk survived the night. My daughters also. Have one of your men find their quarters – ask a servant. Bring me the news as quickly as you can. And find my chancellor, Yao Shu – and Baras'aghur. Get them moving. See who still lives.'

'Your will, my lord,' Jebe said quickly, bowing his head. Ogedai seemed almost manic, his mood hard to read. It was more than the excitement that can come after a battle, when life courses more strongly in the veins.

Ogedai rushed on, his wife and Guards struggling to keep up. Somewhere ahead, he could hear marching feet and he darted down another corridor away from the sound. He needed fresh clothes and to wash the blood and filth off him. He needed time to think.

Kachiun had become cold and pale as they rode through the streets, approaching Ogedai's palace. There seemed to be bodies everywhere, with pools of darkening blood staining the polished stone gutters. Not all of them bore the marks of Ogedai's Guard tuman. Others wore dark deels or armour rubbed with lamp-black, dull and greasy in the dawn light. The night had been bloody and Kachiun dreaded what he would see in the palace itself.

71

Chagatai rode lightly, shaking his head at such destruction until Khasar considered cutting his throat and wiping the expression off his face. The presence of three of Chagatai's bondsmen kept his hand from his sword hilt. They did not stare at the dead. Their eyes were only for the two men riding with their lord, the man who would be khan before the end of the day.

The streets were silent. If any workers had left their homes after the clashes and screams of the night, the sight of so many bodies had sent them scurrying back to bar the doors. The six horsemen made their way to the steps leading up to the palace doors. Dead men lay splayed on the pale marble, their blood in patterns along the veins of stone.

Chagatai did not dismount, but urged his pony up the steps, clicking his tongue as it trod gingerly past the corpses. The main door to the first courtyard stood open and there was no one to challenge his right to enter. Crows called to each other and there were hawks and vultures already overhead, drawn by the scent of death on the breeze. Kachiun and Khasar looked at each other in grim surmise as they passed under a bar of shadow into the yard beyond. The tree of silver shone there in the dawn, beautiful and lifeless.

The generals could read the patterns of dead well enough. There had been no fixed battle, with lines of men cut down. Instead, the bodies lay randomly, killed from behind or taken by shafts they never saw. They could almost sense the defenders' surprise as men dressed in shadows had appeared and killed, cutting through them before anyone could organise a defence. In the silence, Chagatai was rapt as he dismounted at last. His pony was skittish with the smell of blood and he made a point of tying the reins securely to a post.

'I begin to fear for my brother,' Chagatai said.

Khasar tensed and one of the bondsmen raised a hand to him, reminding him of their presence. The man was grinning, enjoying his master's show.

72

'You need not fear,' came a voice, making them all jump.

Chagatai spun instantly, his sword leaping out of its scabbard in one movement. His bondsmen were barely slower, ready for any attack.

Tsubodai stood there under an arch of carved limestone. He wore no armour and the morning breeze had not dried the patches of sweat on his silk tunic. A strip of cloth bound his left forearm and Chagatai could see a smear of blood seeping through it. Tsubodai's face was weary but strong and his eyes were terrible as they met those of the man responsible for the death and destruction all around them.

Chagatai opened his mouth to demand some explanation, but Tsubodai went on.

'My lord Ogedai is waiting for you in his audience hall. He bids you welcome in his home. He guarantees your safety.' He spoke the last words as if they stuck in his throat.

Chagatai looked away from the rage he saw in the general. For an instant, his shoulders sagged as he understood his defeat. He had gambled it all on a single night. He did not look up at the slight sound of boots on stone above his head as archers appeared. He bit his lower lip and nodded to himself. Even so, he was his father's son. He stood straight and sheathed his sword with the care of ritual. No trace of his shock or disappointment showed on his face as he smiled wryly at Tsubodai.

'Thank the spirits he has survived,' Chagatai said. 'Take me to him, general.'

CHAPTER SIX

Chagatai's bondsmen remained in the courtyard. They would have fought if he had asked them. Instead, he clapped one of them on the shoulder and shook his head before striding into the cloister behind Tsubodai. Chagatai did not look back as his men were surrounded by warriors of Ogedai and beaten to the ground. When one of them cried out, Chagatai set his jaw, disappointed the man could not die quietly for the honour of his master.

Khasar and Kachiun followed in silence. They watched Chagatai fall in beside Tsubodai, neither man looking at the other. At the audience chamber, Guards were all around and Chagatai merely shrugged and gave up his sword.

The door was of polished copper, red-gold in the morning light. Chagatai expected to enter, but the Guard officer tapped him on the armour and stood back, waiting. Chagatai grimaced, but he removed his long, scaled jacket and thigh pieces, as well as the heavy gloves and arm protectors. It was not long before he stood in just his jerkin, leggings and boots. It might have diminished another man to be so stripped, but Chagatai had been training for the festival for many months, wrestling, running and shooting hundreds of arrows each day. He was in superb physical condition and he made most of those around him look smaller and weaker than they were.

Not so Tsubodai. None of the Guards dared to come close to that man as he stood and silently dared Chagatai to protest. Though Tsubodai remained still, it was the stillness of a snake, or a sapling bent and ready to spring back.

Finally, Chagatai faced the Guard officer with one eyebrow raised. He endured being patted down, but he had no hidden weapons and the door swung open. He walked in alone. As it closed behind him, he heard Khasar begin to argue as he was held back. Chagatai was pleased Tsubodai and his uncles would not be witnesses. He had gambled and lost, but there was no shame in it, no humiliation. Ogedai had gathered loyal men to him, just as Chagatai had. His brother's generals had proved more resourceful than his own. As it had been the night before, one brother would still be khan, and the other? Chagatai grinned suddenly as he saw Ogedai at the far end of the hall, sitting on a throne of white stone inlaid with patterns of gold. It was an impressive sight, as it was intended to be.

As he walked closer, Chagatai saw Ogedai's hair was damp, loose and black on his shoulders. A purple mark on his cheek was the only visible proof of the night before. Despite the grandeur of the throne, his brother wore a simple grey deel over leggings and a tunic, with no more decoration than any herder of the plains.

'I am glad to see you well, brother,' Chagatai said.

Ogedai tensed as Chagatai walked smoothly towards him, his steps echoing.

'Let us not play games,' he replied. 'I have survived your attacks. I will be khan at sunset today.'

75

Chagatai nodded, still smiling. 'No games then, but you know, the strange thing is I spoke the truth. Part of me was dreading finding you killed. Ridiculous, yes?' He chuckled, amused at the complexity of his own emotions. Family was a peculiar thing. 'Still, I did what I thought best. I have no regrets or apologies. I think father would have enjoyed the risks I took.' He bowed his head. 'You'll forgive me if I don't congratulate you on your triumph.'

Ogedai relaxed subtly. He had spent years thinking of Chagatai as an arrogant idiot. He had almost missed him growing into a man used to responsibility and power. As Chagatai came to stand before him, Ogedai's Guards stepped out and commanded him to kneel. He ignored them, remaining on his feet and looking around the room with an interested expression. It was a huge space to a warrior more used to the gers of the plains. The morning light flooded in from a window overlooking the city.

One of the Guards turned to Ogedai for permission and Chagatai smiled slightly. With any other prisoner, the man would have struck him down, or even hamstrung him to make him kneel. The hesitation acknowledged Chagatai's power even as they sought to humble him.

Ogedai could almost admire his brother's careless courage. No, he *could* admire it, even after such a night. The shadow of Genghis hung over them both and perhaps it always would. Neither they nor Tolui could ever match their father's achievement. By any standard, they were lesser souls and had been from the moment they were born. Yet they had to live and grow and become men, skilful in their crafts. They had to thrive in that shadow – or let it smother them.

No one else understood Ogedai's life as Chagatai did, not even their brother Tolui. He wondered again if he was making the right decision, but in that too he had to be strong. A man could waste his life worrying, that was all too clear. Sometimes

76

you simply had to choose and shrug, however it came out, knowing that you could not have done more with the bones you were given.

Ogedai faced his brother and wished one last time that he could know how long he had to live. Everything depended on it. His son did not have the ruthless will to inherit. If Ogedai died that very day, Guyuk would not follow in the line of their father, the line of Genghis. It would pass to the man standing before him. Ogedai searched for calm, though his heart thumped and pattered in his chest, spreading a constant ache until it became like a blade between his ribs. He had not slept and he knew he ran the risk of collapse in dealing with Chagatai that morning. He had drunk a jug of red wine to steady his nerves and used a pinch of the foxglove powder. He could still taste the bitterness on his tongue and his head ached as if it was being slowly crushed.

For all he knew, he might rule as khan for just days before his heart gave out and burst in his chest. If that was his fate and he had killed Chagatai, the nation would tear itself apart in civil war. Tolui was not strong enough to hold them together. Neither he nor Ogedai's son had gathered loyal generals to protect them through such an upheaval. Power would triumph over blood in that struggle.

The man who stood before him, his tension hidden, was perhaps the best hope for the nation. More, Chagatai was the one Genghis would have chosen if their brother Jochi had never been born. Ogedai felt his damp hair itch and he rubbed it unconsciously. The Guards still looked to him, but he would not let them beat Chagatai to his knees, not that day, though part of him yearned to see it.

'You are safe here, brother,' he said. 'I have given my word.'

'And your word is iron,' Chagatai murmured, almost automatically.

Both of them recalled their father's beliefs and honoured

them. The great khan's shadow clung to them like a cloak. The shared memories made Chagatai look up and frown, suddenly at a loss. He had expected to be killed, but Ogedai seemed troubled rather than triumphant or even vengeful. He watched with interest as Ogedai turned to his Guard officer.

'Clear the room. What I have to say is for my brother alone.' The man began to move but Ogedai stopped him with a raised hand. 'No, bring Orlok Tsubodai as well.'

'Your will, my lord,' the officer replied, bowing deeply.

In just moments, the Guards along the walls were marching to the great copper doors. Tsubodai came in at their call. Outside, Khasar could be heard still arguing with the officers before the door swung shut, leaving the three men alone in the echoing space.

Ogedai rose from the throne and stepped down so that he was at Chagatai's level. He crossed to a small table and poured himself a cup of airag from a jug, drinking deeply and wincing as it stung ulcers in his mouth.

Chagatai glanced at Tsubodai only to find the man glaring at him like an enemy. He winked at the general and looked away.

Ogedai took a slow breath and his voice shook at the strain of saying what he had kept hidden for so long.

'I am my father's heir, Chagatai. Not you, or Tolui, or Kachiun, or Jochi's son, or any of the generals. As the sun sets today, I will accept the oath of the nation.' He paused and neither Chagatai nor Tsubodai interrupted as the silence stretched. Ogedai looked out of the tall window, enjoying the sight of his city, though it was quiet and frightened after such a night.

'There is a world outside the one we know,' he said softly, 'with cultures and races and armies who have never heard of us. Yes, and cities greater than Yenking and Karakorum. To survive, to grow, we must remain strong. We must conquer new lands, so that our army is always fed, always moving. To stop is to die, Chagatai.'

'I know this,' Chagatai said. 'I am not a fool.'

Ogedai smiled wearily. 'No. If you were a fool, I would have had you killed in the courtyard with your bondsmen.'

'Then why am I still alive?' Chagatai said. He tried to keep his tone casual, but this was the question that had burnt him ever since he saw Tsubodai in the courtyard of the palace.

'Because I may not live to see the nation grow, Chagatai,' Ogedai said at last. 'Because my heart is weak and I could die at any moment.'

The two men facing him stared as if struck. Ogedai couldn't bear to wait for their questions. Almost with relief, he went on, the words spilling out.

'I remain alive with the help of bitter Chin powders, but I have no way of knowing how long I have left. I wanted just to see my city finished and to be khan. Here I am, still alive, though I live in pain.'

'Why was I not told this before?' Chagatai said slowly, stunned by the implications. He knew the answer before Ogedai replied and nodded as his brother spoke.

'Would you have given me two years to build a city, a tomb? No, you would have challenged me as soon as you heard. Instead, I have made Karakorum and I will be khan. I think father would have appreciated the risks *I* took, brother.'

Chagatai shook his head as things he had puzzled over began to fall together.

'Then why . . . ?' he began.

'You said you are no fool, Chagatai. Think it through, as I have done a thousand times. I am my father's heir, but my heart is weak and I could fall at any moment. Who would lead the nation then?'

'I would,' Chagatai said softly.

It was a hard truth, that Ogedai's son would not live to

79

inherit, but neither man looked away from the other. Chagatai began to appreciate something of what Ogedai had gone through in the years since their father's death.

'How long have you known of the weakness?' he asked.

Ogedai shrugged. 'I've had twinges as long as I can remember, but it has grown worse in the last few years. There have been . . . more serious pains. Without the Chin powders, I do not think I have much time.'

'Wait,' Chagatai said, frowning. 'You say I am safe? You will let me leave with this information? I don't understand.'

It was Tsubodai who replied and he too stared at Ogedai as if seeing him for the first time.

'If you died, Chagatai, if you were killed as you deserve for the attacks last night, who would keep the nation whole when the khan falls?' Tsubodai's face twisted into a furious sneer. 'It seems you will be rewarded for your failures, my lord.'

'That is why you too had to hear this, Tsubodai,' Ogedai said. 'You must put aside your anger. My brother will be khan after me and you will be his first general. He too is a son of Genghis, the bloodline of the man you gave oath to serve.'

Chagatai struggled to take in what he had heard.

'You expect me to wait then, to be quiet and peaceful while I wait for you to die? How do I know this is not some ruse, something dreamed up by Tsubodai?'

'Because I could kill you *now*,' Ogedai snapped, his temper fraying visibly. 'I still could, Chagatai. Why else would I offer you your life, after last night? I speak from a position of strength, brother, not failure. That is how you should judge my words.'

Reluctantly, Chagatai nodded. He needed time to think and he knew he was not going to be given that luxury.

'I have made promises to those who have supported me,' he said. 'I cannot simply live the life of a herder while I wait. It would be a living death, unworthy of a warrior.' He paused for a moment, thinking quickly. 'Unless you make me your heir, publicly. Then I will have the respect of my generals.'

'That I will not do,' Ogedai said immediately. 'If I die in the next few months, you will be khan whether I have made you heir or not. If I survive longer, I will not deny the chance to my son. You must take your chances with him, as he must with you.'

'Then you offer me nothing!' Chagatai replied, raising his voice almost to a shout. 'What sort of a deal is this, based on empty promises? Why even tell me? If you die soon, yes I will be khan, but I will not spend my life waiting for a messenger who might never come. No man would.'

'After the attacks last night, you had to be told. If I let it pass, if I just sent you back to your tuman, you would see only weakness. How long before you or another challenged me then? Yet I am not leaving you with *nothing*, Chagatai. Far from it. My task is to expand the lands we have conquered, to make the nation safe to thrive and grow by doing so. To our brother Tolui, I will give the homeland, though I will keep Karakorum as my own city.' He took a deep breath, seeing the light of anticipation and greed in his brother's eyes. 'You will take Khwarezm as the centre of your lands, with the cities of Samarkand, Bukhara and Kabul. I will give to you a khanate two thousand miles across, from the Amu Darya river to the Altai mountains. You and your descendants will rule there, though you will pay tribute to me and to mine.'

'My lord . . .' Tsubodai began, appalled.

Chagatai chuckled derisively. 'Let him speak, general. This is a matter for family, not for you.'

Ogedai shook his head. 'I have planned this for almost two years, Tsubodai. My challenge is to put aside the rage I feel for the attacks on my family and make the right choices, even now.'

He raised his head to stare at Chagatai, and his brother felt the surging emotions in his gaze.

'My son and daughters survived, Chagatai. Did you know that? If they had been killed by your warriors, I would be watching you slow-roasted at this moment and listening to you scream. Some things I will not bear in the name of my father's empire, his vision.' He paused, but Chagatai said nothing. Ogedai nodded, satisfied he had been understood.

'You have a position of strength, *brother*,' Ogedai said. 'You have generals loyal to you, while I have a vast empire that must be administered and controlled by able men. After today, I will be the gur-khan, the leader of nations. I will take your oath and honour mine to you and your descendants. The Chin showed us how to rule many lands, Chagatai, with tribute flowing back to the capital.'

'You have not forgotten what happened to that capital?' Chagatai asked.

Ogedai's eyes glinted dangerously. 'I have *not*, brother. Do not think that one day you will lead an army into Karakorum. Our father's blood runs in my veins as much as it does in yours. If you ever come to me holding a sword, it will be against the *khan* and the nation will answer. I will destroy you then with your wives and children, your servants and followers. Do not forget, Chagatai, that I survived the night. Our father's luck is mine. His spirit watches over me. Yet I am offering you an empire greater than anything outside the lands of the Chin.'

'Where I will *rot*,' Chagatai said. 'You would have me lock myself in a pretty palace, surrounded by women and gold . . .' he struggled for something suitably appalling, '. . . chairs and crowns?'

Ogedai smiled slightly to see his brother's horror at such a prospect.

'No,' he said. 'You will raise an army for me there, one I may call on. An army of the West, as Tolui will create an army of the Hearth and I will gather one of the East. The world has grown too large for one army of the nation, my brother. You will ride where I tell you to ride, conquer where I tell you to conquer. The world is yours, if you can put aside the base part of you that tells you to rule it all. That you may not have. Now give me an answer and your oath. Your word *is* iron, brother and I *will* take it. Or I can just kill you now.'

Chagatai nodded, overcome with the sudden shift from fatalistic numbness to new hope and new suspicions.

'What oath will you accept?' he said at last, and Ogedai knew he had won. He held out the wolf's-head sword that Genghis had worn.

'Swear with your hand on this sword. Swear by our father's spirit and honour that you will never raise a hand in anger against me. That you will accept me as gur-khan and be a loyal vassal as khan of your own lands and peoples. Whatever else happens is the will of the sky father, but on that, you can make an oath I will respect. There will be many others today, Chagatai. Be the first.'

The nation knew that Chagatai had gambled for the horsetails, throwing his men at the city of Karakorum. When Ogedai and his officers rode around the city that morning in a show of strength, they saw that the attempt had failed. Yet somehow Chagatai too rode proudly as he rejoined his tuman outside the city. He sent his bondsmen to collect the corpses and carry them far beyond Karakorum, out of sight. In just a short time, only rusty marks were left on the streets, the dead as well hidden as the plans and stratagems of great men. The warriors of the nation shrugged and continued to prepare for the festival and the great games that would begin that day.

For Kachiun and Khasar, it was enough for the moment to know Ogedai had survived. The games would go ahead and there would be time to think of the future once he was made khan. Tumans that had faced each other in anger the night before sent teams of bowmen to the archery wall outside Karakorum. For those men, the battles of princes were a different world. They were pleased their own generals had survived; more pleased that the games had not been called off.

Tens of thousands gathered to watch the first event of the day. No one wanted to miss the early rounds, especially as the final would be seen by only thirty thousand, in the centre of the city. Temuge had organised the paper tokens that gained entry to that final enclosure. They had been changing hands for horses and gold for days before the event. While Ogedai had fought for his life, women, children and the elderly were quietly sitting in darkness where they could watch the greatest skills of their people demonstrated. Even the game of thrones had come second place to that desire.

The archery wall loomed above the east gate of Karakorum, bright in the rising sun. It had been built over the previous days, a massive construction of wood and iron that could hold more than a hundred small shields, each no larger than a man's head. Around it, a thousand iron stoves added smoke to the air, cooking a feast for those who watched. The smell of fried mutton and wild onions was strong around the camp and the knowledge that civil war had been as close as a breath the night before did not diminish their appetites or still the ready laughter as the wrestlers practised with friends on the dry grass. It was a good day, with the sun strong on their backs as the nation prepared to celebrate a new khan.

CHAPTER SEVEN

Khasar stood with nine of his tuman's best archers, waiting for his turn. He had to struggle to find the calm he needed and he took long, slow breaths while he held up each of the four arrows he had been given. In theory, they were all identical, products of the best fletcher in the tribes. Even so, Khasar had rejected the first three he had been handed. It was nerves in part, but he had not slept and he knew the day would be hard as it caught up with him. He was already sweating more than usual, as his body complained and ached. The only consolation was that every other archer had been awake as well. Yet the young ones were bright-faced and cheerful as they saw the grey pallor of more senior men. For them, it was a day of great potential, a better chance than they could have hoped to win recognition and Temuge's precious medals of gold, silver and bronze, each stamped with the face of Ogedai. While he waited, Khasar wondered what Chagatai would have done if he had been successful. No doubt the heavy discs would have been

85

quietly taken away and lost. Khasar shook his head to clear it. Knowing Chagatai, he would have used them anyway. The man felt no embarrassment about small things. In that at least, he was the true son of his father.

The festival would last for three days, though Ogedai would be khan at sunset on the first. Khasar had already seen Temuge running himself ragged trying to organise the events so that all those who qualified to compete could do so. Temuge had complained to Khasar about the difficulties, saying something about archers who were also riding in the horse races, and runners who were wrestling. Khasar had waved him away rather than listen to the tedious detail. He supposed someone had to organise it all, but it did not sound like a warrior's work. It was well suited to his scholarly brother, who could use a bow hardly better than a child.

'Step forward, Bearskin tuman,' the judge called.

Khasar looked up from his thoughts to watch the competition. Jebe was a talented archer. His very name meant 'arrow' and had been given to him after a shot that brought down Genghis' own horse. The word was that his men would be in the final. Khasar noted that Jebe did not seem to be suffering after the night's exertions, though he had fought through the night to save Ogedai. Khasar felt a twinge of envy, remembering when he too could have ridden all night and still fought the following day, without rest or food beyond a few gulps of airag, blood and milk. Still, he knew he had not wasted the good times. With Genghis, he had conquered nations and made a Chin emperor kneel. It had been the proudest moment of his life, but he could have wished for a few more years of uncaring strength, without the painful clicking of his hip as he rode, or the sore knee, or even the small, hard lumps under his shoulder where a lance tip had broken off years before. He rubbed at the spot absently, as Jebe and his nine toed the line, a hundred paces from the archery wall. At that distance, the targets looked tiny.

Jebe laughed at something and clapped one of his men on the back. Khasar watched as the general bent and slow-released his bow a few times, limbering up his shoulders. Around them, thousands of warriors, women and children had gathered to watch, growing still and silent as the team waited for the breeze to die.

The wind dropped to nothing, seeming to intensify the sun on Khasar's skin. The wall had been placed so the archers cast long shadows, but their aim was not spoiled by light in their eyes. Temuge had planned such tiny details.

'Ready,' Jebe said, without turning his head.

His men stood on either side of him, one arrow on the string and three on the ground before them. There were no marks for style, only accuracy, but Khasar knew Jebe would make it as silky smooth as he could, as a matter of pride.

'Begin!' the judge called.

Khasar watched closely as the team breathed out together, drawing at the same time and loosing just before they took the next breath. Ten arrows soared out, curving slightly as blurs in the air before they thumped home on the wall. More judges ran out and held up flags to show the hits. Their voices carried in the silent air, calling 'Uukhai!' for every shot in the centre of the target.

It was a good start. Ten flags. Jebe grinned at his men and they loosed again as soon as the judges were clear. To go on to the next round, they had to hit only thirty-three shields with forty arrows. They made it look easy, hitting a perfect thirty and only missing two on the last shot for a score of thirty-eight. The crowd cheered and Khasar glowered at Jebe as he passed back through the other competitors. The sun was hot, but they were alive.

Khasar did not understand why Ogedai had let Chagatai live. It would not have been his choice, but he was no longer one of the inner circle around the khan, as he had been with

Genghis. He shrugged to himself at the thought. Tsubodai or Kachiun would know, they always did. Someone would tell him.

Khasar had seen Chagatai just before he joined the archers. The younger man had been leaning on a wooden corral, watching the wrestlers prepare with a few of his bondsmen. There had been no visible tension in Chagatai and it was only then that Khasar had begun to relax. Ogedai seemed to have won through to some sort of peace, at least for a time. Khasar put such things out of his mind, an old skill. One way or another, it was going to be a good day.

By the low, white walls of Karakorum, forty riders waited for the signal to begin. Their animals had been groomed and their hooves oiled in the days leading to the festival. Each rider had his own secret diet for his mount, guaranteed by his family to produce the long-distance stamina that the animal would need.

Batu ran his fingers through his pony's mane, a nervous habit that he repeated every few moments. Ogedai would be watching, he was almost certain. His uncle had overseen all aspects of his training with the tumans, giving his officers a free hand to work him bloody and then force him to study each battle and tactic in the nation's history. He ached as he had ached almost constantly for more than two years. It showed in the new muscle on his shoulders and the dark circles under his eyes. It had not been in vain. No sooner had he mastered a task or a post than he was moved again on the order of Ogedai.

The race that day was a respite of sorts from his training. Batu had tied his own hair back in a club, so that it would not whip his face and irritate him during the race. He had a chance, he knew that. He was older than the other boys, a man grown, though he had his father's whip-lean frame. The extra weight

88

would count over the distance, yet his pony was truly strong. It had shown its speed and endurance as a colt and, at two years of age, it was bursting with energy, as fit and ready as its rider.

He looked to where his second in command turned a small, pale mare on the spot. He met Batu's eyes for a second and nodded. Zan's blind white eye gleamed at him, reflecting his excitement. Zan had been Batu's friend when only his mother knew the shame of his birth, when she still hid the disgrace of the name. Zan too had grown up with vicious dislike, beaten and tormented by those pure-blood boys who mocked his golden skin and delicate Chin features. Batu thought of him almost as a brother: thin and fierce, with enough hatred for both of them.

Some of the tumans had supplied teams of riders. Batu hoped Zan alone would be enough to make a difference. If he had learned anything from his father's fate, it was to win, no matter how you did it. It was not important if someone else was hurt, or killed. If you won, you would be forgiven anything. You could be taken from a stinking ger and forced through the ranks until a thousand men followed your orders as if they came from the khan himself. Blood and talent. The nation was built on both.

As the judge stepped up to the mark, another rider crossed Batu's line, as if struggling with his mount. Batu kicked forward instantly, using his strength to shove the boy away. It was Settan of the Uriankhai, of course. Tsubodai's old tribe had been a thorn in his side ever since their valiant general returned to Genghis with Batu's father's head in a sack. He had met their silent dislike a hundred times since Ogedai had raised him. Not that they were open in their disdain or their transparent loyalty to their own blood. Genghis had outlawed the ties of tribe for his new nation, but Batu could smile at the thought of his grandfather's arrogance. As if anything mattered but blood. Perhaps that was what his father Jochi had forgotten when he rebelled and stole away Batu's birthright.

It was ironic that the Uriankhai still chose to visit the sins of the father on his son. Jochi had not known that his tumble with a virgin produced a boy. As an unmarried girl, Batu's mother had no claim on Jochi. She had been scorned by her own family, forced to live on the edges. She had rejoiced when Jochi became an outcast, the traitor general, to be hunted down and killed. Then she had heard that the great khan had decreed all bastard children were to be legitimate. Batu still remembered the night she realised all she had lost, drinking herself into a stupor, then gashing weakly at her wrists with a cooking knife. He had washed and bound the wounds himself.

No one in the world hated the memory of Jochi like his son. In comparison to that seething white flame, the Uriankhai were simply moths that would be burnt by it.

Batu watched out of the corner of his eye as the judge began to unfurl a long flag of yellow silk. His father's men had all left wives and children behind in the camp of Genghis. Zan was one of those abandoned children. Some had returned with Tsubodai, but Zan's father had died somewhere far away, his body lost on strange ground. It was one more thing for which Batu could not forgive his father's memory. He nodded to himself. It was a good thing he had enemies in the group of riders. He fed on their dislike, adding to it so that he could suck strength from their jibes and taunts, their sly blows and tricks. He thought once again of the human shit he had found in his feedbags that dawn and it was like a draught of black airag in his blood. That was why he would win the race. He rode with hatred and it gave him a power they could only imagine.

The judge raised the flag. Batu felt his pony's haunches bunch as he rocked back, ready to explode forward. The flag whipped down, a streamer of gold in the morning sun. Batu kicked and in a heartbeat he was galloping. He did not take the lead, though he was almost sure he could have made them watch his back all the way round the city. Instead, he settled down to a steady pace midway down the group. Six times around Karakorum was forty-eight miles: no sprint, but a test of stamina. The horses had been bred for it and they could last the distance. The skill would come in the manoeuvres of the boys and men on their backs. Batu felt his confidence swell. He was a minghaan officer. He was seventeen years old and he could ride all day.

One thousand and twenty-four men of the nation raised their right arms to the crowd as they prepared for the first, massive round of wrestling. The first day would weed out the injured and the older men, or simply the ones who were unlucky. There were no second chances and with ten rounds to survive, the final two days would depend in part on those who came through the first with the fewest injuries.

The warriors had their favourites and for days there had been a stream of them strolling by the training fields, assessing the strengths and weaknesses, looking for those worth a bet and those who would not last through the gruelling trial.

None of the generals had entered for this part of the festival. They were too dignified to allow themselves to be thrown and broken by younger men. Even so, the first wrestling bout had been delayed so that Khasar and Jebe could take part in the archery competition. Khasar was a huge fan of the wrestling and sponsored the man no warrior wanted to meet in the first rounds. Baabgai, the Bear, was of Chin stock, though he had the compact build of a Mongol wrestler. He beamed tooth-lessly at the crowd and they cheered his name. Herds of the best ponies had been wagered on him, but ten rounds or an injury could wear him down. Even a stone could be cracked with enough blows.

Khasar and Jebe both went through their first round, then

jogged with their teams across the summer grass to where the wrestlers waited patiently in the sun. The air tasted like metal and smelled of oil and sweat. The clashes and bloodshed of the night before were deliberately forgotten.

The archers knelt on mats of white felt, laying their precious bows carefully beside them, already unstrung and wrapped in wool and leather.

'Ho, Baabgai!' Khasar called, grinning at the bulky man he had found and trained. Baabgai had the mindless strength of an ox and seemed to feel no pain. In all his previous bouts, he had never shown the slightest discomfort and it was that stolid quality that most intimidated his opponents. They could not see a way to hurt the fool. Khasar knew some of the wrestlers called him the 'empty one' for his low intelligence, but Baabgai took no offence at anything. He just smiled and threw them over the horizon.

Khasar waited patiently through a song of beginning. The rough voices of the wrestlers swelled as they vowed to stand firm in the earth and to remain friends whether they were victor or vanquished. There would be other songs, in later rounds. Khasar preferred those and he barely listened as he looked across the plains.

Ogedai was in Karakorum, no doubt being washed, oiled and preened. The nation was already drinking hard and if Khasar hadn't been taking part in the archery rounds, he would have joined them.

He watched as Baabgai took his first hold. The big man was not blisteringly fast, but once an opponent came within reach of his hands, once he found a grip, that was it. Baabgai's fingers were short and fleshy, his hands always looking as if they had swollen badly, but Khasar had felt their strength and wagered heavily on him.

Baabgai's first bout ended as he wrenched his opponent's shoulder, grabbing the wrist and then throwing his weight onto the arm. The crowd cheered and beat drums and gongs in appreciation. Baabgai smiled at them, toothless as a huge baby. Khasar could not help chuckling at the simple pleasure in the wrestler. It would be a fine day.

Batu did not cry out as a whip lashed him across the cheek. He could feel the welt rise and his skin became as hot and angry as he was himself. The race had begun well enough and he had moved into the first six by the second lap of the city. The ground was harder and drier than he expected, which favoured some horses more than others. As they took the same path for the third lap, dust whitened their skin and dried the spit in their mouths to a gritty paste. Thirst grew steadily in the sun until the weaker ones gasped like birds.

Batu ducked as the whip came again, a strip of oiled leather. It was one of the Uriankhai, he saw, to his right. A dusty boy, small and light, on the back of a powerful stallion. Through gritty eyes, Batu saw the animal was strong and the boy full of malevolent enjoyment as he drew back his arm to lash him once more. Even over the close-packed thunder of hooves, Batu heard one of the others laugh and felt fury engulf him. They did not command men, as he did. What did he care for the blood of the Uriankhai, except to see it splashed in the dust? He looked to Zan, who raced close by. His friend was ready to aid him, but Batu shook his head, watching the Uriankhai boy all the time.

When the whip came again, Batu simply raised his arm, so the thong wrapped around his wrist. He closed his hand on a length of it. The boy gaped, but it was too late. Batu yanked hard, using all his weight and strength and heaving his own mount away in the same moment.

The stirrups almost saved the boy. For an instant, one leg flailed, but then he went down under the hooves and his mount

93

whinnied and bucked, almost unseating another rider, who shouted angrily. Batu did not look back. He hoped the fall had killed the little bastard. They had stopped laughing at the front, he noticed.

Five Uriankhai riders had entered the race for two-year-olds. Though they came from two tumans, they rode instinctively as a group. Batu had brought them together somehow with his challenge, with his dislike. Settan of the Uriankhai led them. He was tall and lithe, with soft eyes that watered in the wind and a tail of hair that hung down his back. He and his friends exchanged glances as they passed the western gate of Karakorum for a fourth time. Sixteen miles to go and the horses' mouths were white with foam, their skins dark and rimed with sweat. Batu and Zan moved up to challenge for the lead.

He could see the Uriankhai riders looking back at him. He made sure he showed only the cold face as he drew closer and closer. Behind the leading group, thirty other ponies stretched out like a long tail, already falling behind.

Khasar was still smiling as he walked back to the archery wall, where the judges and crowds waited impatiently for him. He ignored their stares as he strode to the line and strung his bow. As a brother to Genghis and one of the founders of the nation, he really couldn't care less if he annoyed the senior men, or spoiled Temuge's beautiful organisation.

Jebe's ten had already taken their shots for the second round and the general stood relaxed, revealing his confidence. Khasar frowned at the younger man, though this seemed to make Jebe chuckle. Khasar steadied himself, knowing he would pass his mood to his own group of archers. No one in the archery rounds was weak or a poor shot. Not a single man there doubted he could win on the right day. There was always an element of luck, if the breeze shifted just as you loosed or a muscle cramped, but the main test was of nerves. Khasar had seen it many times. Men who could stand against a line of screaming Arabs without a qualm found their hands sweating as they walked up to the line in silence. Somehow, they could not take a full breath, as if their chest had swelled to block their throats.

Knowing that was part of the secret of conquering it. Khasar took long, slow breaths, ignoring the crowd and letting his own men settle themselves and grow calm. The forty targets on the wall even seemed to grow a fraction, an illusion he had seen before. He looked over his men and found them tense but steady.

'Remember, lads,' he murmured. 'Every one is a virgin, sweet and willing.'

Some of his men chuckled, rolling their heads on their shoulders to ease the last tension that might spoil their aim.

Khasar grinned to himself. Weary or not, old or not, he was going to give Jebe a good run, he could feel it.

'Ready,' he called to the judges. He looked at the high banner on the archery wall. The wind had risen to a steady blow from the north-east. He adjusted his stance slightly. One hundred paces. A shot he had made a thousand times, a hundred thousand. One more long, slow breath.

'Begin,' the judge said curtly.

Khasar notched his first shaft to the string and sent it soaring to the line of shields he had marked as his own. He waited until he was sure it had struck home, then he turned and glanced at Jebe, raising his eyebrows. Jebe laughed at the challenge and turned away.

The line of pounding, sweating ponies had lengthened like beads on a cord, stretching a mile around the walls of Karakorum.

Three of the Uriankhai still led the field, with two stocky boys almost herding Settan towards the finish. Batu and Zan were within reach of them and the group of five had opened a gap on the rest of the riders. It would be decided between them, and their mounts were snorting to clear their mouths and nostrils, spraying mucus and foaming sweat. The walls were lined with watching warriors as well as thousands of Chin workers. For them, the day was also a celebration, the end of two years of labour, with their purses full of coins.

Batu was blind to the watchers, to everything except Settan and his two companions. The dry ground rose as a cloud of dust, so that it would be hard to see what he was about to do. He felt in his pockets and removed two smooth stones, river pebbles that felt right in his hand. He and Zan had discussed knives or barbing his whip, but such wounds would be public. Some of the judges would not approve. Even so, Zan had offered to gash Settan's neck. He hated the taller Uriankhai boy who took such pride in Tsubodai's achievements. Batu had refused the offer, so that he would not lose his friend to vengeance. A stone could always have been thrown up from the hooves as they raced. Even if Settan saw what he and Zan were doing, he would not dare to complain. It would seem like whingeing and the warriors would laugh at him.

As they began the last lap, Batu fondled the stones. Past the racing horses, he could see wrestlers like brightly coloured birds against the grass; beyond them was the archery wall. His people were out on the plains and he was among them, riding hard. It was a good feeling.

He squeezed with his knees and his mount responded, though it was heaving for breath. Batu moved up and Zan followed closely. The Uriankhai were not sleeping and they moved to block him from Settan's horse. Batu smiled at the closest boy and moved his mouth as if he was shouting something. All the while, he brought his mount closer.

The boy stared at him and Batu grinned, pointing vigorously at something ahead. He watched in delight as the boy finally leaned closer to hear whatever it was Batu was shouting into the wind. Batu swung the stone hard and connected with the side of his head. The boy vanished almost instantly under the hooves, just a rolling, dusty strip behind them.

Batu took his place as the riderless horse ran ahead. Settan looked back and stared to see him so close. They were caked in dust, their hair and skin a dirty white, but Settan's gaze was bright with fear. Batu held his eyes, drinking in strength.

The other Uriankhai boy swerved his mount between them, crashing his leg into Batu so that he was almost unseated. For thumping heartbeats, Batu had to cling on to the mane as his feet lost the stirrups and he endured blows with a whip that came in a wild frenzy, striking his mount as often as himself. Batu kicked out instinctively and connected with the boy's chest. It gave him a moment to regain his seat. He had dropped one stone, but he had another. As the Uriankhai boy turned back to face him, Batu threw it hard and yelled to see the stone crack into his nose, rocking him and sending bright red blood over the pale dust, like a river bursting. The boy fell back, and Batu and Zan were alone with Settan, with two miles still to ride.

As soon as he saw what was happening, Settan went all out to open a gap. It was his only chance. All the horses were at the end of their endurance, and with a cry of rage, Zan began to drift back. There was nothing he could do, though he threw his stones with furious strength, managing to hit Settan's mount on the haunches with one, while the other disappeared in the dust.

Batu cursed under his breath. He could not let Settan leave him behind. He kicked and whipped his horse until they drew level and then Batu went half a length ahead. He felt strong, though his lungs were full of dust that he would cough up for days to come.

The final corner was in sight and Batu knew he could win. Yet he had known from the beginning that winning would not be enough for him. Tsubodai would be on the walls, Batu was certain. With one of his Uriankhai so close to the finishing line, the general would no doubt be cheering him on. Batu wiped his eyes, clearing them of gritty dust. He had no love for his father's memory. It did not change his hatred for the general who had cut Jochi's throat. Perhaps Ogedai would be there too, watching the young man he had raised.

Batu allowed Settan to cut inside him as they rushed towards the corner. The edge of the wall was marked by a marble post, decorated with a stone wolf. Judging it all finely, Batu let Settan come up beside him, almost head to head for the finish line. He saw Settan grin as he scented a chance to go through.

As they reached the corner, Batu wrenched his reins to the right and slammed Settan against the post. The impact was colossal. Both horse and rider stopped almost dead as the Uriankhai boy's leg shattered and he screamed.

Batu rode on, smiling. He did not look back as the high sound faded behind him.

As he crossed the line, he wished his father could have lived to see it, to take pride in him. His eyes were wet with tears and he scrubbed at them, blinking furiously and telling himself it was just the wind and the dust.

CHAPTER EIGHT

As the sun sank towards the horizon, Ogedai breathed out slowly. There had been times when he thought he would not live to stand in his city on this day. His hair was oiled and tied into a club on his neck. His deel was simple and dark blue, without ornament or pretension. He wore it belted, over leggings and herders' soft boots of sheepskin, tied with thongs. He touched his father's sword at his waist, taking comfort from it.

At the same time, he felt a spasm of irritation at the choices his father had left him. If Jochi had become khan, it would have established a line of the first born. Instead, the great khan had made Ogedai his heir, the third of four sons. In the shadow of that man, Ogedai's own line might wither. He could not expect the nation simply to accept his eldest son Guyuk as khan after him. More than twenty others had a blood claim from Genghis, and Chagatai was just one of the more dangerous. Ogedai feared for his son in such a tangle of thorns and teeth. Yet Guyuk had survived so far and perhaps that showed the sky father's approval of him. Ogedai took a slow breath.

'I am ready, Baras'aghur,' he told his servant. 'Stand back now.'

He strode forward into a swelling sea of noise, onto a balcony of polished oak. His drummers thundered his arrival and the warriors of his Guard tuman roared and beat their armour, making a clash of sound that could be heard across the city. Ogedai smiled, acknowledging the crowd as he took his seat overlooking the vast amphitheatre. His wife Torogene sat down beside him, with Baras'aghur fussing over the folds of her Chin dress. Unseen by the watching masses, Ogedai reached out. She took his hand and squeezed it. They had survived two years of intrigue, poison, attempts on their lives and, finally, open insurrection. Ogedai's face and body were stiff and battered from his exertions, but he was in one piece.

As the crowd waited patiently, the wrestlers who had survived the first two bouts came to take their places in the centre ground below Ogedai. Two hundred and fifty-six men formed up in pairs ready for their last struggle that day. Bets flashed around the rows of seats, from shouted instructions to wooden tokens or even Chin printed money and coins. It was possible to bet on any aspect of the competition and the entire nation followed the sport. The weak and injured, the ageing and unlucky, had already been weeded out. Those who remained were the strongest and fastest in a nation which revered martial skill above all else. It was his father's nation and creation, his father's *vision* of a people: horse and warrior, sword and bow together.

Ogedai turned in his seat as Guyuk stepped onto the balcony. He felt his heart contract in the pride and sadness he always felt on seeing the young man. Guyuk was tall and handsome, fit to command a thousand, perhaps even a tuman, in peacetime. Beyond that, he had no spark of tactical awareness, or the subtle touch with his men that would have had them following him into flames. He was in all ways an unremarkable officer and he had not yet taken a single wife, as if continuing the khan's own line meant nothing to him. The fact that he resembled Genghis in face and eyes only made his weaknesses harder to bear for his father. There were times when Ogedai could not understand his son at all.

Guyuk bowed elegantly to his parents and took his seat, staring out in wonder at the massed crowd. He had known little of the struggle in the palace. He had barricaded himself into a room with two friends and some servants, but no one had come to that part of the palace. Apparently, they had drunk themselves into a stupor. Despite Ogedai's relief at seeing him alive, it summed his son up, that no one had considered him worth killing.

Temuge rushed by the rear of the balcony, almost hidden from view by a swarm of his runners and scribes. Ogedai heard him snapping out orders in his waspish voice and allowed himself a grin as he remembered the conversation with his uncle weeks before. Despite the old fool's fears, Ogedai had won through. He reminded himself to offer the libraries of Karakorum to Temuge once again, as soon as the festival was over.

In the great oval, the twilight began the slow summer drift to grey. Because of the low city walls, the huge structure could be seen from the sea of grass outside. It would not be long before a thousand torches were lit, making a shape of light that all the nation could witness from the plains. Ogedai looked forward to the moment, the visible signal that he was khan. It also meant Karakorum was finished at last, barring the bloodstains that waited for rain. Perhaps that too was fitting.

Far below, Temuge signalled the wrestling judges. After a short song to the earth mother, the judges blew horns and the men crashed together, their hands and legs moving swiftly to take and break grips. For some, it was over in an instant, as with Baabgai's opponent. For others, the match became a test of stamina as they heaved and sweated, long red marks appearing on their skin.

Ogedai looked down on the field of athletes. He knew Temuge had planned the events to the last detail. He wondered idly if his uncle would manage the whole festival without flaws. His people were warriors and shepherds to the last man and woman – not sheep, *never* sheep. Still, it was interesting to see.

The final pair collapsed with legs kicking to a roar and a howl from the crowd. A hundred and twenty-eight men were victors and they stood, flushed and pleased, before the nation. They bowed to Ogedai on the balcony and he got to his feet and raised his sword hand to them, showing his pleasure.

More horns sounded, great Chin tubes of brass and bronze that droned notes across the field. The wrestlers retired at a jog and the heavy gate swung open, revealing the main street of the city beyond. Ogedai squinted to see, just as thirty thousand others did their best to catch a glimpse.

In the distance came a group of runners, bare-chested in the summer heat. They had run three laps of the city, some twenty-four miles, before entering the western gate and heading for the centre ground. Ogedai leaned out as far as he could to see them, and for once Guyuk took an interest, craning forward with him, his face alight with excitement. Ogedai glanced at him and wondered if he had wagered some huge sum.

The Mongol people were not long-distance runners as a rule. They had the stamina but not the build, as Temuge had explained it. Some of them limped visibly as they came closer, before trying to hide their weakness as the noise surged around them.

Ogedai nodded to himself when he saw that Chagatai led them. His brother ran smoothly, a head taller than most of the other men. It was true Ogedai feared him, even hated his arrogance, yet he could not disguise his pride at seeing his own brother leading the way into the amphitheatre, pounding up the dusty track to the centre. Chagatai even began to pull away from the rest, but then a small, wiry warrior moved up to challenge him, forcing a sprint when they had nothing left.

As they drew level, Ogedai felt his own heart tremble, his breath coming faster.

'Come *on*, brother,' he whispered.

At his side Torogene frowned, her hands on the oak bar, gripping it. She had no interest in the man who had nearly killed her husband. She could happily have seen Chagatai burst his heart in front of the crowd. Yet she felt her husband's excitement and she loved Ogedai more than anything in the world.

Chagatai threw himself forward at the last, crossing the line no more than a head's length before the challenger. Both men were close to collapse and Chagatai struggled visibly for breath, his chest heaving. He did not rest his hands on his knees. Ogedai felt a twinge of nostalgia as he remembered his father's words on the subject. *If an opponent sees you clinging to your knees, he will think you are beaten.* It was a hard voice to escape as they moved on with the years, leaving Genghis behind.

Out of a sense of decency, Guyuk could not cheer his uncle, but his skin glowed with a light perspiration. Ogedai grinned at him, pleased to see his son enthralled for once. He hoped he had won his bet, at least.

Ogedai remained on his feet as the horns sounded once more, spilling a note across tens of thousands. He closed his eyes for an instant, breathing long and slow.

The crowd fell silent.

Ogedai raised his head as his brass-lunged herald bellowed out the words at last.

'You are here to confirm Ogedai, son of Temujin who was Genghis, as khan of the nation. He stands before you as the heir chosen by the great khan. Is there any other who will challenge for the right to lead?'

103

If there had been silence before, this one had the stillness of death as every man and woman froze, not even daring to breathe as they waited. Guyuk stood back and, for a moment, raised his hand to touch Ogedai's shoulder, before letting it fall without his father knowing.

Thousands of eyes turned towards Chagatai as he stood on the dusty ground with his chest heaving, streaked in sweat. He too looked up at Ogedai on the balcony of oak and his face was strangely proud.

The moment passed and the release of breath was like a summer breeze, followed by a ripple of laughter as people were amused at their own tension and tight expressions.

Ogedai stepped forward, so that they could all see him. The amphitheatre had been influenced by drawings made by Christian monks from Rome who had come to Karakorum. As they had promised, it seemed to magnify sound, so that his voice flew to every ear. He drew the wolf's-head sword and held up the blade.

'I make my own oath before you. As khan, I will protect the people, so that we grow strong. We have had too many years of peace. Let the world fear what will come next.'

They cheered his words and in the enclosed bowl, the sound was immense, almost rocking Ogedai back where he stood. He could feel it on his skin like a physical force. He raised the sword again and they quieted slowly, reluctantly. Down in the field, he thought he saw his brother nod to him. Family was indeed a strange thing.

'Now I will take *your* oath,' he shouted to his people.

The herald took up the chant: 'Under one khan we are a nation.'

The words crashed back at Ogedai and he gripped the sword tighter, wondering if the band of pressure on his face was his father's spirit. He heart thumped slower and slower until he thought he could feel every beat.

The herald called once more to complete the oath and they replied: 'I offer you gers, horses, salt and blood, in all honour.'

Ogedai closed his eyes. His chest was shuddering and his head felt swollen and strange. A sharp pain made him almost stumble as his right arm buckled, suddenly weak. Part of him expected it to end then.

When he opened his eyes, he was still alive. More, he was khan of the nation, in the line of Genghis. His vision cleared slowly and he took a deep breath of the summer air, feeling himself tremble in reaction. He felt the thirty thousand faces turned to him, and as his strength returned, he raised his arms suddenly in joy.

The sound that followed almost deafened him. It was echoed by the rest of the nation who waited outside the city. They heard and they responded, seeing the torches lit for the new khan.

That night, Ogedai walked through the corridors of his palace, with Guyuk strolling at his side. After the excitement of the day, neither man could sleep. Ogedai had found his son throwing bones with his Guards and summoned him for company. It was a rare gesture from father to son, but on that night Ogedai was at peace with the world. Somehow, weariness could not touch him, though he could hardly remember when he had last slept. The bruise on his face had grown colourful. It had been masked for the oath-taking with pale powder, but Ogedai did not know he had streaked it when he scratched his skin.

The corridors became cloisters that opened out onto the palace gardens, still and quiet. The moon was dim behind clouds and only the paths could be seen, as if they walked pale threads through the dark.

'I would prefer to go with *you*, father, to the Chin lands,' Guyuk said.

Ogedai shook his head. 'That is the old world, Guyuk, a task begun before you were born. I am sending you out with Tsubodai. You will see new lands with him. You will make me proud, I do not doubt it.'

'You are not proud now?' Guyuk asked. He had not meant to ask the question, but it was rare for him to be alone with his father and he spoke his thoughts aloud. To his distress, Ogedai did not answer immediately.

'. . . Of course, but that is a father's pride, Guyuk. If you intend to follow me as khan, you must lead warriors in battle. You must make them see you are not as they are – do you understand?'

'No, I don't,' Guyuk replied. 'I have done everything you have asked of me. I have led my tuman for years. You saw the bearskin we brought back. I carried it into the city on a lance and the workers cheered me.'

Ogedai had heard every detail. He struggled to recall the words of his own father on the subject.

'Listen to me. It is not enough to lead a pack of young men in a hunt as if it is some great triumph. I have seen them with you, like . . . dogs, puppies.'

'You told me to choose my officers, to raise them by my own hand,' Guyuk replied.

There was a sulky tone to his voice and Ogedai found himself growing angry. He had seen the beauty of the young men Guyuk had chosen. He could not put words to his unease, but his son's companions did not impress him.

'You will not lead the nation with songs and drunken revels, my son.'

Guyuk came to a sudden halt and Ogedai turned to face him.

'*You* will lecture me on drinking?' Guyuk said. 'Didn't you tell me once that an officer must be able to match his men, that I should develop a taste for it?'

Ogedai winced as he recalled the words. 'I did not know then that you would spend *days* in your revels, taking men from their training. I was trying to make you a warrior, not a drunken fool.'

'Well, you must have failed then, if that is what I am,' Guyuk snapped. He would have left, but Ogedai took him by the arm.

'I did not fail, Guyuk. When have I criticised you? Have I complained that you have not given me an heir? I have not. I have said nothing. You are the image of my father. Is it any surprise that I look for some spark of him in you?'

Guyuk pulled away from him in the darkness and Ogedai heard his breathing grow harsh.

'I am my *own* man,' Guyuk said at last. 'I am not some weaker branch of the line of Genghis, *or* you. You look for him in me? Well, stop it. You will not find him here.'

'Guyuk . . .' Ogedai began again.

'I will go with Tsubodai, because he is riding as far away from Karakorum as anyone,' his son replied. 'Perhaps when I return, you will find something to like in me.'

The young man stalked off over the shining paths while Ogedai struggled with his temper. He had tried to impart a little advice and somehow the conversation had slipped from his control. On such a night, it was a bitter draught to take before sleep.

It was another two days of feasting and triumphs before Ogedai summoned his most senior men to the palace. They sat with bloodshot eyes, most of them still sweating from too much meat, airag and rice wine. Considering them, Ogedai saw they were almost a council of the sort the Chin lords used to rule their lands. Yet the final word was always with the khan. It could be no other way.

He looked down the table, past Chagatai, Tsubodai and his uncles, to Batu who had won in the horse races. Batu still glowed with the news that he would lead ten thousand and Ogedai smiled and nodded to him. He had placed good men in the new tuman, experienced warriors who would be able to guide Batu as he learned. Ogedai had done his best to honour Jochi's memory, to right the sins of Genghis and Tsubodai. In face and gesture, the young man bore a strong resemblance to Jochi in his youth. In a moment or a glance, Ogedai could almost forget his brother had died years before. It hurt him every time it happened.

Across from Batu sat Guyuk, staring fixedly into space. Ogedai had not broken through the cool reserve his son had adopted since their words in the garden. Even as they sat at the table, Ogedai could not help wishing Guyuk had half the fire of Jochi's boy. Perhaps Batu felt he had to prove himself, but he sat as a Mongol warrior, silent and watchful, filled with pride and confidence. Ogedai saw no sign that Batu was intimidated in that company, even among renowned leaders such as Chagatai, Tsubodai, Jebe and Jelme. The blood of Genghis ran in many of the men there and in their sons and daughters. It was a fruitful line and a strong one. His son would learn to be a man on the great trek, Ogedai was certain. It was a good beginning.

'We have grown beyond the tribes my father knew, beyond a single encampment drifting across the plains.' Ogedai paused and smiled. 'We are too many now to graze in one place.'

He used words that tribal leaders had used for thousands of years, for when it came time to move on. Some of them nodded automatically and Chagatai thumped his fist on the table in approval.

'Not all my father's dreams will come true, though he dreamed of eagles. He would approve of my brother Chagatai ruling as khan in Khwarezm.'

Ogedai would have gone on, but Jelme reached out and

clapped Chagatai on the back, setting off a chorus of approval for the son of Genghis. Tsubodai inclined his head in silence, but even he did not stand apart from it. When the noise died down, Ogedai spoke again.

'He would approve of the sacred homeland in the hands of my brother Tolui.'

It was Tsubodai who reached out and gripped the shoulder of the younger man, shaking him slightly to show his pleasure. Tolui beamed. He had known what was coming, but the reality of it brought joy. To him had fallen the mountains where their people had roamed for thousands of years, the sweet grass plains where their grandfather Yesugei had been born. Sorhatani and his sons would be happy there, safe and strong.

'And you, brother?' Chagatai said. 'Where will you rest your head?'

'Here in Karakorum,' Ogedai replied easily. 'This is my capital, though I will not rest here yet. For two years I have sent out men and women to learn about the world. I have welcomed scholars of Islam and priests of the Christ. I know now of cities where the slaves walk bare-breasted and gold is as common as clay.'

He smiled to himself at the images in his mind, but then his expression became stern. His eyes sought out Guyuk and held his gaze as he spoke.

'Those who cannot conquer must bend the knee. They must find strength, or serve those of us who have. You are my generals. I will send you out: my hunting dogs, my wolves with iron teeth. When a city closes its gates in fear, you will destroy it. When they make roads and walls, you will cut them, pull down the stones. When a man raises a sword or bow against your men, you will hang him from a tree. Keep Karakorum in your minds as you go. This white city is the heart of the nation, but you are the right arm, the burning brand. Find me new lands, gentlemen. Cut a new path. Let their women weep a sea of tears and I will drink it *all*.'

PART TWO

AD 1232

'He who controls the heartland controls the world.'

CHAPTER NINE

The palace gardens of Karakorum were still young. The Chin gardeners had done their best, but some of the plants and trees would take decades to reach their full growth.

Despite its youth, it was a place of beauty. Yao Shu listened to the rush of water running through the grounds and smiled to himself, marvelling once again at the sheer complexity of souls. For a son of Genghis to commission such a garden was nothing short of a miracle. It was a blaze of subtle colours and variety, impossible, but there it was. Whenever he thought he understood a man, he would find some contradiction. Lazy men could work themselves to death; kind ones could be cruel; cruel ones could redeem their lives. Each day could be different from all the ones that had gone before it; each man different, not just from others, but from the tumbling pieces of himself stretching back into the past. And women! Yao Shu paused to stare up through branches to where a lark sang sweetly. At the thought of the complexity of women, he laughed aloud. The bird leapt and vanished, calling its panic all the way.

Women were even worse. Yao Shu knew he was a fine judge of character, more so than many men. Why else would Ogedai have trusted him with such authority in his absence? Yet talking to a woman like Sorhatani was like staring into an abyss. Just about anything could be looking back at you. Sometimes, it was a kitten, playful and adorable. At other times, it was a tigress with a bloody mouth and claws. Tolui's wife had that quicksilver quality. She was utterly fearless, but if he made her laugh, she could giggle as helplessly as a girl.

Yao Shu glowered to himself. Sorhatani had allowed him to teach her sons to read and write, even to share his Buddhist philosophy though she was herself Christian. Despite her own faith, she could be utterly pragmatic about her sons as she prepared them for the future.

He shook his head as he crested a rise in the park. At that point in the gardens, the architect had indulged a whim, building the hill high enough for a walker to see over the garden walls. Karakorum lay all around him, but his thoughts were not with the city. He affected the air of a scholar, wandering through the gardens without a thought for the world outside. Yet he was aware of every rustling leaf around him and his eyes missed nothing.

He had spotted two of Sorhatani's sons. Hulegu was in a young ginkgo tree over to his right, obviously unaware that the fan-shaped leaves quivered delicately with his breathing. Arik-Boke should not have worn red in a garden with few red blossoms. Yao Shu had located him almost immediately. The khan's chancellor moved through the gardens at the centre of the young hunters, always aware of them as they shifted their positions to keep him in sight. He would have enjoyed it more if he'd been able to complete the triangle with Kublai. He was the true threat.

Yao Shu walked always in balance, gripping the earth through his sandals. His hands were loose, ready to intercept whatever came at him. It was perhaps not the behaviour of a good Buddhist to take delight in his reflexes, but Yao Shu knew it would also be a lesson for the boys, a reminder that they did not yet know everything – if he could locate Kublai, the only one of them with a bow.

With the garden less than five years old, there were only a few large trees, all of them fast-growing willows and poplars. One of them stretched across the path ahead of him and Yao Shu sensed the danger in the spot when he was still far off. It was not just that it was suitable for an ambush; there was a silence about it, a lack of butterflies and movement. Yao Shu smiled. The boys had gaped at him when he suggested the game, but a man had to move to draw and shoot a bow. To get in range, they had to ambush him or reveal their presence with movement. It was not so hard to outwit the sons of Tolui.

Kublai exploded out of the bush, his right arm coming back in the classic archer's pull. Yao Shu dropped and rolled off the path. Something was wrong, he knew it even as he moved. He heard no arrow, no slap of a bowstring. Instead of rising as he had intended, he tucked in his shoulder and rolled back to his original position. Kublai was still visible, covered in leaves and grinning. There was no bow in his hands.

Yao Shu opened his mouth to speak and heard a low whistle behind him. Another man would have turned, but he dropped again, skittering off the path and into a jerking run towards the source of the sound.

Hulegu was smiling down the length of the single arrow Yao Shu had given them that sunny afternoon. The Buddhist monk skidded to a stop. The boy had fast hands, he knew. Too fast, maybe. Still, there would be a moment.

'That was clever,' Yao Shu said.

Hulegu's eyes began to crinkle as his smile broadened. Moving smoothly, without a jerk, Yao Shu stepped close and snatched the arrow off the string. Hulegu released instinctively and, for an instant, Yao Shu thought he had it completely clear. Then his hand jumped as if it had been kicked by a horse and he spun away. The string of woven hide had struck his knuckles, jerking the arrow almost out of his grip. Yao Shu's fingers ached and he hoped he had not broken one. He did not show the boy his pain as he held out the arrow, and Hulegu took it from him with a shocked expression. It had all happened in a heart-beat, almost too fast to see.

'That was good, getting Kublai to give you the bow,' Yao Shu said.

'It was his idea,' Hulegu said a little defensively. 'He said you would be watching for his green jacket and ignoring my blue.'

Hulegu held the arrow gingerly, as if he could not believe what he had just witnessed. Kublai came up beside them and touched it almost reverently.

'You took it from the string,' Kublai said. 'That's impossible.'

Yao Shu frowned at such sloppy thinking and clasped his hands behind his back. To the boys he was the picture of relaxation. The pain in his right hand was still growing. He was sure by then that he had cracked a bone, perhaps snapped it cleanly. In truth, it had been a vain move. There were a hundred ways he could have removed the threat from Hulegu as soon as he was in range. A simple nerve block to the elbow would have made him drop the bow. Yao Shu repressed a sigh. Vanity had always been his weakness.

'Speed is not everything,' he said. 'We practise slowly until you move well, until your body has been trained to react without thought, but then, when you unleash, you must move as quickly as you can. It gives you force and power. It makes you hard to block, hard even to see. The strongest enemy can be defeated with speed and you are all young and of good

116

stock. Your grandfather was like a striking snake until the day he died. You have that in you, if you train hard.'

Hulegu and Kublai looked at each other as Arik-Boke joined them, his face flushed and cheerful. He had not seen the khan's chancellor snatch an arrow right off the string of a drawn bow.

'Return to your studies, my young lords,' Yao Shu said. 'I will leave you now to hear reports of the khan and your father.'

'And Mongke,' Hulegu said. 'He will smash our enemies, he told me.'

'And Mongke,' Yao Shu agreed with a chuckle. He was pleased to see the flicker of disappointment in their faces as they realised their time with him was over.

For a moment, Yao Shu contemplated Kublai. Genghis would have been proud of his grandsons. Mongke had grown strong, avoiding the ravages of disease and injury. He would be a warrior to trust, a general to follow. Yet it was Kublai who impressed his tutors most, whose mind leapt on an idea and tore it to pieces before it could breathe. Of course it had been Kublai who suggested the switch with the bow. It was a simple trick, but it had almost worked.

Yao Shu bowed to the young men and turned away. He smiled as he left them on the paths, hearing the whispers as Kublai and Hulegu described again what they had seen. His hand had begun to swell, Yao Shu realised. He would have to soak and bind it.

As he reached the edge of the gardens, Yao Shu repressed a groan at the sight of the men waiting for him. Almost a dozen scribes and messengers were craning for their first sight of Ogedai's chancellor, sweating in the morning sunlight. They were his senior men. In turn, they commanded many others, almost another army of ink and paper. It amused Yao Shu to think of them as his minghaan officers. Between them, they controlled the administration of a vast and expanding area, from taxes to import licences and even public works such as the new toll bridges. Ogedai's uncle Temuge had wanted the post, but the khan had given it to the Buddhist monk who had accompanied Genghis on almost all his victories and trained his brothers and sons, with varying degrees of success. Temuge had been given the libraries of Karakorum and his demands for funds were increasing. Yao Shu knew Temuge would be one of those trying to reach him that day. The chancellor had six layers of men between supplicants and himself, but Genghis' own brother could usually browbeat them into obedience.

Yao Shu reached the group and began fielding their questions, snapping answers and making the quick decisions that were the reason Ogedai had chosen him. He needed no notes or scribes to aid his memory. He had found he could retain huge amounts of information and put it all together as he needed it. It was through his work that the Mongol lands were becoming settled, though he used Chin scholars as his bureaucracy. Slowly but surely, he was bringing a civilising influence to the Mongol court. Genghis would have hated it, but then he would have hated the very idea of Karakorum. Yao Shu smiled to himself as the questions came to an end and the group went scurrying back to their work. Genghis had conquered from a horse, but a khan could not rule from a horse. Ogedai seemed to understand that, as his father would never have done.

Yao Shu entered the palace alone, walking towards his offices. More serious decisions waited for him there. The treasury was supplying armour, weapons, food and cloth to three armies and dwindling by the day because of it. Even the immense sums Genghis had amassed would not last for ever, though he had a year or two yet before the treasury ran dry of gold and silver. By then, though, the taxes would surely have increased from a trickle to a good-sized river.

He saw Sorhatani walking with two of her maidservants and

had a moment to appreciate her before she noticed him. Her posture marked her out, a woman who walked like an empress and always had. It made her seem much taller than she really was. Four sons she had borne and yet she still walked lithely, her oiled skin gleaming with health. As he stared, the women laughed at something, their voices light in the cool corridors. Her husband and eldest son campaigned with the khan, thousands of miles to the east. By all accounts they were doing well. Yao Shu thought of a report he had read that morning that boasted of enemies piled like rotten logs. He sighed to himself at the thought. Mongol reports tended to lack a sense of subtle understatement.

Sorhatani saw him and Yao Shu bowed deeply and then endured her taking his hands in both of hers, as she insisted on doing whenever they met. She did not notice the heat in the broken finger.

'Have my boys been working hard for you, chancellor?' she asked.

He smiled briefly as she released his hands. He was still young enough to feel the force of her beauty and he resisted as best he could.

'They are satisfactory, my lady,' he said formally. 'I took them into the gardens for exercise. I understand you are to leave the city.'

'I should see the lands my husband has been given. I can barely remember them from my childhood.' She smiled distantly. 'I would like to see where Genghis and his brothers ran as boys.'

'It is a beautiful land,' Yao Shu admitted, 'though harsh. You will have forgotten the winters there.'

Sorhatani shuddered slightly. 'No, the cold is one thing I do remember. Pray for warm weather, chancellor. And what about my husband? My son? Do you have news of them?'

Yao Shu replied more carefully to the innocent-sounding question.

119

'I have heard of no misfortunes, mistress. The khan's tumans have secured a tract of land, almost to the borders of the Sung territory in the south. I think they will return in a year, perhaps two.'

'That is good to hear, Yao Shu. I pray for the khan's safety.'

Yao Shu responded, though he knew it amused her to goad him on their religions. 'His safety will not be affected by prayers, Sorhatani, as I'm sure you know.'

'You do not pray, chancellor?' she asked in mock amazement.

Yao Shu sighed. She made him feel old, somehow, whenever she was in this mood.

'I do not ask for anything, except more understanding, Sorhatani. In meditation, I merely listen.'

'And God, what does he say when you listen?'

'The Buddha said, "Gripped by fear, men go to the sacred mountains and sacred groves, sacred trees and shrines." I am not afraid of death, my lady. I need no god to comfort me in my fear.'

'Then I will pray for you too, chancellor, that you find peace.'

Yao Shu raised his eyes, but he bowed to her again, aware that her maids were watching with amused interest.

'You are very kind,' he murmured.

Her eyes were twinkling, he saw. His day would be full of a thousand details. He had the khan's army to supply in the Chin lands, another in Khwarezm under Chagatai and a third under Tsubodai ready to strike further into the north and west than the Mongol nation had ever ventured before. Yet he knew he would spend much of the day thinking of the ten things he should have said to Sorhatani. It was simply infuriating.

Ogedai had not brought the war to Suzhou. The city lay beyond the Sung border, on the banks of the Yangtze river. Even if it had not been in Sung territory, it was a place of extraordinary beauty and he could not see it destroyed. Two tumans rested outside the city walls, while only a jagun of a hundred accompanied the khan.

As Ogedai walked with two guards through an enclosure of ponds and trees, he felt at peace. He wondered if the gardens in Karakorum would ever equal such a beautifully planned wilderness. He tried not to show his wistful envy to the Sung administrator who trotted nervously at his side.

Ogedai had thought Karakorum a model of the new world, but Suzhou's position against a great lake, its ancient streets and buildings, made his capital look rough, unfinished by the centuries. He smiled at the thought of his father's response to such inequity. It would have amused Genghis to take their creation and leave it as smoking rubble, his personal comment on the vanities of man.

Ogedai wondered if Yao Shu had come from a place like Suzhou. He had never asked the monk, but it was easy to imagine men like him walking the perfectly clean streets. Tolui and Mongke had gone to the market square, looking for gifts for Sorhatani. They had just a dozen warriors with them, but there was no sense of threat in the town. Ogedai had passed word to his men that there would be no rape or destruction. The penalty for disobeying his edict was clear and Suzhou remained terrified, but untouched.

The khan's morning had been filled with wonders, from the municipal store of black firepowder, where the workers all wore soft slippers, to the astonishment of a watermill and huge looms producing cloth. Yet they were not his reason for taking his tumans into Sung territory. The small city had storehouses of silk and every one of his warriors wore a shirt of that material. It was the only weave capable of trapping an arrow as it twisted into the flesh. In its own way, it was more valuable than armour. Ogedai could not guess how many lives it had saved.

Unfortunately, his men knew its value and few of them ever took off the silk shirts to wash them. The smell of rotting silk was part of the miasma that hung around the tumans, and as the cloth crusted with salt and sweat, it lost its pliability. He needed the entire output of Suzhou and other places like it. Destroying the fields of ancient white mulberry bushes that fed the grubs would end production for ever. Perhaps his father would have burnt them. Ogedai could not. He had spent part of the morning viewing the vats where the grubs were boiled in their cocoons before being unravelled. Such things were true wonders. The workers had not stopped as he passed, pausing only to chew the latest grub as they revealed it to the air. No one went hungry in the silk sheds of Suzhou.

The khan had not bothered to learn the name of the little man bobbing and sweating at his side, struggling to keep up as Ogedai toured the water gardens. The Sung administrator chattered like a frightened bird when he was asked a question. At least they could communicate. Ogedai had Yao Shu to thank for that, and years spent learning the language.

His time in the water gardens would be brief, he knew. His tumans were restless among such prosperity. For all their discipline, there would be problems if he kept them near the city for long. He had noticed the men of Suzhou had the sense to remove their women from sight, but there were always temptations.

'One thousand bolts of silk a year,' Ogedai said. 'Suzhou can produce that much, yes?'

'Yes, lord. High weight, good colour and lustre. Dyed well, without spotting or tangled threads.'

The administrator nodded miserably as he spoke. Whatever happened, he suspected he was ruined. The Mongol armies would go and the emperor's soldiers would arrive to ask him why he had brokered trade deals with an enemy of their master. He wanted nothing more than to find a quiet place in the gardens, write his last poem and open a vein.

Ogedai saw the man's eyes were glassy and assumed he was terrified. He made a gesture with his hand and his guard stepped forward and took the administrator by the throat. The glassy look vanished, but Ogedai continued talking as if nothing had happened.

'Let him go. Are you listening now? Your masters, your emperor are not your concern. I control the north and they will trade with me, eventually.'

Ogedai's chest was hurting him and he walked with a cup of red wine in his hand, constantly refilled. With the foxglove powder, it eased the ache, though his senses swam. He drained the cup and held it out. The second guard stepped forward instantly with a half-full skin of the wine. Ogedai cursed as he spilled some of the dark liquid on the cuff of his sleeve.

'I will send my scribes to your house at noon,' he said. He had to speak slowly and firmly so as not to slur his words, but the little man did not seem to notice. 'They will work out the details. I will pay in good silver, do you understand? Noon – not tonight, or days from now.'

The administrator nodded. He would be dead by noon; it did not matter what he agreed with this strange man and his ugly way of speaking. The smell alone of the Mongols took his breath away. It was not just rotten silk and mutton fat, but the dense odour of men who had never grown used to washing their skins in the far north, where the air was dry. In the south, they sweated and stank. The administrator was not surprised their khan enjoyed the gardens. With the pools and the stream, it was one of the coolest spots in Suzhou.

Something in the man's manner caught Ogedai's attention and he stopped on a stone bridge over a stream. Lilies floated serenely on the surface, their roots disappearing into the black water.

'I have dealt with Chin lords and traders for many years,' Ogedai said, holding his cup over the water and watching the reflection below. His mirror soul looked back at him, kin to the shadow soul that dogged his steps in sunlight. Its face looked puffy, he saw, but he drained the cup anyway and held it for another in an action that had become as natural as breathing. The ache in his chest subsided yet again and he rubbed idly at a spot on his sternum. 'Do you understand? They lie and delay and make lists, but they do not act. They are very good at delays. I am very good at getting what I want. Must I make clear to you what will happen if you do not complete my contracts by today?'

'I understand, master,' the man replied.

It was there again, some glint in his eyes that made Ogedai unsure. The little man had somehow moved beyond fear. His eyes were darkening, as if he cared for nothing. That too Ogedai had seen before and he began to raise his hand to have the man slapped awake. The administrator jerked back and Ogedai laughed, spilling more wine. Some of it fell into the water like drops of blood.

'There is no escape from me, not even in death.' He knew he was slurring by then, but he felt good and his heart was just a distant, thumping pressure. 'If you take your own life before the agreements are finished, I will have Suzhou destroyed, each brick removed from its companion, then shattered in fire. What is not wet will burn, administrator, do you understand? Heh. What is not wet will burn.'

He saw the spark of resistance die in the man's eyes, replaced by fatalism. Ogedai nodded. It was hard to govern a people who could calmly choose death as a response to aggression. It was one of many things he admired about them, but he did not have the patience that day. From past experience, he knew he had to make the choice to die result in such grief that they could *only* live and continue to serve him.

'Run and make your preparations, administrator. I will enjoy this little garden for a while longer.'

He watched as the man scurried away to do his bidding. His guards would hold back the messengers that came constantly to him, at least until he was ready to leave. The stone under his bare forearms was very cool. He drained the cup once again, his fingers clumsy.

In the late afternoon, twenty thousand warriors mounted up outside Suzhou with Ogedai and Tolui. Ogedai's elite Guard made up half his forces, named men with a bow and sword. Seven thousand of his tuman rode black horses and wore black armour with red facings. Many of the grizzled warriors had served with Genghis and they deserved their reputation for ferocity. The remaining three thousand were his Night and Day Guards, who rode horses of pale brown or piebald and wore more common armour. Baabgai the wrestler had joined them, the personal gift of Khasar to his khan. With the sole exception of the wrestling champion, they were men selected for intelligence as well as force. It was Genghis who had begun the rule that a man had to serve in the khan's guards before he could lead even a thousand in battle. It was said that the least of them could command a minghaan if he chose to. Princes of the blood held the tumans, but the khan's Guards were the professionals who made them work.

The sight of them never failed to please Ogedai. The sheer power he could wield through them was intoxicating, exciting. Khasar's tuman was to the north, with lines of scouts between them. It would not be hard to find him again and Ogedai was satisfied with the morning's work.

As well as warriors, he had brought an army of scribes and administrators to Chin lands, in order to take a tally of everything he won. The new khan had learned from his father's conquests. For a people to be at peace, there had to be a foot on their necks. Taxes and petty laws kept them quiet, even

125

comforted them somehow, though he found that mystifying. It was no longer enough to destroy their armies and move on. Perhaps the existence of Karakorum was the spur, but he had men in every Chin city, running things in his name.

He had punished skins of wine and airag that day, more than he could remember. As they rode north, Ogedai knew he was very drunk. He didn't care. He had his contracts for silk, sealed by the terrified local lord after he was dragged from his town house to witness the deal. The Sung emperor would either honour them or give Ogedai an excuse to invade his territory.

His buttocks were still rubbed raw each day by the wooden saddle, so that his clothes stuck to the pale fluids that seeped out of the broken skin. He could no longer undress without first soaking himself in a warm bath, but that too was just a minor hardship. He had not expected to live even so long and each day was a joy.

He saw the dust clouds ahead after just a short ride that cracked his scabs and made them weep all over again. Sung lands were ten miles behind by then. Ogedai knew he would not be expected from the south. He smiled to think of the panic that would follow the appearance of his tumans. In the distance, Khasar was engaging the last remaining army the Chin could field. Outnumbered on an open plain, all Khasar could do was hold them, but he knew the tumans with Ogedai and Tolui were coming. There would be a bloody slaughter and Ogedai began to sing as he rode, enjoying himself.

CHAPTER TEN

Khasar's sharp eyes picked out the banners of Ogedai Khan. The ground was far from perfect, a grassy plain where there had been no herds for years, so that saplings and scrub bushes grew everywhere. He stood on his saddle, balancing casually while his mount cropped the grass.

'Good lad, Ogedai,' he muttered.

Khasar had taken a position on a small rise, outside arrow range, but close enough to the enemy to direct his attacks. The army of the emperor was visibly battered after days fending off the Mongol horsemen. Yet the Chin regiments were disciplined and tough, as Khasar had learned to his cost. Time and again, they had held a solid line of pikes against his men. The ground prevented a full charge with lances and reduced him to picking them off with waves of arrows. As the morning passed, his archers had killed dozens, over and over, but all the while the Chin soldiers moved steadily south and the Mongol tuman drifted with them. Khasar saw weary heads turn to see the new threat, staring at the streaming orange banners of the Mongol khan.

Somewhere in those shining Chin ranks, a particular young man would be raging at the sight, Khasar thought. As a boy emperor, Xuan had knelt to Genghis when the great khan had burnt his capital. Khasar himself had trapped the young man in the city of Kaifeng before being called home. It was like hot blood and milk in his stomach to know the Chin emperor was once again in play, his life in Khasar's hands. It was an ending long in coming.

Even then, the emperor had almost reached the southern empire, where his family still ruled in splendid isolation. If Genghis had been given just a few more years, he would have entered those lands, Khasar was certain. He knew nothing of the twists and turns of politics between the two nations, except that the Sung seemed to have armies in the millions. It was enough for the moment to bring death to the emperor of the north. It was enough to ride with his tuman. He was only sorry Genghis had not lived to see it.

Lost in wistful memories, Khasar half-turned to give an order to Ho Sa and Samuka before he remembered they were both dead, years before. He shivered slightly in the wind. There had been so many dead since he and his brothers had hidden from their enemies in a tiny fold of ground, with winter on the way. From those frightened and starving children a new force had entered the world, but only Kachiun, Temuge and Khasar himself had survived. The cost had been high, though he knew Genghis had not begrudged it.

'The best of us,' Khasar whispered to himself, watching Ogedai's forces ride steadily closer. He had seen enough. He dropped back into the saddle and whistled sharply. Two messengers galloped up to his side. They were both bare-armed, black with dirt and wearing only silk tunics and leggings to be fast and light.

'Minghaans one to four to bring pressure on their western flank,' Khasar snapped to the first. 'Do not let the enemy drift out of the path of the khan.'

The messenger raced away across the battlefield, his young face alight with excitement. The other waited patiently while Khasar watched the ebb and flow of men like an old hawk over a field of wheat. He saw hares racing towards him from some burrow, before his delighted bondsmen shot them through with arrows and dismounted to pick them up. It was another sign that the ground was rough and filled with obstacles. A charge would be even more dangerous when a horse could snap a leg in a hole and kill its rider with the impact.

Khasar winced at the thought. There was no easy victory to be snatched, not that day. The Chin army outnumbered his by more than six to one. Even when Ogedai and Tolui arrived, it would be two to one. Khasar had harried and cut them as they moved south, but he had been unable to force the emperor to stand and fight. It had been Ogedai himself who suggested the vast circle around to come back from the south. Three days had gone past with agonising slowness, until he had begun to think the emperor would find his way to the border and safety before Ogedai even returned.

Khasar found himself wishing it was Genghis coming from the south. It broke his heart to imagine it and he shook his head to clear it of an old man's dreams. There was work to do.

'Take this order to Yusep,' he told the messenger. 'Grip the east wing, force them into a funnel towards the khan. Use all the shafts if they must. He is to command minghaans five to eight. I have two thousand as a reserve. Acknowledge your orders.' Khasar waited impatiently as the scout repeated them, then dismissed him to gallop away.

Staring across the open plain, Khasar wondered how the Chin emperor had grown. No longer a proud little boy, he would be a man in his prime, but denied his birthright. The lands he had

129

known were ruled by Mongolian princes. The huge armies of his father had been crushed. All he had left were these. Perhaps that was why they fought so hard, he thought. They were the last hope of their emperor and they knew it. The Sung border lay tantalisingly close and they were still strong, still many, like multicoloured wasps.

Khasar rode back to his reserve, where they sat their mounts easily and watched the enemy, resting their elbows on the saddle horns. They straightened as Khasar took his position with them, knowing he would notice every small detail.

Ahead, they watched the Chin ranks re-form to deal with the new threat, bristling with pikes and spears. As Khasar had expected, they began to manoeuvre away from the direct route south. He would not have minded if Ogedai had not been there. The Chin emperor wanted to reach the Sung border. If he could be forced along its edges without crossing, eventually his army would tire and the Mongol tumans would tear slices off its flanks. Sunset was still some way off and the foot soldiers of the emperor would weaken before the Mongol riders. The Chin cavalry had been Khasar's first targets, torn away from those they protected over days of blood and arrows. Those who survived were deep in the centre, humiliated and broken.

When Ogedai reached the Chin, they would be trapped between two foes. Khasar hummed under his breath, enjoying the prospect. Nothing sapped morale like the fear of being attacked from behind.

He watched as his first four thousand warriors rode slowly through a swarm of bolts, ducking low in their saddles and trusting their armour. Some crashed down, but the rest forced their way closer and closer. Small trees lashed at them and Khasar saw animals stumble. One fell to its knees as the ground subsided, but the rider heaved the animal up by main force and went on. Khasar whitened his own grip on his reins as he watched.

At fifty paces, the air was thick with whining bolts and the closest Chin ranks were throwing spears, though most fell short or tumbled in the grass. The Mongol lines were ragged over the poor ground, but their bows bent as one. The emperor's soldiers flinched back, despite their roaring officers. They had faced the same storm too many times and they were desperate. From the rapidly closing range, the Mongol bows could hammer through almost anything. His men heaved with writhing shoulder muscles, holding the strings with bone thumb rings. No other bows had that power, nor men the strength to use them.

They released with a snap that echoed to where Khasar watched. The volley tore a great hole in the enemy lines, yanking men backwards so that their pikes and crossbows jerked up all along the line. Khasar nodded sharply. Neither he nor Jebe had won the gold at the festival. That honour had gone to Tsubodai's archers. Even so, this was work he knew.

Bodies fell with many shafts in them and screaming carried on the breeze to where Khasar sat. He grinned. They had broken through the army's skin. He longed to give an order to follow with axe and lances, deep into them. He'd seen armies cut into strips in such a way, for all their strength and drums and coloured banners.

The Mongol discipline held, hardened in battles across the world. His men loosed shaft after shaft, picking their targets from men trying to turn away or hiding behind shields as they were battered to pieces. The outermost fringes met with swinging swords, and more men fell on both sides before the minghaan officers blew a low note and pulled them back, jubilant.

A ragged cheer sounded from untouched Chin ranks further back, but then Khasar's men turned in the saddle and loosed a final shaft, just as the enemy stood tall again. The sound choked off and the minghaans whooped as they wheeled to a

131

new position and prepared to come in again. The movement of the Chin army had been slowed over half a mile and the wounded were left behind in wailing, writhing heaps.

'Here they come,' Khasar murmured. 'The khan enters the field.'

He could see Ogedai's bannermen in the host that trotted across the broken land. The Chin ranks braced to meet them, lowering shields and pikes that could gut a charging horse. As they reached two hundred paces, the Mongol arrows started to come in black waves. The crackle of thousands of bows releasing was like a raging bonfire, a sound that Khasar knew as well as any other. He had them, he was suddenly certain. The emperor would not pass to safety that day.

Another thump sounded, far louder than the bowstring rattle he had known from childhood. It boomed like rolling thunder and was followed by a breath that washed across his men. Khasar stared at a rising cloud of smoke that obscured part of the lines where Ogedai and the Chin force had clashed.

'What was that?' he demanded.

One of his bondsmen answered immediately. 'Gunpowder, my lord. They have fire-pots.'

'In the *field*?' Khasar said. He cursed loudly. He had seen the weapons used on city walls and he knew their effect. Iron pots filled with black powder could rip shards of hot metal through the packed ranks of his men. They had to be thrown far enough for the defenders not to be torn apart themselves. He could not imagine how the Chin were using them without killing their own people.

Before he could gather his stunned thoughts, another great crack sounded. At a distance, the sound was muted, but he saw men and horses blown back from the explosion, landing brokenly on the grass. The smell came to him then, acrid and bitter. Some of his men coughed in the breeze. The Chin cheered with more energy and Khasar's face became savage.

Every instinct urged him to gallop towards the enemy before they could use the small advantage they had won. Ogedai's advance had lost its momentum and only the edge of the two armies were in contact, like struggling insects over the distance. Khasar forced himself under control. This was no raid against tribesmen. The Chin had numbers and nerve enough to lose half their men just to gut the khan of the Mongols. The sky father knew the Chin emperor had the desire. Khasar felt his men staring at him, waiting for the word. He clenched his jaw, grinding his teeth.

'Hold. Wait,' he ordered, watching the battle. His two thousand could mean the difference between victory and defeat or just be lost in the mass. The choice, the decision, was his.

Ogedai had never heard thunder like it. He had been riding well back in the ranks as the armies came together. He had roared as the arrows flew, thousands at a time, again and again before his warriors drew swords and hit. The men around him had surged forward, each man keen to show courage and win the khan's approval. It was a rare opportunity for them to be within sight of the man who ruled the nation. No one wanted to waste it and they prepared to fight like maniacs, showing no pain or weakness.

As they went forward, a thumping blast threw men backwards and left Ogedai's ears ringing. Dirt spattered him as he tried groggily to understand what had happened. He saw a man unhorsed, standing numbly with blood running down his face. A small group lay dead, while many more twitched and pulled at metal stuck in their flesh. The explosion had deafened and stunned those closest. As the ranks surged forward, Ogedai saw one unhorsed man stumble into the path of a rider and go down under the hooves.

Ogedai shook his head to clear the sound of rushing air, the emptiness. His heart pounded in his ears and a wide band of pressure had grown in his head. He thought of a man he had once seen tortured, a flashing image of leather thongs bound around the head and tightened with a stick. It was a simple device, but it produced appalling agony as the skull shifted and eventually broke. Ogedai's head felt like that, as if the band were slowly tightening.

Another booming explosion seemed to raise the ground beneath them. Horses squealed and reared, their eyes wild as the warriors fought savagely to control them. Ogedai could see black specks hurled high into the air from the Chin forces. He did not know what they were, or how to counter them. With a sudden shock that cut through even his drunken state, he realised he could die on that stony plain. It was not a matter of courage or even endurance, but mere luck. He shook his head again to clear it and his eyes were bright. His body was weak, his heart feeble, but above all things, he had luck. Another crack whipped across the field, followed by two more. Ogedai's men were wavering, shocked into immobility. To his right, Tolui's tuman had gone further, but they too were stunned by massive explosions that killed men on both sides.

Ogedai drew his father's sword in one swift gesture, bellowing defiance as he held it up. His bondsmen saw his recklessness and it lit their blood. They came with him as he kicked his mount forward, already grinning at the maniac khan, charging the enemy on his own. They were all young men. They rode with the most beloved son of Genghis, marked by the sky father, khan of the nation. Their lives were not worth as much as his and they threw them away as carelessly as they would a broken rein.

The explosions came faster as more of the black balls were flung sputtering into the air to land around Mongol feet. As he thundered forward, Ogedai saw one unhorsed warrior pick one up. The khan shouted, but the man was blown into a bloody mass. The air was suddenly full of whining flies. Horses and men screamed as needles of iron tore into them all around.

Ogedai's bondsmen plunged into the fray, protecting their khan at the centre. Lowered pikes stopped the horses, but more and more of his men had been unhorsed and they killed the pike-wielders with knives and swords, clearing a path as horses shoved and sweated at their backs. Ogedai saw another black ball drop almost at his feet and one of his men threw himself on top of it. The whump of sound was muted, though a small red crater appeared in the man's back and a piece of bone jumped out, almost to the height of a man. Those around Ogedai flinched, but they stood immediately straight, ashamed that the khan might have seen their fear.

Ogedai realised he had seen some sort of answer to the weapons. He raised his voice to carry across the lines.

'Fall on them as they land, for your khan,' he shouted.

The order was repeated down the lines as the next wave of missiles were thrown high. There were six of the flying iron balls, each fizzing with a short fuse. Ogedai watched in pride as warriors struggled to reach them, smothering the threat so that their friends might live. He turned back to the enemy and saw fear in the Chin faces. There was only vengeful fury in his own.

'Bows!' he roared. 'Clear a path and bring up lances. Lances here!'

There were tears in his eyes, but not for those who had given their lives. There was joy in every waking, breathing moment. The air was cold and bitter in his throat, filled with the strange smell of burning powder. He breathed it deeply, and for a time the band across his face and head seemed to ease as his men ripped a gash in the Chin ranks.

Khasar beat his fist against his armour in unconscious approval of Ogedai's manoeuvres. The two Mongol tumans had been rocked back by the explosions, moving instinctively away from the source of such sound and snaps of light. Khasar had seen the khan's own bondsmen overcome their fear and hack open the Chin lines. The thumps of explosions were suddenly muffled and he no longer saw the spray of stones and dirt each time one of them went up. It was as if they dropped into the Mongol army and were swallowed. He grinned at the thought.

'I think the khan is eating those iron balls,' he said to his men. 'Look, he is still hungry. He wants more to fill his stomach.' He hid his own fear at such a reckless charge from Ogedai. If he died that day, Chagatai would rule the nation and everything they had struggled for would have been in vain.

His experienced eye ran over the battlefield as he trotted his horse south, keeping them in range. In that at least, the Chin emperor had not wavered. His men moved as quickly as they could, struggling over the dead as they marched. Such an army could not easily be stopped by half its number. It was a tactical problem and Khasar struggled with it. If he ordered thinner lines spread like a net, the Chin could break through with a spear thrust. If he kept the depth of men, they could be passed on the flanks as the emperor forced each dogged step towards the border. It must be an agony for him, Khasar thought, to be so close and yet have an enemy boiling around him.

His own minghaans killed almost at their leisure in the enemy rear, leaving a trail of bodies on the rough grass. The Chin would not turn, so intent were they on reaching the border. As he trotted south behind them, Khasar came across one soldier draped on the limbs of a low thorn tree. He glanced at the man and saw his face twitch and the eyes open in sightless agony. Khasar reached out with his sword and flicked the tip across the throat. It was not mercy. He had not killed that day and he longed to be part of the battle.

The action bit away a piece of his control and he snapped an order to the two thousand warriors with him.

'Ride forward, with me. We do no good here and the khan is in the field.'

He cantered to just a hundred paces behind the enemy, looking for the best place and opportunity to strike. He sat as tall as he could in the saddle, staring into the distance in the hope of seeing the emperor's own bannermen. They would be somewhere close to the heart of the massed ranks, he was certain, a barrier of men, horses and metal to bring just one desperate ruler to safety. Khasar wiped his sword clean on a rag before sheathing it. His men picked their targets and sent shafts into the Chin soldiers with pitiless accuracy. It was hard to hold himself back and his control was wearing thin.

Ogedai's charge had brought him past the outer lines of pikemen. The Chin regiments were disciplined, but discipline alone could not win the day. Though they did not break, they were cut down by the marauding horsemen. Their lines were sundered, driven back or reduced to cores and knots of struggling men to be spitted on shafts.

Horns sounded in the Chin ranks and ten thousand swordsmen drew their blades and charged, screaming defiance. They ran into a constant barrage of arrows, shot from close range. The front lines were ground down and trampled. They ran forward as a mass, then each rank found themselves in twos, threes and lonely dozens, facing the swords of horsemen. Seeing such a slaughter, those behind hesitated as the Mongols came lunging forward in a line. In a few heartbeats, they accelerated to a full gallop and struck the charge cleanly, unstoppably. The Chin lines crumpled further back.

Tolui saw his brother had gone deep into the enemy formations, the khan's wedge of bondsmen killing as if they thought they could win right through to the other side. He was in awe of Ogedai then. He had not expected to see him go insane on a battlefield, but there was no holding him back and his bondsmen were hard-pressed to keep up. Ogedai rode as if he was immortal and nothing touched him, though the air was filled with death and smoke.

Tolui had never before seen smoke on a battlefield. It was a new element and his men hated to see it drifting towards them. He was becoming used to the strange odour, but the thunderous cracks and thumps were some of the most terrifying moments he had ever known. He could not hold back, not with Ogedai moving into the mass. The frustration of being unable to prevent the drift south was telling on all of them. It was close to becoming a chaotic brawl, with the Mongol advantages of speed and accuracy sacrificed to vengeful fury.

Tolui directed his minghaan officers to protect the khan, moving swiftly to bolster Ogedai's flanks and widen the wedge he pressed into the Chin army. He felt a surge of pride as his son Mongke passed on the order to his thousand and they followed him without hesitation. There had been few occasions when Genghis rode to war with his sons. Amidst the fear for Mongke's safety, Tolui could grin with pleasure at seeing such a strong young man. Sorhatani would be proud when he told her.

The rolling smoke cleared again and Tolui expected another wave of thunder to follow. He was closer by then and the Chin army was spiralling around his men, moving south, always south. Tolui cursed them as a Chin soldier passed almost under his horse's head blindly, trying to stay in marching rank. Tolui killed him with a brief thrust from above, choosing a point on the neck where armour did not protect him.

He looked up and found hundreds more marching rapidly towards his position. They were armoured like common soldiers, but each carried a black iron tube. He saw they struggled with the weight, but they strode closer with a strange confidence. Their officers barked orders to load and brace. Tolui knew instinctively that he should not give them time.

Tolui bawled his own orders, his voice already hoarse. A thousand of his men turned to charge the new threat, letting Ogedai's wedge move on without them. They followed their general without hesitation, swinging swords and loosing arrows at anything in his path.

The Chin soldiers were hacked down as they struggled with fuses and iron tubes. Some were crushed by horses, others died as they pressed a spluttering taper to the weapon. Many of the tubes fell to the ground and, in response, Mongol warriors yanked their mounts away or even threw themselves on top with their eyes tightly shut.

They did not catch them all. A rattle of lighter cracks sounded, rippling across the lines. Tolui saw a man snatched away from him, torn from his saddle before he could even cry out. Another horse crashed to its knees, its chest running with blood. The sound was appalling and then the smoke rolled in a great grey wave and they were blind. Tolui laid about him with his sword until it snapped and he stared at the hilt in disbelief. Something fell against him, whether an enemy or one of his own men he did not know. He felt the life go out of his mount and staggered clear before it could roll on him. He drew a long knife from his boot, holding it high as he limped across the smoking ground. More of the strange cracks sounded around him as the tubes fired their load of stone and iron, some of them spinning uselessly on the ground as their owners lay dead.

Tolui did not know how long they had been fighting. In the thick smoke, he was almost overwhelmed with fear. He calmed himself with calculations, forcing his mind to work amidst the noise and chaos. The Chin army could reach the border by sunset. It lay no more than a few miles to the south by then, but they had suffered and died for every step. As the smoke cleared, Tolui darted one look at the sun, seeing it closer to the horizon as if it had dropped while he was wreathed in smoke. He could hardly believe it as he grabbed a riderless horse and held the reins while he searched the ground for a good sword. The grass was slick and bloody as he walked. His stomach heaved at the stench of bowels and death mingled with burnt black powder, a bitter combination he never wanted to know again.

Xuan, the Son of Heaven, rode untouched by bloodshed, though he could smell the odour of gunpowder in the evening air. Around him the Mongol tumans tore and screeched at his noble soldiers, ripping at them with teeth and iron. Xuan's face was cold as he stared south above their heads. He could see the border, but he did not think the Mongols would hold back as he passed the simple stone temple that marked the boundary between two nations. By some chance, the Chin army had wound its way back onto the main road. The white stone building was a distant speck, an oasis of peace with clashing armies converging on it.

Xuan sweated in his armour, shamed by the thought that he could race his mount alone along that road. His horse was a fine, cut stallion, but Xuan was not a fool. He could not enter Sung lands as a beggar. His army protected his body, but also the last wealth of the Chin kingdoms, in a thousand sacks and bags. His wives and children were there as well, hidden by the walls of iron and loyal men. He could not leave them to the mercies of the Mongol khan.

With his wealth, he would be welcomed by his cousin. With an army, he would have the Sung emperor's respect. He would have a place at the table of nobles as they planned a campaign to take back his ancestral lands.

Xuan winced at the thought. There was little love for his

bloodline in the Sung court. The emperor, Lizong, was a man of his father's generation who viewed Chin territory as his own, claiming a mere error of history that it was not already his by right. There was a chance that Xuan was putting his hand into a rat hole by placing himself in Sung power. There was no other choice. Mongol goatherders strode his lands as if they owned them, peering into every storehouse, tallying the wealth of every village for taxes they would never know how to spend. The shame of it should have been overwhelming, but Xuan had never known peace. He had grown used to the humiliation of losing his kingdom piece by piece to an army of locusts and seeing his father's capital burn. Surely his Sung cousin would not underestimate the threat. Yet there had been conquerors before, tribal leaders who raised an army and then died. Their empires always fell apart, broken by the arrogance and weakness of lesser men. Xuan knew Emperor Lizong would be tempted to ignore them and simply wait for a century or two. He wiped sweat from his eyes, blinking at the sting of salt. Time cured so many ills in the world, but not these cursed tribesmen. The Mongols had lost their great conqueror at the height of his power and simply carried on, as if one man did not matter. Xuan did not know if it made them more civilised, or just a pack of wolves, with another taking the lead.

He clenched his fist in pleasure as he heard the rippling snaps of his gunners. He had so few, but they were wonderful, fearsome weapons. That too was something he took to the Sung: vital knowledge of the enemy as well as ways to destroy him. A wolf would not stand against a man with a burning brand. Xuan knew he could be that weapon, if he had the time and space to plan.

He was jerked from his reverie by the shouting of his officers. They were pointing to the south and he shaded his eyes from the setting sun to look into the distance.

An army was approaching the border, barely two miles away. He could see huge fast-moving square formations pouring over the hills. Like wasps, the Sung regiments were reacting to the threat, he thought. Or answering the arrogance of a khan who had dared to enter their lands. As Xuan watched, concentrating, he began to realise that it was no minor force, no regional governor. The emperor himself would never leave his capital for the filthy business of warfare. It had to be one of his sons, perhaps even his heir. No one else could command so many. The squares layered the ground like a cloth pattern, each at least five thousand fresh men, well trained and supplied. Xuan tried to count them, but it was impossible with the dust and distance. The men around him were already jubilant, but he narrowed his eyes to think, staring around him at the Mongol forces who still growled at his heels.

If his cousin closed the border, he would not survive. Xuan scratched irritably at a line of sweat on his face, leaving a red mark from his fingernails. Surely they would not stand by and watch him killed? He did not know. He *could* not know. The tension made bile rise in his stomach as his horse brought him closer and closer, the calm centre of a whirling storm.

Taking a deep breath, Xuan summoned his generals and began to bark orders to them. The commands rippled out and the edges of his army hardened. Men carrying heavy shields raced into position, setting up a strong defence that would hold the Mongols long enough to reach the border. It was his last-ditch plan, just to survive, but at that point, it might also serve to keep as many soldiers alive as possible. He had fought a defensive battle for days. If the border was closed, he would have to turn at bay and strike down the khan. He had the numbers still and his men were hungry to give back the blows they had taken.

The thought was intoxicating and Xuan wondered if he should attack even if the border army opened to let him through. All he had wanted was to find safety with enough men to make him a powerful voice in the councils that would follow. Yet the Mongol khan remained outnumbered. The grubby Mongol shepherd would be dumbstruck and unnerved at the sight of so many pristine regiments.

The first Sung ranks had reached the border and halted, perfect lines of coloured armour and Sung banners streaming. As Xuan stared at them, he saw a puff of smoke in the line and heard a crack as a rock ball came flying over the grass. It hit no one, but the message was not for him. The Sung prince had brought cannon to the field, huge metal tubes on wheels that could smear a line of horses and men with a single shot. Let the khan digest that little detail.

Xuan's army marched on, his heart beating like a bird's as they approached the dark lines.

CHAPTER ELEVEN

Khasar could hardly believe the size of the army that had raced to the Sung border, stretching back over the land. The southern nation had not had its battle of the Badger's Mouth, as the north had. Their emperor had not sent out armies and seen them battered, destroyed, routed. His soldiers had never run in terror from Mongol riders. Khasar hated them for their splendour and he wished again that Genghis was there, if only to see his brother's anger kindle at the sight.

The Sung lines stretched for miles, dwarfing the marching squares of their Chin cousins as they drifted in. Khasar saw the pace to the border had slowed. He wondered if the Chin emperor knew whether he would be allowed to escape or be turned away. That thought gave some hope, the only small comfort to be weighed against Khasar's fury and indignation. He had won the battle! The Chin regiments had fought to keep him away for days, but not once had they sallied out. They had only attacked when his men pierced their ranks. His tuman had soaked the ground in their blood, suffered explosions and storms of hot metal. His men had been burnt and broken, cut and maimed. They had earned the victory, and now it was to be snatched from them.

His reserve of two thousand were still fresh. Khasar sent up a flag signal to the camel riders keeping pace with him. The boys on the beasts rode with the naccara drums strapped on either side. All along the lines, they began a thunder, striking left and right with both hands. The armoured horses leapt forward at the signal and the warriors brought their heavy lances down slowly, balancing them in a casual display of strength and skill. The wall of riders matched the drums with a screaming roar from their throats that terrified their enemies.

Khasar's two thousand hit their full speed just twenty paces from the shaken Chin. The general had time to see some of them jam their long shields into the earth, but only a solid shield wall could have stopped his charge. Good officers would have halted them, mingled shields and pikemen together in an unbroken barrier. The emperor's men had to march, terrified.

The Mongol ponies had lightly armoured cloth covering their faces and chests. The warriors themselves wore layered scale armour and helmets, and carried lances and swords as well as saddlebags full of supplies. They crashed into the Chin lines like a mountain falling.

Khasar saw the closest ranks collapse, the men broken by lances and hooves. Some of the horses refused and whinnied in wild-eyed distress as their riders sawed at their mouths, shouting angrily as they brought them round again. Others plunged straight through the Chin, their lances snapping with the force of the strike. They tossed aside the broken hilts and followed with swords, using the muscles from twenty years of bow work to lay about them tirelessly, cutting down, always down, onto the snarling faces.

Khasar was spattered with warm red drops as his horse was

killed and he jumped clear. He tasted someone's blood on his lips and he spat in disgust, ignoring the outstretched arm of one of his bondsmen as the man tried to grab him up into a saddle. His fury at the emperor's looming escape blurred his judgement. On foot, he stalked the enemy soldiers, his sword held low until they attacked. His counters were vicious and accurate, and as he strode forward with his men, the Chin backed away rather than engage him.

He could feel the sullen gaze of the emperor's soldiers, watching in silence as they marched away from him. Khasar grunted as he trapped his sword in a shield, leaving it and backhanding a soldier before snatching another one from the ground. Only then did he mount behind a warrior, to see what was happening.

In the distance, the front ranks of the Chin army had reached the Sung lines.

'Find me a horse,' Khasar shouted into the ear of the bondsman.

The man wheeled and rode out of the cup they had cut for themselves. It closed behind them, the battered shields rising once again.

Khasar looked for Ogedai, his blood cooling as he considered the threat. A child could have seen the position was hopeless. Faced with such an army, all the tumans could do was get clear. If the Sung regiments attacked, the Mongols would be forced away, routed on the border. The only choice was between a dignified retreat and running as if there were wolves after them. Khasar ground his teeth until his jaw hurt. There was no help for it.

His back straight, Xuan trotted his horse towards the Sung line, flanked by three generals in ornate armour and cloaks. They were all dusty and tired, but Xuan rode as if there were no possibility of being turned away. He knew he had to be the first one there. Of course the Sung would refuse common soldiers the right to enter their realm. Only Xuan could shape the rules around him, as the reigning emperor. He was the Son of Heaven. It was a title without a nation, an emperor without cities, yet he kept his dignity as he reached the first line of soldiers.

They did not move and Xuan reached down to brush a speck of dust from his gloves. He showed no discomfort as he stared over the heads of the Sung army. He could hear the Mongols ripping at his own men, but he did not move or acknowledge it. There was a chance that his cousin Lizong would allow his army to be destroyed while they all waited. Xuan seethed at the thought, but there was nothing he could do. He had come as a supplicant to the Sung lands. If the emperor chose to remove his strength in such a way, Xuan knew he could not react. It was a bold stroke and he could almost applaud it. Let the damaged Chin emperor enter, but let him see his army withered to just a few men first. Let him come on his knees, begging for favour.

All Xuan's choices, all his plans and stratagems, had been reduced to one course of action. He had ridden up to the lines. If they opened to let him in, he could pass to safety with whoever remained alive in his army. Xuan tried not to think what might happen if his poisonous Sung cousins had decided to remove him from the balance. It was not beyond them to have manoeuvred him to exactly this position, waiting, waiting, waiting. He could sit his horse in front of them until the Mongols had finished slaughtering his army and came for him. There was a chance Lizong would not lift a hand to save him even then.

Xuan's face was utterly without emotion as he studied the Sung soldiers. Whatever happened was his fate and not to be denied. Some hidden spark of him was white with fury, but

147

nothing showed. As casually as he could, he turned to one of his generals and asked about the cannon the Sung had used.

The general was sweating visibly, but he replied as if they were at a military inspection.

'It is a field-piece, imperial majesty, similar to the ones we have used on city walls. Bronze is poured into a mould and then filed and polished. Black powder burns with great fierceness, sending a ball leaping out to cause terror in the enemy.'

Xuan nodded as if he was fascinated. By the spirits of his ancestors, *how long must he wait?*

'Such a large cannon would be very heavy,' he said stiffly. 'It must be difficult to move over rough terrain.'

The general nodded, pleased that his master had engaged him in conversation, though he knew the stakes as well as anyone.

'It sits on a wooden cart, imperial majesty. It is wheeled, but yes, it takes many men and oxen to drag it into position. More are needed to carry the stone balls, the powder bags, the swabs and fuses. Perhaps you will have the chance to inspect one more closely when we enter Sung territory.'

Xuan looked at the general in reproof for his lack of subtlety.

'Perhaps, general. Tell me now about the Sung regiments. I do not know all these banners.'

The man began to recite the names and histories, an expert in his field, as Xuan knew very well. He cocked his head to listen to the droning voice, but all the time, Xuan watched the Sung lines. The Son of Heaven glanced up as an officer rode a magnificent stallion through to the borderline. He tried not to show how his heart leapt.

It was hard to allow his general to finish the litany of names, but Xuan forced himself to listen, making the Sung officer wait for both of them. His precious army was being butchered as he nodded at tedious detail, but Xuan's face was calm and interested.

At last, his general had the sense to subside and Xuan thanked him, appearing to notice the Sung officer for the first time. The man dismounted as soon as their eyes met. He came forward and prostrated himself on the dusty ground before touching his forehead to the general's stirrup. He did not look at Xuan as he spoke.

'I bear a message for the Son of Heaven.'

'Speak your message to me, soldier. I will tell him,' the general replied.

The man prostrated himself again, then rose. 'His imperial majesty bids you welcome in his lands, Son of Heaven. May you live ten thousand years.'

Xuan would not lower himself to reply to a mere soldier. The message should have been delivered by someone of noble rank and he wondered what to make of the subtle insult. He barely listened as his general completed the formalities. Xuan did not glance behind him as he walked his mount forward. Sweat trickled down his back and from his armpits under his armour. He knew his undertunic would be sopping wet.

The Sung lines stood apart as he moved, a rippling motion that spread along them for half a mile. In this way the last Chin army could walk between the ranks and the border was still held against their mutual enemy. Xuan and his generals crossed the invisible line, showing no emotion to those who watched them. The Chin ranks began to follow them, like a blister collapsing into skin.

Ogedai watched in furious disbelief. He saw pavilions rise amidst the Sung ranks, great squares of peach-coloured silk. Banners floated on the wind, marking out regiments of bowmen, pikemen, lancers. It was the sight of the fresh cavalry that broke through his battle madness. Regiments of horsemen stared out onto the broken plain with its trail of dead. Would the Sung be able to resist a sudden charge, as soon as the Chin emperor was safe? Only the setting sun would stay their hand and perhaps not even then. The Mongol ponies had ridden for days. They were as weary as their riders and, for once, the khan himself was in the field, vastly outnumbered and with every advantage taken away. Ogedai shook his head. He had seen the puff of smoke that revealed the presence of heavy guns. It was a thought for another day, but he did not see how he could ever bring such weapons to a battlefield. They were too slow, too heavy for an army whose chief strength had always been in its speed and manoeuvres. In the distance, he saw a small group of horses move through the Sung lines. Perhaps ten thousand still marched to follow them, but the Chin emperor had passed through the net.

Ogedai felt a wave of weariness replace the thrilling energy of the fighting. He could hardly believe he had walked without fear. He had faced his enemies and survived unmarked. For just an instant, a heartbeat, pride swelled in him.

Even so, he had failed. The band across his head returned, tightening. He imagined mockery in every concerned face. He could almost hear the whispered voices among his warriors. Genghis would not have failed. His father would somehow have plucked victory from disaster.

Ogedai gave fresh orders and the three tumans pulled back from the retreating Chin ranks. The men had been expecting the command and the minghaans moved quickly and easily into squares of horse, facing the Sung border.

The sudden silence was like a pressure and Ogedai rode slowly along the lines of his own men, his face flushed and sweating. If the Sung generals wanted him badly enough, they would not even wait for the rest of the Chin to come across. Half the Sung army could launch an attack at that moment. Ogedai swallowed, working his tongue around a mouth so dry he thought he would choke. He gestured to a messenger and the man brought him a skin of red wine. It moistened his lips and he gulped at it, sucking desperately on the leather teat. The pain in his head was growing all the time and he realised his vision was blurred. He thought at first it was just sweat in his eyes, but it remained no matter how roughly he rubbed at them.

As the Mongol tumans came to order, hundreds were still panting or binding gashes. Ogedai saw Tolui trotting a mare across the broken ground towards him. The two brothers met with a quick glance of resignation and Tolui turned his mount to watch the Chin emperor escape them once again.

'He has a lot of luck, that man,' Tolui said softly. 'But we have his land and his cities. We have taken away his armies except for that rabble of survivors.'

'Enough,' Ogedai snapped, rubbing his temples. 'You do not need to add honey. I must bring an army into Sung lands now. They have given sanctuary to my enemies and they know I must respond.' He winced and sucked again on the wine-skin. 'There will be other days to avenge the dead. Form the men up to go back to the north, with haste, but not too visible, do you understand?'

Tolui smiled. No commander liked to be seen retreating, but the men would understand far better than Ogedai realised. They could see the wall of Sung soldiers as well as anyone. None of the Mongol warriors were clamouring to be first against that solid border.

As Tolui turned away, a single crack sounded in the distance. He jerked back and saw the puff of smoke rising above the row of Sung cannon. Only one had fired and both men saw a tumbling object rise only a short way and bounce across the ground.

It came to rest just a few hundred paces from the khan and his brother. For a moment, no one moved, then Tolui shrugged and rode over to it. He kept his back straight as he went, knowing he was watched by more men than at the festival in Karakorum.

By the time he returned to Ogedai carrying a cloth bundle, Khasar had ridden across the tumans to see what was happening. He nodded to his nephews and reached for the cloth bag. Tolui shook his head a fraction before he held it out to Ogedai.

The khan kept blinking at it, his vision doubling. Tolui waited for an order, but when none came, he cut the rope around the bag himself and snorted in disgust as he pulled out a mottled head by its hair, its eyes upturned.

Khasar and Tolui both looked blank as it dangled, spinning slowly. Ogedai squinted, frowning as he recognised the administrator from his morning ride. Had it been that very same day? It seemed impossible. There had been no army in Sung lands then, though they must have been marching almost in his wake. The message was as clear as the silent ranks who stood and moved not a foot from the border. He was not to enter Sung lands for any purpose.

Ogedai opened his mouth to speak and a sudden pain flared in his head, worse than anything he had ever known. He made a soft sound in his throat, helplessly. Tolui saw his distress and dropped the bloody object, moving his mount to take his brother by the arm.

'Are you unwell?' Tolui hissed at him.

His brother swayed in the saddle and Tolui feared he might fall in front of the tumans. The khan would never recover from such an omen, not in sight of the enemy. Tolui jammed his horse up against his brother's mount and kept his hand on Ogedai's shoulder to steady him. Khasar fell in on the other side, awkward with worry. Step by painful step, they forced the pony into the Mongol lines, then dismounted as soon as they were surrounded by staring warriors.

Ogedai had been holding on, his hands gripping the saddle horn like death. His face had twisted somehow, his left eye weeping in a constant stream. His other eye was wide and clear with agony, but he did not let go until Tolui began to prise his fingers away. Then he slumped and slid into his brother's arms, his body as limp as a sleeping child.

Tolui stood aghast, staring down at the pale face of his brother. He looked up at Khasar suddenly, seeing his own expression mirrored.

'I have a good shaman in the camp,' Tolui said. 'Send yours to me also, with any Chin or Moslem healers, the best you know.'

For once, Khasar did not argue. His gaze kept drifting to his nephew, aware but helpless. It was a fate that made Khasar shudder.

'Very well, general,' he said. 'But we must put some distance between that army and ours before they decide to test our strength.'

'Command the tumans, uncle. I will take my brother.'

Tolui gestured and Khasar helped him heave Ogedai onto Tolui's pony, making the animal snort at the double weight. Tolui gripped his brother around the chest, holding him in place. Ogedai's legs dangled loosely and his head lolled as Tolui broke into a trot.

As the sun set, the warriors of the khan were still moving slowly towards their camp, more than a hundred miles north across the plain. Behind them, the Sung soldiers lit torches all along the line, making a false horizon they could see for many miles as they retreated.

Chagatai reined in at the top of a hill, reaching down to pat his mare and rub her ears. Two tumans halted behind him, his sons and wives waiting patiently with them. He had chosen the high place deliberately, wanting a view of the khanate Genghis had won and Ogedai had granted to him. Chagatai could see for many miles and his breath caught in his throat at the sheer vastness of the land he now owned. It was the only true wealth.

Many years had passed since the armies of Genghis had stormed through the region. The marks of that violent passage would take generations to vanish. He smiled at the thought. His father had been a thorough man. Some of the cities would remain ruins for ever, dust-blown and empty of all but ghosts. Yet Ogedai's gift was not a false one. The citizens of Samarkand and Bukhara had rebuilt their walls and markets. Of all peoples, they knew the khan's shadow was long, his vengeance unforgiving. Under that protective wing, they had grown and gambled on peace.

Chagatai squinted into the setting sun and saw black lines in the far distance, caravans of carts, oxen and camels stretching to the east and west. They were heading for Samarkand, a blur of white on the horizon. Chagatai cared little for traders, but he knew the roads kept cities alive, made them strong. Ogedai had given him a land of good earth, of rivers and fine herds. The vista before him was enough to make him wonder at his own ambition. Was it not enough to rule such a land, with water and good grass? He smiled. For the son and heir of Genghis, no, it was not enough.

A hot wind blew across the hill as the sun set and he closed his eyes and faced it, enjoying the breeze as it tugged at his long, black hair. He would build a palace on the river. He would hunt with arrows and falcons along the hills. He would make a home in his new lands, but he would not sleep or dream. He had spies and informants with Ogedai, Tsubodai, all the men of power in the nation. There would come a time when he would put aside the khanate of milk and honey and reach once again for what he had been promised. It was in his blood to be khan, but he was no longer a foolish young man. With such a dominion, he could wait for the call.

He thought of the women such cities produced, soft of flesh

and fragrant. Their beauty and youth was not worked out of them in the life of the plains. Perhaps that was the purpose of cities, to keep women soft and fat instead of hard. It was a good enough reason to let them exist. As he prepared to ride on, he chuckled at the thought of the wolf entering the sheepfold. He would not ride with fire and destruction. The shepherd did not frighten his own pretty lambs.

CHAPTER TWELVE

The ger stank of something unpleasant, the air thick. Tolui and Khasar sat on low beds in the corner, watching uncomfortably as Ogedai's shaman manipulated the khan's limbs. Mohrol was a man of powerful build, short and stocky with a thick grey tuft of beard at the point of his chin. Khasar had tried not to stare at his right hand, which had marked him from birth as one who would never hunt or fish. A sixth finger, brown and twisted against the others, had made Mohrol a shaman.

The status of his craft had suffered hugely since the betrayal of Genghis years before by one whose name was no longer spoken. Yet Mohrol had conferred only briefly with robed healers and other shamans before sending them away. The khan's own shaman still had some power to command, at least among those of his own craft.

Mohrol seemed unaware of the two men watching him. He straightened and bent each of Ogedai's limbs, letting them fall limp while he worked his thumbs into the joints and murmured to himself. He took particular care with the head and neck. As the generals waited, Mohrol sat on the bed with his legs crossed and pulled Ogedai's head and shoulders into his lap, so that the khan stared sightlessly upward. The shaman's thin fingers tested and pressed the bones of his skull, clasping the dome of Ogedai's head while Mohrol looked into the middle distance. Khasar and Tolui could make nothing of it as Mohrol nodded and tutted to himself.

The khan's body was slick with sweat. Ogedai had not said a word since his collapse at the Sung border two days before. He had no wound, but his breath was as sweet as rotting fruit and it was that smell that filled the ger and made Khasar want to gag. The Chin healers had lit tapers of soothing incense, saying the smoke would help him to heal. Mohrol had allowed such things, though his disdain was poorly hidden.

The shaman had already worked on Ogedai for a full day, dipping his flesh into icy water, then pummelling his body with coarse cloth so that the blood bloomed under the surface. The khan's eyes stared throughout and sometimes they moved, but he did not wake. When he was turned to the side, he drooled long tendrils of spit, his lips slack.

Ogedai would not survive if he stayed like that, Khasar realised miserably. Water, even warm blood and milk, could be forced into his stomach with a thin bamboo tube, though he choked and bled from the mouth as it scored his throat. Cared for like a helpless baby, he could be kept alive almost indefinitely. Yet the nation was without a khan and there were other things that could kill a man.

Khasar had refused all permission to leave the camp. As messengers came in, they were unhorsed and put under guard. For a short time, the news could be contained. Chagatai would not yet be readying his forces for a triumphant return to Karakorum. Even so, there were ambitious men in the tumans who knew only too well how they would be received if they brought that news. Chagatai would reward them with gold, promotion and horses, whatever they wanted. Sooner or later, one or more would be tempted to slip away in the night. If nothing changed before that moment, even if Ogedai still lived, he was finished. Khasar winced at the thought, wondering how long he had to stay in the khan's ger. He did no good sitting there, shifting about like an old man with piles.

Ogedai's face seemed even puffier than before, as if fluid was building up underneath the skin. Yet he was hot to the touch, his body burning its reserves. Time crept slowly in the ger while outside the sun rose and passed noon. Tolui and Khasar watched as Mohrol took each of Ogedai's arms and pierced them at the crook of the elbow, letting the blood flow into a brass bowl. The shaman peered closely at the colour of the liquid, pursing his lips in disapproval. Putting aside the bowls, he chanted over the khan, suddenly striking his chest with an open palm. Nothing changed. Ogedai stared on, blinking rarely. They did not know if he could even hear them.

At last, the shaman fell silent, tugging irritably at his chin-beard as if he wanted to yank it out. He laid Ogedai's head back on the coarse blankets and rose. His servant moved in to bandage the cuts his master had made, silent with awe at treating the khan of the nation.

With the unthinking authority of his calling, Mohrol gestured to the two watching men to follow him out into the clean air. They joined him, breathing deeply in the breeze to clear the foul sweetness from their lungs. Around them, warriors of the khan stood with hope on their faces, waiting for good news. Mohrol shook his head and many of them turned away.

'I have no medicines for this,' the shaman said. 'His blood flows well enough, though it seems dark to me, without the life spirit. I do not think it is his heart, though I am told that is weak. He has been using Chin syrups.' He held up an empty blue bottle with distaste. 'He took a terrible risk in trusting their potions and filth. They use anything, from unborn children to the penis of a tiger. I have seen it.'

'I don't care about any of that,' Khasar snapped. 'If you can do nothing for him, I will find others with more imagination.'

Mohrol seemed to swell with anger and Khasar responded by stepping in instantly, deliberately standing too close and using his height to advantage.

'Watch yourself, little man,' Khasar murmured. 'If I were you, I'd try and remain useful.'

'You do Ogedai no service by arguing out here,' Tolui said. 'It does not matter what has gone before, or what potions or powders he has taken. Can you help him now?'

Mohrol still glowered at Khasar as he replied. 'Physically, there is nothing wrong with him. His spirit is weak, or made weak. I do not know if he has been cursed, brought to this by some enemy, or whether it is something of his own doing.' He blew air out in a gust.

'Sometimes, men just die,' he said. 'The sky father calls and they are snatched, even khans. There is not always an answer.'

Without warning, Khasar's hand shot out and grabbed the shaman's robe, twisting the cloth as he yanked him close. Mohrol struggled in reaction before his instinct for survival made him drop his hands. Khasar was a man of power and Mohrol's life hung on the single thread of his goodwill. The shaman mastered his outrage.

'There is a dark magic,' Khasar snarled. 'I have seen it. I have eaten a man's heart and felt the light bursting in me. Do not tell me there is nothing to be done. If the spirits demand blood, I will spill lakes of it for the khan.'

Mohrol began to stammer a reply, but then his voice steadied. 'It will be as you say, general. I will sacrifice a dozen mares this evening. Perhaps it will be enough.'

Khasar let go and Mohrol stumbled back.

'Your life rests with his, do you understand?' Khasar said. 'I have heard too many of your kind with their promises and lies. If he dies, you will be sky-buried with him, staked out on the hills for the hawks and foxes.'

'I understand, general,' Mohrol replied stiffly. 'Now I must prepare the animals for sacrifice. They must be killed in the right way, their blood for his.'

There had been a city on the site of Jiankang for almost two thousand years. Fed by the immense Yangtze river that was the lifeblood of all China, it had been the capital of ancient states and dynasties, made wealthy on the back of dyes and silk. The sound of looms was always present, clicking and thumping day and night to provide Sung nobles with clothing, shoes and tapestries. The smell of frying grubs was heavy in the air as they fed the workers at every meal, tumbled golden brown with herbs, fish and oils.

In comparison to the small city of Suzhou to the north, or the fishing villages that fed the workers, Jiankang was a true stronghold of power and wealth. It was visible in the colourful soldiers who stood on every corner, in the palaces and bustling streets of a million workers, their lives revolving around a moth grub that made a cocoon of thread so perfect it could be unwound and made into extraordinarily beautiful sheets of cloth.

At first, Xuan had been treated reasonably well as he left the border miles to the north. His wives and children had been placed in palaces away from him. His soldiers had been moved further south, where they could not be a danger. He had not been told the location of their barracks. Sung officials had shown the bare courtesy due his rank, and the emperor's own son had deigned to receive him and use words of honeyed sweetness. Xuan controlled the spasm of anger that threatened to

engulf him as he remembered the meeting. He had lost everything and they let him know his status by the most subtle
insults. Only a man used to perfection could have detected the
faint tinge of age in the tea they offered him, or the fact that
the servants they sent to him were coarse of feature, even
clumsy. Xuan did not know if the emperor intended to humili-
ate him, or whether the man's soft and perfumed son was
simply a fool. It did not matter. He was already aware that he
was not among friends. He would never have come to Sung
lands if his situation had not been desperate.

His weapons had caused some excited interest at first as
Sung soldiers began to catalogue his baggage and supplies.
That too brought a moment of irritation as Xuan recalled their
sly grins. His most precious possessions had been laid out in
a vast courtyard that dwarfed the remnant of his father's wealth.
Even then, Xuan was not certain he would see any of it again.
Chests of gold and silver coins had vanished into some hidden
treasury, perhaps not even in the city. In return, Xuan had only
a sheaf of ornate papers, stamped with the marks of a dozen
officials. He was completely in the power of men who thought
of him at best as a weak ally, at worst as an obstacle to lands
they claimed as their own.

As he stared out across Jiankang, Xuan ground his teeth
silently, the only sign of his tension. They had scorned his fire-
pots and hand-cannon. The Sung had such things in their
thousands and of more advanced designs. It was clear they
thought themselves untouchable. Their armies were strong and
well supplied, their cities wealthy. Some bitter part of him almost
wanted the Mongols to reveal the folly of such arrogance. It
made his stomach churn to see the way the Sung officers glanced
at him and whispered, as if he had just *given* Chin lands away
to herdsmen. It was a peculiar thing to take pleasure in the
image of the Mongol khan riding his warriors into Jiankang,
sending the Sung armies running in disarray.

Xuan smiled at the thought. The sun had risen and the silk looms could be heard tapping like insects deep in a beam of wood. He would spend the day with his senior advisers, talking endlessly and pretending they had some purpose while they waited for the Sung emperor to notice their existence.

As Xuan looked over the roofs of Jiankang, a bell sounded nearby, one of a hundred different tones that rang across the city at different times in the day. Some signalled the changing hours or announced the arrival of messengers, others called children to school. As the sun set, the words of a poem from Xuan's youth came back to him and he murmured the lines, taking pleasure in the memories.

'The sun grows dim and sinks in the dusk. People are coming home and the bright peaks darken. Wild geese fly to the white reeds. I think of a northern city gate and I hear a bell tolling between me and sleep.'

Tears sprang into his eyes as he thought of his father's kindness to the thin little boy he had been, but he blinked them away before someone could see and report his weakness.

The horses Mohrol had chosen were all young mares, capable of bearing foals. He had taken them from the herd of spare mounts that followed the tumans, spending half a day selecting each mare for perfection of colour and unblemished skin. One of the owners stood in mute misery as two of his best white mares were marked for sacrifice, the product of generations of careful selection and breeding. Neither had borne foals and their bloodlines would be lost. Ogedai's name made all resistance vanish, despite the near-sacred relationship between herdsmen and their beloved mounts.

Such a thing had never been seen before on the plains. The tumans pressed so closely around the ger where Ogedai lay that Mohrol had to ask for them to be kept away. Even then, the warriors crept forward with their wives and children, desperate to see magic and great sacrifice. The life of no other could have been worth such a price and they watched with fascination and dread as Mohrol sharpened his butcher's knives and blessed them.

Khasar sat close to where Ogedai lay on a silk-covered pallet in the setting sun. The khan had been dressed in polished armour, and at intervals, his mouth opened and shut slowly, as if he gasped for water. It was impossible to see his pale skin and not think of Genghis laid out for death. Khasar winced at the thought, his heart beating faster at an old grief. He tried not to stare as the first white mare was brought forward with two strong men holding her head. The other horses were kept well back where they would not see the killing, but Khasar knew they would smell the blood.

The young mare was already nervous, sensing something in the air. She pranced, jerking her head up and down and whinnying aloud, fighting the tight grip of fingers in her mane. Her pale skin was perfect, unmarked by scars or ticks. Mohrol had chosen well and some of the watching warriors were tight-mouthed at such a sacrifice.

Mohrol built a bonfire taller than himself in front of the khan's ger, then lit a branch of cedar wood, snuffing the flames so that the wood gave off a trail of fragrant white smoke. The shaman walked to Ogedai and held the smoking branch over his body, cleansing the air and blessing the khan for the ritual to come. With slow steps, he made a path around the supine form, muttering an incantation that made the hair on Khasar's neck stand up. Khasar glanced at his nephew Tolui and found him rapt, fascinated by the shaman. The younger man would never understand how Khasar had once heard Genghis speaking an ancient tongue, with the blood of enemies fresh on his lips.

The darkness seemed to come quickly after looking into the flames of Mohrol's fire. Thousands of warriors sat in silence and even those who had been injured in the fighting had been moved far away so that their cries of pain would not disturb the ritual. The quiet was so perfect that Khasar thought he could hear their keening cries even so, thin and distant, like birds.

With great care the mare's front and rear legs were bound in pairs. Whinnying in distress, she struggled briefly as warriors pushed at her haunches, rolling them so that she could not remain upright. Unable to take a step, she fell clumsily, lying with her head raised. One of the warriors took her muscular neck in his arms, holding her steady. The other gripped the back legs and they both looked up for Mohrol.

The shaman would not be rushed. He prayed aloud, singing and whispering in turn. He dedicated the life of the mare to the earth mother who would receive the blood. He asked again and again for the khan's life to be spared.

In the middle of the ritual, Mohrol approached the mare. He had two knives and continued to sing and pray as he chose a place below the neck, where the smooth white skin began to sweep down into the mare's chest. The two warriors braced themselves.

With a quick jerk, Mohrol jammed the blade in to its hilt. Blood streamed out, pumping rich and dark, covering his hands. The mare shuddered and whinnied in panic, snorting and struggling to rise. The warriors sat on her haunches and the blood continued to gout with every beat of her heart, covering the warriors as they struggled to hold her slippery flesh.

Mohrol placed a hand on her neck, feeling how the skin grew cold. The mare was still struggling, but more weakly. He pulled back her lips and nodded at the sight of the pale gums. In a loud voice, the shaman called once more to the spirits of the land and reached out with his second knife. It was a heavy-hilted block of metal, as long as his forearm and fine-edged. He waited until the blood flow was sluggish, then sawed quickly, back and forth across the mare's throat. The blade disappeared into the flesh. More blood rushed and he watched her pupils grow large and infinitely dark.

Mohrol's arms were red as he walked over to the khan. Unaware of all that was being done in his name, Ogedai lay unmoving, pale as death. Mohrol shook his head slightly and marked the khan's cheeks with a red stripe from his finger.

No one dared to speak as he returned to the dead mare. They knew there was magic in sacrifice. As Mohrol brushed a biting insect from his face, many of them made a sign against evil at the thought of spirits gathering like flies on carrion.

Mohrol did not look discouraged as he nodded to the men to drag away the dead animal and bring in the next. He knew the mares would struggle as they smelled the blood, but he could at least spare them the sight of a dead horse.

Once again, he began the chant that would end in sacrifice. Khasar looked away and many of the warriors drifted off rather than witness such wealth being ruined with a blade.

The second mare seemed quieter than the first, less spirited. She allowed herself to be walked in, but then she sensed something. In just a moment, she was panicking, whinnying loudly and using all her strength to pull the rein away from the man holding her. As they heaved in opposite directions, the halter snapped and she was free. In the darkness, she cannoned into Tolui, knocking him to the ground.

She did not get far. The warriors spread their arms and herded her, turning her around until they were able to get a new halter on and lead her back.

Tolui rose to his feet with no more than bruises, dusting himself off. He saw Mohrol was looking strangely at him and

165

he shrugged under the shaman's stare. The chanting began again and the second mare was hobbled quickly, ready for the knives. It would be a long night and the bitter smell of blood was already strong.

CHAPTER THIRTEEN

The ground around the khan was sodden red. Blood from a dozen mares had soaked into the earth until the soil could take no more and it pooled. Fat, black flies buzzed and dipped all around them, driven to frenzy by the smell. Mohrol was dark with it, his bare arms and deel still wet as the torches guttered out and the sun began to rise. His voice was hoarse, his face filthy. Mosquitoes had gathered in clouds in the warm, damp air. The shaman had exhausted himself, but the khan lay motionless on the pallet, with eyes like shadowed holes.

The warriors were sleeping on the grass, waiting for news. They had not taken the mares for meat and the bodies lay sprawled in a heap, their thin legs outstretched as their bellies began to swell with gas. No one knew whether the sacrifice might be lessened if they consumed the meat, so it would be left to rot untouched as the camp moved on. Many of them had left the scene of the slaughter for their own gers and women, unable to watch such fine mares being killed any longer.

167

In the dawn, Mohrol knelt on the wet grass and his knees sank into the soft ground. He had killed twelve horses and he felt leaden, weighed down by death. He refused to let his despair show while the khan lay helpless, his face marked with a script of dry blood. Mohrol felt light-headed as he knelt and his voice began to fail completely, so that he whispered the ancient spells and divinations, rhythmic chants that rolled over and over until the words blurred into a stream of sound.

'The khan is in chains,' he croaked. 'Lost and alone in a cage of flesh. Show me how to break his bonds. Show me what I must do to bring him home. The khan is in chains . . .'

The shaman could feel the weak dawn sunlight on his closed eyes. He had grown desperate, but he thought he could sense the whisper of spirits around the still figure of Ogedai. In the night, Mohrol had taken the khan's wrist and checked for a pulse, he was so still. Yet without warning Ogedai would jerk and twist, his mouth opening and closing, his eyes bright for a few moments with something like awareness. The answer was there, Mohrol was certain, if he could only find it.

'Tengri of the blue sky, Erlik of the underworld, master of shadows, show me how to break the chains,' Mohrol whispered, his voice scratching. 'Let him see his mirror soul in water, let him see his shadow soul in sunlight. I have given you blood in rivers, sweet mares bleeding their lives into the ground. I have given blood to the ninety-nine gods of white and black. Show me the chains and I will strike them free. *Make* me the hammer. By the ninety-nine, by the three souls, show me the way.' He raised his right hand to the sun, splaying the fingers that were his mark and his vocation. 'This is your ancient land, spirit lords of the Chin. If you hear my voice, show me how you will be appeased. Whisper your needs into my ears. Show me the chains.'

Ogedai moaned on the bier, his head falling to one side. Mohrol was with him in an instant, still chanting. After such a night, with the dawn still grey and the dew half-frozen on the red grass, he could *feel* the spirits around the khan. He could hear them breathe. His mouth was dry from a bitter paste that left a black crust on his lips. He had soared with it in the darkness, but there had been no answers, no flash of light and understanding.

'What will you take to let him go? What do you want? This flesh is the cage for the khan of a nation. Whatever you want you may have.' Mohrol took a deep breath, close to collapse. 'Is it my life? I would give it. Tell me how to break the chains. Were the mares not enough? I can have a thousand more brought to mark his skin. I can weave a web of blood around him, a skein of dark threads and dark magic.' He took faster breaths, forcing his body to pant, raising the heat within him that might lead to more powerful visions. 'Shall I bring virgins to this place? Shall I bring slaves or enemies?' His voice fell lower, so that no one else could hear. 'Shall I bring children to die for the khan? They would give their lives gladly enough. Show me the chains that I may strike them away. Make me the hammer. Is it a kinsman that he needs? His family would give their lives for the khan.'

Ogedai moved. He blinked rapidly, and as Mohrol watched in astonishment, the khan began to sit up, falling backwards as his right arm crumpled. The shaman caught him and tipped his own head back to howl in triumph like a wolf.

'Is it his son?' Mohrol went on desperately as he held the khan. 'His daughters? His uncles or friends? Give me the sign, strike off the chains!'

At the shaman's howl, men had jerked from sleep all around them. Hundreds came running from all directions. The news spread and as they heard, men and women raised their hands and cheered, hammering pots or swords together, whatever they had. They crashed out a rippling thunder of joy and Ogedai sat up, flinching from it.

'Bring me water,' he said, his voice weak. 'What is happening?' He opened his eyes and saw the field of blood and the corpse of the last mare lying dark in the dawn light. Ogedai could not understand what had happened and he rubbed his itching face, staring in confusion at the flakes of dried blood on his palms.

'Raise a fresh ger for the khan,' Mohrol ordered, his voice barely a wheeze, but growing stronger in his jubilation. 'Make it clean and dry. Bring food and clean water.'

The ger was raised around Ogedai, though he was able to sit up. The weakness in his arm drained away in slow stages. By the time the rising sun was blocked by felt and wood, he was drinking water and calling for wine, though Mohrol would not hear of it. The shaman's authority had grown with his success and the khan's servants could not ignore his stern expression. For just a short time, the shaman could overrule his own khan. Mohrol stood tall with a new dignity and visible pride.

Khasar and Tolui joined Ogedai in the new ger, as the most senior men in the camp. The khan was still pale, but he smiled weakly at their worried expressions. His eyes were sunken and dark and his hand quivered as Mohrol handed him a bowl of salt tea, telling him to drink it all. The khan frowned and licked his lips at the thought of wine, but he did not protest. He had felt death pressing and it had frightened him, for all he thought he had prepared for it.

'There were times when I could hear everything, but not respond,' Ogedai said, his voice like an old man's breath. 'I thought I was dead then, with spirits in my ears. It was ...' His eyes darkened as he sipped and he did not go on to tell them of the sick terror he had felt, trapped in his own body, drifting in and out of consciousness. His father had told him never to speak of his fears. Men were fools, Genghis had said, always imagining others were stronger, faster, less afraid. Even in his weakness, Ogedai remembered. The terror of that dark had hurt him, but he was still the khan.

Servants laid sheets of rough felt on the bloody ground around him. The thick mats drew up the blood in an instant, becoming heavy and red. More were brought in and piled on top of the lower layers until the whole floor of the ger was covered. Mohrol knelt then at Ogedai's side and reached out to examine his eyes and gums.

'You have done well, Mohrol,' Ogedai said. 'I did not expect to be coming back.'

Mohrol frowned. 'It is not over, my lord. The sacrifice of mares was not enough.' He took a long breath and fell silent while he bit at a ragged nail on his hands, tasting the specks of blood there. 'The spirits of this land are full of bile and hatred. They released their grip on your soul only when I spoke of another in your place.'

Ogedai looked blearily at the shaman, struggling not to show his fear.

'What do you mean? My head is full of wasps, Mohrol. Speak clearly, as if to a child. I will understand you then.'

'There is a price for your return, lord. I do not know how long you have before they snatch you back into the darkness. It could be a day, or even a few more breaths, I cannot tell.'

Ogedai stiffened. 'I cannot go through that again, do you understand, shaman? I could not breathe . . .' He felt his eyes prickle and rubbed furiously at them. His own body was a weak vessel, it always had been. 'Bring me wine, shaman.'

'Not yet, my lord. We have just a little time and you need to think clearly.'

'Do what you must, Mohrol. I will pay any price.' Ogedai had seen the dead mares and he shook his head wearily, looking through the walls of the ger to where he knew they still lay. 'You have my own herds, my slaughtermen, whatever you need.'

171

'Horses are not enough, my lord, I'm sorry. You came back to us . . .'

Ogedai looked up sharply. 'Speak! Who knows how much time I have!'

For once, the shaman stammered, hating what he had to say.

'Another sacrifice, lord. It must be someone of your own blood. That was the offer that pulled you back from death. That was the reason you returned.'

Mohrol was so intent on watching Ogedai's response that he did not sense Khasar coming towards him until he was heaved into the air to face the older man.

'You little . . .' Khasar's mouth worked in rage, sending flecks of spit onto Mohrol's face as he held the shaman and shook him like a dog with a rat. 'I have heard these games before from men like you. We broke the back of the last one and left him for the wolves. You think you can scare my family? *My* family? You think you can demand a blood debt for your shabby spells and incantations? Well, after *you*, shaman. You die first and then we'll see.'

As he spoke, Khasar had drawn a short skinning knife from his belt, keeping his hand low. Before anyone could speak, he flicked his wrist, cutting into Mohrol's groin. The shaman gasped and Khasar let him fall onto his back. He wiped blood from the knife, but kept it ready in his hand as Mohrol writhed, his hands cupped.

Ogedai rose slowly from his pallet. He was thin and weak, but his eyes were furious. Khasar looked coldly at him, refusing to be cowed.

'In my camp, you cut my own shaman, uncle?' Ogedai growled. 'You have forgotten where you are. You have forgotten who *I* am.'

Khasar stuck his chin out defiantly, but he put away the blade.

'See him clearly, Ogedai . . . my lord khan,' Khasar replied. 'This one wants my death, so he whispers that it has to be one of your blood. They are all hip-deep in games of power and they have caused my family – *your* family – enough pain. You should not listen to a word from him. Let us wait a few days and see how you recover. You will be strong again, I'd bet my own mares on it.'

Mohrol rolled to his knees. The hand he pressed to his groin was red with fresh blood and he felt sick and shaky with the pain. He glared at Khasar.

'I do not know the name yet. It is not my choice. I wish it was.'

'Shaman,' Ogedai said softly. 'You will not have my son, even if my own life depends on it. Nor my wife.'

'Your wife is not your blood, lord. Let me cast another divination and find the name.'

Ogedai nodded, easing himself back down to the pallet. Even that small exertion had brought him to the edge of fainting.

Mohrol got to his feet like an old man, hunched over against the pain. Khasar smiled coldly at him. Spots of blood fell from between the shaman's legs, vanishing instantly into the felt.

'Do it quickly then,' Khasar said. 'I do not have patience for your kind, not today.'

Mohrol looked away from him, frightened by a man who used violence as easily as breathing. He could not untie his robe and examine the wound with Khasar leering at him. He felt ill and the gash throbbed and burned. He shook his head, trying to clear it. He was the khan's shaman and the divination had to be correct. Mohrol wondered what would happen if the spirits gave him Khasar's name. He did not think he would live long after that.

As Khasar watched with contempt, Mohrol sent his servants running for tapers of incense. Soon the air of the ger was thick, and Mohrol added other herbs to his burning bowl, breathing in a coolness that made the ache in his groin just a distant irritation. After a time, even that faded and was gone.

At first, Ogedai coughed as the harsh smoke entered his lungs. One of the servants dared Mohrol's disapproval at last and a skin of wine had appeared at the khan's feet. He drank it like a man dying of thirst and a bloom of colour came back to his cheeks. His eyes were bright with fascination and dread as Mohrol clutched the bones for divination, holding them to the four winds and calling for the spirits to guide his hand.

At the same time, the shaman took a pot of gritty black paste and rubbed a stripe of it along his tongue. It was dangerous to release his spirit again so soon, but he steeled himself, ignoring the way his heart fluttered in his chest. The bitterness brought tears to his eyes, so that they shone in the gloom. When Mohrol closed his mouth, his pupils grew enormous, like the eyes of dying horses.

The blood was slowly seeping into the layers of felt and the smell of it was pungent. With the narcotic incense, the exhausted men could hardly stand it, but Mohrol seemed to thrive in the thick air, the paste giving strength to his flesh. His voice rolled out a chant as he moved the bag of bones to the north, east, south and west, over and over, calling for the spirits of home to guide him.

At last he threw the bones; too hard, so that the yellow pieces scattered across the felt. Was it an omen to see them leap and jump away from him? Mohrol cursed aloud and Khasar laughed as the shaman tried to read the way they fell.

'Ten . . . eleven . . . where is the last one?' Mohrol said, speaking to no one.

None of them noticed that Tolui had grown almost as pale as the khan himself. The shaman had not seen the yellow ankle bone resting against Tolui's boot, touching the soft leather.

Tolui had seen. He had kept to himself the sick fear he had felt on hearing that it had to be one of Ogedai's blood. From that moment, he had been gripped by a numb helplessness, a resignation to a fate he could not avoid. The bolting mare had knocked him from his feet, no other. He thought he had known then. Part of him wanted to tread the bone deep into the felt, to hide it with his foot, but with an effort of will, he did not. Ogedai was the khan of the nation, the man his father had chosen to rule after him. No life was worth as much as his.

'It is here,' Tolui whispered, then repeated himself as no one heard him.

Mohrol looked up at him and his eyes flashed with sudden understanding.

'The mare that struck you,' the shaman said in a whisper. His eyes were dark, but there was something like compassion in his face.

Tolui nodded, mute.

'What?' Ogedai broke in, looking up sharply. 'Do not even think of that, shaman. Tolui is not part of this.' He spoke firmly, but the terror of the grave was still on him and his hands trembled on the wine cup. Tolui saw.

'You are my older brother, Ogedai,' Tolui said. 'More, you are the khan, the man our father chose.' He smiled and rubbed his hand across his face, looking almost boyish for a moment. 'He told me once that I would be the one to remind you of things you have forgotten. That I would guide you as khan and be your right arm.'

'This is madness,' Khasar said, his voice tight with suppressed rage. 'Let me spill this shaman's blood first.'

'Very *well*, general!' Mohrol snapped suddenly. He stepped forward to face Khasar with his arms open. 'I will pay that price. You have spilled my blood already this morning. Have the rest if you wish. It will not change the omens. It will not change what must be done.'

Khasar touched his hand to where his knife lay under his belt, tucked into the grubby folds of cloth, but Mohrol did not

175

look away from him. The paste he had consumed had stolen away any fear, and instead he saw Khasar's love for Ogedai and Tolui, coupled with his frustration. The old general could face any enemy, but he was lost and confused by such a decision. After a time, Mohrol dropped his arms and stood patiently, waiting for Khasar to see the inevitable.

In the end, it was Tolui's voice that broke the silence.

'I have much to do, uncle. You should leave me now. I have to see my son and have letters written to my wife.' His face was stiff with pain, but his voice remained steady as Khasar glanced at him.

'Your father would not have given up,' Khasar said gruffly. 'Believe me, as one who knew him better than any man.'

He was not as certain as he seemed. In some moods, Genghis would have thrown his life away without a thought, enjoying the grand gesture. In others, he would have fought to the last furious breath, doomed or not. Khasar wished with all his heart that his brother Kachiun were there. Kachiun would have found an answer, a way through the thorns. It was just ill luck that Kachiun was riding with Tsubodai and Batu into the north. For once, Khasar was alone.

He felt the pressure from the younger men as they looked to him in hope for some stroke that would cut through the decision. All he could think of was to kill the shaman. That too was a useless act, he realised. Mohrol believed his own words, and for all Khasar knew, the man spoke the perfect truth. He closed his eyes and strained to hear Kachiun's voice. What would he say? Someone had to die for Ogedai. Khasar raised his head, his eyes opening.

'I will be your sacrifice, shaman. Take my life for the khan's. I can do that much, for my brother's memory, for my brother's son.'

'No,' Mohrol said, turning away from him. 'You are not the

one, not today. The omens are clear. The choice is as simple as it is hard.'

Tolui smiled wearily as the shaman spoke. He came close to Khasar and the two men embraced for a moment while Ogedai and the shaman looked on.

'Sunset, Mohrol,' Tolui said, looking back at the shaman. 'Give me a day to prepare myself.'

'My lord, the omens are set. We do not know how long the khan has left before his spirit is taken.'

Ogedai said nothing as Tolui looked at him. His younger brother's jaw tensed as he struggled with himself.

'I will not run, brother,' he whispered. 'But I am not ready for the knife, not yet. Give me the day and I will bless you from the other side.'

Ogedai nodded weakly, his expression tortured. He wanted to speak out, to send Mohrol away and dare the malevolent spirits to come back for him. He could not. A wisp of memory of his helplessness came to him. He could not suffer it again.

'Sunset, brother,' Ogedai said at last.

Without another word, Tolui strode out of the ger, ducking to pass through the small door into the clean air and sun.

Around him, the vast camp was arrayed in all directions, busy and alive with the noise of horses and women, children and warriors. Tolui's heart thumped with pain at such a pleasant, normal scene. He realised with a stab of despair that it was his last morning. He would not see the sun rise again. For a time, he simply stood and watched it, holding one hand above his eyes to shade them from its brilliant glare.

CHAPTER FOURTEEN

Tolui led a small group of ten riders to the river that ran by the camp. His son Mongke rode at his right shoulder, the young man's face pale with strain. Two slave women ran at Tolui's stirrups. He dismounted on the banks and the slaves removed his armour and underclothes. Naked, he walked into the cold water, feeling his feet sink into the cool mud. Slowly he washed himself, using silt to work the grease from his skin, then dipping under the surface to sluice himself down.

His female slaves both stripped to enter the water with him. They shivered as they worked bone tools under his fingernails to clean them. Both women stood up to their waists in the water, their breasts firm with goosebumps. There was no lightness or laughter from them and Tolui was not aroused by the sight, whereas any other day might have had him playing in the shallows and splashing to make them squeal.

With care and concentration, Tolui accepted a flask of clear oil and rubbed it into his hair. The prettier of his slaves tied it into a black tail that hung down his back. His skin was very white at the nape of his neck, where the hair protected it from the sun.

Mongke stood and watched his father. The other minghaans were senior men who had seen battle a thousand times. Next to them, he felt young and inexperienced, but they could not look at him. They were quiet with respect for Tolui, and Mongke knew he had to maintain the cold face for his father's honour. It would have shamed the general to have his son weeping, so Mongke stood like a stone, his face hard. Yet he could not take his eyes off his father. Tolui had told them his decision and they were all bruised by it, helpless in the face of his will and the khan's need.

One of them gave a low whistle when they saw Khasar ride out from another part of the camp. The general had earned their respect, but they were still willing to block him from the river as he came close. On that day, they did not care that he was the brother of Genghis.

Tolui had been standing with blank eyes as his hair was tied. The whistle brought him out of himself and he nodded to Mongke to let Khasar through, watching as his uncle dismounted and came to the bank.

'You will need a friend to help you in this,' Khasar said.

Mongke's stare bored into the back of Khasar's head, but he did not notice.

Tolui looked up in silence from the river and finally dipped his head in acceptance, striding out of the water. His slaves came with him and he stood patiently as they rubbed him down. The sun warmed him and some of his tension seeped away. He looked at the armour that lay waiting, a pile of iron and leather. He had worn something like it for all of his adult life, but suddenly it seemed an alien thing. Of Chin design, it did not suit his mood.

'I will not wear the armour,' he said to Mongke, who was

179

standing ready for orders. 'Have it bundled up. Perhaps in time you will wear it for me.'

Mongke struggled with his grief as he bent and gathered the pieces into his arms. Khasar looked on with approval, pleased to see how Tolui's son kept his dignity. The father's pride was shining in his eyes, though Mongke turned away without seeing it.

Tolui watched as his women yanked on clothes to cover their nakedness. He sent one barefoot over the grass with instructions to find a particular deel and leggings from his ger, as well as new boots. She ran well and more than one of the men turned to watch her legs flash in the sun.

'I am trying to believe this is really happening,' Tolui said softly. Khasar looked at him and reached out to grip his bare shoulder in silent support as he went on. 'When I saw you coming, I hoped that something had changed. I think some part of me will expect a shout, a reprieve, up to the last moments. It is a strange thing, the way we torture ourselves.'

'Your father would be proud of you, I know that,' Khasar replied. He felt useless, unable to find the right words.

Strangely, it was Tolui who saw his uncle's distress and he spoke kindly. 'I think I will be better on my own for the moment, uncle. I have my son as a comfort to me. He will take my messages home. I will need you later on, at sunset.' He sighed. 'I will need you to stand by me then, without a doubt. Now though, I still have words to write and orders to give.'

'Very well, Tolui. I will come back as the sun sets. I tell you one thing: when this is over, I am going to kill that shaman.'

Tolui chuckled. 'I would expect nothing else, uncle. I will need a servant in the next world. He would do very well.'

The young slave returned bearing an armful of clean, woollen clothes. Bare-chested, Tolui pulled rough leggings up his thighs, concealing his manhood from view. The slave tied the thong at his waist while Tolui stood with his arms out, staring into the distance. His women had begun to weep and neither man rebuked them for it. Tolui was pleased to hear the crying of women for him. He dared not think of Sorhatani and how she would react. He watched as Khasar mounted his horse once more, the older man silent with misery as he held up his right hand and turned to ride away.

Tolui sat on the grass and the slaves knelt before him. The boots were new, soft leather. The women bound his feet in untreated wool and then pulled the boots over them, tying them with quick, neat movements. Finally, he rose.

The deel robe was the simplest he owned, a lightly padded cloth with almost no decoration beyond buttons shaped like tiny bells. It was an old piece that had once belonged to Genghis and it was marked with the stitching of the Wolf tribe. Tolui ran his hands over the coarse design and found he could take comfort from it. His father had worn it and perhaps there was a hint of his old strength left in the cloth.

'Walk with me for a time, Mongke,' he called to his son. 'There are things I want you to remember for me.'

The sun dipped on the last day, spreading a cool light that slowly lost its colours, so that the plains softened into grey. Sitting cross-legged on the grass, Tolui watched the sun touch the hills in the west. It had been a good day. He had spent some of it rutting with his slaves, losing himself for a time in the pleasures of the flesh. He had appointed his second in command to lead the tuman. Lakota was a good man and loyal. He would not shame Tolui's memory, and in time, when Mongke had more experience, he would step aside for the son.

Ogedai had come to him in the afternoon, saying that he would appoint Sorhatani the head of Tolui's family, with all the rights her husband had known. She would retain his wealth and the authority over his sons. On his return home, Mongke would be given Tolui's other wives and slaves as his own, protecting them from those who would take advantage. The khan's shadow would keep his family safe. It was the least Ogedai could offer, but Tolui felt lighter after hearing it, less afraid. He only wished he could speak to Sorhatani and his other sons one last time. Dictating letters to his scribes was not the same and he wished that he could hold his wife, just once, that he could crush her to him and breathe in the scent of her hair.

He sighed to himself. It was hard to find peace as the sun went down. He tried to hold on to every moment, but his mind betrayed him, drifting and coming back to clarity with a start. Time slipped like oil through his hands and he could not hold a single instant of it.

The tumans had gathered in ranks to witness his offering. Ahead of him on the grass, Ogedai stood with Khasar and Mohrol. Mongke waited slightly apart from the other three. Only he looked directly at his father, a constant gaze that was the sole sign of the horror and disbelief that he felt.

Tolui took a deep breath, enjoying the scent of horses and sheep on the evening breeze. He was pleased he had chosen the simple garb of a herdsman. Armour would have choked him, confined him in iron. Instead, he felt loose-limbed, clean and calm.

He walked towards the small group of men. Mongke stared at him like a stunned calf. Tolui reached out and drew his son into a brief embrace, releasing him before the shuddering he felt against his chest turned into sobs.

'I am ready,' he said.

Ogedai lowered himself to sit cross-legged on one side of him, Khasar on the other. Mongke hesitated, before sitting to one side.

There was a certain shared animosity as they all watched

Mohrol set a taper to brass pots. Thin trails of smoke dragged their way across the plain and the shaman began to sing.

Mohrol was bare-chested, his skin marked in stripes of red and dark blue. His eyes looked out from a mask that seemed barely human. The four men faced west, and as the shaman worked his way through six verses of the song of death, they stared at the setting sun, slowly eaten by the horizon until there was just a fat line of gold.

Mohrol stamped the ground as he finished his verse to the earth mother. He jabbed a knife into the air as he called on the sky father. His voice grew in strength, a double tone from his nose and throat that was one of the earliest sounds Tolui could remember. He listened distractedly, unable to look away from the golden thread that bound him to life.

As the verses to the four winds ended, Mohrol passed a knife into Tolui's cupped hands. Tolui stared at the blue-black blade in the last light. He found the calm he needed. Everything around him was sharp and defined and he breathed deeply as he pressed the blade against his skin.

Ogedai reached out and clasped his left shoulder. Khasar did the same with his right. Tolui felt their strength, their grief, and it steadied the last of his fear.

He looked at Mongke and saw the young man's eyes were brimming with tears. There was no shame in it.

'Look after your mother, boy,' Tolui said, then looked down and took a deep breath. 'It is time,' he said. 'I am a fitting sacrifice for the khan. I am tall and strong and young. I will take the place of my brother.'

The sun vanished in the west and Tolui pushed the knife into his chest, finding the heart. All the air in his lungs came out in a long, rasping breath. He found he could not breathe in and struggled to control his panic. He knew the cuts that had to be made. Mohrol had explained every detail of the ritual. His son was watching and he had to have the strength.

Tolui's body had gone tight and hard, every muscle straining as he sipped air back in and wrenched the blade between his ribs, cutting his heart. The pain was a burning brand in him, but he pulled out the knife and looked in astonishment at the rush of blood that came with it. His strength was fading, and as he began to fall forward Khasar reached out and took his hand in fingers that were impossibly strong. Tolui turned his eyes to him in gratitude, unable to speak. Khasar guided his hand higher, holding the grip closed so he could not drop the blade.

Tolui sagged as Khasar helped him draw the edge across his neck. He was frozen, a man of ice, as his warm blood drained into the grass. He did not see the shaman hold a bowl to his throat. His head lolled forward and Khasar gripped him by the back of the neck. Tolui could feel the warm touch as he died.

Mohrol offered the brimming bowl to Ogedai. The khan knelt with his head down, staring into darkness. He did not let go of Tolui's body, so that it remained upright, held between the two men.

'You must drink, my lord, while I finish,' Mohrol said.

Ogedai heard and took the bowl in his left hand, tipping it back. He choked on the warm blood of his brother and some of it dribbled down his chin and neck. Mohrol said nothing as the khan steeled himself and fought the urge to vomit. When it was empty, Ogedai tossed the bowl away into the gloom. Mohrol began to sing the six verses once again from the beginning, drawing the spirits close to witness the sacrifice.

Before he was halfway through, Mohrol heard Ogedai vomiting onto the grass. It was already too dark to see and the shaman ignored the sounds.

Sorhatani rode hard, calling 'Chuh!' and forcing her mare to gallop across the brown plains. Her sons galloped with her and,

184

with the remounts and pack animals, they made a fine plume of dust, rising behind them. Under the hot sun, Sorhatani rode bare-armed in a yellow silk tunic and deerskin leggings, with soft boots. She was grubby and she had not bathed in a long time, but she exulted as her horse flew across the ancient land of the tribes.

The grass was very dry, the valleys thirsty. Drought had drained all but the widest rivers. To refill the waterskins, they had to dig into the river clay until water seeped into the hole, brackish and full of silt. Silk had proved its value yet again to strain muck and wriggling insects out of the precious liquid.

As she rode, she saw the pale bones of sheep and oxen, the white shapes cracked to shards by wolves or foxes. To anyone else, it might not have seemed a great reward for her husband to be given such a dry land. Yet Sorhatani understood there were always hard years there, that such a land made strong men and stronger women. Her sons had already learned to eke out their supplies of water and not gulp it as if there would always be a stream within reach. The winters froze and the summers burned, but there was freedom in its immensity – and the rains would come again. Her childhood memories were of hills like rippled green silk, stretching away to the horizon on all sides. The land endured the droughts and the cold, but it would be reborn.

In the distance, she could see the mountain of Deli'un-Boldakh, a peak of almost mystical significance in the legends of the tribes. Genghis had been born somewhere near that place. His father Yesugei had ridden with his bondsmen there, protecting his herds from raiders through the coldest months.

Sorhatani kept her eyes on a different crag, the red rock that Genghis had climbed with his brothers when the world was smaller and all the tribes were at each other's throats. Her three sons kept pace with her and the red hill grew before them. There, Genghis and Kachiun had found an eagle's nest and brought down two perfect chicks to show their father. Sorhatani could imagine their excitement, even see their faces in the features of her own sons.

She only wished Mongke could have been there, though she knew that was a mother's foolishness. Mongke had to learn to lead, to campaign with his father and uncles. The warriors would not respect an officer who knew nothing about terrain or tactics.

She wondered if Genghis' mother had loved Bekter as she loved her own first born. As the legends told it, Bekter had been solemn in spirit, just as Mongke was. Her eldest son was not easily given to laughter, or the lightning flashes of insight and humour that characterised a boy like Kublai.

She watched Kublai ride, his Chin tail of hair whipping in the wind. He was slim and wiry like his father and grandfather. Her boys raced each other through the dust and she gloried in their youth and strength as well as her own.

Tolui and Mongke had been gone for many months. It had been hard for her to leave Karakorum, but she knew she had to prepare a camp for her husband, to scout the land. It was her task to raise gers in the shadow of Deli'un-Boldakh and find good grazing on the river plains. Thousands of men and women had come with her to the homeland, but for the moment they would wait on her pleasure while she rode to the red hill.

Perhaps one day Mongke would command an army like Tsubodai, or become a man of power under his uncle Chagatai. It was easy to dream on such a day, with the wind making her hair flow back in a river of silk threads.

Sorhatani glanced behind her, checking on the presence of her husband's bondsmen. Two of the most ferocious warriors at his command rode within easy reach of the family. As she watched them, she saw their heads turning to the left and right, looking for the slightest danger. She smiled. Before he left, Tolui had given very clear orders about keeping his wife and sons safe. It might have been true that the hills and steppes of their homeland were practically empty of nomadic families, but still he worried. He was a fine man, she thought. With just a fraction of his father's ambition, he would have risen far. Sorhatani's mood did not sink at the thought. The destiny of her husband had never been hers to shape. He had always been the youngest son of Genghis and from the earliest age he had known his brothers would lead and he would follow.

Her sons were a different matter. Even her youngest, Arik-Boke, had been trained as a warrior and a scholar from the moment he could walk. All could read and write the court script of the Chin. Though she prayed to Christ and his mother, they had been taught the religion of the Chin and Sung, where true power lay. Whatever the future held, she knew she had prepared them as best she could.

The small group dismounted at the foot of the red hill and Sorhatani cried out in pleasure as she saw the circling specks of eagles high above. Part of her had thought the rumour of their presence was just a herdsman's boasting, a way of honouring the story of Genghis. Yet they were there and their nest would be somewhere in the crags.

Her husband's bondsmen came up and bowed deeply before her, waiting patiently for her orders.

'My sons are going to climb for the nest,' she said, as excited as a girl. She did not need to explain. Both of the warriors had squinted up at the circling birds. 'Scout the area for water, but do not go too far.'

In moments, the men had leapt back into the saddle and were cantering away. They had learned that Sorhatani expected the same sort of instant obedience as her husband. She had grown up around men of power and had married into the great khan's family at a very young age. She knew that men prefer to follow, that it takes an effort of will to lead. She had that will.

Kublai and Hulegu were already at the base of the red hill,

shading their eyes against the sun for the location of the nest. It was later in the year than the ideal. If there were chicks there, they would already be strong, perhaps even able to leave the nest and fly on their own. Sorhatani did not know if her sons would be disappointed, but it did not matter. She had made them part of a tale from Genghis' life and they would never forget the climb, whether they brought down a chick or not. She had given them a memory they would tell to their own children one day.

The boys removed their weapons and began to scramble up the easy section as Sorhatani pulled a bag of soft curds from under her saddle. She had hammered the chips of hard cheese herself, breaking them small enough so that they would not gall the mare's skin as they softened in water. The thick yellow paste was bitter and refreshing, a particular favourite of hers. She licked her lips as she dipped her hand inside, then sucked her fingers clean.

It did not take long to fetch water from the packhorses and water the animals with a leather bucket. When the chore was done, Sorhatani rummaged further in her saddlebags until she found some sweet dried dates. She looked guiltily at the hill as she nibbled one, knowing that her sons loved the rare deli-cacy. Still, they were not there. She could see them rising higher, climbing easily on strong, thin legs. It would be sunset by the time they returned and for once she was on her own. She hobbled the pony with a length of rope so it would not wander far, then sat on the dry grass, spreading a saddle blanket for herself.

Sorhatani dozed through the afternoon, enjoying the peaceful solitude. At times, she took up a deel robe she was embroidering in gold thread for Kublai. It would be very fine when it was finished and she worked with bowed head over the stitches, cutting lengths of thread with strong, white teeth. In the sun's warmth, it was easy to nod over the cloth and she dozed for a time. When she came awake again, it was to find the afternoon had faded to coolness. She rose and stretched, yawning. This was a good land and she felt at home here. She had dreamed of Genghis as a young man and her face was flushed with perspiration. It had not been a dream to share with her sons.

In the distance, the movement of a rider caught her eye. It was an instinctive talent, born of generations for whom spotting an enemy was the key to survival. She frowned and shaded her eyes, then made her hands into a tube to focus her sight further. Even with the old scout's trick, the dark figure was just a speck.

Her husband's bondsmen had not slept in the afternoon and already they were galloping to intercept the lone rider. Sorhatani felt her sense of peace dwindle and fade as they reached the man and the single point became a larger knot.

'Who *are* you?' she muttered to herself.

It was hard not to feel a twinge of worry. A single rider could only be one of the yam messengers who criss-crossed thousands of miles for the khan and his generals. With fresh horses, they could ride a hundred miles in a day, sometimes even further if it was a matter of life and death. The khan's forces in Chin territory were only ten days away by the reckoning of such men. She saw the three riders begin to approach the red hill together and her womb clenched in sudden premonition.

Behind her, she heard the sound of her sons back from their climb. Their voices were light and cheerful, but there were no calls of triumph. The fledgling eagles had left the nest, or flown from their grasping hands. Sorhatani began to pack away her supplies, folding her precious needles and spools of thread back into their roll and tying the knots with unconscious expertise. She did it rather than stand helplessly waiting and she took her time with the saddlebags, stowing the waterskins carefully.

When she turned back, her hand flew to her mouth as she recognised the lone rider flanked by the bondsmen. They were still some way off and she almost cried out to them to go faster. As they drew nearer, she saw how Mongke swayed in the saddle, close to utter exhaustion.

He was coated in dust and the sides of his horse heaved with caked muck from where he had emptied his bladder without dismounting. She knew the scouts did that only when the news had to be brought home with all speed and her heart skipped with dread. She did not speak as her eldest son dismounted and staggered, almost falling as his legs betrayed him. He clung to the saddle horn, using his strong right hand to rub out the cramps. At last their eyes met and he did not have to speak.

Sorhatani did not weep then. Though some part of her knew her husband was gone, she stood tall, her mind racing. There were so many things she had to do.

'You are welcome in my camp, my son,' she said at last.

Almost in a trance, she turned to the bondsmen and told them to make a fire and salt tea. Her other sons stood in silent confusion at the sight of the small group.

'Sit with me, Mongke,' she said softly.

Her son nodded, his eyes red-rimmed with weariness and grief. He took his place on the grass beside her and nodded to Kublai, Hulegu and Arik-Boke as they made a tight circle around their mother. When the salt tea was ready, Mongke drained the first bowl in a few gulps to cut the dust in his throat. The words still had to be spoken. Sorhatani almost cried out to stop him, her emotions in turmoil. If Mongke did not speak, it would not be completely true. Once the words were out, her life, her son's lives, would all change and she would have lost her beloved.

'My father is dead,' Mongke said.

His mother closed her eyes for a moment. Her last hope was torn away. She took a long breath.

190

'He was a good husband,' she whispered, choking. 'He was a warrior who commanded ten thousand for the khan. I loved him more than you will ever know.' Tears made her eyes large and her voice roughened as her throat closed on grief. 'Tell me how it happened, Mongke. Leave nothing out.'

CHAPTER FIFTEEN

Tsubodai reined in at the edge of a cliff, leaning out of his saddle to peer down on the valley below. It had taken him a day of following goat trails to reach the place, but from such a height he could see for twenty miles, his gaze encompassing hills and villages, rivers and towns. The wide Volga river ran to the west, but it was not a serious obstacle. He had already sent men wading across its sandbars to scout islands and the banks beyond. He had raided these lands years before. He smiled as he remembered taking his men across the frozen rivers. The Russians had not believed anyone could withstand their winter. They had been mistaken. Only Genghis could have called him back then. When the great khan had ordered him home, Tsubodai had returned, but it would not happen again. Ogedai had given him a free hand. The Chin borders were secure to the east. If he could crush the lands of the west, the nation would hold the central plains from sea to sea, an empire so vast it beggared the imagination. Tsubodai hungered to see the lands beyond the Russian forests, all the way to the legendary cold seas and the ghostly white peoples there who never saw the sun.

With such a view, it was easy to imagine the threads of his influence stretching back to him. Tsubodai stood at the centre of a web of messengers and spies. For hundreds of miles around the spot where he stood, he had men and women in every market, village, town and fortress. Some of them had no idea the coins they were paid came from the Mongol armies. A few of his scouts and informants were from the Turkic tribes, who lacked the eye-folds that marked his warriors. Others came from those Tsubodai and Batu had already recruited or taken by force. They staggered out of the ashes of every town, homeless and desperate, ready to accept whatever their conquerors asked in exchange for their lives. The khan's silver flowed like a river through Tsubodai's hands and he bought information as much as meat and salt – and valued it more.

The general turned his head as Batu came around the last turn and brought his pony onto the ridge crest before dismounting. Batu stared at the valleys below with an expression of bored resentment. Tsubodai frowned to himself. He could not change the past, any more than he could challenge Ogedai Khan's right to raise a sullen young man to command ten thousand. A green adolescent with an army could do a great deal of damage. The strange thing was that Tsubodai persisted in training him to be the most efficient destroyer he could be. Time alone would give him perspective and wisdom, all the things Batu currently lacked.

They sat for a long time in silence before Batu's patience frayed as Tsubodai had known it would. There was no calm at the centre of the angry young warrior, no internal peace. Instead, he simmered with constant rage and all those around him sensed it.

'I have come, Tsubodai *Bahadur.*' Batu pronounced the

general's nickname with a sneer, making 'the valiant' sound like mockery. 'What is it that only your eyes can see?'

Tsubodai replied as if it was nothing, his voice as infuriatingly relaxed as he could make it.

'When we move on, your men will not be able to see the terrain, Batu. They might become lost, or be stopped by some obstacle. You see those low hills, there?'

Batu peered where Tsubodai pointed.

'From here, you can see how they run almost together, leaving a central ground free for . . . a mile, perhaps two. Four or five *li*, as the Chin measure distance. We could hide two minghaans on either side in ambush. If we bring the Russians to battle a few miles further on, a false retreat will drag them back to those hills and they will not get out.'

'This is nothing new,' Batu said. 'I know about the feigned retreat. I thought you would have something more interesting to make it worth dragging my horse up here.'

Tsubodai kept his cold eyes on the younger man for a moment, but Batu held his gaze with insolent confidence.

'Yes, Orlok Tsubodai?' he asked. 'Is there something you wish to say to me?'

'It is important to choose the ground, then scout it well for hidden obstacles,' Tsubodai replied.

Batu chuckled and stared down again. For all his bluster and arrogance, Tsubodai saw he was taking in every detail of the land, his eyes flickering back and forth as he memorised it. He was an unpleasant student, but his mind was as sharp as anyone Tsubodai had known. It was hard not to think of his father at times, the memories robbing the general of his irritation.

'Tell me what you see in our tumans,' Tsubodai went on.

Batu shrugged. Down below, he could see five columns moving slowly across the land. It took just a glance for him to read them.

'We march apart and attack together. Five fingers covering

as much ground as possible. The messengers keep them in contact for quick response to any show of force. I believe my grandfather began the practice. It has worked well enough since then.'

He grinned without looking at Tsubodai. Batu knew the general was responsible for the formation that allowed a small army to sweep across huge areas, clearing towns and villages before them so that they left a smoking landscape behind. They came together only when the enemy appeared in strength, when the arrow messengers would bring the tumans racing, a fist to smash the resistance before they moved on.

'Your eyes are strong, Batu. Tell me what else you see.'

Tsubodai's voice was maddeningly calm and Batu rose to the bait, determined to show the older man that he needed no lessons from him. He spoke quickly and used his hand to chop the air.

'For each column, there are scouts at the front in groups of ten. They ride up to eighty miles out, looking for the enemy. The centre is the families, the baggage, gers, oxen, camels, drummers and collapsed gers by the thousand. There are mobile forges on carts with spoked wheels, iron-reinforced. I believe you are responsible for those, general. Boys and foot warriors march there, our final defence if the warriors are ever overrun. Around them are the herds of sheep, goats and of course remounts, three to a man or more.' He spoke faster, enjoying the chance to show his knowledge: 'Beyond *those* are the heavy tuman cavalry in minghaan ranks. Further still, we have the light cavalry screen, the first to meet any attack with arrows. Finally, we have the rearguard, who plod along and wish they were closer to the front instead of riding through everyone else's shit. Shall I begin naming the officers? You are the orlok, in overall command, I am told. You have no bloodline worth mentioning, so I am the prince whose name appears on the orders, the grandson of Genghis Khan. It is an odd arrangement, but we

195

will discuss it another time. I lead a tuman, as do generals Kachiun, Jebe, Chulgetei and Guyuk. The minghaan officers, in order of seniority are . . .'

'That is enough, Batu,' Tsubodai said quietly.

'Ilugei, Muqali, Degei, Tolon, Onggur, Boroqul . . .'

'Enough,' Tsubodai snapped. 'I know their names.'

'I see,' Batu said, raising an eyebrow. 'Then I do not understand what you wanted me to learn by losing half a day riding up this rock with you. If I have made mistakes, you must feel able to bring them to me. Am I in error, general? Have I displeased you in some way? You must tell me, so I can remove the fault.'

His eyes bored into Tsubodai, allowing his bitterness to show for once. Tsubodai controlled his temper, felt it rise in him and took a firmer grip before he ruined a young man guilty of nothing more than spite and arrogance. He looked too much like Jochi for Tsubodai not to know he had reason.

'You have not mentioned the auxiliaries,' Tsubodai said calmly, at last. In response, Batu chuckled, an unpleasant sound.

'No, and I will not. Our ragged conscripts are good for nothing more than soaking up the missiles of our enemies. I am going to rejoin my tuman, general.'

He began to turn his mount and Tsubodai reached out and took his reins. Batu glared at him, but he had the sense not to reach for the sword that hung at his waist.

'I have not yet given you permission to leave,' Tsubodai said.

His face was still emotionless, but his voice had hardened and his eyes were very cold. Batu smiled and Tsubodai could see he was on the point of saying something that would tear down the strained courtesy between them. This was why he preferred to deal with more senior men, who had some idea of consequences and would not throw their entire lives away on a bad-tempered moment. Tsubodai spoke quickly and firmly to head him off.

'If I have the slightest doubt about your ability to follow

196

my orders, Batu, I will send you back to Karakorum.' Batu
began to take a breath, his face twisting as Tsubodai went on
relentlessly. 'You may take your complaints to your uncle there,
but you will no longer ride with me. If I give you a hill to take,
you will destroy your entire tuman rather than fail. If I tell
you to ride to a position, you will break your horses to reach
it in time. Do you understand? If you fail me in *anything*, there
will be no second chance. This is not a game, general, and I
do not care what you think of me, not at all. Now, if you have
something to say to me, say it.'

At almost twenty, Batu had matured in the years since
winning the horse race at Karakorum. He took command of
his temper with a swiftness that surprised Tsubodai, reining
in his emotions and shuttering them away so that his eyes were
blank. It showed he was more man than boy, but it made him
a far more dangerous adversary.

'You may put your faith in me, Tsubodai Bahadur,' Batu
said, this time without the sneer in his voice. 'With your permission, I will return to my column.'

Tsubodai inclined his head and Batu trotted his mount back
down the goat path that led to the base of the hill. Tsubodai
stared after him for a time, then grimaced to himself. He should
have sent him back to Karakorum. With any other officer, he
would have had him whipped and strapped to a horse to be
ridden home in disgrace. Only the memories of Batu's father
and, yes, his grandfather held Tsubodai's hand. They had been
men to follow. Perhaps the son could be made in their image,
unless of course he got himself killed first. He needed to be
tested, to gain the soul weight that came only from true knowledge of skill, rather than empty arrogance. Tsubodai nodded
to himself as he looked over the lands ahead. There would be
many opportunities to temper the young prince in fire.

*   *   *

The Russian lands had been wide open for the sort of attack Tsubodai had perfected. Even the nobles there had homes and towns protected by little more than a wooden palisade. Some of them had the solidity of decades or even centuries, but the Mongol war machine had overcome such obstacles in Chin territory. Their catapults smashed apart the ancient logs, sometimes crushing those who sheltered behind them. It was true that the Mongol archers had to contend with thicker forests than they had ever seen, sometimes stretching for thousands of miles and able to hide large forces of horsemen. The last summer had been hot and heavy rainfall meant the ground was often too soft to move forward with any speed. Tsubodai disliked the marshes intensely, but he was coming to the opinion that if it hadn't been for those, Genghis had made an error in attacking to the east. The lands to the west were still ripe, and as yet, Tsubodai had seen no force worthy to challenge his tumans as they scoured the land. The Mongol sweep took them hundreds of miles into the north and winter brought blessed relief from the flies and rain and disease.

For the first year, he had kept to the east of the Volga river, preferring to crush any possible threat from the area that would become his rear and be part of the supply route to Karakorum. Though the distances were vast, there was already a constant stream of riders. The first yam waystations were rising behind his tumans, as well fortified as anything else in Russian territory. Tsubodai cared nothing for the buildings, but they housed grain, saddles and the fastest mounts from the herds, ready for whoever needed to race through.

It was a spring morning when Tsubodai gathered his most senior officers on a meadow by a lake filled with wildfowl. His scouts had spent the morning trapping thousands of birds in nets, or taking them in flight for sport. The women in the camps were plucking the birds to be roasted that evening, creating great drifts of feathers that tumbled over the grass like spilt oil.

198

Batu watched with carefully hidden interest as Tsubodai brought forward one of his strongest warriors. The man's face could not be seen under the helmet of polished iron. Everything he wore had been captured further to the west. Even the horse was a monster, black as night and half as high again at the shoulder as any Mongol pony. Like its rider, it was sheathed in iron, from plates around its eyes to a skirt of hardened leather and metal to protect its hindquarters from arrows.

Some of the men looked on it with greed in their eyes, but Batu scorned such a beast. As large as it was, with such a burden of armour he was certain it would be slow, at least in the thrust and parry of battle.

'This is what we will face as we move west,' Tsubodai said. 'Men like this in cages of iron are the most feared force on a battlefield. According to the Christian monks in Karakorum, they are unstoppable in the charge, a weight of metal and leather that can crush anything we have.'

The senior men shifted uncomfortably, unsure whether to believe such a wild claim. They watched in fascination as Tsubodai brought his pony close to the larger animal. He looked small next to the man and horse, but he used his reins lightly to take his pony around in a tight circle.

'Raise your hand when you can see me, Tangut,' he said.

It was not long before they understood. The line of sight Tsubodai had revealed was just a small strip to the front.

'Even with the visor raised, he can see nothing at the side or behind, and that iron will be hard to turn quickly.' Tsubodai reached out and clanged his fist against the warrior's breast-plate. It rang like a bell.

'His chest is well protected. Under this is a layer of iron links, like metal cloth. It serves a similar purpose to our silk tunics, but is made to withstand axes and knives more than arrows.'

Tsubodai gestured to a boy holding a long lance and the

boy ran to the armoured warrior and handed it up to him, tapping his leg for attention.

'This is how they are used,' Tsubodai said. 'Like our own heavy horse, they ride head-on against an enemy. In a charge, they have no flaw or hole in their armour.'

He nodded to Tangut and they all watched as the warrior trotted away, his ungainly metal carapace jingling with every step.

At two hundred paces, the man turned his heavy mount, which reared and flattened its ears. He dug in his heels and the animal lunged forward, the thick legs thumping the ground. Batu saw how dropping the horse's head brought the armour of chest and skull together, forming an impenetrable shell. The lance lowered, the point cutting the air in circles as it centred on Tsubodai's chest.

Batu found he was holding his breath and he let it go, annoyed with himself for falling under Tsubodai's spell. He watched coldly as the warrior hit full gallop, his lance a deadly weapon. The hooves thundered and Batu had a sudden vision of a line of such men sweeping across a battlefield. He swallowed at the thought.

Tsubodai moved quickly, darting to one side with his pony. They saw the armoured warrior try to correct, but he could not turn at full speed and swept past.

Tsubodai raised and drew his bow in a fluid motion, aiming casually. The front of the horse was as well armoured as its rider. There was even a crest of armour running along the line of the mane, but below that the great neck was open and bare.

Tsubodai's arrow punched into the flesh and the horse screamed, spattering bright blood from its nostrils.

'From the sides, to a good bowman, they are unprotected,' Tsubodai shouted over the noise. He spoke without pride: any one of the men watching could have made the shot. They smiled at the thought of such powerful enemies brought down by speed and arrows.

They could all hear the tortured snorting of the horse as it wrenched its head back and forth in pain. Slowly, it sank to its knees and the warrior stepped clear. He dropped his lance and drew a long sword, advancing on Tsubodai.

'To defeat such armoured men, we must first kill the horses,' Tsubodai went on. 'Their armour is designed to deflect arrows shot from the front. Everything is made for the charge, but on foot, they are like turtles, slow and ponderous.'

To make his point, he selected a thick arrow with a long steel tip. It was a wicked-looking thing, smooth and polished, with no barbs to slow its speed.

The approaching warrior saw the action and hesitated. He did not know how far Tsubodai was willing to go to make his point, but the general would be equally ruthless with a man whose nerve failed. The moment of indecision passed and the warrior clumped forward, straining to pump his heavy legs and arms quickly so that he could bring his sword to bear.

From the saddle, Tsubodai guided his mount with his knees, sending the pony dancing back out of sword range. He drew again, feeling the immense power of the bow as he pulled the three-foot shaft right back to his ear. With the warrior just a few paces away, Tsubodai loosed and watched closely as the shaft passed straight through the side plates.

The warrior went down hard with a crash of metal. The arrow was lodged in his armour, the feathers showing clearly as he toppled. Tsubodai grinned.

'They have just one strength – in a line, facing forward. If we allow them to use that strength, they will sweep us away like wheat to a scythe. If we scatter and ambush them, stage false retreats and flank them, they will be as children to us.'

Batu watched as Tsubodai's serving men carried the dying warrior away between them, sweating and struggling under the massive burden. At a distance, they stripped the armour, revealing a mailed body spitted through by the shaft. They had to break the arrow to get the plate free and bring it back to Tsubodai.

'According to those boastful Christians who wished to frighten us, these knights have had no equal on the battlefield for a hundred years.' He held up the metal plate and everyone there could see the sunlight gleam through the neat hole. 'We cannot leave a major force or city behind us or on our flanks, but if this is the best they have, we will surprise them, I think.'

They raised their own bows and swords then, cheering Tsubodai's name. Batu joined them, careful not to be the only one who remained outside the group. He saw Tsubodai's gaze flicker over him. A look of satisfaction crossed the general's face at seeing Batu shout with the others. Batu smiled at the thought of holding Tsubodai's head up in just such a way. It was only a fantasy. The army was strong, but he knew they needed Tsubodai to lead them west against the great armies of horsemen and further to these men of iron. For Batu, men like Tsubodai were old and approaching the end of their time. His chance would come naturally; he did not need to force its progress.

Chagatai had built a summer palace on the banks of the Amu Darya river, the western edge of his empire that led as far south as Kabul. For the site, he had chosen a high ridge over the river where there was always a cool breeze, even in the hottest months. The sun of his khanate had baked him lean and dark, as if all the moisture had been boiled out, leaving him as hard as ancient birch. He ruled the cities of Bukhara, Samarkand and Kabul, with all their wealth. The citizens there had learned to deal with the summer heat, sipping cool drinks and sleeping through the afternoon before rising again. Chagatai had chosen almost a hundred new wives from those cities alone and many of them had already given birth to sons and daughters. He had taken

Ogedai's order to breed a new army literally and he enjoyed the sound of the squalling children in the infant rooms of his seraglio. He had even learned the new word for his collection of beautiful women, as there was nothing like it in his own tongue.

Yet there were times when he missed the frozen plains of his homeland. Winter was a passing thing in his new lands, always with the promise of a return to green life. Though their nights could be bitter, the people of his new khanate had no concept of the endless, crushing cold that had shaped the Mongol people, the desolate high plains that had to be fought for every meal, with life and sudden death as the stakes. His heartland had groves of figs and fruit, rolling hills and rivers that flooded every few years and had not run dry in living memory.

His summer palace had been built to the same specification and measurements as Ogedai's in Karakorum – then carefully reduced in all dimensions. Chagatai was nowhere near the fool some believed him to be. No great khan would enjoy hearing of a building to rival his own and Chagatai was careful to remain a support rather than any kind of threat.

He heard his servant approaching along the marble corridor that led to the audience room over the river. Suntai's sole concession to the climate was wearing open sandals with iron studs that clacked and echoed long before he could be seen. Chagatai stood on the balcony, enjoying the sight of the ducks sweeping in to settle in the reed beds along the banks. Above them, a lone white-tailed eagle hung in perfect stillness, silent and deadly.

As Suntai entered, Chagatai turned and gestured to a bottle of arack on the table. Both men had developed a taste for the aniseed drink so popular among the Persian citizens. Chagatai turned back to the river as Suntai clinked the cups together and poured, adding a dash of water so that it whitened like mare's milk.

Chagatai accepted the cup without taking his eyes off the eagle over the river. He squinted against the setting sun as it stooped, dropping suddenly to the waters and rising again with a squirming fish in its claws. The ducks rose in mindless panic and Chagatai smiled. When the air cooled in the evenings, he found he had grown affectionate towards his new home. It was a fitting land for those who would come after him. Ogedai had been generous.

'You have heard the news,' Chagatai said. It was a statement rather than a question. Any message that reached his summer palace would have passed through Suntai's hands at some point.

Suntai nodded, content to wait to hear his master's mind. To those who did not know him, he looked like any other warrior, though one who had marked his cheeks and chin with heavy lines of knife scars as some did, removing the need to shave on campaign. Suntai was always grubby and his hair was thick with ancient, rancid oil. He scorned the Persian habits of bathing and he suffered worse than most with boils and spreading rashes. With his dark eyes and lean frame, he looked like a rough killer. In fact, the mind behind the carefully created image was sharper than the knives he carried hidden against his skin.

'I did not expect to lose another brother so soon,' Chagatai said softly. He emptied the cup down his throat and belched. 'Two are gone. Just two of us remain.'

'Master, we should not stand at a window to discuss such things. There are always ears to hear.'

Chagatai shrugged and gestured with his empty cup. Suntai walked with him, deftly snatching up the jug of arack as he passed the table. They sat facing each other at an ornate table of gold-inlaid black wood, once the property of a Persian king. It was not symbolism that placed it at the very centre of the room. Suntai knew they could not be overheard by the keenest listener with his ears pressed to the outer walls. He suspected

204

Ogedai would have spies in the new summer palace, just as Suntai had placed them with Tsubodai and Ogedai, Khasar and Kachiun, all the senior men he could reach. Loyalty was a difficult game, but he loved it.

'I have reports of the fit suffered by the khan,' Suntai said. 'I cannot say how close he was to death without interviewing the shaman who tended him. He is not one of mine, unfortunately.'

'Nevertheless, I must be ready to move at the first messenger to come galloping in.' Despite the placing of the table, Chagatai was unable to resist glancing around to be sure no one could hear him and he leaned forward, his voice very low.

'It took *forty-nine* days for me to hear this, Suntai. It is not good enough. If I am to take the great khanate as my own, I must have better news and faster. The next time Ogedai falls, I want to be there before he is cold, do you understand?'

Suntai touched his forehead, mouth and heart with his fingertips in the Arab gesture of respect and obedience.

'Your will commands me, my lord. One of my closest servants was gored in a boar hunt. It has taken time to replace him in the great khan's retinue. However, I have two others ready for promotion to his personal staff. In just a few months, they will be part of his innermost councils.'

'Make it so, Suntai. There will be only one chance to take the reins. I do not want his weakling son gathering the tribes before I can act. Serve me well in this and you will rise with me. The nation of my father is too strong for a man who cannot command even his own body.'

Suntai smiled tightly, rubbing the ugly ridged skin of his cheeks. The instinct of years prevented him from agreeing with the treason, or even to nod his head. He had spent too long with spies and informants and he never spoke without carefully weighing the words. Chagatai was used to his silences and merely refilled the cups, adding the splash of water that took the edge off the bitterness.

'Let us drink to my brother Tolui,' Chagatai said.

Suntai looked closely at him, but there was real grief in his eyes. The khan's spymaster raised his cup and dipped his gaze.

'He would have made my father proud with such a sacrifice,' Chagatai went on. 'It was insane, but by the sky father, it was a glorious insanity.'

Suntai drank, aware that his lord had been drinking most of the day already. It showed in his bloodshot eyes and clumsy movements. In comparison, Suntai only sipped from his cup. He almost choked when Chagatai slapped him on the shoulder and laughed, spilling the white liquid across the lacquer.

'Family is everything, Suntai, never think that I forget that . . .' He trailed off, staring into memories for a time. 'But I was my father's choice to succeed him. There was a time when my destiny was written in stone and carved *deep*. Now, I must make it for myself, but it is nothing more than fulfilling the old man's dreams.'

'I understand, my lord,' Suntai said, refilling Chagatai's cup. 'It is a worthy aim.'

CHAPTER SIXTEEN

The rain could not last, Tsubodai was almost certain. The sheer force of it was astonishing, drumming across his tumans. The sky was a wall of black cloud and lightning flashed at irregular intervals, revealing the battlefield in stark images. Tsubodai would never have fought on such a day if the enemy had not moved into position in the darkness. It was a bold move, even for mounted horsemen armed much as his own warriors.

The Volga river was behind them. It had taken another year to secure the lands beyond the river, the second since leaving Karakorum. He had chosen to be thorough, to sting the great men, attacking their walled towns and cities on a wide front until they were forced to unite against him. In that way, his tumans could destroy them all, rather than spend many years hunting down each duke and minor noble, whatever they called themselves. For months, Tsubodai had seen strangers watching his columns from hilltops, but they vanished when challenged, disappearing back into the damp forests. It seemed their masters knew no loyalty to each other and for a time he had been forced to pick them off one by one. It was not enough. To cover the sort of ground he intended, he dared not leave a major army or city untouched. It was a complex web of terrain and information and it grew harder to manage with each passing month. His spearhead was widening further and further, his resources stretched. He needed more men.

His scouts had ridden out as usual in a constant relay. A few days before, without warning, some had not come back. As soon as the first ones were missed, Tsubodai prepared for attack, almost two full days before an enemy was in sight.

Still in darkness, with a cold drizzle soaking them all to the skin, horn warnings sounded, relayed from man to man. The Mongol columns had come together from miles apart, forming a single mass of horses and warriors. There was no separate camp for those who could not fight. From children to old women on carts, Tsubodai preferred them to move in the safety of the main army. His light cavalry took positions on the outskirts, each man covering his bow and dreading the moment when he would have to shoot arrows in the rain. They all carried spare bowstrings, but rain ruined them quickly, stretching the skin strips and robbing the shafts of force.

The ground was already soft as the grey morning lightened almost imperceptibly. It would bog down the carts. Tsubodai began to arrange a corral for them behind the battlefield. All the time, he continued to gather information. Many of his scouts had been ridden down, but others struggled through to bring him news. Some of them were wounded and one had an arrow lodged in his back, near the shoulder blades. Before Tsubodai could even see the horizon, he had estimates of the enemy numbers. They were moving quickly towards him, risking life and mounts to surprise the Mongol columns, to catch them out of formation.

He smiled at the thought. He was no wild tribesman, to be

surprised at dawn. His men could not be routed with a sudden charge. The Russian noblemen were reacting like ants to repulse an invader, without a pause for thought.

The tumans moved smoothly in formation, each jagun of a hundred following the next in the darkness, calling back and forth to keep position. The five generals spoke to Tsubodai in turn and he gave them their orders without hesitation. They split apart at a gallop to pass them down the line of command.

It was Tsubodai's practice to interrogate prisoners, if gold would not buy what he needed. Moscow lay ahead, a centre of power in the region. The prisoners had known its location on the Moskva river. Now Tsubodai knew as well. The Russians had a record of arrogance, considering themselves masters of the central plains. Tsubodai smiled again to himself.

The downpour had begun after the enemy horsemen had begun the attack, but they had not called it off. The soft ground would hamper them as much as his own warriors. His tumans were outnumbered, but they always were. The auxiliary forces Batu had poured scorn on were good enough to hold the flanks and prevent encirclement. Tsubodai had his best men among them, training them constantly and setting up chains of command. They were already more than just a rabble of peasants and he would not throw them away without good reason. To his experienced eye, their formations of foot soldiers were ragged compared with the discipline of his tumans, but they were still many, standing in the mud with axes, sword and shields.

Tsubodai had given his orders and the rest was up to the individuals who led. His men knew the plans could change in an instant, if some new factor showed itself. The ripple of orders would run again and the formations would change faster than an enemy could possibly react.

The light did not brighten under the cloud. The rain became suddenly heavier, though the thunder fell silent for a time. By then, Tsubodai could make out horsemen moving across the hills like a stain. He rode alongside his own tumans, checking every detail as messengers raced across the field. If it had not been for the rain, he would have split his force and sent Batu to one side to flank or encircle the enemy. As it was, he had chosen to appear slow and clumsy, a single mass of warriors riding blindly at the enemy. It was what the Russians would expect from armoured knights.

Tsubodai looked across to where Batu rode with his tuman. The younger man's position was marked in the third rank by a host of banners, though Tsubodai knew he was not there. That too was an innovation. Armies concentrated their arrows on officers and kings. Tsubodai's orders had been to reveal those spots with flags, but have the generals in the ranks to one side. The bannermen carried heavy shields and their morale was high at the thought of fooling an enemy in such a way.

A clot of cold mud flung from a hoof touched Tsubodai's cheek and he wiped it away. The Russians were no more than a mile off and his mind clicked through calculations as the armies closed. What else could he have done? He grimaced at the thought. Much of the plan depended on Batu following his orders, but if the younger general failed or disobeyed, Tsubodai was ready. He would not give Batu another chance, no matter who his father and grandfather had been.

The rain died away without warning, the morning suddenly filled with the sounds of horses and men, orders suddenly clear where they had been muffled. The Russian prince had widened the line when he saw their numbers, preparing to encircle. One of the Russian flanks was struggling to keep up with the rest over boggy ground, their horses plunging and rising. It was a weakness and Tsubodai sent scouts to his generals to make sure they had noted it.

Eight hundred paces and he kept the columns together. It was too far for arrows, and cannon would have been left behind on such a slog over soft ground. Tsubodai saw that the Russian warriors carried spears and bows. He could not see the huge horses ridden by knights in iron. This Russian noble seemed to favour light armour, speed over power, much as Tsubodai did himself. If the enemy truly understood those qualities, Tsubodai knew they would be hard to pin down, but they showed no sign of such an understanding. They had seen his smaller force, lumbering along in a single block. Whoever led them had chosen a simple hammerhead formation to crush mere tribesmen and sheepherders.

At four hundred paces, the first shafts were sent high, shot by young fools on both sides who should have known better. None reached his men from the Russian side and most of his own warriors guarded their bowstrings, keeping them covered until the last moment. Men who had fashioned a bow themselves would not risk it being destroyed by a snapping string. The weapons were precious, sometimes the only thing of value they owned apart from a pony and saddle.

Tsubodai saw the Russian prince who led the force. Like Batu's false position, he was surrounded by flags and guards, but there was no mistaking the enormous horse at the centre of the army, its rider sitting in armour that shone like silver in the rain. The man's head was bare and at two hundred paces, his eyes still sharp over distance, Tsubodai could see a blond beard. He sent another rider to Batu to be sure he had marked his man, but it was unnecessary. As soon as the messenger had hared away, Tsubodai saw Batu point and exchange commands with his minghaans.

Thunder grumbled again above their heads and for an instant Tsubodai saw thousands of lighter faces among the enemy as men looked up. Many were bearded, he realised. Compared to the Mongol face, where little hair grew, they were like great lumbering bears. Arrows followed as his light cavalry released thousands of shafts, sending them high. For the first shots, every tenth man used a whistling head, carved and fluted to scream in the air. They did less damage than the steel-head shafts, but the sound was unearthly and terrifying. In the past, armies had broken and run from that first volley. Tsubodai grinned to hear the naccara drums hammer out their own thunder, answering the storm as it dwindled to the east.

The arrows curved upwards, dropping hard. Tsubodai noted the way the Russians protected the blond leader with shields, ignoring their own safety. Some of the man's guards fell, but then the steady approach seemed to go faster and the distance between them dwindled rapidly. The Mongol light horsemen released another storm of arrows before falling back at the last moment and letting the lancers through. It was Batu's moment of madness, exactly as Tsubodai had ordered. The grandson of Genghis would challenge the blond leader personally. A knight of iron would expect just such a challenge.

The naccara drums roared, the strikes blurring as the camel boys hit the great kettles at their sides. As Batu's minghaans cantered into a spear formation, lunging ahead of the tumans, the warriors screamed, an ululating bellow to send men white.

Arrows rained down from the Russian horsemen. They fell most heavily on the bannermen in the third rank of the main formation, surrounded by the snapping flags. They raised their shields above their heads and endured. Ahead of them, Batu took three thousand in a charge for the very centre of the Russian force.

Tsubodai watched coldly, satisfied that the younger man's nerve was up to the task. The spearhead was to serve one purpose. Tsubodai watched as they punched a hole with arrows in the Russian lines, then rode lances at it, crashing deeper in. The blond leader was pointing at them, shouting to his men as Batu's minghaans threw down broken lances and drew the lightly curved swords of good steel. Horses and men went down, but they pushed on. Before he was lost to sight in the

212

mass, Tsubodai saw Batu at the bloody tip of the spear, pushing his mount on and on.

Batu seethed as he chopped down on a roaring face, dragging his blade across a man's mouth so that his jaw hung slack. His sword arm ached, but his blood was on fire and he felt as if he could fight all day. He knew Tsubodai would be watching: the ruthless tactician, the Orlok Bahadur who threw warriors away as if they were nothing to him. Well, let the old men see how it was done.

Batu's strike minghaans crashed on into the Russians, aiming at the prince and his long flags. There were moments when Batu could see the blond warrior in his shining armour. He knew they were coming for him, risking it all on a single blow to his throat. It was the sort of attack a Russian army might have made.

Batu knew the true plan. Tsubodai had given him that much before sending him out. He was to hit hard until his men began to be overwhelmed. Only then could he fight his way out again. He smiled bitterly to himself. It would not be hard to feign panic at that point. The false retreat would collapse the Mongol centre, quickly turning into a rout as the tumans withdrew. The enemy horsemen would be drawn through the wings of foot soldiers, further and further, stretched thin over the ground. Then the jaws would close. If any of them made it through the trap, Kachiun's reserve would hit from both sides, hidden two miles back in heavy forest. It was a good plan, if the auxiliaries could hold the flanks, if Batu survived it. As he backhanded his sword across a horse's cheek, tearing a great flap, he recalled the challenge in the general's eyes as he had given him the order. Batu had shown him none of the roiling fury that filled him. Of course Tsubodai had chosen him. Who else had been a thorn in his side for so many months? His minghaan officers had exchanged resigned glances when they heard, but they had still volunteered. Not one of them had stood back rather than ride with the grandson of Genghis.

Fresh fury filled Batu at the thought of their wasted loyalty. How far had he come? Two hundred paces, three, more, into the enemy? They milled around him, their blades flickering, their shields taking his blows. Arrows whipped past his face. They wore leather armour and his blade was sharp enough to pierce it with a thrust, or even gash it as he went past, leaving them gasping over bloody ribs. He had no idea how long he had been pressing forward in the mass of horses, further and further away from safety and the tumans. All he knew was that he had to choose the moment well. Too soon and the Russians would sense a trap and simply close ranks behind him. Too late and there would not be enough battered warriors left to stage the false retreat. His men had chosen to follow into the mouth of the beast. Not because of Tsubodai, but because of him.

He felt his charge slowing as the Mongol warriors were hemmed in. Every step brought more Russian warriors against their flanks, stretching their force thinner and thinner, like a needle into flesh that gripped it tight. Batu felt fear rise in his throat like acid. He grabbed a shield of leather and wood and yanked it towards him with his left hand, stabbing down over the edge into the man behind it. He thrust the blade with all his fury and then punched with the hilt, so that the enemy fell away, his face a mass of blood.

Three warriors stayed in line with him as he forced his mount another four steps forward, killing a man to make space. Without warning, one of his companions was gone, taken by an arrow in the throat and falling backwards out of the saddle so that the horse snorted and lashed out with its hooves, its own panic growing. It was time. It was surely time. Batu looked around him. Had he done enough? The agony of the choice ate at him. He could not come back too early and face Tsubodai's stern expression. Better to die than have that man consider he had lost his nerve.

It had always been hard to look in the eyes of a man who had known Genghis. How could he ever match up to those memories? The grandfather who had conquered a nation, who had never known Batu at all. The father who had betrayed the nation and been killed like a dog in the snow. It was time.

Batu took a sword blow on his armoured sleeve, letting it slide uselessly past him as he gashed the arm that held it. More blood coated him and there was screaming everywhere. The Russians he faced were pale with rage or fear, holding heavy shields that bristled with Mongol arrows. Batu turned to begin the retreat and, for a single moment, he saw through the ranks of enemies to where the blond leader sat calmly watching him, a huge sword ready across his saddle horns.

Tsubodai had never expected the spearhead to get so close. Batu saw that his men were ready to cut their way back. Though he bore no marks of rank that would have made him the target for every Russian archer, his warriors watched him, risking their lives to glance his way. Most of the Russians were still facing the front, where the tumans were clashing with them. They would howl and chase as the Mongols turned to run, but Batu thought his men would win through, beginning the rout. He was so *close*. Who would have thought his spearhead thrust could reach the Russian prince?

Batu took a deep breath. 'No retreat!' he roared, warning his men.

He dug in his heels and his pony kicked out with its front hooves, knocking a shield from its owner's broken fingers. Batu lunged for the gap, swinging his blade wildly. Something hit him from the side and he felt a wave of pain that vanished before he knew whether it was serious. He saw the blond leader raise his sword and shield and the enormous horse snorted.

The Russian prince had decided not to wait, his blood lighting up at the challenge. His own shield-bearers were knocked to one side as the warhorse started forward.

Batu yelled in excitement, a babble of insult and fury. He had not known if he could break through the final solid ranks, but there was the prince himself coming to cut down the impudent horsemen. Batu saw the man's sword rise up behind his shoulder. The two horses were head-on, but Batu's mount was weary and battered, bruised by constant impact and the thousand scrapes and cuts that came from running through a fighting line.

Batu brought his own sword high, trying to remember Tsubodai's words on the weaknesses of knights. The blond-bearded man seemed like a giant as he came closer, wrapped in steel and unstoppable. Yet he wore no helmet and Batu was young and fast. As the Russian blade swept down with enough force to cut him in half, Batu nudged his pony to the right, away from the sweeping sword. His own blade licked out in a thrust, holding it just long enough to caress the man's throat under the beard.

Batu swore as his weapon scraped across metal. A piece of the beard had been cut loose, but the man himself was untouched, though he roared in shock. The horses were passing in the press, unable to ride free, but both men were side-on to each other, their weaker left sides exposed. The prince's sword came back up, but he was slow and heavy. Before he could land a blow, Batu had struck three times into his face, chopping at the cheeks and teeth, cutting away part of the jaw. The Russian prince lurched as Batu hammered at his armour, denting the plate metal that protected his chest.

The prince's face was a bloody ruin, his teeth broken and his jaw hanging loose. He would surely die from such a terrible wound, but his eyes cleared and he swung his left arm like a mace. Clad in iron, it struck Batu across the chest. He was guiding his pony with pressure from his knees and he had no reins. The high wooden saddle horns saved him and he twisted at an impossible angle. His sword had gone and he could not remember it leaving his hand. Spitting anger, he pulled a blade from a sheath on his calf and jammed it into the red mess of the prince's jaw, sawing back and forth at the blond beard that was thick and shining red.

The prince fell and a wail of horror went up from his shield-bearers and retainers. Batu raised both hands in victory, roaring long and loud at being alive and victorious. He did not know what Tsubodai was doing, or what the orlok would think. It had been Batu's decision and the prince had faced him. He had defeated a strong and powerful enemy and, for a time, he did not care if the Russians killed him. It was Batu's moment and he relished it.

At first, he did not see the ripple that spread across the Russians as the word spread. For half the army, it had happened behind them and the news of the death of the prince had to be shouted from unit to unit. Before Batu lowered his arms, some of the furthest nobles had turned their mounts and begun to withdraw, taking thousands of fresh horsemen with them. Those who tried to continue the fight saw them go and shouted angrily across the battlefield, blowing horns. The prince was dead and his armies shook with the suddenness of the omen. This was not to be their day, their victory. They went from determined fighters to frightened men as they heard, backing away from Tsubodai's tumans while they waited to be rallied, to have someone else take command.

It did not happen. Tsubodai sent minghaans racing along the flanks, the wiry ponies spattering clots of earth like rain as they went. Arrows poured into the Russian ranks once again and Tsubodai's heavy horse peeled off from the front and then came back in spearpoints like the one Batu had led into the heart of their army. Three separate strikes tore at the milling ranks. Even then, the defenders were half-hearted. They had seen their senior noblemen leaving and regiments and units beginning to withdraw. It was too much to ask that they stay to be slaughtered. Someone else could take the brunt of the Mongol warriors, now that their blood was up. More and more Russians marched clear, looking back at the shrinking heart where their companions still rode and died. It was enough. The prince was dead and they had done enough.

Tsubodai watched calmly as the Russian army fell apart. He wondered how his own tumans would fare if he was seen to fall, but he knew the answer. They would go on. They would endure. In the tumans, the warriors hardly ever saw the orlok or even their own generals. They knew the leader of their ten, a man they had elected among themselves. They knew the officer of the hundred, perhaps even the minghaan officer by sight. Those were the ones who spoke with authority, not some distant commander. Tsubodai knew that if he fell, the nation would complete his task and promote another to lead in his stead. It was a cold business, but the alternative was to witness the destruction of an army from the death of one man.

Tsubodai sent messengers to his generals, congratulating them as they took new orders. He wondered if those who had left the field expected him to let them go. He could not always understand the foreign soldiers he encountered, though he learned everything he could. He knew that some of them might expect to return to their homes, but that was foolish. Why leave alive men who could one day face you again? That was war as a game, and Tsubodai knew it would be a long hunt, weeks or even months, before his men had killed the last of them. He did not need to teach them their foolishness, only to destroy them and move on. He rubbed his eyes, suddenly weary. He would have to face Batu, if the young man still lived.

He had disobeyed his orders. Tsubodai wondered if he could have a general whipped after handing him such a victory.

Tsubodai looked around as men cheered nearby. His lips thinned in irritation as he saw Batu was at the centre of it. Half the Russian army was still in the field and his minghaans were passing around wineskins and whooping like children.

Tsubodai turned his horse and trotted slowly towards the scene. Silence fell among those he passed as they realised the orlok was among them. His bannermen unfurled long strips of silk that fluttered and snapped in the breeze.

Batu sensed or heard the approach. He had already begun to feel the battering he had taken. One eye and cheek were swelling, making his face look lopsided. He was filthy with blood, sweat and the strong smell of wet horses. Scales from his armour hung loose and he had a line of crusted red marking the skin from one ear down into his tunic. Yet he was jubilant and the sour face of Tsubodai could not spoil his mood.

'General, you are throwing away a morning,' Tsubodai said.

The men around Batu choked off their cheering. As it died away, Tsubodai continued coldly.

'Pursue the enemy, general. Let not one of them escape. Locate their baggage and camp and secure it from looting.'

Batu looked at him, suddenly quiet.

'Well, general?' Tsubodai went on. 'Will you face them again tomorrow, when you have thrown away this advantage? Will you allow them to reach the safety of Moscow or Kiev? Or will you hunt the Russians down now, with the other tumans under my command?'

The warriors around Batu turned away with sudden jerkiness, like boys caught stealing. They would not look at Tsubodai and only Batu held his gaze. Tsubodai expected some sort of retort, but he misjudged his man.

Another group of riders came cantering across the lines. The slaughter of the enemy was beginning, with lancers and archers picking them off almost as sport. Tsubodai saw that the group was led by the khan's son, Guyuk, his face fixed on Batu as he approached. He did not seem to see Tsubodai.

'Batu *Bahadur!*' Guyuk called, bringing his horse alongside. 'That was very fine, cousin. I saw it all. By the sky father, I thought you would never make it back, but when you reached the nobleman!' Lost for words, he clapped Batu on the back, patting him in admiration. 'I will put it in the reports to my father. What a moment it was!'

Batu glanced at Tsubodai to see how he was taking such generous praise. Guyuk noticed and turned.

'My congratulations on such a victory, Tsubodai,' Guyuk said. He was bluff and cheerful, apparently unaware of the strained moment he had interrupted. 'What a stroke! Did you see any of it? I thought I would choke when I saw the prince come forward to take him on.'

Tsubodai inclined his head in acknowledgement. 'Even so, the Russians must not be allowed to regroup. It is time to pursue, to hunt them all the way to Moscow. Your tuman will ride out as well, general.'

Guyuk shrugged. 'A hunt, then. It has been a *good* day.'

Oblivious, he thumped Batu on the shoulder again and rode clear with his men, bawling orders to another group to come with him. The quiet swelled as he moved away and Batu grinned as he waited. Tsubodai said nothing, and Batu nodded to himself, turning his horse and joining his minghaan officers. He left Tsubodai staring after him.

CHAPTER SEVENTEEN

Sorhatani swept around the corner in full array, sons and servants marching with her. She was a member of the khan's own family by marriage! She had thought he might never return from Chin lands. For the longest time, they seemed to have swallowed his army, with no word of their return. Yet when he came home at last, there was no summons, nothing from him at all. She would *not* accept any other delays from petty, pompous officials. Her messengers and servants had been baulked and sent back without even an excuse. Finally, she had come to Karakorum herself.

Instead of simply being allowed to see the khan, to talk of the grief and loss they shared, she had been stopped by a Chin official with jowls and soft hands. What was Ogedai thinking in using such perfumed courtiers in his own palace? What sort of message of strength would that send to those less benign than Sorhatani?

The courtier had stopped her once, but today all four of her sons were with her. She would see Ogedai today! No matter his sorrow, she could share it. The khan had lost a brother, but she had lost her husband, the father to her sons. If there had ever been a time when Ogedai could be persuaded of anything, it was then. The idea was intoxicating. A man with as much power as Genghis lay in his rooms like a broken reed. The palace was full of rumours that he hardly even spoke or ate. Whoever reached him could surely have whatever they wanted, yet he had given orders to keep visitors away. Well, she would tell him how the insult had hurt her and begin the negotiations with that. One last corner lay ahead in the labyrinth of the palace corridors. She passed under painted murals without looking up, her concentration focused on more important things.

The final corridor was a long one and in the stone halls the footsteps of her group echoed back. Though she saw there were men and Guards in front of the polished copper door, Sorhatani stormed on, forcing her sons to keep up. Let the fat little courtier sweat when he heard her coming. The khan was her brother-in-law, ill and weak in sadness. How *dare* a Chin eunuch bar her entry to her own family?

As she approached, she looked in vain for the bright-coloured silks the man preferred. She almost missed a step as she saw Yao Shu was there in his place. There was no sign of the man with whom she had argued that very morning. Yao Shu had turned to face her, his attitude clear from his stance. Sorhatani revised her plan as she went, shedding anger like a snakeskin with every step.

By the time she reached the shining metal door, she was walking at a normal pace and smiled as sweetly as she knew how at the khan's chancellor. Still, she seethed to have another Chin stop her at the door, especially one with such authority. Yao Shu could not be browbeaten into submission, nor threatened. She did not have to look at her younger sons to know they were cowed by the man who had tutored them. At one time or other, Yao Shu had thrashed all four of the boys for some transgression. He had beaten Kublai like a rug when the boy put a scorpion in the chancellor's boot.

Now he faced her, his face as forbidding as the Guards at his sides.

'The khan is not receiving visitors today, Sorhatani. I am sorry you came across the city. I did send a runner at dawn to warn you not to come.'

Sorhatani hid her irritation behind a smile. Giving her a house well away from the palace was another sign of voices other than Ogedai's at work. The khan would have given her rooms in the palace if he knew she had come, she was certain.

Sorhatani rose to the challenge in Yao Shu's impassive face.

'What plot is this?' she hissed at him. 'Have you murdered the khan, Yao Shu? How is it that only Chin men seem to roam the corridors of Karakorum these days?'

As Yao Shu took a breath in shock, she spoke to her sons without looking away from the chancellor.

'Ready your swords, Mongke, Kublai. I do not trust this man any longer. He claims the khan will not see the wife of his beloved brother.'

She heard the jingle of metal behind her, but more importantly, she saw the sudden doubt come into the faces of the Mongol Guards on either side of Yao Shu.

'The khan has an army of servants, scribes, concubines and wives.' she said. 'Yet where is his wife Torogene? Why is she not here to tend him in his illness? How is it that I can find no one who can say they have seen him alive for days, even weeks?'

It thrilled her to see Yao Shu's unnatural control crack at the accusations. He was immediately flustered, off balance as her words struck.

'The khan has been very ill, as you say,' he replied. 'He has asked for quiet in his palace. I am his chancellor, Sorhatani. It is not up to me to say where his family has gone, or to discuss it in a corridor.'

She saw that he was truly struggling with difficult orders and she pressed on, sensing the weak point of the man's essential kindness.

'You say the family have gone, Yao Shu? Guyuk is with Tsubodai. I do not know Ogedai's daughters, or the children of other wives. Torogene is not here then?'

His eyes flickered at the simple question.

'I see,' she went on. 'The summer palace perhaps, on the Orkhon river. Yes, that is where I would have sent her if I intended to steal power in this city, Yao Shu. If I intended to murder the khan in his bed and replace him with who? His brother Chagatai? He would be here in an instant. Is that your plan? What lies beyond this door, Yao Shu? *What have you done?*'

Her voice had risen, louder and higher. Yao Shu winced at the strident tone, but he was at a loss. He could not have the Guards take her away by force, not with her sons ready to defend their mother. The first one to lay a hand on Sorhatani would lose it, that much was obvious. Mongke in particular was no longer the sullen boy he had known. Yao Shu deliberately kept his eyes on Sorhatani, but he could feel Mongke staring coldly at him, daring him to meet his gaze.

'I must follow the orders I have been given, Sorhatani,' Yao Shu tried again. 'No one is to pass through this door. No one is to be granted an audience with the khan. He does not have to answer to you and neither do I. Now please, spend the day in the city, rest and eat. Perhaps he will see you tomorrow.'

Sorhatani tensed as if to attack him. Yet Yao Shu had not been made weak with his duties. Her sons had told her how he snatched an arrow from the bowstring in the palace gardens. It seemed an age ago, when her husband was still alive. She felt

224

tears start in her eyes and blinked them away. This was a time for anger, not sorrow. She knew if she let herself start weeping, she would not pass the door that day.

She took a deep breath. 'Murder!' she shouted. 'The khan is in danger! Come quickly!'

'There is no danger!' Yao Shu shouted over her. The woman was insane! What did she hope to gain, yelling like a scalded cat in his corridors? He heard running footsteps coming closer and cursed her under his breath. The night before Ogedai had become khan was still a painful memory among the Guards. They reacted to any perceived threat with a massive show of force.

In just a few heartbeats, the corridor was blocked at both ends by sprinting warriors. They were led by minghaans in black and red lacquered armour, their swords already drawn. Yao Shu held up both hands with palms clearly open and empty.

'There has been a mistake . . .' he began.

'No mistake, Alkhun,' Sorhatani snapped, turning to the senior man.

Yao Shu groaned to himself. Of course she knew the officer's name. Sorhatani had a prodigious memory for such things, but it was probably part of her plan to learn the names of the officers of the watch. The chancellor struggled for words that would rescue the situation.

'The lady is distraught,' he said.

The minghaan officer ignored him and spoke to Sorhatani directly. 'What is the difficulty here?'

Sorhatani looked down, shaking her head. To Yao Shu's irritation, there were tears showing in her eyes.

'This Chin official claims the khan cannot be seen by anyone. For days now, there has been no word. He speaks suspiciously, Alkhun, I do not trust his word.'

The soldier nodded, a man of quick thought and action, as would be expected for one of his rank. He turned to Yao Shu.

225

'You'll have to stand aside, chancellor. I need to check on the khan.'

'He gave orders,' Yao Shu started, but the officer merely shrugged.

'I will see him. Step aside, *right now.*'

The two men stood very still, glowering at each other as if they were the only ones in the corridor. Yao Shu had been put in an impossible position and Sorhatani saw there could be a brief and bloody struggle in the corridor at any moment. She spoke to break the deadlock.

'You will accompany us, of course, Yao Shu,' she said.

His head snapped round towards her, but she had given him a way out and he took it.

'Very well,' he said, his expression tight with anger. He turned to Alkhun. 'Your concern does you credit, minghaan. However, you are not to allow armed men such as these into the presence of the khan. All must be searched for weapons first.'

Sorhatani began to protest, but Yao Shu was adamant.

'I insist,' he said, reclaiming the balance of power.

'They will remain here,' Sorhatani said, rather than lose the moment. In truth, she did not mind that her sons were to remain outside, with their armour and blades. They had served their purpose by backing her at the door. She did not need them to hear everything after that.

With a grimace, Yao Shu lifted the small bar of brass that made the central lock. It was an ornate piece, carved and marked like a dragon curled around the centre of the door. Yet another sign of the Chin influence on the khan, Sorhatani thought as the door opened. A rush of wind chilled them all as she followed Yao Shu and Alkhun inside.

There were no lamps lit, but dim light came from one open window. The shutters had been thrown back with such force that one of them lay askew, a hinge broken. Long silk curtains billowed into the room, rustling and snapping at the walls with each gust.

The room was incredibly cold and their breath showed instantly as white mist. The outer door closed behind them and Sorhatani shivered as her eyes fell on the figure on a couch in the centre of the room. How could Ogedai withstand such a chill wearing only a thin silk tunic and leggings? His arms were bare and his feet looked bluish as he lay on his back and stared up at the ceiling.

He had not acknowledged them and Yao Shu had a moment of dread that they had found the khan's body. Then he saw pale mist rise from the still figure and he breathed again.

For a moment, none of them were sure how to proceed. The minghaan officer had seen that the khan still lived. His task was at an end, though his dignity forbade him from simply leaving, at least until he had apologised for invading the khan's privacy. Yao Shu too was quiet, guilty that he had failed in his orders. Sorhatani had manipulated them all.

Of course she was the first to speak.

'My lord khan,' Sorhatani said. She pitched her voice to carry over the noise of the wind, but Ogedai did not react. 'I have come to you in my grief, my lord.'

Still there was nothing and Yao Shu watched with interest as she firmed her jaw, visibly controlling irritation. The chancellor motioned for her to be taken away and the officer raised a hand to take her arm.

Sorhatani shrugged off the touch. 'My husband gave his life for you, my lord. How will you use his gift? Like this? Waiting for death in a frozen room?'

'That is *enough*,' Yao Shu said, horrified.

He took Sorhatani's arm in a firm grip and turned her back towards the door. All three froze as they heard a creak behind them. The khan had risen from his couch. His hands shook slightly as they turned to face him and his skin was a sickly yellow, his eyes bloodshot.

Under that cold gaze, the senior minghaan of the khan's Guards knelt and dipped his head to the floor.

'Rise, Alkhun,' Ogedai said in a hoarse whisper. 'Why are you here? Did I not say I was to be left alone?'

'My lord khan, I am sorry. I was led to understand you might be ill or dying.'

To his surprise, Ogedai smiled mirthlessly. 'Or indeed both, Alkhun. Well, you have seen me. Now get out.'

The officer moved with great speed to leave the room. Ogedai stared at his chancellor. He did not yet look at Sorhatani, though he had risen at her voice.

'Leave me, Yao Shu,' Ogedai said.

His chancellor bowed deeply, then tightened his hold on Sorhatani's arm as he began to guide her out.

'My lord khan!' she cried out.

'Enough!' Yao Shu snapped, yanking her. If he had released his grip, she would have fallen, but instead she swung around, helpless and furious.

'Take your hands away,' she hissed at him. 'Ogedai! How can you see me attacked and do nothing? Did I not stand with you on the night of knives, in this very palace? My husband would have answered this insult. Where is he now? Ogedai!'

She was in the doorway when the khan replied.

'You are dismissed, Yao Shu. Let her approach.'

'My lord,' he began, 'she . . .'

'Let her approach.'

Sorhatani shot a look of pure venom at the chancellor as she rubbed her arm and stood straight. Yao Shu bowed again and left the room without looking back, his face cold and emotionless. The door clanged softly behind him and she breathed slowly, hiding her delight. She was in. It had been close and even dangerous, but she had won through to the khan, alone.

Ogedai watched her come. He felt guilt, but he met her eyes. Before she could speak again, footsteps sounded, and a clinking of glass and metal. Sorhatani paused at the sight of the khan's manservant Baras'aghur carrying a tray into the room.

'I have a visitor, Baras,' Ogedai murmured.

The servant stared at Sorhatani with open hostility.

'The khan is not well. You should come back another time.'

He spoke with the confidence of a trusted man, his service to the khan beyond dispute. Sorhatani smiled at him, wondering if he had taken on a more motherly role during the khan's illness. He certainly seemed happy fussing around Ogedai.

When she did not move, Baras'aghur tightened his lips and set the tray down by his master with a gentle clinking. Then he faced her.

'The khan is not well enough for visitors,' he insisted, a little too loudly.

Sorhatani saw his growing indignation, so she spoke louder still. 'Thank you for the tea, Baras'aghur. I will serve the khan in your place. You *do* remember your place?'

The servant spluttered for a moment, looking to Ogedai. When the khan said nothing, Baras'aghur bowed with icy dislike and left the room. Sorhatani added a sprinkling of brown salt to the steaming golden liquid, salt that was so precious for life. Finally, she added milk from a tiny jug, its surface smooth in her hands. Her fingers were quick and sure.

'Serve me,' Ogedai said.

Gracefully, she knelt before him and held out the cup, bowing her head.

'I am yours to command, my lord khan,' she said.

She shivered slightly at the touch of his hands as he took it from her. He was like ice in that room where the wind blew constantly. From under lowered eyelids, she could see his face was mottled and dark, as if there were bruises deep within. Up close, his feet were veined like marble. His eyes were pale yellow as they regarded her. He sipped the tea, the plume of steam whipped away in the breeze.

Sorhatani settled herself, kneeling at his feet and looking up into his face.

'Thank you for sending me my son,' she said. 'It was a comfort to me to hear the worst from him.'

Ogedai looked away from her. He changed the cup from one hand to another as its heat burned his frozen flesh. He wondered if she knew how beautiful she was, kneeling with her back so straight and the wind snatching at her hair. It looked like a living thing and he watched in silence, mesmerised. Since his return to Karakorum, he had not spoken of Tolui's death. He could feel Sorhatani edging towards the subject and he shrank back physically on the low couch, cradling the cup as his only warmth. He could not explain the lassitude and weakness that beset his days. Months fled from him without his notice and the challenges of the khanate went unanswered. He could not rouse himself from the dim dawns and sunsets. He waited for death and cursed its slowness in coming.

Sorhatani could hardly believe the changes in Ogedai. He had left Karakorum full of life, constantly drunk and laughing. Fresh from the triumph of becoming khan, he had gone with his elite tumans to secure the Chin borders, thriving on a difficult task in the field. Recalling those days was like looking back on youth. The man who had returned had aged visibly, deep wrinkles appearing on his forehead and around his eyes and mouth. The pale eyes no longer reminded her of Genghis. There was no spark there, no sense of danger in the quiet gaze. It would not do.

'My husband was in good health,' she said suddenly. 'He would have lived for many years, seen his sons grow into fine men. Perhaps he would have had other children, taken more wives. In time, he would have been a grandfather. I like to think of the joy he would have taken in those years.'

Ogedai shrank back as if she had attacked him, but she went on without hesitating, her voice firm and clear so that he could hear every word.

'He had a sense of duty that is too rare today, my lord khan. He believed the nation came before his health, his life. He believed in something greater than himself, or my happiness, or even the lives of his sons. Your father's vision, my lord, that a nation can spring from the tribes of the plains, that they can find a place of their own in the world. That they *deserve* such a place.'

'I . . . I have said that he . . .' Ogedai began.

Sorhatani interrupted him and, for an instant, anger showed in his eyes before it faded.

'He threw his future into the wind, but not just for you, my lord. He loved you, but it was not just for love. It was also for his father's will and dreams; do you understand?'

'Of course I understand,' Ogedai said wearily.

Sorhatani nodded, but went on. 'He gave you life, a second father to you. But not just for you. For those who come after you, in his father's line, for the nation to come, the warriors who are children yet, the children who will be born.'

He gestured with his hand, trying to fend off her words. 'I am tired now, Sorhatani. Perhaps it would be best . . .'

'And how did you use this most precious gift?' Sorhatani whispered. 'You send your wife away, you leave your chancellor to roam an empty palace. Your Guards are left to make trouble in the city on their own, untended. Two of them were hanged yesterday – did you know that? They murdered a butcher for a haunch of beef. Where is the breath of the khan on their necks, the sense that they are in the nation? Is it in this room, in this freezing wind, while you sit alone?'

'Sorhatani . . .'

'You will die here. They will find you stiff and cold. And Tolui's gift will have been thrown away. Tell me then how I will justify what he did for you.'

His face twisted, and in astonishment she saw that he was struggling not to weep. This was not Genghis, who would have sprung up in rage at her words. This was a broken man before her.

'I should not have let him do it,' Ogedai said. 'How long do I have? Months? Days? I cannot know.'

'What is this foolishness?' Sorhatani said, forgetting herself in her exasperation. 'You will live for forty years and be feared and loved throughout a huge nation. A million children will be born with your name, in your honour, if you leave this room and this weakness behind you.'

'You don't understand,' Ogedai said. Only two other men knew of the weakness that plagued him. If he told Sorhatani, he was risking it becoming common knowledge in the camps and tumans, yet they were alone and she knelt before him, her eyes wide in the gloom. He needed someone.

'My heart is weak,' he said, his voice just a breath. 'I truly do not know how long I have. I should not have let him sacrifice himself for me, but I was . . .' He stumbled over the words.

'Oh, my husband,' Sorhatani said to herself as she understood at last. A sudden upwelling of grief choked her. 'Oh, my love.'

She looked up at him, her eyes shining with tears. 'Did he know? Did Tolui know?'

'I think so,' Ogedai said, looking away.

He was not sure how to respond. He had learned that his shaman had discussed the weakness of his body with his brother and uncle, but he had not asked Tolui himself. Having surfaced from a dark river, choking and gasping back to life, Ogedai had grasped at anything offered to him. At that time, he would have done anything, just for a day in the light. Now, it was hard to remember that yearning for life, as if it had been someone else The cold room with its billowing silk jarred somehow with the memories. He looked around him, blinking like one awakening from sleep.

'If he knew, it was an even greater sacrifice,' she said. 'And even more reason why you must not waste another day of it.

232

If he can see you now, Ogedai, will he consider he gave his life for something worthwhile? Or will he be ashamed of you?'

Ogedai felt a stab of anger at her words.

'You dare to speak to me in such a way?' he demanded.

He had stopped blinking like a day-old lamb. The gaze he fixed on her had a touch of the old khan in it. Sorhatani welcomed it, though she still reeled at what she had heard. If Ogedai died, who would lead the nation? The answer followed on the question, without a pause. Chagatai would be back in Karakorum in just days, riding in triumph to accept the beneficent will of the sky father. She ground her teeth at the very thought of his pleasure.

'Get up,' she said. 'Get up, my lord. If you do not have long, there is still much to do. You must not waste another day, another morning! Take hold of your life with both hands and crush it to you, my lord. You will not have another in this world.'

He began to speak and she reached out and pulled his head towards her, kissing him hard on the mouth. His breath and lips were cool with the scent of tea. When she released him, he lurched backwards, then came to his feet, staring incredulously at her.

'What was that?' he said. 'I have enough wives, Sorhatani.'

'That was to see if you were still alive, my lord. My husband gave his life for these precious days, no matter how long or short they are. In his name, will you trust me?'

He was still dazed, she knew it. She had awoken some part of him, but the fog of despair, perhaps of the Chin drugs, was still weighing heavily, dulling his wits. Yet she saw a gleam of interest in his eyes as he looked at her kneeling before him. He summoned his will like a stick borne aloft on a flood, visible for an instant before vanishing into the depths.

'No, Sorhatani, I don't trust you.'

She smiled. 'That is to be expected, my lord. But you will learn I am on your side.'

She rose and closed the windows, shutting out the moaning wind at last.

'I will call your servants, lord. You will feel better when you have eaten proper food.'

He stared at her as she yelled for Baras'aghur, snapping instructions to the man in a torrent. Baras looked to Ogedai over her shoulder, but the khan just shrugged and acquiesced. It was a relief to have someone else who knew what he needed. The thought sparked another.

'I should have my wife and daughters brought back to the palace, Sorhatani. They are at the summer house on the Orkhon.'

Sorhatani considered for a moment.

'You are still unwell, my lord. I think I should wait a few days before restoring your family and servants. We will take it slowly.'

For a short time, she would be the only one with the ear of the khan. With his seal, she could have her son Mongke join Tsubodai on the great trek, where the future was being written. She was not ready to throw that influence away so quickly.

Ogedai nodded, unable to resist her.

CHAPTER EIGHTEEN

The ground was covered in autumn frost and the horses snorted white mist as Mongke rode past yet another pair of Tsubodai's scouts, He was already in awe of the general, but nothing had prepared him for taking ten thousand warriors through the man's trail of destruction. From beyond the Volga river, for hundreds of miles west, towns and villages had been looted or destroyed. He had passed the site of three major battles, still marked with a host of birds and small animals made bold at the presence of so much rotting flesh. The odour seemed to have seeped into him, so that Mongke could smell it on every breeze.

He saw scouts galloping ahead of him for days before he caught sight of the main Mongol army. It had spent the summer in an encampment equal to Karakorum as it had been before the khan's city was built. It was a host of white gers, a peaceful scene of morning fires and vast herds of horses in the distance. Mongke shook his head in silent wonder as he trotted closer.

His banners had been recognised, of course, but still Tsubodai sent a minghaan out to meet him before the tuman was in striking distance of the main camp. Mongke accepted the silent scrutiny of the orlok's men. He recognised their officer and saw the man nod to himself. Mongke knew then that Tsubodai had sent a man who could confirm his identity by sight. He watched with fascination as the officer gestured to a companion who raised a long brass tube to his lips. The note blared out and Mongke looked around in astonishment as it was answered to the left and right. Horses and men appeared less than a mile away on both sides. Tsubodai had sent out a flanking force to contain him, lying with their horses concealed in trees and behind a ridge of ground. It went some way to explain how the ice general had fought his way so far from home.

By the time they reached the main camp, a space had been cleared, a vast empty field with access to a small river. Mongke was nervous.

'Show them the cold face,' he said quietly to himself.

As his tuman fell into the routines of the camp and began to set up gers with quick efficiency, Mongke dismounted. His ten thousand and the horses they brought needed land the size of a large town just to rest. Tsubodai had prepared for their arrival.

He turned sharply at a cry of pleasure to see his uncle Kachiun walking over the torn grass. He looked much older than when Mongke had last seen him and he limped heavily. Mongke watched him with a guarded expression, but gripped his hand when Kachiun held it out.

'I have been waiting for days to see you,' Kachiun said. 'Tsubodai will want to hear news of home this evening. You are invited to his ger as a guest. You will have fresh information.' He smiled at the young man his nephew had become. 'I understand your mother has sources our scouts can't match.'

236

Mongke tried to hide his confusion. Karakorum was three thousand miles to the east. It had taken him four months of hard travel to reach the general. There had been times over the previous month when Tsubodai was moving so fast he thought he would never catch up with him. If the general had not stopped for a season to refresh his herds and men, Mongke would still have been travelling. Yet Kachiun spoke as if Karakorum was just over the next valley.

'You are well informed, uncle,' Mongke said after a pause. 'I do have a number of letters from home.'

'Anything for me?'

'Yes, uncle. I have letters from two of your wives as well as the khan.'

'Excellent, I'll take those now then.'

Kachiun rubbed his hands together in anticipation and Mongke suppressed a smile as he realised it was the main reason for his uncle coming to greet him in such a way. Perhaps they were not too busy to want fresh news of home. He crossed to his pony as it munched on ice-rimed grass and he opened the saddlebags, pulling out a sheaf of greasy yellow parchments.

Kachiun looked around him as Mongke sorted through them.

'You would not have brought your father's tuman to protect letters, Mongke. You are staying then?'

Mongke thought of the efforts his mother had made to have Ogedai assign her oldest son to this army. She believed that the future of the nation lay in the battle honours he could win there, that whoever returned from the sweep west would have a hand on the reins of fate. He wondered if she was correct.

'With the permission of Orlok Tsubodai, yes,' he said, handing over the letters marked for his uncle.

Kachiun smiled as he took them and clapped his nephew

on the shoulder. 'You are dusty and tired, I see. Rest and eat while your gers are constructed. I will see you tonight.'

Both Mongke and Kachiun looked up as another rider came trotting across the camp towards them.

Men covered the entire valley floor, the camp and its smoky fires stretching away as far as Mongke could see. With the constant need for water, food, wood, toilet pits and the thousand details of simply living, it was a place of constant bustle and movement. Children ran around, yelling and pretending to be warriors. Women watched them indulgently while they worked at a thousand different tasks. Real warriors trained or just stood guard over the herds.

Through them all, Tsubodai rode with his eyes fixed on Mongke, his pace brisk. He wore a new set of scale armour, clean and well oiled, so that it moved easily with him. His horse was copper-brown, almost red in the sunlight. The orlok looked neither left nor right as he rode.

It was an effort for Mongke to hold his gaze. He saw Tsubodai frown slightly, and then the general dug in his heels and increased his speed, bringing the pony up quickly so that it stood blowing and pawing the ground.

'You are welcome in my camp, general,' Tsubodai said, giving Mongke his official title with no hesitation.

Mongke bowed calmly. He was aware that he owned the rank only because his mother seemed to have a hold on the khan. Yet his father's sacrifice had raised the son and that was only right. He had ridden in war against the Chin. He would do better with Tsubodai, he was certain.

As if in echo of his thoughts, Tsubodai looked over the tuman from Karakorum.

'I was sorry to hear of your father's death,' Tsubodai said. 'He was a fine man. We can certainly use you here.' The orlok was obviously pleased at the sight of so many additional warriors. It brought his tumans up to six, with almost as many again in his auxiliaries. Surely the sky father smiled on this campaign.

'You have a month or two yet before we move,' Tsubodai went on. 'We must wait for the rivers to freeze solid. After that, we will ride against the city of Moscow.'

'In winter?' Mongke said, before he could stop himself. To his relief, Tsubodai only chuckled.

'Winter is *our* time. They shut up their cities for the cold months. They put their horses in stables and sit around great fires in enormous houses of stone. If you want a bearskin, do you attack in summer when it is strong and fast, or cut its throat as it sleeps? We can stand the cold, Mongke. I took Riazan and Kolomna in winter. Your men will join the patrols and training immediately. It will keep them busy.'

Tsubodai nodded to Kachiun, who bowed as the orlok clicked in his cheek and trotted the red horse away.

'He is . . . impressive,' Mongke said. 'I am in the right place, I think.'

'Of course you are,' Kachiun said. 'It is incredible, Mongke. Only your grandfather had his touch on campaign. There are times when I think he must be possessed of some warlike spirit. He *knows* what they will do. Last month, he sent me to the middle of nowhere to wait. I was there just two days when a force came galloping over the hill, three thousand armoured knights riding to relieve Novgorod.' He smiled in memory. 'Where else would you rather be? Safe at home? You were right to come out here. We have one chance to knock the world back on its heels, Mongke. If we can do it, there will be centuries of peace. If not, everything your grandfather built will be ashes in just a generation. Those are the stakes, Mongke. This time, we will not stop until we reach the sea. I swear, if Tsubodai can find a way to put horses on ships, perhaps not even then!'

*   *   *

239

Chagatai rode along the cliffs of Bamiyan with his eldest son, Baidur. North-west of Kabul, the red-brown crags ran outside the lands granted him by Ogedai, but then his family had never truly recognised borders. He grinned at the thought, pleased to be riding in the fading heat, in the shadow of dark peaks. The town of Bamiyan was an ancient place, the houses built of the same dun stone that formed its backdrop. It had suffered conquerors and armies before, but Chagatai had no quarrel with the farmers there. He and his men patrolled areas outside the Amu Darya river, but there was no cause to leave the villages and towns as smoking ruins.

With the khan's shadow stretching over them, they were actually thriving. Thousands of migrant families had come to live in the lands around his khanate, knowing that no one would dare move an army in reach of Samarkand or Kabul. Chagatai had made his authority clear in the first two years, as he took control of an area populated by wild bandits and aggressive local tribes. Most were slaughtered, the rest driven away like goats to take word to those who did not hear. The message had not been lost and many of the townspeople believed that Genghis himself had returned. Chagatai's men had not bothered to correct the error.

Baidur was already tall, with the pale yellow eyes that marked the line from the great khan, ensuring instant obedience among those who had known Genghis. Chagatai watched him closely as he guided his mare across broken ground. It was a different world, Chagatai thought, a little ruefully. At Baidur's age, he had been locked in a struggle with his older brother, Jochi, neither willing to give up the prospect of being khan after their father. It was a bitter-sweet memory. Chagatai would never forget the day when their father had denied them both and made Ogedai his heir.

The air had been baked all day, but as the sun sank, it grew cooler and Chagatai could relax and enjoy the sights and sounds around him. His khanate was a huge area, larger even than the homeland. It had been won by Genghis, but Chagatai would not scorn the gift of his brother. The cliffs were looming closer and he saw Baidur look back at him to see where he wanted to go.

'To the foot of the cliffs,' he said. 'I want you to see a wonder.'

Baidur smiled and Chagatai felt a burst of affection and pride. Had his own father ever felt such an emotion? He did not know. For a moment, he almost wished Jochi alive so he could tell him how different things were, how his world had grown larger than the small inheritance they had fought over. The horizons were wide enough for them all, he realised now, but the wisdom of age is bitter when those you have failed have gone. He could not bring back the years of his youth and live them with greater understanding. How impatient he had been once, how foolish! He had vowed many times not to make the same mistakes with his own sons, but they too would have to find their path. He thought then of another son of his, killed in a raid by some ragged tribesmen. It had just been his bad luck that he had come across them as they camped. Chagatai had made them suffer for the death of that boy. His grief swelled and vanished just as quickly. There had always been death in his life. Yet somehow Chagatai survived where other, perhaps better, men had fallen. His was a lucky line.

At the base of the cliffs, Chagatai could see hundreds of dark spots. From his previous trips, he knew they were caves, some natural, but most hewn from the rock by those who preferred the cool refuges to a brick-built house on the plain. The brigand he sought that day had his base in those caves. Some of them went back into the earth for a great distance, but Chagatai did not think it would be too hard a task. The tuman that rode at his back had brought enough firewood to bank at the entrance to every cave, smoking them out like wild bees from their nest.

In among the dark fingernail smudges of the cave mouths,

241

two fingers of shadow rose above them, immense alcoves cut into the rock. Baidur's sharp eyes picked them out from a mile away and he pointed excitedly, looking to his father for an answer. Chagatai smiled at him in response and shrugged, though he knew very well what they were. It was one reason he had brought his son out on the raid. The dark shapes grew before them as they came closer, until Baidur reined in his mare at the foot of the largest of the pair. The young man was awestruck as his eyes made out the shape inside the cliff.

It was a huge statue, larger than any man-made thing Baidur had ever seen before. The drapes of robes could be seen cut into the brown stone. One hand was held up with an open palm, the other outstretched as if in offering. Its partner was only slightly smaller: two smiling figures looking out onto the fading sun.

'Who made them?' Baidur asked in wonder. He would have walked even closer, but Chagatai clicked his tongue to stop him. The cave-dwellers were sharp-sighted and good with a bow. It would not do to tempt them with his son.

'They are statues of the Buddha, some deity of the Chin,' he said.

'Out here? The Chin are far away,' Baidur responded. His hands opened and closed as he stood there, obviously wanting to walk up and touch the enormous figures.

'The beliefs of men know no borders, my son,' Chagatai said. 'There are Christians and Moslems in Karakorum, after all. The khan's own chancellor is one of these Buddhists.'

'I cannot see how statues could be moved . . . no, they were cut here, the rock removed around them,' Baidur said.

Chagatai nodded, pleased at his son's sharp wits. The statues had been chiselled out of the mountains themselves, revealed with painstaking labour.

'According to the local men, they have stood here as long as anyone can remember. Perhaps even for thousands of years.

There is another one in the hills, a huge figure of a man lying down.'

Chagatai felt an odd pride, as if he were somehow responsible for them himself. His son's simple pleasure was a joy to him.

'Why did you want me to see them?' Baidur asked. 'I am grateful – they are . . . astonishing – but why have you shown them to me?'

Chagatai stroked the soft muzzle of his mare, gathering his thoughts.

'Because my father did not believe in building a future,' he said. 'He used to say there was no better way for a man to spend his life than in war with his enemies. The spoils and land and gold you have seen came almost by accident from those beliefs. He never sought them for themselves. Yet here is proof, Baidur. What we build can last and be remembered, perhaps for a thousand generations to come.'

'I understand,' Baidur said softly.

Chagatai nodded. 'Today, we will smoke out the thieves and brigands who inhabit the caves. I could have hammered the cliffs with catapults. In months or years, I could have reduced them to rubble, but I chose not to because of those statues. They remind me that what we make can survive us.'

As the sun set, father and son stood and watched the shadows move across the faces of the huge stone figures. Behind them, minghaan officers shouted and whistled to their men until the khan's ger was up and the fires lit for the evening meal. The men in the caves would wait another night. Some of them would escape in the darkness, perhaps, though Chagatai had warriors hidden on the other side, waiting for anyone who tried.

As they sat down to eat, Chagatai watched as Baidur crossed his legs and took salt tea in his right hand, the left cupping the elbow automatically. He was a fine young warrior, coming into his prime years.

Chagatai accepted his tea and a plate heaped with pouches of unleavened bread and mutton, well spiced and fragrant.

'I hope you understand now why I must send you away, my son,' he said at last.

Baidur stopped chewing and Chagatai went on.

'This is a beautiful land, ripe and rich. A man could ride all day here. But this is not where the nation will make its history. There is no struggle here, even if you count a few rebels and cattle thieves. No, the future is being written in the sweep west, Baidur. You must be part of that.'

His son did not reply, his eyes dark in the gloom. Chagatai nodded, pleased that he did not waste words. He reached into his deel robe and withdrew a sheaf of bound parchments.

'I sent messages to the khan, my brother, asking that you be allowed to join Tsubodai. He has given me that permission. You will take my first tuman as your own and learn all you can from Tsubodai. He and I have not always fought on the same side, but there is no better teacher. In years to come, the fact that you knew the orlok will be worth much in the eyes of men.'

Baidur swallowed his mouthful with difficulty, bowing his head. It was his greatest wish and he did not know how his father had understood. Loyalty had kept him in the khanate, but his heart had been with the great trek, thousands of miles west and north. He was overcome with gratitude.

'You honour me,' he said, his voice tight.

Chagatai chuckled and reached over to ruffle his son's hair. 'Ride fast, boy. If I know Tsubodai, he will not slow down for anyone.'

'I thought you might send me to Karakorum,' Baidur said.

His father shook his head, his face suddenly bitter.

'There is no future being written there. Trust me in this. It is a place of stagnant water, where nothing moves and no life stirs. No, the future is in the west.'

CHAPTER NINETEEN

The wind moaned and then whispered like a living thing, biting into their lungs as they breathed. Snow fell constantly, though it could not obscure the path. Tsubodai and his men walked their horses along the line of the frozen Moskva river beneath them. The ice was like bone; white and dead in the dark. The city of Moscow lay ahead, its cathedrals and churches rising high on the horizon. Even in the darkness, lights gleamed behind wooden shutters in the walls: thousands of candles lit to celebrate the nativity of Christ. Much of the city was shuttered and closed for the heart of winter, the terrible cold that stole away the old and the weak.

The Mongols trudged on, heads down, hooves and reins muffled in cloth. The river they walked ran right through the centre of the city. It was too wide to guard or block, a natural weakness. Many of the warriors looked up as they passed under a bridge of wood and stone, spanning the icy road in arches that were anchored in huge columns. There was no outcry from the bridge itself. The city nobles had not considered any invading army could be insane enough to walk the ice into their midst.

Only two tumans followed the course of the river into Moscow. Batu and Mongke roamed to the south, raiding towns and making certain there were no forces on their way to intercept the Mongol armies. Guyuk and Kachiun were further north, preventing a relief army from force-marching to save the city. It was not likely. The tumans seemed to be the only ones willing to move in the coldest months. The chilled air was brutal. The cold numbed their faces, hands and feet, leaching away their strength. Yet they endured. Many of them wore deel robes as cloaks over their armour. They slathered thick mutton fat on exposed skin and wrapped themselves in layers of silk and wool and iron, their feet frozen despite the lambswool stuffed into their boots. Many of them would lose toes, even so. Their lips were already raw, gummed shut with frozen spit. Yet they survived, and when the rations ran short, they took blood from their mounts, filling their mouths with the hot liquid that could sustain them. The ponies were thin, though they knew to dig through the snow to crop frozen grass beneath. They too had been bred in a harsh land.

Tsubodai's scouts moved faster than the main force, risking their mounts on the icy ground to bring back the first warning of any organised defences. The city seemed eerily silent, the snow lending such a stillness to the air that Tsubodai could hear hymns being sung. He did not know the language, but the distant voices seemed to suit the cold. He shook his head. The ice road was strangely beautiful in the shadows and moonlight, but it was no place for sentiment. His aim was to crush anyone with the strength to stand before him. Only then could he move on, knowing his flanks and rear were safe.

The city itself was not large. Its cathedrals had been built on high ground above the river, and around them clustered the houses of churchmen and wealthy families. In the moon-light, they could be seen spreading down the hills into a town of smaller buildings, haphazard across the landscape. The river fed them all, gave them life as it would now bring death. Tsubodai's head jerked up as he heard a voice call nearby, high and broken. The panic was unmistakable. They had been seen at last. He was only surprised it had taken so long. The voice yelled and yelled, then was choked off as one of the scouts riding along the banks used the sound to guide himself in. There would be bright red blood on the snow, the first of the night. Yet the watcher had been heard and it was not long before bells began to sound in the distance, tolling a warning through the still darkness.

The cathedral was silent, the air heavy with incense issuing from the censer in a trail of white smoke. Grand Duke Yaroslav sat with his family in the pews reserved for him, his head bowed as he listened to the plainsong words of a prayer written eight centuries before.

'If He was not flesh, who was laid in a manger? If He is not God, whom did the angels who came down from heaven glorify?'

The duke was not at peace, no matter how he tried to put the cares of the world aside and take comfort from his faith. Who could know where the damned Mongols would strike next? They moved with incredible speed, making children of the armies he had sent. Three thousand of his finest knights had been slaughtered at the beginning of winter. They had ridden out to find the Mongol army and report their pos-ition, not to engage them. They had not come back. All he had were rumours of a bloody streak in the hills, already covered in snow.

Duke Yaroslav twisted his hands together as the heavy incense filled his lungs.

247

'If He was not flesh, whom did John baptise?' Father Dmitri intoned, his voice strong and resonant in the echoing church.

The benches were full and not just to celebrate the birth of Christ. Yaroslav wondered how many of them had heard of the red-mouthed wolf hunting through the hills and snow. The cathedral was a place of light and safety, though it was cold enough to need the heavy furs. Where better to come on such a night?

'If He is not God, to whom did the Father say: This is my beloved Son?'

The words were comforting, summoning an image of the young Christ. On such a night, Yaroslav knew he should be focusing his thoughts on birth and rebirth, but instead he thought of crucifixion, of pain and agony in a garden, more than a thousand years before.

His wife's hand touched his arm and he realised he had been sitting with his eyes closed, silently rocking like the old ladies at prayer. He had to keep up a calm front, with so many eyes watching. They looked to him to protect them, but he felt helpless, lost. Winter did not stop the Mongol armies. If his brothers and cousins had trusted him, he could have put a force in the field to destroy the invaders, but instead they thought he schemed for power and ignored his letters and messengers. To be surrounded by such fools! It was hard to find peace, even on such a night.

'If He was not flesh, who was invited to the marriage in Cana? If He is not God, who turned the water into wine?'

The priest's voice echoed, rolling in a rhythm of its own that should have been comforting. They would not read the darker verses on the night of Christ's birth. Yaroslav did not know if the Mongol host would attack his cities of Vladimir and Moscow. Would they reach even Kiev? It was not so many years since they had struck so deep into the forests and tundra, killing at will and then vanishing again. There were many stories and legends of the fearsome 'Tartars'. It was all they had left behind the last time. Like a storm, they had struck and then vanished.

He had nothing that could stop them. Yaroslav began to wring his hands again, praying with all his heart that his city, his family might be spared. God had mercy, he knew. The Mongols had none.

Far away, thin shouts could be heard. The duke looked up. His wife was staring at him, her expression confused. He turned at the sound of running feet. Surely he would not be called out at this hour? Could his officers not handle one night without him, while he found solace in the Mother Church? He did not want to rise from the hard-won warmth of his seat. As he hesitated, more running steps could be heard as someone raced up the stairs to the bell tower. Yaroslav's stomach clenched in sudden terror. No, not here, not this night.

The bell began to toll above his head. Half the congregation looked up as if they could see it through the wooden beams. Yaroslav saw Father Dmitri walking towards him and stood quickly, struggling to master his fear. Before the priest could reach him, he bent down and spoke into his wife's ear.

'Take the children now. Take the carriage to the barracks, for your life. Find Konstantin; he will be there, with my horses. Get out of the city. I will come when I can.'

His wife was white-faced with terror, but she did not hesitate as she gathered his daughters and sons, herding them like sleepy geese. Duke Yaroslav was already moving, leaving his pew and striding down the central aisle. All eyes were on him as Father Dmitri caught up with the duke and dared to take his arm. The priest's voice was a harsh whisper.

'Is it an attack? The Tartars? Can you hold the city?'

Duke Yaroslav stopped suddenly, so that the elderly man stumbled into him. On another night, he might have had the priest whipped for his insolence. Yet he would not lie in the presence of the born Christ.

'If they are here, I cannot hold them, father, no. Look to your flock. I must save my own family.'

The priest fell back as if he had been struck, his mouth open in horror. Above their heads, the bell tolled on, calling despair across the city and the snow.

The duke could hear screaming in the distance as he raced outside, his riding boots skidding on the icy cobbles. His family's coach was already moving, a black shape slipping into the darkness with the driver's whip-crack echoing on either side. He could hear his son's high voice fading into the distance, unaware of the danger as only a child can be.

Snow had begun to fall again and Yaroslav shivered as he stood there, his mind racing. For months he had heard reports of the Mongol atrocities. The city of Riazan had been reduced to smoking rubble, with wild animals tearing at bodies in the streets. He had ridden there himself with just a few of his guards and two of them had vomited into the snow at what they saw. They had been hard men, used to death, but what they had encountered was utter desolation, on a scale they had never known. This was an enemy with no concept of honour, who fought wars and destroyed cities to crush the will of an enemy. The duke stepped towards the snorting mount of his aide. It was a stallion, uncut, fast and black as night.

'Dismount,' he snapped. 'Return to the barracks on foot.'

'Yes, your grace,' the man said immediately, swinging his leg over and jumping down to the snow.

As the duke mounted in his place, finding the saddle still warm, the aide stood back and saluted. Yaroslav didn't look at him, already turning the animal and digging in his heels. The hooves clattered on the stone road as he trotted away. He could not gallop on the ice without risking a fall that could kill both him and the horse. He heard shouting voices nearby and then a single clash of steel on steel, a sword blow that carried in the frozen air from God alone knew how far away.

Around him, the sleeping city was waking up. Candles and lamps appeared in the windows and swung in the hands of men as they came out to stand in the street and shout questions to each other. None of them knew anything. More than once, they stumbled and fell as they tried to avoid the black horse and its rider.

The barracks were not far away. He half-expected to see his family's coach up ahead. The driver could force his horses to more speed, held steady by the weight of the carriage and those within. Duke Yaroslav prayed under his breath, asking the innocent virgin to take care of his little ones. He could not hold the city against the wolves that came in the snow. All he could do was escape. He told himself it was the correct tactical decision, but the shame of it burned him even against the cold.

As he rode, he ignored the voices calling behind him. There would be few survivors, not now the enemy had come in the depths of winter. No one could have expected it, he told himself. He had gathered his main army near Kiev, ready for the spring. They sat in a winter camp behind vast wooden palisades, almost three hundred miles to the south-west. He had just two thousand men in Moscow and they were not his best troops. Many were injured soldiers wintering in the comfort of the city rather than the army camps, where dysentery and cholera were a constant threat. The duke hardened his heart to their fate. They had to fight, to give him time to get free. He could only hope that the Mongol army had not yet blocked the roads out of the city. One of them must still be open, for his family.

Moonlight gleamed through the falling snow above him as he crossed a wooden bridge, the frozen Moskva river below. He glanced at it as he clattered over the ancient wood and stiffened in the saddle at the sight of the white river covered with horses and men. They were already spreading onto the banks like spilt blood, black in the night. He could hear more screaming as they tore into homes near the river. He put his head down and rode on, drawing the ornate dress sword on his hip. In terror, he saw dark figures clambering over the wooden bridge railings: two, no four, men. They had heard his horse, and as he saw them, something buzzed by his face, too fast even to flinch from it. He hoped the black horse made a difficult target and dug in his heels again, suddenly heedless of the slippery ground. A man loomed up on his right flank and Yaroslav kicked, feeling a spike of pain up his leg as the impact twisted his knee. The man fell away in silence, his chest crushed from the blow. The duke was through then, the white road opening before him as the bridge came to an end.

He felt the arrow strike as a shudder in his mount. The animal whinnied in pain, snorting harder and harder with every step. The gallop slowed and Yaroslav kicked and leaned forward, trying for the last burst of speed. His hands had held reins from a young age and he could almost feel the life drain out of the stallion as it struggled on, panic and duty keeping it going. He rounded a corner, leaving the bridge behind, but the animal's great heart could take him no further. The stallion went down hard, without warning, the front legs collapsing. Yaroslav tumbled, tucking in his head and trying to roll as he hit. Even with the snow, the ground was like iron and he lay winded and stunned, knowing he had somehow to regain his feet before they came looking. Dazed and helpless, he struggled up, wincing as his knee crackled and shifted under him. He would not cry out. He could hear their guttural voices just around the corner.

He began to stagger away, more from instinct than with any sense of purpose. His knee was on fire and when he reached down to it, he bit his lip to stop a shout of pain. It was already swelling. How far was the barracks? Walking had become agony and he could only shuffle on the bad leg. His eyes filled with unwanted tears as he was forced to put his weight on it, lurching over it with each step and beginning again. If anything, the pain worsened until he thought he might pass out in the snow. Surely he could not endure much longer? He reached another corner and behind him he heard the voices grow louder. They had found the horse.

The duke had seen the burnt dead in Riazan. He forced himself to go faster for a few steps, but then his leg crumpled as if he had no control over it. He hit the ground hard and bit his tongue, feeling sour blood fill his mouth.

Weak and still dazed, he turned over and spat. He could not kneel to gasp and recover. His knee was still too painful even to touch. Instead, he reached out to a wall and dragged himself up with his arms. At any moment, he expected to hear running footsteps as the Mongol animals caught him, drawn by the scent of blood perhaps. Yaroslav turned to face them, knowing he could run no longer.

From the deep shadows by the wall of a house, he saw a group of Mongols on foot, leading their horses as they followed his tracks. He groaned at the sight. The snow was still falling, but his prints would be visible for another hour, more. They had not yet seen him, but a child could follow that path. He looked around desperately for some bolt-hole, painfully aware that all his soldiers were at the barracks. His family would already be on the road west and south to Kiev. If he knew Konstantin, the grizzled old soldier would send a hundred of the best men and horses with them.

Yaroslav did not know if the rest would stay and fight or simply melt away into the darkness, leaving the citizens to their fate. He could already smell smoke on the air, but he could not drag his gaze from the men hunting him. In his delirium, he thought he had come further, but they were no more than fifty or sixty paces away. They were already pointing in his direction.

A rider came trotting down the road from the bridge. Yaroslav saw the men straighten from where they stared at his tracks. To his eyes, they looked like dogs faced with a wolf and they stood with their heads down. The man snapped orders at them and three of the four immediately began to move. The last one stared into the shadows that hid the duke as if he could see him. Yaroslav held his breath until his senses swam. Finally, the last man nodded grimly and mounted his pony, turning the animal back to the bridge.

The duke watched them go with mixed emotions. He could hardly believe he would live, but at the same time he had discovered the Mongols had discipline, ranks and tactics. Someone higher up had told them to take and hold the bridge. The brief chase had dragged them away, but the structure of some sort of regular army had found them and dragged them back. He had survived, but he had yet to face them in the field and the task ahead had suddenly become a great deal harder.

He staggered as he set off again, the pain making him swear under his breath. He knew the street of weavers. The barracks was not too far away. He could only pray there was someone still there waiting for him.

Tsubodai stood alone in a stone tower, looking out over the frozen city. To reach the window, he had inched past a massive bronze bell, dark green with age. As he stared across the night, parts of it were lit by flames, spots of gold and flickering yellow. He drummed his fingers on the engraved surface of the bell, listening idly to the deep tone that went on for a long time.

The vantage point suited him perfectly. In the light of distant flames, he could see the result of his sudden strike along the ice road. Below him, Mongol warriors were already running wild. He could hear their laughter as they tore silk hangings from the walls and threw goblets and chalices across the stone floors, unimaginably ancient. There was screaming below, as well as laughter.

There had been little resistance. What soldiers there were had been slaughtered quickly as the Mongols spread through the streets. The conquering of a city was always bloody. The men received no gold or silver from Tsubodai or their generals. Instead, they expected to loot and take slaves wherever he led them. It made them hungry as they stared at city walls, but when they were inside, his officers had to stand back.

Not one of them could control the minghaans after that. It was their right to hunt women and men through the streets, drunk on wine and violence. It offended Tsubodai's senses to see the warriors reduced to such a state. As a commander, he had to keep a few minghaans sober in case a counter-attack appeared, or a new enemy hove into view in the morning. The tumans had drawn lots for those unlucky ones who would stand and shiver all night, listening to the screams and revelry and wishing they were allowed to join in.

Tsubodai thinned his lips in irritation. The city had to burn, he had no qualms about that. He cared nothing for the fate of the citizens within. They were not his people. Still, it seemed . . . wasteful, undignified. It offended his sense of order to have his tumans run riot the moment a city wall fell. He smiled wearily at the thought of how they would respond if he offered them regular pay and salt instead of loot. Genghis had once told him he should never give an order they would not obey. He should never let them see the limits of his authority. The truth was that he *could* have called them back from the city. They would form up at his order, dropping everything, drunk or sober, to ride back. They would certainly do it once. Just once.

He heard raucous laughter coming closer. A woman's voice whimpered and he blew air out in irritation as he realised the men were coming up the steps. In just moments, he saw two

255

of his warriors dragging a young woman as they looked for a quiet place. The first one froze as he saw the orlok, standing at the bell-tower window of the cathedral. The warrior was roaring drunk, but Tsubodai's gaze had a way of cutting through the fog. Caught by surprise, the man tried to bow on the steps and stumbled. His companion behind him called out an insult.

'I will leave you in peace, orlok,' the warrior said, slurring and dipping his head. His companion heard and fell silent, but the woman continued to struggle.

Tsubodai turned his gaze on her and frowned. Her clothes were well made, of good materials. She was the daughter of some wealthy family, probably already killed before her. Her dark brown hair had been bound in a silver clasp but it had torn half-free, so it hung in long tresses, swinging as she tried to pull away from the grip of the warriors. She looked at Tsubodai and he saw her terror. He almost turned and let them retreat. The warriors were not so drunk that they would dare move until he dismissed them. He had no living children himself, no daughters.

'Leave her here,' Tsubodai snapped, surprising himself even as he spoke. He was the ice general, the man without emotion. He understood the weaknesses of others, he did not share them. Yet the cathedral was beautiful in its way, with great fluted arches of stone that appealed to him. He told himself it was those things that touched his sensibilities, not the girl's animal panic.

The warriors let go of her and vanished back down the steps at a great pace, pleased to get away without a punishment or extra duties. As the clatter of their boots faded, Tsubodai turned again to look out over the city. There were more fires by then and parts of Moscow glowed red with flame. By morning, much of it would be ashes, the stones so hot they would crack and burst apart in the walls.

He heard her panting and the slight scrape as she sank down the wall.

'Can you understand me?' he asked in the Chin tongue, turning.

She looked blankly at him and he sighed. The Russian language had little in common with either of the tongues he knew. He had picked up a few words, but nothing that would let her know she was safe. She stared at him and he wondered how a father would feel in such a position. She knew she could not escape back down the stairs. Violent, drunken men roamed the church and streets around it. She would not get far. It was quieter in the bell tower and Tsubodai sighed as she began to sob softly to herself, bringing her knees up to her chest and keening like a child.

'Be silent,' he snapped, suddenly irritated with her for spoiling his moment of peace. She had lost her shoes somewhere, he noticed. Her feet were scratched and bare. She had fallen silent at his tone and he watched her for a while until she looked up at him. He held up his hands, showing they were empty.

'Menya zavout Tsubodai,' he said slowly, pointing at his chest. He could not ask her name. He waited patiently and she lost some of her tension.

'Anya,' she said. A torrent of sound followed that Tsubodai could not follow. He had all but exhausted his stock of words.

In his own language, he went on. 'Stay here,' he said, gesturing. 'You are safe here. I will go now.'

He began to walk past her and at first she flinched. When she realised he was trying to step past onto the stone steps, she cried out in fear and spoke again, her eyes wide.

Tsubodai sighed to himself. 'All right. I will stay. Tsubodai stay. Until the sun comes up, understand? Then I will leave. The soldiers will leave. You can find your family then.'

She saw he was turning back to the window. Nervously, she crept further into the room so that she sat at his feet.

'Genghis Khan,' Tsubodai muttered. 'Have you heard the name?'

He saw her eyes widen and nodded to himself. A rare bitterness showed in his expression.

'They will talk of him for a thousand years, Anya. Longer. Yet Tsubodai is unknown. The man who won his battles for him, who followed his orders. The name of Tsubodai is just smoke on the breeze.'

She could not understand him, but his voice was soothing and she pulled her legs in tighter, making herself small against his feet.

'He is dead now, girl. Gone. I am left to atone for my sins. You Christians understand that, I think.'

She looked blankly at him and her lack of understanding freed words that were lodged deep in his chest.

'My life is no longer my own,' Tsubodai said softly. 'My word is worthless. But duty goes on, Anya, while there is breath. It is all I have left.'

The air was frozen and he saw she was shivering. With a sigh, he removed his cloak and draped it over her. He watched as she curled into its folds until only her face showed. The cold intensified without the warm cloth around his shoulders, but he welcomed the discomfort. His spirits were in turmoil and sadness swelled in him as he rested his hands on the stone sill and waited for the dawn.

CHAPTER TWENTY

Yao Shu fumed as he faced Sorhatani. Even the air in the room was subtly scented as it had not been before. She wore her new status like heavy robes, taking delight in the number of servants attending her. Through Ogedai, she had been given the titles of her husband. At a single stroke, she controlled the heartlands of the Mongol plains, the birthplace of Genghis himself. Yao Shu could not help but wonder if the khan had considered all the implications when he made the offer to Tolui before his death.

Another woman would have quietly managed the lands and titles for her sons until she passed them on. Surely that was what Ogedai had intended. Yet Sorhatani had done more. Only that morning, Yao Shu had been forced to stamp and seal an order for funds from the khan's treasury. Tolui's personal seal had been used on the papers and, as chancellor, Yao Shu could not refuse it. Under his sour-faced glare, vast sums of gold and silver had been packed into wooden crates and delivered to her guards. He could only imagine what she would do with enough precious metal to build herself a palace or a village, or a road into the wilderness.

As Yao Shu sat in her presence, he ran a Buddhist mantra through his mind, bringing calm to his thoughts. She had granted him an audience as his superior, fully aware of how her manner irked the khan's chancellor. It was not lost on him that Ogedai's own servants scurried to serve them tea. No doubt Sorhatani had chosen ones he would know personally, to demonstrate her power.

Yao Shu remained silent as he was handed the shallow bowl. He sipped, noting the quality of Chin leaf that had been used. It was probably from the khan's personal supply, brought at immense cost from the tea plantations at Hangzhou. Yao Shu frowned to himself as he put the cup down. In just a few months, Sorhatani had made herself indispensable to the khan. Her energy was extraordinary, but Yao Shu could still be surprised at how deftly she had read the khan's needs. What was particularly galling was that Yao Shu had respected the orders he had been given. He had accepted Ogedai's need for privacy and seclusion. The chancellor had done nothing wrong, yet somehow she had bustled into the palace, wielding her sudden authority over servants as if she had been born to it. In less than a day, she had furnished and aired a suite of rooms close by Ogedai's own. The servants assumed the khan's approval and though Yao Shu suspected she had overreached his favour a hundred times over, Sorhatani had dug herself into the palace like a tick burrowing under skin. He watched her closely as she sipped her own tea. Her robe of fine green silk was not lost on him, nor the way her hair was bound in silver and her skin dusted with pale powder, so that she looked almost like porcelain, cool and perfect. The robes and manner of a Chin noblewoman were deliberately assumed, but she returned his gaze with the calm directness of her own people.

In itself, her stare was a challenge to him and he struggled not to respond.

'The tea is fresh, chancellor?' she asked.

He inclined his head. 'It is very good, but I must ask . . .'

'You are comfortable? Shall I have the servants bring a cushion for your back?'

Yao Shu rubbed one of his ears before settling himself again.

'I need no cushions, Sorhatani. What I need is an explanation of the orders that were delivered to my rooms last night.'

'Orders, chancellor? Surely such things are between you and the khan? It is certainly no business of mine.'

Her eyes were wide and guileless and he covered his irritation by signalling for more of the tea. He sipped the pungent liquid once more before trying again.

'As I'm sure you know, Sorhatani, the khan's Guards will not let me speak to him.'

It was a humiliating admission and he coloured as he spoke, wondering how she had come between Ogedai and the world with such neatness. All the men around the khan had respected his wishes. She had ignored them, treating Ogedai as if he were an invalid or a child. The gossip in the palace was that she doted on him like a mother hen with a chick, but instead of being irritated, Ogedai seemed to find relief in being cosseted. Yao Shu could only hope for his swift recovery, that he might throw the she-wolf out of the palace and rule again in earnest.

'If you wish, chancellor, I can ask the khan about the orders you say were sent to you. However, he has been unwell in spirit and body. Answers cannot be demanded from him until he is strong again.'

'I am aware of that, Sorhatani,' Yao Shu said. He clenched his teeth for an instant, so that she saw the muscles ripple in his jaw. 'Nonetheless, there has been some mistake. I do not think the khan wishes me to leave Karakorum for some

261

pointless tax-gathering tally in the northern Chin towns. I would be away from the city for months.'

'Still, if those are your orders,' she said, shrugging. 'We obey, Yao Shu, do we not?'

His suspicions hardened, though he could not see how she could have been the author of the command to send him away. It made him more determined to remain and challenge her control of the khan in his weakened state.

'I will send a colleague. I am needed here, in Karakorum.'

Sorhatani frowned delicately. 'You take great risks, chancellor. In the khan's state of health, it would not do to anger him with disobedience.'

'I do have other work, such as bringing the khan's wife back from the summer palace where she has languished these long months.'

It was Sorhatani's turn to look uncomfortable.

'He has not called for Torogene,' she said.

'She is not his servant,' he replied. 'She was most interested in your care of her husband. When she heard you were in such close contact, I am told she was keen to return and thank you personally.'

Sorhatani's eyes were cold as she regarded the chancellor, their mutual loathing barely hidden by the facade of manners and calm.

'You have spoken to her?'

'By letter, of course. I believe she will be arriving in just a few days.' In a moment of inspiration, he embroidered the truth a little for his benefit, playing the game. 'She has asked that I be here to receive her, so that she can be told all the latest news of the city. You see now why I cannot go haring off at such a time.'

Sorhatani bowed her head slightly, giving him the point.

'You have been . . . conscientious in your duties, I see,' she said. 'There is a great deal to do to welcome back the wife of the khan. I must thank you for letting me know in time.'

A tic had begun high on her forehead, evidence of internal strain. Yao Shu watched it in delight, knowing she felt his gaze on that spot. He chose his moment to add to her discomfort.

'For my own part, I would also have wanted to discuss the permission Ogedai gave for his nephew to travel to Tsubodai.'

'What?' Sorhatani said, shaken from her reverie. 'Mongke will not be an observer of the future, chancellor. He will help to shape it. It is right that my son is present as Tsubodai secures the west. Or should the orlok take all the credit for giving us a safe border?'

'I'm sorry, I did not mean your own son. I meant Baidur, the son of Chagatai. He too is following in Tsubodai's steps. Oh, I thought you would have heard.'

He tried not to smile as he spoke. For all her connections at the heart of the city, Sorhatani had no access to his network of spies and gossip-mongers stretching for thousands of miles in every direction, at least not yet. He watched as she mastered her surprise and her emotions settled. It was impressive control and he had to remind himself that her beauty hid sharper wits than most.

Yao Shu leaned forward so the servants around them could not easily overhear.

'If you are truly one who looks to the future, I am surprised you did not consider Baidur joining the great trek west. His father is next in line to be khan, after all.'

'After Ogedai's son, Guyuk,' Sorhatani snapped.

Yao Shu nodded. 'All being well, of course, but it was not so many years ago that these corridors and rooms were full of armed men contesting just such an event. May it never happen again. The princes are gathering, Sorhatani, with Tsubodai. If you are planning to have your sons reach for the khanate one day, you should be aware of the stakes involved. Guyuk, Batu and Baidur have as strong a claim as your own, don't you think?'

She glared at him as if he had raised a hand to her. He smiled and stood, the meeting at an end.

'I will leave you to your tea and fine things, Sorhatani. I have found such luxuries are fleeting, but do enjoy them for the moment.'

As he left her sitting in thought, he promised himself that he would be there to witness the khan's wife returning to Karakorum. It was one pleasure he would not deny himself after so many months of strain.

The soldiers stood and shivered in the shadow of the huge gate. Like the stockade around them, it was made of ancient black logs, lashed together with ropes that became brittle in the winter cold. There were men in the stockade whose daily task was to walk the outer line, stepping carefully along a tiny walkway. With frozen hands, they checked each rope was still like iron in the cold. It took them the best part of the day. The stockade was more like a town than a camp and many thousands were crammed inside.

The yard in front of the gate was a good place to stand, Pavel thought, a safe place. He was there because he had been among the last to come in the night before. Yet the soldiers who stamped and shoved their hands into their armpits for warmth felt its strength looming over them. They tried not to think of the moments to come when the gate would be heaved open by snorting oxen and they would go out among the wolves.

Pavel stood back from the men close to the gate. He felt his sword nervously, wanting to draw it again and look at it. His grandfather had told him the importance of keeping it sharp. He had not told him what to do if he was given a blade older than he was himself, with more nicks, cuts and scratches than he could believe. Pavel had seen some of the real soldiers run a whetstone along their swords, but he had not had the courage to ask to borrow one. They did not look like the sort of men who would lend anything to a boy. He had not seen the grand duke yet, though Pavel had craned his neck and stood as tall as he could. That would be something to tell his grandfather when he went home again. His dedushka remembered Krakow and, in his cups, the old man claimed to have seen the king when he was young, though it might have been just a story.

Pavel longed for a glimpse of the freemen adventurers, the Qasaks the duke had bought for the campaign with a river of gold. He tried not to get his hopes up that his father could be among them. Part of him saw the sadness in his grandfather's eyes whenever he spoke of the brave young man who had gone to join the horsemen. Pavel had seen his mother weep in the house when she thought he couldn't hear. He suspected his father had simply abandoned them, as so many did when the winters were too hard. He had always been a wanderer. They had left Krakow looking for land of their own to buy, but farm work had turned out to be one step from starvation and with little more joy. If anything, the Russian farmers were worse off than those they had left behind.

There were always men who travelled to Kiev or Moscow looking for work. They promised they would send money to their families, but few ever did and fewer still came back. Pavel shook his head. He was not a child, hoping for a little truth in all the lies. He had a sword and he would fight for the duke alongside those fierce, coarse riders. He smiled, amused at himself. He would still look for his father's face among them, tired and lined with hard work, with the hair cropped close to the skull against lice. He hoped he would be able to recognise him after so long. The Qasaks were somewhere outside the stockade, riding their horses in the snow.

The cold was biting as the sun came up, the ground rubbed to slush by men and horses. Pavel wrung his hands together and cursed aloud as he was jostled from behind. He enjoyed cursing. The men around him used terms he had never heard before and he growled a good blasphemy at his unseen assailant. His irritation faded as he saw it was just a runner boy carrying dough balls stuffed with meat and herbs. Pavel's hands were quick and he lifted two of the steaming lumps as the boy struggled to get past him. The boy swore at the theft, but Pavel ignored him, cramming one into his mouth before someone noticed and took it away. The taste was glorious and the juices dribbled down his chin and under the mailed jerkin he had been given just that morning. He had felt like a man then, with a man's weight to carry. He had thought he would be frightened, but there were thousands of soldiers in the stockade and many more Qasaks outside. They did not seem afraid, though many of the faces were stern and quiet. Pavel did not speak to those who wore beards or heavy moustaches. He was still hoping to grow whiskers of his own, but there was nothing there yet. He thought guiltily of his father's razor in the barn. For a month or so, he'd gone out there every evening to run it up and down his cheeks. The boys in the village said it made the hair grow faster, but there was precious little sign of it on him, at least so far.

Horns sounded somewhere distant and men began shouting orders all around him. There was no time to eat the second dough ball, so Pavel shoved it down his jerkin, feeling the heat spread against his skin. He wished his grandfather could have been there to see him. The old man had been away from home, gathering firewood from miles out so that the easy stocks would still be there as winter tightened its grip. His mother had wept, of course, when Pavel brought the duke's recruiter to the back door. With the man watching, she hadn't been able to refuse him, just as he'd planned it. He'd walked tall behind the recruiter and he still remembered the combination of excitement and nervousness in the faces of the others on the road. Some of them were older than Pavel and one had a beard that reached almost to his chest. He'd been disappointed not to see any of the other village lads there. No doubt they had run from the recruiters. He'd heard of boys hiding in hay barns and even lying down with cattle to avoid the duke's call. Their fathers were not Qasaks. Pavel hadn't looked back at the village as he'd left, or only once at least, to see his mother come to the boundary and hold up her hand to him. He hoped his grandfather would be proud when he heard. Pavel wasn't sure how the old man would react, but at least he'd miss the beating, if that was the result. He grinned at the thought of the old devil standing in the yard with the chickens, with no one to take his strap to.

Something was happening, that much was obvious. Pavel saw his sotski march past, the one officer he knew. The man looked tired and though he didn't notice Pavel, instinct made him fall in behind. If they were going out, his place was in the hundred, as he'd been told. Pavel didn't know any of the ones walking with him, but that was where he was meant to be and his sotski at least seemed to be marching with purpose. Together, they crossed the gate and the officer finally saw Pavel standing behind him.

'You are one of mine,' he said, then pointed to a slightly larger group without waiting for an answer.

Pavel and six more walked over, smiling sheepishly at each other. They looked as ungainly as he felt, standing with their swords and iron jerkins that draped almost to their knees, rubbing their frozen hands as they went red and pale blue in the cold. The sotski had gone off to shepherd in a few more of those in his charge.

Pavel jumped as horns sounded again, this time from the walls of the stockade. One of the men with him laughed unpleasantly at his reaction, revealing brown and broken teeth. Pavel's cheeks burned. He had hoped for the sort of brotherhood his grandfather had described, but he couldn't see it in the frozen yard, with men pissing in the slush, their thin faces pinched with cold. Snow began falling out of the white sky above and many of the men cursed it, knowing it would make the day harder in all ways.

Pavel watched as steaming brown oxen were driven past him and roped to the gates. Were they going out already? He could not see the sotski anywhere. The man seemed to have vanished, just when Pavel needed to ask him all sorts of things. He could see daylight through the gates as they groaned inwards. Those in the yard were forced back by shouting officers, the crowd swaying in like a drawn breath. Some of the men were facing the widening gap, but a new commotion started somewhere far back and heads turned to see what it was. Pavel could hear voices raised in pain and anger. He craned his neck to look behind him and the one who had laughed shook his head.

'The whips are out, boy,' he said gruffly. 'They'll send us into battle like animals being driven. It's the way of the duke's fine officers.'

Pavel did not like the man who spoke, especially as he seemed to be criticising the duke himself. He looked away rather than answer, then shuffled forward as those behind began to press into the open yard. The gate yawned wider and the whiteness was almost blinding after so long in its shadow.

The air was painful in his lungs and throat, the cold so intense that Batu could hardly breathe. The mounts of his tuman cantered in together, judging the range to the Russian horsemen. They were already sweating from the manoeuvres as the sun came up. All they could do then was keep moving. To stop was to let the sweat freeze and begin to die slowly, unaware of the spreading numbness.

Shortly after first light, Tsubodai had sent his right wing

forward, Batu at the head. They did not fear the levies and conscripts the duke had gathered in his great stockades. Those could be torn apart by arrows. The enemy cavalry were the danger and Batu felt pride at being first against them. They had feinted left at dawn, forcing the Russians to bolster their lines there. As the duke pulled men from his other wing, Batu had waited for Tsubodai's signal, then gone in fast. He could see huge numbers of horses, and as he rode, he saw the lines accelerate towards his tuman, rippling forward as the orders came. The duke had gathered a massive force to defend Kiev, but none of them had expected to fight in winter. It was a killing cold.

Batu tested his bowstring, easing and heaving back on the bow as he rode, feeling the action loosen the great muscles in his shoulders. The arrows were thick in the quivers on their backs and he could hear the feathers crackle against each other by his ear.

The duke had spotted the threat. Batu could see the man and his pretty flags off to one side. Horns blew his orders, but Tsubodai had sent Mongke in on the left, the two wings drawing ahead of the main force. The orlok held the centre with Jebe and Kachiun, his heaviest horsemen armed with lances. Whoever came out of the stockade would be met with a massed black line, ready for them.

Batu nodded to his bannerman and a great streak of orange silk began to swing back and forth, visible all along the line. The creak of thousands of bows bending sounded, a groan that seemed to hum in the air. Four thousand shafts soared as the first ranks released, reaching behind them for another arrow and fitting it at a canter as they had learned to do as children. They lifted themselves slightly off the saddle, letting their knees balance against the lunge of the horse beneath. There was no great need for accuracy at full range. The arrows flew high, then sank into the Qasak horsemen, blurring the air and leaving it clean and dead in their wake.

Horses collapsed among the enemy. Those who had bows responded, but they could not match the range of the Mongol weapons and their shafts fell short. Batu slowed the pace, rather than throw away such an advantage. His signal brought the cantering line down to a trot and then a walk, but the arrows continued to fly out, one every six heartbeats, like hammer blows on an anvil.

The Russian horsemen forced their mounts through the barrage, racing blindly forward as they held shields high and crouched as low as they could on the saddles. The two wings would clash around the stockaded town and Batu eased himself into the front rank. His men expected to see him there since his wild ride against the Russian prince and his blood ran faster and hot when he was facing down the enemy, his tuman around him.

There was no break, no respite in the arrow waves. From soaring arcs, the Mongol riders adjusted and sent them lower, then began to pick targets. The Russian charge was not clad in steel like the duke's personal guard. Tsubodai would have to take those on in the centre. The duke's Qasaks continued to fall, riding into a gale of shafts that seemed to leave no space for man or horse.

Batu found his quiver empty and he grimaced, tucking his bow on the saddle hook without thought. He drew his sword and that action was copied all along the line. The Russian wing had been battered, hundreds of them left behind the charge. Those who remained were still coming on, but many were wounded, swaying in the saddle, breathing blood from shafts through their lungs. They wheezed defiance still, but the Mongols cut them down as they passed, striking out with armoured fists and forearms, using the swords with neat precision.

Batu's tuman swept over the remnants of the wing and on past the stockade walls. He had a glimpse of the great gates opening, but then it was behind him and he was chasing an enemy half-hanging out of his saddle as he tried to get away. The Mongol warriors hooted as they rode, calling out prime targets to each other. Batu could feel their pride and pleasure as they nodded to him. This was the best of times, when the enemy were in disarray and could be hunted like a herd of deer.

As the gates swung open, Pavel was shoved out into the bright light, the snow making the dawn blinding. He blinked in confusion and fear. There were too many voices shouting. He could not make sense of any of it. He drew his sword and marched forward, but the man in front of him stopped suddenly, the one who had spoken earlier.

'Keep moving!' Pavel said.

Already, he was being shoved from behind. The man with the broken teeth hawked and spat as he stared out at the Mongol army riding towards them. The lances came down in a line.

'Jesus Christ save us,' the man muttered and Pavel did not know if it was a prayer or a curse. He heard the men behind him begin a martial shout, trying to spur each other on, but it was thin on the wind and Pavel felt his hands weaken, his stomach clench.

The Mongol line grew larger, bringing with them a swelling vibration of the ground beneath their feet. They could all feel it and many of them turned to each other. The officers were shouting, pointing to the Mongols, red in the face and spraying spittle in their urging. The column still moved, unable to stop as those behind pressed them out into the snow. Pavel tried to slow his steps, but he was shoved by men as reluctant as he was.

271

'For the duke!' one of the officers shouted. A few took up the cry, but their voices were feeble and they soon fell silent. The Mongol tuman came on, a line of darkness that would sweep them all away.

CHAPTER TWENTY-ONE

Kachiun heard the laughter before the group was even in sight. He winced as his bad leg throbbed. An old wound had suppurated in the thigh and he had to drain it twice a day, according to Tsubodai's Moslem healer. It didn't seem to help. The wound had troubled him for months, flaring up without warning. It made him feel old to approach the young officers limping like a cripple. He *was* old, of course. Limping or not, they would have made him feel his years.

He heard Guyuk's voice rise above the others, telling some story of Batu's triumphs. Kachiun sighed to himself as he walked past a final ger. The noise stopped for a moment as Guyuk spotted him. The others turned to see what had caught the young man's attention.

'The tea has just boiled, general,' Guyuk called cheerfully. 'You're welcome to share a cup with us, or something stronger if you prefer.' The others laughed as if this was a great jest and Kachiun repressed his grimace. He had been young too, once.

The four of them were sprawled around like young lions and Kachiun grunted as he lowered himself to the mat of felt, easing his leg out carefully. Batu noticed the swollen thigh, of course. That one missed nothing.

'How is the leg, general?'

'Full of pus,' Kachiun snapped.

Batu's face closed at his tone, shuttering his emotions away. Kachiun cursed himself. A little pain and sweating and there he was, snapping at boys like a bad-tempered old dog. He looked around the little group, nodding to Baidur, who was hard-pressed to contain the sheer excitement he felt at joining the campaign. The young warrior was jittery and bright-eyed to be in such company and be treated as an equal. Kachiun wondered if any of them knew the treacheries of their fathers, or whether they cared if they did.

Kachiun accepted the bowl of tea in his right hand, and tried to relax as he sipped. The conversation did not resume immediately in his presence. He had known all their fathers and, for that matter, Genghis himself. The years weighed heavily on him at that thought. He could see Tolui in Mongke and the memory saddened him. The promise of Chagatai's strong features looked out from Baidur's face in its lines and jutting jaw. Time would tell if he had the man's stubborn strength as well. Kachiun could see the lad had something to prove yet in this company. He was not among the leaders of the group, by any means.

That brought Kachiun's thoughts to Batu, and as he glanced over, he found the young man watching him with something like a smile, as if he could read his thoughts. The others deferred to him, that much was obvious, but Kachiun wondered if their new-found friendship would survive the challenges of the years. When they were rivals for the khanates, they would not be so relaxed in each other's presence, he thought, sipping.

Guyuk smiled easily, one who expected to inherit. He had

not had Genghis as a father to harden him and make him understand the dangers of easy friendship. Perhaps Ogedai had been too soft on him, or perhaps he was just a normal warrior, without the ruthless quality that set men like Genghis apart.

'And men like me,' Kachiun thought to himself, considering his own dreams and past glories. Seeing the future in the relaxing cousins was bitter-sweet for him. They showed him respect, but he did not think they understood the debt they owed. The tea tasted sour in his mouth at the thought, though his teeth were rotting at the back and everything tasted bad to him.

'Did you have a reason to visit us on this cold morning?' Batu said suddenly.

'I came to welcome Baidur to the camp,' Kachiun replied. 'I was away when he brought in his father's tuman.'

'His *own* tuman, general,' Guyuk said immediately. 'We have all been raised by the hands of our fathers.'

He did not notice how Batu stiffened. His father Jochi had done nothing for him, yet he sat with the others, cousins and princes, as strong and perhaps harder than they were. Kachiun did not miss the flicker of emotions that played across the younger man's face. He nodded to himself, silently wishing them all luck.

'Well, I cannot waste a morning sitting here,' Kachiun said. 'I have to walk this leg, I'm told, to keep the bad blood moving.'

He clambered painfully to his feet, ignoring Guyuk's outstretched arm. The useless thing was throbbing again, in time with his heart. He would go back to the healer and endure another knife in the flesh to release the brown filth that filled the thigh. He frowned at the prospect, then inclined his head to the group as one, before limping away.

'He's seen a few things in his time,' Guyuk said wistfully, looking after him.

'He's just an old man,' Batu replied. 'We will see more.' He grinned at Guyuk. 'Like the bottom of a few skins of airag, for a start. Bring out your private store, Guyuk. Don't think I haven't heard of your father's packages to you.'

Guyuk blushed to be the centre of attention, as the others clamoured for him to bring out the drink. He rushed away to fetch the skins for his friends.

'Tsubodai told me to report to him at sunset,' Baidur said, his voice worried.

Batu shrugged. 'And we will, though he didn't say we had to be sober. Don't worry, cousin, we'll put on a show for the old devil. Perhaps it's time he realised *we* are the princes of the nation. He is just an artisan we employ, like a painter ... or a maker of bricks. Good as he is, Baidur, that's *all* he is.'

Baidur looked uncomfortable. He had joined the army after the battles around Kiev and he knew he had yet to prove himself to his cousins. Batu had been the first to greet him, but Baidur was enough of a judge to see the spite in the older man. He was wary of the group, for all they were his cousins and princes of the same nation. He chose to say nothing and Batu relaxed back into a pile of grain sacks. It was not long before Guyuk returned, bearing fat skins of airag over each shoulder.

Yao Shu had put a lot of effort into being ready for the meeting of Sorhatani and the khan's wife. The summer palace on the Orkhon river was barely a day's ride away for a scout, but the khan's wife had never travelled at that sort of speed. For all her apparent urgency, moving her staff and baggage had taken the best part of a month. Yao Shu had enjoyed the secret pleasure of watching Sorhatani's strain grow daily as she bustled about the palace and city, checking the tallies in the treasury and coming up with a thousand things for which she might be reproached in her care of the khan.

In that time, with just a few letters and messengers, he had won back the freedom of his office. No longer was he troubled by Sorhatani's constant enquiries and demands on his time and resources. No longer was he summoned at all hours of the day and night to explain some matter of policy, or some aspect of the titles and powers she had been granted in her husband's stead. It was a perfect application of power, he decided: the minimum force to achieve the desired outcome.

For the previous two days, the palace corridors had been scrubbed by an army of Chin servants. Anything made of cloth had been sent to the courtyard and beaten free of dust before being carefully replaced. Fresh fruit had been packed in ice barrels and brought to the kitchens below ground, while cut flowers were placed in such profusion that the entire building was heavy with their scent. The khan's wife was coming home and she must not be disappointed.

Yao Shu strolled along an airy corridor, enjoying the weak sunshine on a cold, clear day with blue skies. The joy of his position was that no one would challenge the khan's own chancellor if he chose to be there when Torogene returned. It was almost his duty to welcome her and there was little Sorhatani could do about it.

He heard a horn blow from the outskirts of the city and he smiled to himself. Her baggage train was in sight at last. He had time to go to his offices and put on his most formal robes. His current deel was grubby and he brushed at the cloth as he jogged to his work rooms. He barely noticed the servant prostrating himself at the doorpost as he passed. He had clean robes in a chest. They would be a little musty, but the cedar wood should have kept the moths at bay. He crossed the room with quick steps and was bent over the chest when he heard the door swing closed behind him. As he spun round in surprise, a click sounded, then the scrape of a key in a lock.

Yao Shu forgot about the chest. He crossed to the door and tried the handle, knowing it would not open. Sorhatani's orders, of course. He could almost smile at the woman's sheer effrontery to lock him in his own rooms. It was all the more irritating that he was the one responsible for introducing locks to the doors of the palace, at least those which guarded valuables. The lessons of the long night had been learned, when Chagatai had sent men into the palace to spread terror and destruction. Only good doors had saved the khan then. Yao Shu ran his hands over the wood, his calloused skin making a sibilant sound. He matched it with a hiss of air through his teeth.

'Really, Sorhatani?' he muttered to himself.

He resisted the pointless urge to rattle the handle or call for help. The whole palace was busy that morning. There could be servants rushing by outside, but it was more than his dignity would take to have to be rescued from his own rooms.

He tapped the door with the palm of his hand, testing its strength. From childhood, he had conditioned his body to hardness. For years he had begun each day with a thousand blows on his forearms. The bones had cracked in tiny fissures, filling and growing dense so that he could unleash all his strength without fearing his wrists would snap. Yet the door felt depressingly solid. He was no longer a young man and, smiling ruefully to himself, he put aside the young man's response of force.

His questing hands moved to the hinges instead. They were simple iron pegs, lowered onto rings of iron, but the door had been put into place while it was open. Now that it was closed, the frame prevented him from lifting it. He looked around his offices, but there were no weapons there. The chest was too heavy to be flung at the door and the rest – his inkstone, his pens and scrolls – were all too light to be of any use. He muttered a curse under his breath. The windows of the room were barred in iron, high and small enough so that the winter wind did not freeze him as he worked.

He felt his anger growing again, as all his attempts at reason failed. It would have to be force. He rubbed the two large knuckles on his right hand. Years of the striking post had given them a sheath of callus, but the bones underneath were like marble, cracked and healed until they were a mass of dense bone.

Yao Shu removed his sandals and stretched his legs for a moment. They too had been hardened. Time would tell if he could break through a door with nothing else.

He chose the weakest spot, where a panel had been fitted into the main frame. He took a deep breath, readying himself.

Sorhatani stood at the main gate to Karakorum. She had fretted for some time over where to receive Ogedai's wife. Would it seem like a challenge to force her to come all the way through the city to the palace before they met? She did not know Torogene well enough to be certain. Her main memory of her was a motherly woman who had remained calm on the long night when Ogedai had come under attack in his rooms. Sorhatani told herself she had done nothing wrong, that she could not be reproached for her care of the khan. Yet she knew well enough that a wife's feeling about a younger woman was not always a rational thing. No matter how it went, the meeting was going to be delicate, to say the least. Sorhatani had prepared herself as best she could. The rest was up to the sky father and earth mother, and Torogene herself.

The retinue was an impressive sight, with outriders and carts stretching back along the road for almost a mile. Sorhatani had ordered the city gates opened, rather than insult Torogene, yet she feared that the khan's wife would just sweep by her as if she did not exist. She watched nervously as the first rows of riders passed under the gate and the largest cart trundled closer. Pulled by six oxen, it moved slowly and creaked loudly enough to be heard some distance away. The khan's wife sat under a canopy, with four poles of birch supporting a silk roof. The sides were open and Sorhatani twisted her hands together at the first sight of Torogene returning to her husband and Karakorum. It was not reassuring, and Sorhatani felt the woman's eyes seek her out at a distance, then rest on her as if fascinated. She thought she could see the gleam of them and knew that Torogene would be seeing a slim and beautiful woman in a Chin dress of green silk, her hair tied with a silver clasp as large as a man's hand.

Sorhatani's thoughts raced as the cart came to a halt just a few paces away from where she stood. Status was the issue and the one thing she had not been able to decide in the days previously. Torogene was the khan's wife, of course. When they had met last, she had been Sorhatani's social superior. Yet in the time since, Sorhatani had been granted all the titles and authority of her husband. There was no precedent in the short history of the nation. Certainly no other woman had ever had the right to command a tuman if she so chose. It was a mark of the khan's respect for her husband's sacrifice that he had made the ruling at all.

Sorhatani took a deep, slow breath as she saw Torogene was moving to the edge of the cart, extending her hand to be helped down. The grey-haired woman was older, but the khan's wife would have bowed to Tolui if he had been standing there. The khan's wife would have spoken first. Without knowing how Torogene would react to her, Sorhatani didn't want to throw away her sole advantage. She had the status to demand respect, but she did not want to make an enemy of the older woman.

The moment when she would have to decide came too quickly, but her attention was dragged away by the sound of running footsteps. Sorhatani and Torogene both looked up at the same time as Yao Shu came through the gate. His face was stiff with anger and his eyes glittered as they took in the scene.

Sorhatani caught a glimpse of bloody knuckles before he clasped his hands behind his back and bowed formally to welcome the khan's wife.

Perhaps it was his example, but Sorhatani stepped aside from her new-found dignity. As Torogene turned to face her, she too bowed deeply.

'Your return is welcome, lady,' Sorhatani said, straightening. 'The khan is on his way to health and he needs you now more than ever.'

Torogene relaxed subtly, a hint of tension vanishing from the way she held herself. As Yao Shu watched in anticipation, the older woman smiled. To his fury, he saw Sorhatani echo the expression.

'I'm sure you'll tell me everything I need to know,' Torogene said, her voice warm. 'I was sorry to hear about your husband. He was a brave man, more so than I ever knew.'

Sorhatani found herself blushing, relieved beyond words that the khan's wife had not snubbed her, or begun hostilities. She bowed again on impulse, overcome.

'Join me on the cart, dear,' Torogene said, fitting her arm through Sorhatani's. 'We can talk on the way to the palace. Is that Yao Shu I see there?'

'My lady,' Yao Shu murmured.

'I will want to see the accounts, chancellor. Bring them to me in the khan's rooms at sunset.'

'Of course, my lady,' he replied.

What trickery was this? He had hoped for two cats spitting rage over Ogedai, and instead they seemed to have assessed each other and found something to like in just a glance and a greeting. He would never understand women, he thought. They were life's great mystery. His hands ached and throbbed from hammering through the door panels and he was suddenly tired. He wanted nothing more than to return to his offices and settle down with something hot to drink. He watched in numb frustration as Sorhatani and Torogene were handed up onto the cart and took seats next to each other, already chattering like birds. The column moved off with cries from the drivers and warriors riding escort. It was not long before he was standing alone on the dusty road. The thought came to him that the accounts were in no state to be perused by anyone apart from himself. He had a great deal of work to do before sunset, before he could rest.

Karakorum was far from quiet as the riders and carts made their way through the streets. The khan's own Guards had been brought out from their barracks to man the roads and keep back crowds of well-wishers, as well as those who just wanted to catch a glimpse of Torogene. The khan's wife was seen as the mother of the nation and the Guards were hard-pressed. Torogene smiled indulgently as they wended their way through the streets to the golden dome and tower of the khan's palace.

'I had forgotten there were so many people here,' Torogene said, shaking her head in wonder. Men and women held children out to her in the vain hope that she would bless them with a touch. Others cried her name, or called out blessings of their own on the khan and his family. The Guards linked arms at crossroads, struggling to hold back a tide of humanity.

When she spoke again, Sorhatani could see a faint flush in Torogene's cheeks.

'I understand that Ogedai is much taken with you,' Torogene began.

Sorhatani closed her eyes for a moment of irritation. Yao Shu.

'Looking after him gave me something to do while I bore my own grief,' she said. Her eyes were clear of guilt and Torogene regarded her with interest. She had never been as beautiful, even when young.

'You seem to have offended my husband's chancellor, at least. That says something for you.'

Sorhatani smiled. 'He feels the khan's wishes should have been respected. I . . . did not respect them. I think I irritated Ogedai into taking a grip on his duties again. He is not fully well, my lady, but I think you will see a change in him.'

The khan's wife patted her knee, reassured by Sorhatani's babbling. By the spirits, the woman had secured her husband's titles with just a few ruffled feathers! If that was not enough, she had nursed the khan back to health, when the man was refusing to see his wife or his chancellor. Some part of her knew Ogedai had chosen to die alone in his palace. He had sent her away with a sort of cold resignation she could not pierce. Somehow, she had thought that to defy him would be to see him break down completely. He had not allowed her into his grief. It still hurt.

Sorhatani had done what Torogene could not and she silently thanked the younger woman, however she had achieved it. Even Yao Shu had been forced to admit Ogedai was in better spirits. It was somehow good to know Sorhatani could be as nervous as a girl. It made her less frightening.

Sorhatani regarded the motherly lady at her side. It had been a very long time since anyone had shown her that sort of affection and she found herself liking the woman more. She could hardly express her relief that there was no bad blood between them. Torogene wasn't the foolish sort to come storming home. If Ogedai had the sense of a marmot, he'd have had her close from the moment he returned. He'd have healed himself in her arms. Instead, he'd chosen to wait for death in a frozen room. He'd seen it as refusing to flinch in the face of death, she knew now. He had tormented himself with past sins and errors until he could no longer move even to save himself.

'I am glad you were there for him, Sorhatani,' Torogene said.

The colour in her cheeks deepened suddenly and Sorhatani prepared for the question she knew would come.

'I am not a young girl, a blushing virgin,' Torogene said. 'My husband has many wives . . . and slaves and servants to attend to every need. I will not be hurt, but I do want to know if you comforted him in *all* ways.'

'Not in bed,' Sorhatani said, smiling. 'He came close to grabbing me once when I was bathing him, but I hit him with a foot-brush.'

Torogene chuckled. 'That's the way to deal with them, dear, when they get warm. You're very beautiful, you see. I think I would have been jealous of you if you had.'

They smiled at each other, each one realising she had found a friend. Both women wondered if the other valued the discovery anywhere near as much.

CHAPTER TWENTY-TWO

Tsubodai moved slowly west over the following spring and summer. Leaving the Russian principates behind, he reached the limits of his maps. His scouts spread out ahead of the tumans, ranging in unknown territory for months at a time as they sketched valleys and towns and lakes, putting together a picture of the land that lay before him. Those who could read and write made notes on the strength of armies they encountered, or the moving columns of refugees fleeing before them. Those who could not write bound sticks in bundles of ten, with each ten representing a thousand. It was a rough system, but Tsubodai was content to move in summer and fight each winter, playing to the strengths of his people. The lords and nobles of these new lands were made weak by such an approach to war. As yet, they had shown him nothing that could threaten his horse warriors.

Tsubodai assumed he would eventually face armies the equal of those wielded by the chin emperor. At some point, the foreign princes would join forces against the sweep west. He heard rumours of armies like clouds of locusts, but he did not know if it was exaggeration. If the foreign lords did not join together, they would be taken one by one and he would not stop, would not *ever* stop, until he saw the sea.

He rode to the front of a column of the closest two tumans, checking on the supplies Mongke had promised to send after a lucky find. Just keeping so many in the field forced them to move constantly. The horses needed vast plains of sweet grass and the sheer number of ragged foot soldiers was becoming a greater problem every day. They served a purpose when used ruthlessly. Tsubodai's tumans sent them in first, forcing the enemy to use all their bolts and arrows before they met the main Mongol forces. In that way, they were valuable enough, but anything that lived or moved had to be shot to feed the men – not just herds of cattle and sheep, but foxes, deer, wolves, hares and wild birds, anything they could find. They scoured the land, leaving almost nothing alive behind them. He thought the destruction of villages was something like a mercy. Better a quick death than being left to starve, without grain or meat for the winter to come. Time and again, Tsubodai's tumans had found abandoned villages, places filled with ghosts from years back, when plague or starvation had forced the people to leave. It was no wonder they gathered in great cities. In such places, they could pretend they were safe and find comfort in numbers and high walls. They did not yet know how weak those walls were for his tumans. He had brought down Yenking, with the Chin emperor inside it. Nothing he had seen in the west could match that stone city.

Tsubodai firmed his jaw as he saw Batu in the company of Guyuk yet again. Mongke and Baidur were a hundred miles away, or he thought he might have found them there as well. The four princes had become friends, which could have been useful enough, if Batu had not been the one holding them

286

together. Perhaps because he was the oldest, or because Guyuk followed his lead, Batu seemed to set the tone for the others. He made a great show of respect whenever Tsubodai spoke to him, but always there was the mocking half-smile. It was never so obvious that the orlok could react, but still, it was there. He felt it like a thorn in his back, too far to reach and pluck out.

Tsubodai reined in as he reached the head of the column. Behind him, Batu's tuman rode alongside Guyuk's. There was none of the usual rough competition between those warriors, as if they took their manner from the generals at the head. Tsubodai grunted at the clean lines. He could not fault them, but it rankled to have Guyuk and Batu talking the day away as if they were riding to a marriage feast and not through hostile territory.

Tsubodai was hot and irritable. He had not eaten that day and he had ridden the best part of twenty miles since dawn, checking on the columns as they clawed their way across the earth. He stifled his temper as Batu bowed in the saddle to him.

'Do you have new orders, orlok?' Batu called.

Guyuk looked up as well and Tsubodai brought his horse in closer, matching their pace. He did not bother to answer the pointless question.

'Has the beef herd reached you from Mongke yet?' Tsubodai said. He knew it had, but he needed to broach the subject. Guyuk nodded immediately.

'Just before dawn. Two hundred head and large. We've slaughtered twenty bulls and the rest are in the herds behind.'

'Send sixty more to Kachiun. He has none,' Tsubodai said, curt and stiff with them. He did not like even the appearance of asking for a favour.

'Perhaps because Kachiun sits on a cart, instead of riding out and finding meat,' Batu muttered.

Guyuk almost choked as he tried to smother laughter. Tsubodai stared them both down coldly. If it was not enough to have the khan's own son act the fool, Batu's insolence was something he would have to face and crush eventually. He hoped Batu would step over the line before it became a killing matter. He was young and headstrong. He would make a mistake, Tsubodai was sure.

A scout raced in to report and Tsubodai turned automatically, only to find the man heading across him towards Batu. He took a slow breath as the scout saw him and started, bowing deeply in the saddle.

'The village by the river is coming up, general,' he said to Batu. 'You asked to be told when we were in range.'

'And the river itself?' Batu asked. He knew Tsubodai had scouted it for fords and bridges days before. The half-smile was playing over his mouth again, knowing Tsubodai could hear every word.

'Two shallow fords in our path, general. The better one is to the north.'

'Very well. That's the one we'll take. Show my bondsmen where it is, then lead us in.'

'Yes, my lord,' the scout replied. He bowed to Batu, then Tsubodai, before kicking in his heels and trotting along the line of moving warriors.

'Was there anything else, orlok?' Batu asked innocently. 'I have things in hand here.'

'Camp as soon as you are over the river, then both of you come and see me at sunset.'

He saw them look at each other and then away before they could laugh. Tsubodai gritted his teeth and left them. He had news of two cities beyond the mountains, cities his scouts said were flooded with refugees running from the Mongol tumans. Yet instead of preparing a campaign against Buda and Pest, he was dealing with generals acting like children. He wondered if he could take Guyuk aside and shame the young man into something resembling duty or dignity. He nodded to himself as he rode. Ever since his charmed strike to the heart of a Russian army, Batu had eaten away at the orlok's authority. If it went on, it would cost lives, perhaps see them all destroyed. It was not too early to grab the problem by the throat, or even the man. There was no place on the march for challenges to his authority, even from the sons and grandsons of khans.

The generals rode to Tsubodai's ger as the sun set. The tumans slept around them, an ocean of pale gers as far as the eye could see. Huddled in their midst was a darker mass of fighting men. The vast majority were Russian, either those who had survived the destruction of their towns and cities or a much smaller number who had come for spoils, tracking the army across the valleys and offering their weapons and strength. Most of those were made officers of the rest, as ones who knew one end of a sword from the other. Their equipment was whatever they could scavenge and the best food went to the tumans, so that they were lean and always hungry.

Pavel was one of them, thin as a wild wolf and always bruised or tired from the training. He did not understand half of what he was made to do, but he did it. He ran in the mornings, loping along behind the tumans for ten miles at a time. He had lost his rusty sword in the only battle of his life and come just a hair's breadth from losing his life with it. The blow that had felled him had torn a flap of skin from his scalp, leaving him stunned. When he finally awoke, it was to find the stockade burning and the tumans arrayed in a vast camp. The dead lay where they had been cut down and some of the bodies had been stripped. His face was stiff with his own blood, frozen in layers from his hair to his chin. He had not dared to touch it, though it had closed his right eye in a solid mass.

Pavel might have slunk away then, if it had not been for the man with the rotting teeth, who had walked past him carrying a skin of some bitter fluid. It had made Pavel vomit, but the man only laughed in that unpleasant way of his and said his name was Alexi and that they had stood together. It was Alexi who had walked him through the camp where Mongol warriors lay sprawled and drunken, half of them asleep. He had taken Pavel to a man so badly scarred it made Pavel flinch.

'Polan blood,' Alexi had said. 'Just a farm boy, but he didn't run.'

The scarred man had grunted, then spoken in Russian and told him they could use another sword. Pavel had held up empty hands. He had no idea where his blade had gone by then and the world still swam around him. He remembered the man saying his skull was probably cracked before he passed out.

His new life was hard. Food was scarce, though he had been given a new sword without the flaws and rust of the last one. He ran with the tumans and endured, until the air in his lungs blew hot enough to burn and his heart pounded as if it would burst. He tried not to think of the farm he had left with his mother and grandfather. They would be tending the small-holding, watching the crops grow ready for harvest. He would not be there to help them that year.

Pavel was still awake when he saw three men ride towards the large ger at the centre of the camp. He knew the tall one with the cruel face was Batu, a grandson of Genghis. Pavel learned all the names he could. It was the only way he could draw threads from the new chaos of his life. He did not know the one who grinned foolishly as Batu made some comment. Pavel fingered his sword hilt in the darkness, wishing he had the strength to stride over to them and cut them down. He had not seen the duke killed, though the other men shook their heads and looked away when he asked about it. They did not seem to care as he did.

Unseen, Pavel wandered closer to the ger. He knew the name of their leader, though it was hard to make his mouth say the sound. Tsubodai, they had called him, the man responsible for burning Moscow. Pavel craned for a glimpse of him, but as the three generals dismounted, their horses blocked a view inside the ger. He sighed to himself. He could run further than he would have believed possible just a few months before. It was tempting to escape when there was no moon, though he had seen the fate of a few men who tried it. They had been brought back in pieces and the haunches of meat had been thrown to the others, as an insult. He had not joined in, but he thought his starving companions had eaten the bloody lumps. Hunger made light of squeamish stomachs.

He could smell tea and roasting lamb on the breeze and his mouth filled with saliva. He had been hungry since leaving the farm, but there would be nothing until the morning and only then after he had run and loaded carts until his arms and shoulders burned. He rubbed a spot on his back at the thought, feeling the new muscle there. He wasn't large, just hard from work. Silently, in the darkness, he told himself he might run at the next new moon. If they caught him, at least he would have tried, but they'd have to ride fast and hard to do it.

Batu ducked his head to enter the ger, straightening up as he greeted those inside. He had brought Guyuk and Baidur with him and he was pleased to see Mongke already there. Batu nodded to him, but Mongke merely glanced over and then went back to filling his mouth with hot mutton. Batu reminded himself that Mongke too had lost a father. It was a way in, perhaps, to share that grief. The fact that he felt only hatred for his own father was no obstacle if he handled the younger man carefully. They were all princes of the nation, with blood ties to Genghis that Tsubodai could never claim. Batu enjoyed the idea, the sense of identity it gave him to know he was part of that group. No, that they were *his* group, to lead. He was the eldest of them, though Mongke had the build and dour manner of an experienced man, heavy with muscle. He would be the hardest to influence, Batu thought. Guyuk and Baidur were just boys in comparison, young and enthusiastic about everything. It was easy to imagine ruling an empire with them.

Before he sat down, he acknowledged Kachiun, Jebe and Chulgetei, bowing briefly. More old men. He noticed Kachiun's thigh was hugely swollen, far worse than before. The general sat on a low pallet with the distended leg stretched out before him. A quick glance at Kachiun's face showed tired eyes and skin a deep yellow from sickness. Batu thought his great-uncle would not survive the winter to come, but that was the way of things. The old died to give way to the young. He did not let it trouble him.

Tsubodai was watching, his eyes cold as he waited for Batu to speak first. Batu made a point of smiling widely, his thoughts making him mellow.

'It is a fine night, orlok,' he said. 'My men say this is the best grassland they have seen since home. The horses have put on a layer of fat you wouldn't believe.'

'Sit, Batu. You are welcome here,' Tsubodai replied curtly. 'Guyuk, Baidur, there is tea in the kettle. There are no servants tonight, so pour your own.'

The two younger men set to the task, with clinking and chuckles as they poured boiling tea from a huge iron urn on the stove at the centre of the ger, under the smoke hole. Tsubodai watched as Baidur handed Batu a cup of the steaming salt liquid. It was natural enough, but such small things were always to do with power. In just a short time, it seemed Batu had found himself another follower. Tsubodai might have admired Batu's gift for leadership, if it had not interfered with his own control of the army. His father Jochi had had the same talent. Tsubodai had heard the name Batu had given the army. It would have been hard not to hear it. Over the years of campaign, the 'Golden Horde' had almost passed into common use, as such things will. Half the men seemed to think Batu was in overall command and he did nothing to dispel their belief. Tsubodai clenched his jaw at the thought.

Ogedai had honoured Jochi's bastard with titles and authority, making a point of it, in the face of Tsubodai's objections. In fact, Batu had not disgraced himself, far from it. His tuman was well organised, his officers carefully chosen. Some men could inspire loyalty and others could only demand it. It was strangely galling to see Batu was one of the first kind. Such men were always dangerous. The difficulty lay in handling them, directing their energies, if it was not already too late.

'The Magyars of Hungary are horsemen,' Tsubodai began, his voice deliberately low so that they had to lean in to listen. 'They have vast herds and they use the central plains much as we do. They are not nomads, however. They have built two cities on the banks of the river Danube. Pest and Buda are the names. Neither is well defended, though Buda rests on hills. Pest stands on a plain.'

He paused for questions.

'Defences?' Batu said immediately. 'Walls? Weapons? Supply lines?'

'Pest has no walls. The scouts report a stone palace on one of the hills by Buda, perhaps the residence of their king. His name . . .'

'Is not important,' Batu went on. 'It does not sound like such a task to take these cities. Why even wait for winter?'

'His name is Bela the fourth,' Tsubodai replied, his eyes dark with anger. 'We will wait for winter because the river can be crossed when it freezes. As with Moscow, it gives us a road between the cities, right into their heart.'

Guyuk sensed the tension between the two men and put a hand on Batu's arm. He shook it off irritably.

'My tuman is ready to ride today, orlok,' Batu continued. 'My scouts tell me the mountains to the west are passable before winter. We could be in these cities before the first snow. You are the one who said speed was important, or is it caution that is important now?'

'Keep your arrogance in your mouth, lad,' Jebe snapped suddenly.

Batu's gaze flickered over the older man. Jebe had ridden with Genghis through the Afghan hills. He was dark and lean, his face seamed with years and experience. Batu snorted in contempt.

'There is no need to leave the major targets to winter, general, as I'm sure the orlok knows. Some of us would like to see an end to the conquests *before* we are old men. For others, of course, it is already too late for that.'

Jebe surged to his feet, but Tsubodai raised a hand across him and he did not move from the spot. Batu chuckled.

'I have carried out all of Tsubodai's orders,' he said. He looked around as he spoke, deliberately including the princes. 'I have taken cities and towns because the great strategist said "Go here. Go there." I have not questioned a single command.' He paused and the ger was very still. No one else would speak if Tsubodai did not and he remained silent. Batu shrugged as if it was nothing and went on.

'Yet I do not forget that the khan himself raised me, not the orlok. I am the khan's man first, as are we all. More than that, I am of the blood, in the line of Genghis, as are Guyuk, Baidur and Mongke. It is not enough to follow blindly and *hope* that it is right. We are the ones who lead, who *question* the orders given, is that not right, Orlok Tsubodai?'

'No,' Tsubodai said. 'It is not right. You obey orders because if you do not, you cannot expect the same from your men.

You are part of the wolf, not the whole wolf. I would have thought you had learned that when you were a boy, but it is not the case. A wolf cannot have more than one head, general, or it tears itself apart.'

He took a deep breath, thinking deeply. Batu had chosen the wrong moment to assert himself, Tsubodai could feel it. The older men were shocked at his words, while the princes were nowhere near ready to overthrow Tsubodai Bahadur, not this season. With hidden satisfaction, he spoke again.

'You have displeased me, Batu. Leave us. I will have fresh orders for you in the morning.'

Batu turned to Guyuk, looking for support. He felt his stomach drop away as the khan's son would not meet his eyes. Batu winced then and nodded.

'Very well, orlok,' he said stiffly. No one spoke as he left.

In the silence, Tsubodai refilled his cup and sipped at the hot tea.

'The mountains ahead are more than just a ridge or a few peaks,' he said. 'My scouts tell me we will have to cross sixty or seventy miles of crags. My scouts have made it through, but without local men, we cannot know the major passes. I could force a few minghaans through to map the valleys, without carts or supplies beyond a few weeks. For the rest, the siege machines, the carts, the families and injured, it will be slow and difficult. We need to know where the passes are, to survive. We may have to build ramps or bridges. Even so, we have to make good speed or we will lose many when winter comes in. We cannot be in the highlands then. There is no grazing up there.'

Tsubodai looked around at the assembled generals. There was one man he needed to make strong, to separate from the rest, but it was not Batu.

'Guyuk. You will go first. Leave tomorrow with two ming-haans. Take tools to cut a path, timber, anything you might need. Make a way through that will be suitable for the heavy carts. Stay in contact with scouts and guide us in.'

The play of authority over Batu had not been wasted on Guyuk. He did not hesitate.

'Your will, orlok,' he said, bowing his head. He was pleased at the responsibility, knowing that the survival of the rest depended on finding a good path. At the same time, it would be grim work and every dead end or false opening would be his to find and mark.

'My scouts say open land lies beyond those mountains,' Tsubodai said. 'They could not see an end to it. We will force the peoples there to meet us in the field. For the khan, we will take their cities, their women and their lands. This is the great raid, the furthest strike in the history of the nation of Genghis. We will not be stopped.'

Jebe grunted in pleasure and hefted a skin of airag, throwing it to Tsubodai, who scored his throat with the liquid. The ger stank of wet wool and mutton, a sweet smell that he had known all his life. Guyuk and Baidur exchanged glances at seeing the orlok so animated, so confident. Mongke watched them all, his face unreadable.

Pavel ran, as fast as he had ever run in his life. The dim lights of Mongol fires faded on the horizon behind him. He fell more than once and the third time winded him badly enough to make him limp. He had struck his head hard on something in the darkness, but the pain was nothing to what the Mongols would do if they caught him.

He was alone in the night, with neither the sound of pursuing horses, nor any companion. Many of the other men had lost their homes in the years of war. Some of them could barely remember another life, but Pavel had not lost his memory. Somewhere to the north, he hoped his grandfather and mother still tended their little farm. He would be safe once he reached them and he told himself that he would never leave again. As he ran, he imagined the other young men looking on him with envy in their eyes for the things he had seen. The village girls would see him as a hardened soldier, something different from the country boys around them. He would never tell them about the bodies heaped like straw bales, or the hot release as his bladder unclenched in fear. He would not mention those things. His sword was heavy and he knew it slowed him down, but he could not bring himself to throw it away. He would walk into the yard and his mother would surely weep to see him return from the wars. He would make it home. The sword tripped him, and as he stumbled, he let it fall and hesitated before going on. He felt much lighter without it.

CHAPTER TWENTY-THREE

Batu cursed as he found himself sweating again. He knew that sweat could freeze under clothes in such cold, making a man listless and sleepy until he just lay down and died in the snow. He snorted at the thought, wondering if his constant, simmering anger would help to keep him alive. It was all very well knowing that sweat should be avoided, but there was no help for it when you were manhandling a heavy cart with eight others, heaving and rocking it until the stubborn thing finally shifted another few feet. Ropes stretched from the cart to a group of men pulling like horses; sullen, trudging Russians who never looked back and had to be struck or whipped to break through to them. It was maddening work, needing to be done over and over again as the carts lurched and spilled their contents. The first time Batu had seen one break free and race back to the bottom of the hill, he'd almost laughed. Then he'd seen a man holding his bloody face where a rope had lashed across it and another nursing a broken wrist. Every day brought injuries, and in the cold, even a small wound sapped the strength and made it harder to get up the next morning. They were all stiff and sore, but Tsubodai and his precious generals drove them on, higher into the Carpathian mountains every day.

The sky had come lower and grown blinding white, threatening snow all morning. When it began to fall again, many of the men groaned. The carts were hard enough to manoeuvre on good ground. With fresh slush, the men slipped and fell at every step, gasping for air and knowing that no one was coming to relieve them. Everyone was involved and Batu wondered how they had come to amass such a weight of carts and equipment. He was used to riding out with his tuman and leaving most of it behind. At times, he thought they could have built a city in the wilderness with all the tools and equipment they had with them. Tsubodai had even brought timber into the mountains, a weight of wood that took hundreds of men to move. It meant they had fires at night, when there was nothing else to burn, but the wind sucked away the small heat, or chilled one side of you while the other roasted. Batu seethed at the way he had been treated, more so because Guyuk had not spoken up for him. All he had done was question Tsubodai's absolute authority over them, not refuse an order. He prided himself on that, but he was being punished almost as if he had.

Batu bent his back again to get his shoulder under a beam with the other men, ready to heave the cart over a rut where the wheels had sunk in.

'One, two, three . . .'

They grunted with effort as he called the rhythm. Tsubodai had not been able to stop his men dismounting to help him with the work. Perhaps at first it was only the loyalty of a warrior to his general, but after days of the back-breaking labour, he thought they felt as disgusted with Tsubodai Bahadur as he was.

'One, two, three . . .' he growled again.

The cart lifted and thumped down. Batu's feet went out from under him and he grabbed the cart-bed to steady himself. His hands were wrapped in wool and sheepskin, but they stung bitterly, raw as fresh meat. He used spare moments to swing his arms, forcing blood to the tips so he would not lose them to frost. Too many of the men had those white patches on their noses, or on their cheeks. It explained the faded scars on the older men who had been through it all before.

Tsubodai had the right to set him any task, but Batu thought his authority was more fragile than the orlok realised. His right to command came from the khan, but even on the march, not all of their actions were purely military. There would be moments when political decisions had to be made and those were the responsibility of princes, not warriors. With Guyuk's support, the orlok could be overruled, even dismissed, Batu was certain. It would have to be the right moment, when the orlok's authority was not so clear-cut. Batu took hold of the cart again as the cursed thing lurched and almost tipped over. He was willing to wait, but he found his temper growing shorter each day. Tsubodai was not of the blood. The princes would make the future, not some broken-down old general who should have retired to tend his goats long before. Batu used his anger in a surge of strength, so that he felt as if he lifted the cart almost by himself, shoving it onwards and upwards.

Ogedai mounted slowly, feeling his hips protest. When had he become so stiff? The muscles in his legs and lower back had grown astonishingly weak. He could make them shudder like a horse shrugging off flies just by raising himself in the stirrups.

Sorhatani was deliberately not watching him, he noticed. Instead, she was fussing around her sons. Kublai was checking his pony's belly strap, while Arik-Boke and Hulegu were very

300

quiet in the presence of their khan. Ogedai knew the younger ones only by sight, but Sorhatani had brought Kublai to talk to him in the evenings. She had made it seem a favour to her, but Ogedai had grown to look forward to the conversations. The boy was sharp and he seemed to have an endless interest in the stories of past battles, particularly if Genghis had been part of them. Ogedai had found himself reliving past glories through Kublai's eyes and spent part of each day planning what he would tell the young man that evening.

The khan tested his legs again surreptitiously, then looked down as Torogene chuckled behind him. He turned his horse to see her standing there. He knew he was thin and pale from too much time indoors. His joints hurt and he ached for wine so that his mouth grew dry at the thought of it. He had promised Torogene he would drink fewer cups each day. More than that, she had made him swear a solemn oath. He had not told her about the set of enormous cups the kilns were firing for him. His word was iron, but wine was one of his few remaining joys.

'Don't stay out if you feel yourself getting tired,' Torogene said. 'Your officers can wait for another day if they have to. You must build your strength back slowly.'

He smiled at her tone, wondering if all wives became mothers to their husbands at some point. He could not help glancing at Sorhatani at that thought, still as lean and strong as a herd-boy. There was one who should not go to waste in a cold bed. He could not remember when he had last felt honest lust outside of dreams. His body felt worn out, withered and old. Yet the sun shone weakly and the autumn sky was blue. He would ride along the canal to see the new works. Perhaps he would even bathe in the river that fed it, if he could bring himself to enter the icy waters.

'Do not set my city on fire while I am gone,' he said gruffly. She smiled at his tone.

'I cannot promise, but I'll try,' Torogene replied. She reached out and touched his foot in the stirrup, holding it hard enough for him to feel the pressure. He did not need to speak the love he felt for her; he just reached down and touched her cheek before digging in his heels and clattering through the gate.

Sorhatani's sons came with him. Kublai held the reins of three packhorses, laden high with supplies. Ogedai watched as the young man clucked to them, so full of life that it was almost painful to see. He had not told Kublai his memories of Tolui's death. He was not yet ready to tell that story, with all the pain that continued to that cold day.

It took half the morning to reach the river. His stamina had melted away over so many months of inactivity. His arms and legs were leaden by the time he dismounted and he had to struggle not to cry out as his thighs cramped. He could already hear the rippling cracks across the valley and in the distance smoke hung like morning mist. The air had the tinge of sulphurous bitterness he remembered from the Sung border. To his surprise, he found it almost pleasant to breathe in the exotic scent.

Sorhatani and her sons made camp around him, setting up a small ger on dry ground by the bank and starting tea on the stove. While it brewed, Ogedai mounted once again. He clicked his tongue to catch Kublai's attention and the young man leapt into his saddle to join him, his face bright with excitement.

Together, both men rode across a sunlit field to where Khasar readied the ordnance crews for inspection. Ogedai could see the old general's pride in the new weapons from a distance. He too had been on the Sung border and seen their destructive potential. Ogedai rode up slowly. He felt no sense of urgency or hurry. His glimpse at the greater night had given him a long perspective. It was just harder to care about the smaller things. Having Kublai with him was a reminder that

302

not everyone shared his long view. The sight of the polished bronze guns had Kublai practically sweating.

Ogedai suffered through the formalities with his uncle. He declined the invitation of tea and food and finally gestured for the gunners to begin.

'You might want to dismount and hold your horse, my lord khan,' Khasar said.

He looked thin and weary, but his eyes were bright in his enthusiasm. Ogedai wasn't touched by uncle's mood. His legs felt weak and he did not want to stumble in front of such men. He took a moment to remind himself that he was in the eye of the nation once again. One slip and his weakness would reach every ear.

'My horse was at the Sung border,' he replied. 'He will not bolt. Kublai? You should do as he says.'

'Very well, my lord,' Khasar said formally. He clasped his hands behind his back as he gestured sharply to the gunnery teams. They stood in groups of four, carrying sacks of black powder as well as a range of odd-looking equipment. Kublai drank it all in, fascinated.

'Show me,' Ogedai said to them.

Khasar snapped orders and Ogedai watched from the saddle as the first team checked their weapon had blocks against the massive, studded wheels. A warrior placed a reed in a hole in the tube, then lit a taper from a lamp. When the taper touched the reed, there was a spark, then an explosion that sent the cannon rocking back. The blocks barely held it and the weapon leapt and crashed back down. Ogedai did not see the ball that came flying out, but he nodded, deliberately calm. His horse flicked up its ears, but then bent to crop at the grass. Kublai had to slap his gelding on the face, shocking it out of panic. The young man snarled at the animal. He would not be shamed by seeing his horse break free and run in front of the khan. However, he was more than thankful he was not in the saddle.

'Fire the rest together,' Ogedai said.

Khasar nodded proudly and eight other teams inserted their reeds into the touch-holes and lit tapers.

'On my mark, gunners. Ready? Fire!'

The crash was extraordinary. The teams had practised outside the city for weeks and the guns fired almost together, with only a slight delay. This time, Ogedai saw blurs vanishing across the valley, one or two skipping along the ground. He smiled at the thought of a line of horses or men in the path of such weapons.

'Excellent,' he said.

Khasar heard and chuckled, still delighted at controlling thunder.

Ogedai's gaze drifted to the lines of heavy catapults beyond the guns. They could launch barrels of gunpowder for hundreds of feet. His engineers had learned from the Chin, but they had improved the powder, so that it burned faster and more fiercely. Ogedai did not understand the process, nor care. What mattered was that the weapons worked.

More men waited by the catapults, standing perfectly at attention. Ogedai suddenly realised that he did not feel tired. The explosions and bitter smoke had invigorated him. Perhaps because of that, he noticed how Khasar's shoulders had slumped. The older man wore his exhaustion for all to see.

'Are you ill, uncle?' he said.

Khasar shrugged with a wince. 'I have lumps in my shoulders. The things make it hard to move my arm, that's all.'

His yellow complexion gave the lie to his words and Ogedai frowned as his uncle went on.

'The shamans say I should have them cut out, but I won't let those butchers have me, not yet. Half the men they cut don't walk out again, maybe more.'

'You should,' Ogedai said softly. 'I don't want to lose you yet, uncle.'

Khasar snorted. 'I'm like the hills, boy. A few lumps won't stop me.'

Ogedai smiled.

'I hope not. Show me more, uncle,' he said.

When Ogedai and Kublai returned to the small camp by the river, the morning was almost over and the tea was long past stewed and undrinkable. The gunnery went on behind them, using vast stocks of the powder to train the men who would play a vital role in future battles. Khasar could be seen striding up and down the lines, in his element.

Sorhatani saw that her son's flushed face was smudged with soot. Both the khan and Kublai reeked of sulphurous fumes and Arik-Boke and Hulegu could only look on with transparent envy. Sorhatani left her sons to make fresh tea and walked over to where Ogedai had dismounted.

He stood at the river's edge and stared over it, shading his eyes against the sun. The noise of the waterfall hid Sorhatani's steps as she came up behind him.

'Kublai is chattering like a bird,' she said. 'I take it the demonstration went well.'

Ogedai shrugged. 'Better than I had hoped. With the new powder mix, Khasar is convinced our guns have the range of the Sung cannon.' He clenched his fist at the thought, his expression fierce. 'That will make a difference, Sorhatani. We will surprise them one day. I only wish I could get some of them out to Tsubodai, but it would take years to drag those heavy things so far.'

'You are getting stronger,' she said, smiling.

'It's the wine,' he replied.

Sorhatani laughed. 'It's not the wine, you great drunkard, it's morning rides like this one and bow work each afternoon. You already look a different man from the one I found in that cold room.' She paused, tilting her head.

'There's a little more meat on you as well. Having Torogene back is good for you, I think.'

305

Ogedai smiled, but the excitement of the great guns was fading and his heart wasn't in it. He sometimes thought of his fears as a dark cloth that draped itself over him, choking off his breath. He had died on that campaign, and though the sun shone and his heart still beat in his chest, it was hard to go on with each day. He had thought Tolui's sacrifice might have given him fresh purpose, but instead he felt the loss as another burden, one too great to bear. The cloth still clung to him, for all Sorhatani had done. He could hardly explain it and part of him wished the woman would leave him alone to find a quiet path onwards.

Under Sorhatani's watchful gaze, Ogedai sat with the family, drank the tea and ate the cold food they had brought. No one brought him wine, so he rummaged for a skin of it in the packs, drinking straight from the teat, like airag. He ignored Sorhatani's expression as the red liquid brought a glow back to his cheeks. Her eyes seemed made of flint, so he spoke to distract her.

'Your son Mongke is doing well,' he said. 'I have reports from Tsubodai that speak highly of him.'

The other sons sat up in sudden interest and Ogedai wiped his lips, tasting the wine. It seemed bitter that day, sour on the tongue as if there was no goodness in it. To his surprise, it was Kublai who spoke, his tone respectful.

'My lord khan, have they taken Kiev?'

'They have. Your brother was part of the battles around that city.'

Kublai seemed to be struggling with impatience.

'Are they at the Carpathian mountains yet then? Do you know if they will breach them this winter?'

'You will tire the khan with your chatter,' Sorhatani said, but Ogedai noticed she still looked for an answer.

'The last I heard, they are going to try and cross before next year,' he said.

306

'That's a hard range,' Kublai murmured to himself.

Ogedai wondered how a young man could presume to know anything of mountains four thousand miles away. The world had grown since he was a boy. With the chains of scouts and way stations, knowledge of the world was flooding into Karakorum. The khan's library already contained volumes in Greek and Latin, full of wonders he could hardly believe. His uncle Temuge had taken the task of building its reputation seriously, paying fortunes for the rarest books and scrolls. It would be the work of a generation to translate them into civilised languages, but Temuge had a dozen Christian monks working on the task. Lost in a reverie, Ogedai dragged himself back and considered the words that had led him to drift away in thought. He wondered if Kublai was worried for his brother's safety.

'With Baidur, Tsubodai has seven tumans and forty thousand conscripts,' he said. 'The mountains will not stop them.'

'And after the mountains, my lord?' Kublai swallowed, trying not to irritate the most powerful man in the nation. 'Mongke says they will ride all the way to the sea.'

The younger brothers hung on his response and Ogedai sighed. He supposed distant battles were exciting compared to a life of study and quiet in Karakorum. Sorhatani's sons would not stay in the nest of stone for long, he could see.

'My orders are to secure the west, to give us a border without enemies clamouring beyond it to invade our lands. How Tsubodai chooses to do that is up to him. Perhaps in a year or two you will travel out to him. Would you like that?'

'Yes. Mongke is my brother,' Kublai replied seriously. 'And I would like to see more of the world than just maps in books.'

Ogedai chuckled. He could remember when the world seemed limitless and he had wanted to see it all. Somehow, he had lost that terrible hunger and for a moment he wondered if it was Karakorum that had taken it from him. Perhaps that was the curse of cities, that they rooted nations in one place and made them blind. It was not a pleasant thought.

'I would like to have a private word with your mother,' he said, realising he would not have a better moment that day.

Kublai moved fastest, shepherding his brothers to their horses and taking them in the direction of Khasar's gun teams, still practising in the afternoon sun.

Sorhatani sat down on the mat of felt, her expression curious.

'If you are going to declare your love for me, Torogene told me what to say,' she said.

To her pleasure, he laughed aloud. 'I'm sure she has, but no, you are safe from me, Sorhatani.' He hesitated and she leaned closer, surprised to see a touch of pink come to his cheeks.

'You are still a young woman, Sorhatani,' he began.

She shut her mouth rather than reply, though her eyes sparkled. Ogedai began twice more, but stopped himself.

'We have established my youth, I think,' she said.

'You have your husband's titles,' he went on.

Sorhatani's light mood dropped away. The one man who could remove the extraordinary authority she had been given was nervously trying to say what was on his mind. She spoke again, her voice harder.

'Earned by his sacrifice and death, my lord, yes. *Earned*, not given as a favour.'

Ogedai blinked, then shook his head.

'They too are safe, Sorhatani,' he said. 'My word is iron and you have those things from my hand. I will not take them back.'

'Then what is sticking in your throat so that it chokes you to say it?'

Ogedai took a deep breath. 'You should marry again,' he said.

'My lord khan, Torogene told me to remind you . . .'

'Not to me, woman! I've told you before. To my son. To Guyuk.'

Sorhatani looked at him in stunned silence. Guyuk was the heir to the khanate. She knew Ogedai too well to think the offer was made in haste. Her mind whirled as she tried to see through to what he truly wanted. Torogene must have known the offer would be made. Ogedai would never have thought of it on his own.

The khan turned away from her, giving her time. As he stared into the middle distance, the cynical part of Sorhatani wondered if this was a way to bring her husband's vast holdings back into the khanate. At a stroke, marriage to Guyuk would reverse the rashness of Ogedai's offer to Tolui. The effects of that unique decision were still rippling out and she did not know where it would end. The original lands of Genghis Khan were ruled by a woman and she had still barely come to terms with it.

She thought of her own sons. Guyuk was older than Mongke, but not by many years. Would her sons inherit, or would their birthright be stolen from them in such a union of families? She shuddered and hoped Ogedai had not seen. He was the khan and he could order her to marry, just as he had given her the titles of her husband. His power was near absolute over her, if he chose to use it. She looked at him without turning her head, weighing up the man she had nursed through fits and darkness so strong that she had thought he would never return. His life was as fragile as porcelain, yet he still ruled and his word was iron.

She could sense his patience was unravelling. A small muscle fluttered in his neck and she stared at it, searching for words.

'You do me great honour with such an offer, Ogedai. Your son and heir . . .'

'Then you accept?' he said curtly. His eyes knew the answer from her tone and he shook his head in irritation.

'I cannot,' Sorhatani replied softly. 'My grief for Tolui is the same. I will not marry again, my lord khan. My life now is my sons and no more than that. I *want* no more than that.'

Ogedai grimaced and the silence came back between them. Sorhatani feared his next words would be to command her, ignoring her will. If he spoke the words, she would have no choice but to obey. To resist would be to throw the bones with the futures of her sons, to see them stripped of authority and power before they had even learned to use it. She had wiped the khan's skin when he had soiled himself unknowing. She had fed him from her own hand when he moaned for peace and death. Yet he was the son of his father. The fate of one wife, one woman, would mean little to him and she did not know what he would say. Keeping silent, she waited with her head bowed, the breeze blowing between them.

It took an age, but at the last, he nodded to himself.

'Very well, Sorhatani. I owe you your freedom, if that is your wish. I will not demand your obedience in this. I have not told Guyuk. Only Torogene knows it was even a thought.'

Relief flooded through Sorhatani. On instinct, she prostrated herself on the grass, placing her head by his foot.

'Oh, get up,' he said. 'A less humble woman I have never met.'

CHAPTER TWENTY-FOUR

Kachiun died in the mountains, above the snowline, where there was neither time nor strength to tend to his body. The general's flesh had swollen with the poison from his infected leg. His last days had been spent in delirious agony, his hands and face mottled with sickness. He had died hard.

The winter had struck early just days afterwards, with blizzards howling through the mountains. Heavy snow blocked the narrow passes Guyuk had scouted through to the plains below. The only blessing of the plummeting temperatures was that it kept the dead from rotting. Tsubodai had ordered Kachiun's body wrapped in cloth and bound to a cart. The brother of Genghis had expressed a wish to be burnt in death, rather than sky-buried, laid out for birds and animals in high crags. The Chin ritual of cremation was becoming more popular. Those of the nation who had become Christian were even buried, though they preferred to go into the ground with the hearts of enemies in their hands, servants for the next life.

Neither Tsubodai nor Ogedai laid down the law on any of the practices. The people of the nation made their own choices at a time that could hurt no one else.

There was no single peak to the Carpathians, but dozens of valleys and ridges to be traversed. At first they were the only presence apart from distant birds, but then they came upon the first of the frozen bodies, high up, where the air was painful in the lungs. It lay alone, the hands and face wind-seared to black, almost as if charred by fire. Snow half-covered the man, and one of the minghaan officers set his warriors to dig at similar humps of snow. There were more bodies, the faces dark or pale, Turkic or Russian, often bearded. Men lay with women, their children frozen between them. They were preserved on the heights, their bodies thin, their flesh made stone for ever.

In all, there were hundreds and the generals could only wonder who they had been, or why they had chosen to risk death in the mountains. The bodies did not look old, but there was no way to tell. They could have lain there for centuries, or starved just months before the Mongols came loping along the tracks after them.

The wind and snow of winter came like a new world. From the first flakes, the animal paths vanished and the drifts built and built, having to be dug out at every step. Only the links between scouts at every pass and the sheer numbers and discipline of the tumans saved them. Tsubodai could relieve those at the front, who had to push through with hands and shovels. Those behind walked a wide trail of brown slush, churned up by tens of thousands of trudging feet and hooves. The snows could not stop them. They had already come too far.

As the cold deepened, the weakest and the wounded struggled to keep up. The tumans passed more and more seated figures, their heads bowed in death. There had been children born in the years away from Karakorum. Their small bodies froze quickly, the wind ruffling their hair as they were left behind

312

in the snow. Only the fallen horses were butchered for meat to sustain the living. The tumans pushed on, never stopping until they saw the plains before them and they had left the mountains and eternity behind. It took them two months longer than Tsubodai had hoped.

On the other side of the Carpathian mountains, the tumans gathered to mourn a general and a founder of the nation. The army of conscripts sat uncomprehending and sullen as they watched the Mongol shamans sing and tell the story of his life. For a man of Kachiun's history, the tales and songs lasted two full days. Those who witnessed it ate where they stood and heated frozen airag from the icy slush it had become, until they could drink to the brother of Genghis khan. At sunset of the second day, Tsubodai himself lit the funeral pyre they had soaked in oil, then stood back as the black smoke poured out.

Tsubodai watched the dark column rise and he could not help thinking of the signal it would send to their enemies. For anyone with eyes to see, the smoke meant the Mongols had crossed the mountains and reached the plains. The orlok shook his head, remembering the white, red and black tents Genghis had raised before cities. The first was simply a warning to surrender quickly. The red cloth went up if they refused and was a promise to kill every male of fighting age. The black tent meant that nothing would survive when the city fell at last. It promised only destruction and bare earth. Perhaps the rising thread of sparks and oily smoke was an omen for those who saw it. Perhaps they would see it and know Tsubodai had come. He could smile at his own vanity, commanding men still thin and weak from the crushing labour they had endured. Yet his scouts were already running. They would find a place to rest and recover, for those who had lost the use of fingers to have them cut away.

The flames gusted and crackled as the wind huffed across the pyre, sending the smoke back into the faces of the men standing around it. They had used a part of the seasoned timber Tsubodai had brought across the mountains, layering it to twice the height of a man over Kachiun's body. The smoke carried the sweetish smell of frying meat and some of the younger ones gagged as they took a breath. Tsubodai could hear pings and creaks from the general's armour as it expanded in the heat, at times sounding like a voice in the fire. He shook his head to clear it of foolishness, then sensed Batu watching him.

The prince of the nation stood with Guyuk, Baidur and Mongke, a group of four all under his command, yet separate from the rest. Tsubodai returned the stare until Batu looked away, his constant half-smile flickering on his mouth.

With a chill, Tsubodai realised Kachiun's death was a personal loss to him. The old general had supported him in council and on the field, trusting Tsubodai to find a way through, no matter what the odds. That blind faith had died with him and Tsubodai knew his flank was exposed. He wondered if he should promote Mongke to some senior post. Of the princes, he seemed least under Batu's spell, but if Tsubodai had misjudged him, there was a chance it would just make Batu's growing power even greater. As the wind gusted stronger still, Tsubodai cursed under his breath. He hated the labyrinth of politics that had sprung up since the death of Genghis. He was used to tactics, to the ruses and stratagems of battle. The city of Karakorum had added layers to those, so that he could no longer predict the knife thrust, the betrayal. He could no longer know the simple hearts of the men around him and trust them with his life.

He rubbed his eyes roughly and found a smear of moisture on his gloves that made him sigh. Kachiun had been a friend. His death had brought home the fact that Tsubodai too was getting old.

'This is my last campaign,' he murmured to the figure in

the pyre. He could see Kachiun in his blackened armour, alone in a furnace of yellow-gold. 'When I am done, I will bring your ashes home, old friend.'

'He was a great man,' Batu said.

Tsubodai gave a start. He had not heard him approach over the crackling flames. Fury welled up in him that Batu would bring his petty bitterness even to the funeral of Kachiun. He began to reply, but Batu held up an open palm.

'No mockery, orlok. I did not know half his story until I heard it from the shaman.'

Tsubodai stifled his retort and held Batu's steady gaze for a few more moments before looking back to the pyre. Batu spoke again, his voice gentle with awe.

'He hid with Genghis and other children from their enemies. They were hardened by starvation and fear. From that family, from those brothers, we all spring. I understand that, orlok. You too were there for some of it. You have seen a nation *born*. I can hardly imagine such a thing.' Batu sighed and gripped the bridge of his nose between his fingers, rubbing the tiredness out. 'I hope there is a tale to tell when it is my turn in the flames.'

Tsubodai looked at him, but Batu was already walking away through the snow. The air was clean and cold, promising more snow on the way.

PART THREE

AD 1240

CHAPTER TWENTY-FIVE

The dancers came to a halt, sweat gleaming on their bodies, the bells on their wrists and ankles falling silent. Incense was strong in the air, pouring in wreaths of white smoke out of censers as they swung at the foot of the marble stairs. The influence of Greece was everywhere in the palace, from columns of fluted marble and busts of King Bela and his ancestors, to the scanty costumes of the dancing girls waiting with their heads bowed. The walls themselves were decorated in gold leaf from Egypt and blue lapis lazuli from the Afghan hills. The ceiling stretched above them in a great dome that dominated the river city of Esztergom. In the inlaid images, it proclaimed the glory of the risen Christ, and of course the glory of the Hungarian king.

The courtiers prostrated themselves, pressed as close as bees in a hive, so that their bodies covered the tiled floor. Only the martial lords remained standing around the walls, looking at each other with poorly concealed irritation. Among them was

Josef Landau, master of the Livonian Brothers. He glanced at his brother-knight, a man who had recently become his commanding officer. Conrad von Thuringen was a powerful figure in all senses, with the build to handle the enormous longsword he wore and a black beard shot through with grey that did nothing to reduce his physical menace. Von Thuringen was the grand master of the Teutonic knights, an order that had been formed in the city of Acre, near Galilee. He bowed only to priests. The pomp and glitter of King Bela's court made little impression on a man who had dined with the Holy Roman Emperor and even Pope Gregory himself.

Josef was a little in awe of the grizzled commander. If the Teutonic Knights had not agreed to amalgamate, his Brothers of Livonia would have been disbanded after their losses in war. The double-headed black eagle he now wore had its twin on Conrad's chest. Together, their landholdings made them almost the equal of the king who made them wait on him like servants. Yet they served a higher power and the delay only served to tighten Josef's nerves and temper.

King Bela's seneschal began to recite the titles of his master and Josef saw Von Thuringen's eyes flicker upwards in frustration. The Holy Roman Emperor ruled a hundred territories, as far-flung as Italy and Jerusalem. King Bela of Hungary could not match those possessions. It pleased Josef that his commander had little patience for vanities. Such things were of the world and the Teutonic Order forced their gaze to heaven, so that the venal sins of men were far beneath them. Josef touched the cross of black and gold that he wore on his chest, proud that his Brothers of Livonia had been taken up by a noble order. If they had not been, he thought he might have put away his armour and sword and become a wandering monk, with a begging bowl and rags to serve the Christ. At times when politics hung as thick in the air as incense, such a life still appealed to him.

The seneschal finished his litany of titles and the crowd in the palace hall grew tense for the arrival of their master. Josef smiled to see Conrad scratch the side of his mouth in boredom, where a sore had scabbed over. Horns sounded a low note across the city to announce the arrival of the king. Josef wondered if the peasants in the markets were meant to prostrate themselves as well. The idea made his own mouth twitch, but he controlled himself as King Bela entered at last, striding to the top of the marble steps, so that he was almost the height of a man above them all.

The king was blond-bearded and wore his hair to his shoulders. A gold crown sat firmly on his head and his pale blue eyes looked out from under it. As his gaze travelled across them, both Josef Landau and Conrad von Thuringen bowed, the angle carefully chosen. King Bela did not acknowledge their presence beyond a brief nod, then took his place on a throne decorated in the same gold and blue as the walls. It glittered behind him as he was handed the ceremonial regalia of his monarchy, including a great staff of gold. As Josef watched, the king lifted it and let it fall three times, striking the ground. The seneschal stood back and some other servant dressed almost as richly came forward to address the crowd.

'There will be no judgments today, no court. The king has spoken. Let those who have such business remove themselves from his presence. You may petition the master of the court at noon.'

Josef could see anger and frustration on the faces of many of the men and women who rose from prostration and turned away. They had more sense than to let the king see their response to his edict. Josef could imagine how they had bribed and waited to get into that room, only to be told to leave before a word was spoken about their cases. He saw one young woman in tears as she left and he frowned to himself. The room emptied quickly, until only a dozen or so men remained, all senior lords or knights.

'The Cuman Lord Köten is summoned!' cried the seneschal.

Some of the lords looked askance at each other, but Josef noted that Conrad appeared relaxed. When their eyes met, the older man shrugged very slightly, all the answer he could give with the king's gaze on them.

Doors at the back opened and a small man walked in, in many ways the opposite of the king above him. Köten's skin was almost as dark as the Moors of Jerusalem to Josef's eyes. He had the sunken face and wiry build of a man who had never known more food than he needed to stay alive, a rarity in that court. His eyes were fierce and he bowed only a fraction deeper than Conrad and Josef had before him.

King Bela rose from his throne and spoke for the first time that morning.

'My lords, honoured knights, freemen. The Tartars have crossed the mountains.'

He repeated the words in Russian and Latin, a demonstration of his scholarship.

Conrad and Josef both crossed themselves at the words, with Conrad going on to kiss a heavy gold ring he wore on his left hand. Josef knew it contained a tiny relic of the True Cross from Calvary. He could only wish he had such a talisman of power to soothe his own nerves.

The reaction of Köten was to lean his head to one side and spit on the floor at his feet. The king and his courtiers froze at the action and high points of colour appeared in Bela's cheeks. Before he could act, perhaps to order the man to lick up his own spittle, Köten spoke.

'They are not Tartars, your majesty, they are Mongol warriors. They move quickly and they slaughter every living thing in their path. If you have friends, my king, call them now. You will need them all.'

The king's eyes were cold as he looked down on the room.

'I gave your people sanctuary here, Köten. Two *hundred*

322

thousand of your tribe, your families. You crossed the mountains to get away from these . . . Mongol warriors, did you not? You were not so well dressed then, Köten. You were ragged and close to death. Yet I took you in. I gave you lands and food from my own hand.'

'In exchange for taking the body and blood, your majesty,' Köten replied. 'I was baptised myself into . . . our faith.'

'That is the gift of the Spirit, God's favour to you. The world's price has yet to be paid, Köten.'

The small man clenched his hands behind his back as he waited. Josef was fascinated. He had heard of the mass exodus of refugees from Russia, leaving their dead in the frozen mountains rather than be hunted down. The stories they had spread of this 'Golden Horde' of Mongols had done the work of an army all on its own. Half of Hungary quaked at the threat and the rumours of black smoke in the mountains. Josef could see the whiteness of Köten's knuckles against the darker skin as King Bela went on.

'If I am to count you friend, I will need every warrior under your command. I will supply what arms they need and I will give them good soup to keep them warm, fuel for their fires, fodder for their horses, salt for their food. Your oath has been sworn, Köten. As your liege lord, my orders are to stand and face the enemy with me. Do not fear for your people. This is my land. I will stop them here.'

He paused and for a time Köten let the silence go on. At last, as if exhausted, his shoulders dipped.

'Will your allies be sending armies? The Pope? The Holy Roman Emperor?'

It was King Bela's turn to grow stiff and still. Pope Gregory and Emperor Frederick were locked in their own struggle. He had entreated them both for men and arms for more than a year, ever since the refugees had arrived from Russia. King Frederick had sent the Teutonic Knights: 1,190 men chosen

323

for the founding year of their order and never exceeding that number. They were legendary fighters, but against a Golden Horde of savage warriors, Bela could imagine them being swept away like leaves in a storm. Still he showed only confidence to the men he needed to support him.

'I have been promised an army from King Boleslav of Krakow, one from Duke Henry of Silesia, another from King Wenceslas of Bohemia. There *will* be fresh reinforcements in the spring. In the meantime, we have my own men of Hungary, Lord Köten: sixty thousand soldiers, all well trained and hungry to defend their land. And we have the knights, Köten. They will hold the line. With your horsemen, I can field a hundred thousand soldiers.' He smiled at the thought of such a colossal number. 'We will take the worst they can offer us and then we will strike back in the thaw and end this threat to peace for ever.'

Köten sighed visibly. 'Very well. I can bring my forty thousand to this dance, my king. We will stand.' He shrugged. 'In winter there is nowhere to run anyway, not where they cannot catch us.'

Conrad von Thuringen coughed into his mailed hand. The king looked across the meeting hall at him and nodded graciously. The knight marshal of the Teutonic Order scratched his beard for a moment, reaching through the heavy thatch to some flea or louse on the skin.

'Your majesty, my lord Köten. The Emperor Frederick did not send us to you. His is the authority over the earth, not the souls of men. We came because of the Christian brothers from Russia, fresh converted to the True Faith. We will stand between those families and the storm. It is no more than our duty.'

Around the room, other noblemen stepped forward to pledge their soldiers and houses to the king's cause. Josef waited until they had finished before he too swore his eight hundred knights of Livonia to service. He saw that Köten looked less than impressed and he smiled slightly at the man. As one of those 'fresh converts' Conrad had mentioned, Köten had no inkling yet of the force of men armed in Christ. The knights were few in number, but each one was a master of weapons, as strong on the field as in his faith in God. For all their fearsome reputation, he was certain the Mongol army would break on the knights like a wave on a rock.

'Every king should have such men to follow him,' Bela said, visibly pleased at their open support. For once he would not have to broker deals and persuade or bribe his lords to save themselves. 'The enemy have gathered in the foothills of the Carpathians. They are no more than three hundred miles away, with the Danube and Sajo rivers between us. We have a month, perhaps two at most, to make ready for them. They will not be here before spring.'

'Your majesty,' Köten said in the pause. 'I have seen them move. It is true the entire camp would take so long to reach us, but the tumans – the raiding armies – could cross that much land in eight days. If they did not spend the summers resting, majesty, they could have been here long before. They came into Moscow on the frozen river. They run like wolves in winter, while other men sleep. We should be ready, at least as ready as it is possible to be.'

King Bela frowned. Standing above them, he twisted an ornate gold ring on one hand with the fingers of the other, a gesture of nerves that was not lost on Köten or the lords present. He had ascended the throne only six years before, on the death of his father. Nothing in his experience had prepared him for the sort of war he now faced. At last he nodded.

'Very well. Marshal von Thuringen, you will decamp today to Buda and Pest to oversee the preparations. We will be ready for them when they come.'

The king put out his hand and his seneschal drew a long sword and handed it to him. In front of them all, Bela raised the blade and cut his forearm. He remained impassive as blood flowed, using his hand to daub it all along the blade, until most of the silver was red.

'My lords, you see the blood royal of Hungary. Make a dozen like this and take the swords out to the villages and towns. Hold them high. The people will answer the call of their noblemen, the call to arms of their king. We *will* defend the kingdom. Let this be the sign.'

Tsubodai stood huddled in furs, stretching out his hands to a crackling fire. The smoke rose and his gaze followed it, drifting up to ancient beams in the barn. It had been long abandoned by the farmer and part of the roof had sagged and broken. It smelled of horses and straw and it was dry enough, at least at one end. It was not much of a place to begin the conquest of a country, but there was nowhere else in the frozen fields that stretched to the horizon. He watched as an icicle on the open door dripped, and frowned at the sight. Surely it was just the warmth from the fire reaching it. Yet this was a new land. He knew nothing of the seasons, or how long the winter would last.

His seven generals waited patiently for him, chewing noisily on pouches of bread and meat and passing a fat skin to take gulps of airag that kept them warm.

Kachiun's senior minghaan, Ilugei, had taken over the tuman. In time, a new general would be appointed at the khan's order, but in the field, Tsubodai had raised Ilugei. It was no coincidence that the man was grey-haired and wiry, almost forty years of age and one of those trained in the personal guard of Genghis. Tsubodai had had enough of the young lions Batu had gathered around him. He would have preferred Khasar, if he had not been almost five thousand miles away in Karakorum. He needed dependable men if he was to take the army on to the sea.

'Attend me,' Tsubodai said, without preamble. He paused only for a beat as the generals stopped eating and came closer to hear. 'The further we go west, the more danger comes from the flanks. If we drive on, it is as a spear thrust into the centre of an army: every step is greater risk.'

He did not look at Batu as he spoke, though the prince smiled. Tsubodai paused to take a draught of airag, feeling the warmth spread in his stomach.

'I am splitting the army in three. Baidur and Ilugei will strike north. My scouts tell me there is an army near a city named Krakow. Your orders are to remove it from the field and burn the city. The small kings there cannot be allowed to form up on our flank.'

He looked Ilugei in the eye.

'You have more years of experience than Baidur, who is new to the role.' Tsubodai sensed Baidur stiffen as the younger man saw his authority threatened before his eyes. He went on. 'Can you accept his command over you, Ilugei?'

'I can, orlok,' Ilugei replied, bowing his head.

Baidur let out a breath. It was a small thing, but Tsubodai had taken one of Batu's supporters and deliberately favoured him.

'Guyuk and Mongke, the lands to the south must be laid waste. You will take your tumans to the south of us. Sweep the land clear of anyone capable of fielding a force of men or horses. When you have scorched the earth, return and support me.'

'What about me, orlok?' Batu said softly. He was frowning deeply at the news that Guyuk would be sent to the south, well away from him. 'Where would you have *me* stand?'

'At my side, of course,' Tsubodai replied with a smile. 'You and I will strike west with Jebe, Chulgetei and the ragged army we command on foot. With three tumans, we will raze Hungary together, while our brothers clear the flanks.'

There was no ceremony as the men walked away from the

327

old barn. Tsubodai noticed how Batu made a point of clapping Guyuk on the back, but there was strain in both men's faces. They had fought and ridden with Tsubodai's eyes on them and other tumans ready to ride in support. They were not afraid of the responsibility. Each man there welcomed the chance to act on his own. It was why they had sought power and it had come upon them in the foothills of the Carpathians, from the hand of Tsubodai. Only Batu, Jebe and Chulgetei would remain. The three men were a little wistful as they watched the others break into a jog to reach their warriors quickly.

'It feels like a race, does it not?' Jebe said.

Batu turned cold eyes on him. 'Not to me. It seems I am to stay with my wet nurse and you.'

Jebe laughed and stretched the stiffness out of his back.

'You think too much, Batu, do you know that?' he said and walked away, still smiling.

Ogedai was in the gardens of Karakorum, watching the sun set from a stone bench. He felt at peace there in a way he could never have explained to his father. He chuckled softly. Even the thought of Genghis was like bringing darker shadows into the groves of trees. Ogedai loved the gardens in summer, but in winter they had a different beauty. The trees stood bare, their branches outstretched and waiting silently for green life. It was a time of darkness and yearning, of snug gers and heated airag, of being wrapped tight against the wind. Life in the gers was one thing he missed in the palace of Karakorum. He had even considered having one built in a courtyard before he dismissed the idea as foolishness. He could not go back to a simpler life, not now he had left it behind. It was the longing of a child, for the days when his mother and father were still alive. His grandmother Hoelun had lived long enough to lose her mind and memories and he shuddered at the thought of her last days. The first mother of the nation had become a babbling child at the end, unable even to clean herself. No one would wish such a fate on an enemy, never mind someone they loved.

He stretched his back, loosening the cramps from a day of sitting and talking. There was so *much* talking in a city. It was almost as if the streets were built on words. He smiled at the thought of his father's reaction to all the meetings he had attended that day. The problems of clean water and sewage pipes would have driven Genghis to apoplexy.

Ogedai shaded his eyes as the sunlight struck across Karakorum. The city was washed in dark gold, making every line of it stand out with extraordinary clarity. His eyes were not as sharp as they had once been and he relished the light and what it revealed. *He* had made Karakorum, no one else, certainly not his father. The palace tower cast a long shadow across the city in the wilderness. It was young yet, but in time it would be the true heart of the nation, the seat of khans. He wondered how they would remember him in the centuries to come.

He shivered slightly as the evening breeze picked up. With a quick gesture, he pulled his deel tighter over his chest, but then let it fall open again. What would his life have been without the weakness of the flesh? He sighed slowly, feeling the erratic thumping in his chest. He had grown weary waiting. He had thrown himself into battle to conquer the terror, ridden into an enemy army as if fear was a snake to be crushed under his sandal. In response, it had sunk its fangs into his heel and dropped him into darkness. There were times when he thought he had not yet climbed out of that pit.

He shook his head in memory, trying not to think of Tolui and what he had done for him. A brave man could conquer fear, he had learned that, but perhaps only for a time. It was something the young did not understand, the way it could gnaw at a man, the way it came back stronger every time, until you were alone and gasping for breath.

He had smothered himself in despair, giving up the struggle; giving in. Sorhatani had pulled him back and given him hope again, though she could never know how it was an *agony* to hope. How could he live with death crouched on his shoulders, gripping him from behind, weighing him down? He had faced it. He had summoned his courage and raised his head, but it had not looked away. No man could be strong *all* day, all night. It had worn him down to nothing.

Ogedai rested his hands on his knees, turning them upwards so he could see the palms. The callus had begun to return, though he had experienced blisters for the first time in years. One or two were still weeping from just an hour with the sword and bow that afternoon. He could feel his strength coming back, but too slowly. In his youth, he had been able to call on his body without thought, but his heart had been weak even then. He raised a hand to his neck and pushed his fingers under his silk tunic over his chest, feeling the thready beat there. It seemed such a fragile thing, like a bird.

A sudden pain made him start. It was as if he had been struck, and as his vision blurred, he turned to see whatever had hit him. He felt his head for blood, bringing his hands close to his eyes. His hands were clean. Another spasm made him hunch over, leaning against his knees as if he could press it away. He gasped aloud, panting. His pulse thumped in his ears, a hammer that throbbed through him.

'Stop,' he snapped, furious. His body was the enemy, his heart the betrayer. He *would* command it. He clenched his fist and pressed it against his chest, still bent over to his knees. Another pain hit him then, even worse than the last. He groaned and threw back his head, staring at the darkening sky. He had survived before. He would wait it out.

He did not feel himself slump, slipping sideways off the bench so that the stones of the path pressed against his cheek. He could hear his heart beat in great, slow thumps, then nothing, just an awful silence that went on and on. He thought he could hear his father's voice and he wanted to weep, but there were no tears left in him, just darkness and cold.

CHAPTER TWENTY-SIX

Sorhatani was tugged from sleep by the creak of the floor. She woke with a start to see Kublai standing by her bed, his expression grim. His eyes were red and she was suddenly afraid of what he would say. Though years had passed, the memory of Tolui's death was still painfully fresh. She sat up sharply, pulling the blankets around her.

'What is it?' she demanded.

'It seems your sons are cursed to bear bad news, mother,' Kublai replied. He looked away as she stood and removed her shapeless nightdress, pulling on clothes from the day before.

'Tell me,' she said, yanking at a tunic's buttons.

'The khan is dead. Ogedai is dead,' Kublai replied, staring out of the window at the night outside the city. 'His Guards found him. I heard them and I went to see.'

'Who else knows?' Sorhatani said, all sleep forgotten as the news sank in.

Kublai shrugged. 'They sent someone to tell Torogene.

The palace is still quiet, at least for the moment. They found him in the gardens, mother, without a mark on him.'

'Thank God for that at least. His heart was weak, Kublai. Those of us who knew have feared this day for a long time. Have you seen the body?' she asked.

He winced at such a question and the memory it evoked. 'I did. Then I left and came to tell you.'

'You were right. Now listen to me. There are things we must do now, Kublai, as the news begins to spread. Or before summer you will see your uncle Chagatai come riding through the gates of Karakorum to claim his birthright.'

Her son stared at her, unable to comprehend her sudden coldness.

'How can we stop him now?' he asked. 'How can *anyone* stop him?'

Sorhatani was already moving towards the door.

'He is not the heir, Kublai. Guyuk stands in line and in his way. We must send a fast rider to Tsubodai's army. Guyuk is in danger from this moment until he is declared khan by an assembly of the nation, just as his father was.'

Kublai gaped at her. 'Have you any *idea* how far away they are?' he said.

She halted, with her hand on the door.

'It does not matter if Guyuk stands at the end of the world, my son. He must be told. The yam, Kublai, the way stations. There are enough horses between us and Tsubodai, are there not?'

'Mother, you don't understand. It is more than four thousand miles, maybe even five thousand. It would take months to bring word.'

'Well? Write the news on parchment,' she snapped. 'Is that not how it works? Send a rider with a sealed message for Guyuk alone. Can these messengers hand a private letter over such a distance?'

'Yes,' Kublai replied, shocked by her intensity. 'Yes, of course.'

'Then *run*, boy! Run to Yao Shu's offices and write the news down. Get the news moving to the one who must have it.' She wrestled a ring from her hand and shoved it into his palm.

'Use your father's ring to seal it in wax and get the first rider on his way. Make him understand there has never been a message as important as this one. If there was ever a reason to create the scout line, this is it.'

Kublai broke into a sprint down the corridors. Sorhatani bit her lip as she watched him go before turning the other way, towards Torogene's rooms. Already, she could hear raised voices somewhere nearby. The news would not be kept in the city. As the sun rose, it would fly from Karakorum in all directions. She felt sadness swell in her at the thought of Ogedai, but pressed it down, clenching her fists. There was no time to grieve. The world would never be the same after the day to come.

Kublai had cause to thank his mother as he sat at Yao Shu's writing desk. The door to the chancellor's workrooms had been replaced by carpenters, but the holes for the new locks still sat ready, clean and sanded. It had swung open at just a push and Kublai had shivered in the cold as he took a Chin tinderbox and scratched sparks with a flint and iron until a wisp of tinder blew into flame. The lamp was small and he kept it well shuttered, but there were already voices and movements in the palace. He looked for water, but there was nothing, so he spat on the inkstone and blackened his fingers rubbing a paste. Yao Shu kept his badger-hair brushes neatly and Kublai worked fast with the thinnest of them, marking the Chin characters on the parchment with delicate precision.

He had barely finished a few stark lines and sanded them dry when the door creaked open and he looked up nervously to see Yao Shu standing there in a sleeping robe.

'I do not have time to explain,' Kublai said curtly as he stood. He folded the vellum parchment, goatskin beaten and stretched until it was as thin as yellow silk. The lines that would change the nation were hidden, and before Yao Shu could speak, Kublai dripped wax and jammed his father's ring down, leaving a deep impression. He faced Ogedai's chancellor with a strained expression. Yao Shu stared at the neat package and the glistening wax as Kublai fanned it in the air to dry. He could not understand the tension he saw in the younger man.

'I saw the light. Half the palace is awake, it seems,' Yao Shu said, deliberately blocking the door as Kublai moved towards it. 'You know what is happening?'

'It is not my place to tell you, chancellor,' Kublai replied. 'I am on the khan's business.' He met Yao Shu's eyes steadily, refusing to be cowed.

'I'm afraid I must insist on an explanation for this . . . intrusion before I let you go,' Yao Shu replied.

'No, you will not insist. This is not your business, chancellor. It is a matter of family.'

Kublai did not let his hand drift to the sword he wore on his hip. He knew the chancellor could not be intimidated with a blade. They locked eyes and Kublai kept silent, waiting.

With a grimace, Yao Shu stepped aside to let him pass, his gaze falling onto the desk with its still-wet inkstone and writing materials scattered in confusion. He opened his mouth to ask another question, but Kublai had already vanished, his footsteps echoing.

It was not far to the yam way station, the central hub of a network that extended as far as Chin lands to the east and beyond. Kublai raced through the palace outbuildings, across a courtyard and along a cloister around a garden, where the wind caught him up and passed him with a cold breath. He could see torches in the garden, lighting a spot in the distance as men gathered by the khan's body. Yao Shu would hear the terrible news soon enough.

Out of the palace, he ran along a street made grey in the dawn. He skidded on the cobbles as he rounded a corner and saw the lamps of the yam. There was always someone awake there, at every hour of the day. He called as he passed under the stone arch into a large yard, with horse stalls on either side. Kublai stood panting, listening as a pony snorted and tapped the door of its stall with its hoof. Perhaps the animal sensed the excitement that gripped him; he did not know.

It was just moments before a burly figure came into the yard. Kublai saw the yam master had only one hand, his job a compensation for losing his ability to fight. He tried not to look at the stump as the man approached.

'I speak with the authority of Sorhatani and Torogene, wife to Ogedai Khan. This has to reach Tsubodai's army as fast as you have ever run before. Kill horses and men if you have to, but get it into the hands of the heir, Guyuk. No other but Guyuk. His hands alone. Do you understand?'

The old warrior gaped at him.

'What is so urgent?' he began. It seemed the news had not yet spread to those who carried it. Kublai made a decision. He needed the man to jump quickly and not waste a moment longer.

'The khan is dead,' he said flatly. 'His heir must be told. Now *move*, or give up your post.'

The man was already turning away and calling for whoever was on duty that night. Kublai stayed to watch the pony brought out to a taciturn young rider. The scout stiffened as he heard the order to kill horses and men, but he understood and nodded. The papers went deep into a leather satchel that the scout strapped tightly to his back. At a run, yam servants brought a saddle that jingled with every movement.

The pony chosen for the task raised its head at the sound,

336

snorting once more and flicking its ears. It knew the sound of saddle bells meant it would run fast and far. Kublai watched the rider kick in his heels and canter under the arch, out into the waking city. He rubbed his neck, feeling the stiffness there. He had done his part.

Torogene was awake and weeping when Sorhatani arrived at her rooms. The Guards at the door let her pass with no more than a glance at her expression.

'You have heard?' Torogene asked.

Sorhatani opened her arms and the older woman came into her embrace. Larger than Sorhatani, her arms came fully round her, so that they clung to one another.

'I'm just going to the gardens,' Torogene said. She was shuddering with grief, close to collapse. 'His Guards are standing over . . . him there, waiting for me.'

'I must speak to you first,' Sorhatani said.

Torogene shook her head.

'Afterwards. I cannot leave him out there alone.'

Sorhatani weighed her chances of stopping Torogene and gave up.

'Let me walk with you,' she said.

The two women moved quickly along the corridors that led to the open gardens, Torogene's guards and servants falling behind. As they walked, Sorhatani heard Torogene choke into her hands and the sound tore at her own control. She too had lost a husband and the wound was still fresh, ripped open by the news of the khan's passing. She had the unpleasant sensation of events slipping beyond her control. How long would it be before Chagatai heard his brother had fallen at last? How long after that would he come to Karakorum to challenge for the khanate? If he moved quickly, he could bring an army before Guyuk could come home.

Sorhatani lost track of the corners and turns in the palace until she and Torogene felt the breeze on their faces and the gardens lay before them through a cloister. The torches of the Guards still lit the spot, though dawn had come. Torogene gave a cry and broke into a run. Sorhatani stayed with her, knowing she could not interrupt.

As they reached the stone bench, Sorhatani stood rooted, letting Torogene cross the last few steps to her husband. The Guards stood in mute anger, unable to see an enemy, but consumed with the failure of their office.

Ogedai had been turned to face the sky by whoever had found him. His eyes had been closed and he lay in the perfect stillness of death, his flesh as white as if he had no blood in him. Sorhatani rubbed tears from her eyes as Torogene knelt at his side and brushed his hair back with her hand. She did not speak, or weep. Instead, she sat on her heels and looked down at him for a long time. The breeze passed through them all and the gardens rustled. Somewhere close, a bird called, but Torogene did not look up or move from the spot.

Yao Shu arrived in the silence, still in his sleeping robe and with a face almost as pale as his master's. He seemed to age and shrink as he looked on the fallen khan. He did not speak. The silence was too deep for that. In misery, he stood as one of the sentinel shadows in the garden. The sun rose slowly and more than one man looked at it almost in hatred, as if its light and life were not welcome there.

As the morning light turned the city a bloody gold, Sorhatani stepped forward at last and took Torogene gently by the arm.

'Come away now,' she murmured. 'Let them take him to be laid out.'

Torogene shook her head and Sorhatani bent closer to her, whispering into her ear.

'Put aside your pain for today. You must think of your son,

Guyuk. You hear me, Torogene? You must be strong. You must shed your tears for Ogedai another day if your son is to survive.'

Torogene blinked slowly and began to shake her head, once, then twice, as she listened. Tears came from under her closed eyelids and she reached down and kissed Ogedai on the lips, shuddering under Sorhatani's hand at the terrible coldness of him. She would never feel his warmth, his arms around her again. She reached out to touch the hands, rubbing her fingers over the fresh calluses there. They would not heal now. Then she stood.

'Come with me,' Sorhatani said softly, as if to a frightened animal. 'I will make you tea and find you something to eat. You must keep up your strength, Torogene.'

Torogene nodded and Sorhatani led her back through the cloister to her own rooms. She looked back almost at every step, until the garden hid her view of Ogedai. The servants ran ahead to have tea ready as they arrived.

The two women swept into Sorhatani's rooms. Sorhatani saw the Guards were taking positions on her door and realised they too were without direction. The death of the khan had taken away the established order and they seemed almost lost.

'I have orders for you,' she said on impulse. The men straightened. 'Send a runner to your commander, Alkhun. Tell him to come to these rooms immediately.'

'Your will, mistress,' the Guard said, bowing his head. He set off and Sorhatani told her servants to leave. The tea urn was already beginning to steam and she needed to be alone with Ogedai's wife.

As she closed the doors, Sorhatani saw how Torogene sat staring, stunned with grief. She bustled about, deliberately making noise with the cups. The tea was not fully hot, but it would have to do. She hated herself for intruding on a private grief, but there was no help for it. Her mind had been throwing sparks from the moment she had woken to find Kublai standing beside her. Some part of her had known even before he spoke.

'Torogene? I have sent a runner to Guyuk. Are you listening? I am truly sorry for what has happened. Ogedai . . .' She choked off as her own grief threatened to overwhelm her. She too had loved the khan, but she forced the sadness away once again, pressing it into a closed part of her mind so that she could go on.

'He was a good man, Torogene. My son Kublai has sent a letter to Guyuk, with the yam riders. He says it will not reach him for months. I do not suppose Guyuk will return as quickly.'

Torogene looked up suddenly. Her eyes were terrible.

'Why would he not come home, to me?' she said, her voice raw.

'Because by then he will know that his uncle Chagatai could be in the city with his tumans, Torogene. Chagatai will hear the news faster and he is far closer than Tsubodai's armies. By the time Guyuk returns, Chagatai could be khan. No, listen to me now. At that point, I would not give a copper coin for your son's life. Those are the stakes, Torogene. Put aside your grief now and listen to counsel.'

The sound of boots on the stones outside made them both look up. The senior minghaan of the khan's Guards entered the room in full armour. He bowed briefly to the two women, unable to hide his irritation at such a summons. Sorhatani glanced at him without warmth. Alkhun may not have realised how power had shifted in the palace since dawn, but she had.

'I do not wish to intrude on your grief,' Alkhun said. 'You will both understand that my place is with the Guard tuman, keeping order. Who knows how the city will react when the news spreads. There could be riots. If you will excuse me . . .'

'Be silent!' Sorhatani snapped. Alkhun froze in amazement, but she did not give him time to think and realise his error. 'Would you walk in on the khan without so much as a knock on the door? Then why show less honour to us? How *dare* you interrupt?'

'I was . . . summoned,' Alkhun stammered, his face flushing. It was many years since anyone had raised a voice to him in anger. Sheer surprise made him hesitate.

Sorhatani spoke slowly, with complete confidence.

'*I* have title to the ancestral lands, minghaan. There is but one in the nation senior to me. *She* sits here.' Sorhatani saw Torogene was staring at her in bewilderment, but went on. 'Until Guyuk arrives in Karakorum, his mother is regent. If it is not obvious to even the least of men, I decree it from this moment.'

'I . . .' Alkhun began, then fell silent as he considered. Sorhatani was willing to wait and she poured more tea, hoping that neither one noticed the way her shaking hands made the cups clink together.

'You are correct, of course,' Alkhun said, almost with relief. 'I am sorry to have disturbed you, mistress. My lady.' He bowed again to Torogene, this time much deeper.

'I will have your head if you displease me again, Alkhun,' Sorhatani continued. 'For the time being, secure the city as you say. I will let you know details of the funeral as I have them.'

'Yes, my lady,' Alkhun replied. The world had ceased spinning wildly, at least in those rooms. He did not know if the sense of chaos would return outside them.

'Bring your nine minghaan officers to the main audience chamber at sunset. I will have further orders for you by then. I do not doubt Chagatai Khan will be considering an assault on Karakorum, Alkhun. He must not set one *foot* in this city, do you understand?'

'I do,' Alkhun replied.

'Then leave us,' Sorhatani said, waving her hand to dismiss him. He closed the door carefully behind him and Sorhatani let out a huge breath. Torogene was watching her with wide eyes.

'May all our battles go so smoothly,' Sorhatani said grimly.

Baidur rode north with a fierce pride in his heart, leaving Tsubodai and Batu behind. He suspected that Ilugei would report back his every action, but he was not daunted by thought of close scrutiny. His father Chagatai had trained him in every discipline and tactic – and his father was a son of Genghis Khan. Baidur had not gone into the wilderness unprepared. He just hoped he would have the chance to use some of the things he had packed onto spare horses. Tsubodai had given his approval to leave carts behind. The vast herd of ponies that travelled with a tuman could carry almost anything except the spars of heavy catapults.

It was difficult to smother his visible joy as he rode with two tumans through lands he had never imagined. They covered around sixty miles a day, by the best reckoning. Speed was important, Tsubodai had made that clear enough, but Baidur could not leave armies in his wake. That was why he had taken a path almost true north of the Carpathian mountains. Once he was in position, he would drive west in concert with Tsubodai, breaking anything that stood in his way. His men had begun to scour the land clear as they reached a position with Krakow to the west and the city of Lublin ahead of them.

As Baidur reined in, he stared at the walls of Lublin with a sour expression. The land around him was barren in winter, the fields black and bare. He dismounted to feel the soil, crumbling the black muck in his hands before moving on. It was good land. Only rich earth and horses could excite a real greed in him. Gold and palaces meant nothing at all; his father had taught him that much. Baidur had never heard of Krakow until Tsubodai had given him the name, but he hungered to claim the Polish principalities for the khan. It was even possible that Ogedai would reward a successful general with a khanate of his own. Stranger things had happened.

Tsubodai had given him vellum skins with all he knew about the land ahead, but he had not yet had a chance to read them. It did not matter. No matter who he faced, they would be as wheat.

He mounted again and rode closer to the city. It was not long till sunset and the gates were closed against him. As he approached, he saw the walls were shored up, showing the patches and marks of generations of poor repairs. In places, there was little more than a barrier of piled wood and stone. He smiled. Tsubodai expected speed and destruction.

He turned to Ilugei, who sat his mount and watched with an impassive expression.

'We will wait for darkness. One jagun of a hundred men will climb the walls on the other side, drawing their guards to them. Another hundred will go in and open the gates from inside. I want this place burning by sunrise.'

'It will be done,' Ilugei said, riding away to pass on the orders of the younger man.

CHAPTER TWENTY-SEVEN

Baidur and Ilugei moved at blistering speed across the landscape. No sooner had Lublin fallen than Baidur was urging
the tumans onwards to the cities of Sandomir and Krakow. At
such a pace, the tumans came across columns of men marching
to relieve cities already taken. Again and again, Baidur was able
to surprise the nobles in the area, his twenty thousand routing
smaller forces, then hunting them down piecemeal. It was the
sort of campaign Baidur's grandfather had relished and his
father Chagatai recounted in detail. The enemy were sluggish
and slow to react against a knife thrust across their lands.
Baidur knew there would be no mercy if he failed, from his
own people or those he faced. Given the chance, the Poles
would wipe out his tumans to the last man. It made sense not
to meet them on their own terms, or fight to their strengths.
He had no reinforcements to call on and he husbanded his
tumans carefully, knowing he had to keep them intact, even if
it meant refusing to engage.

He did not know the name of the man who led out the regiments of bright knights and foot soldiers against him near Krakow. Baidur's scouts reported an army of around fifty thousand and Baidur swore to himself when he heard. He knew what Tsubodai would want him to do, but he had never seen the race across the north as suicide. At least the Polish noble hadn't retreated behind thick walls and dared them to take the city. Krakow was as open as Moscow and as hard to defend. Its strength lay in the massive army that gathered before it, waiting in camp for the Mongol tumans to attack.

Baidur rode dangerously close to the city with his senior minghaans, observing the formations of soldiers and the lie of the land. He had no idea whether the Poles presented a threat to Tsubodai, but it was for exactly this task that he had been sent north. Such an army could not be allowed to join forces with those in Hungary, but it was not enough to pin them down around Krakow. Baidur's task was to tear a strip right through the country, to make sure that no armed force could consider moving south in support, not with such a wolf loose among their own people. Apart from anything else, Tsubodai would have his ears if Baidur ignored those orders.

Baidur rode to a small hill and stared at the sea of men and horses revealed to him. In the distance, he could see his presence had been marked. Polish scouts were already galloping closer, their weapons drawn in clear threat. Other men were mounting on the outskirts, ready to defend or attack, whatever his presence called for. What would his father do? What would his *grandfather* have done against so many?

'That city must be rich to have so many men guarding it,' Ilugei muttered at his shoulder.

Baidur smiled, making a quick decision. His men had almost sixty thousand horses with them, a herd so vast it could never remain in one place for more than a day. The horses stripped the grass like locusts, just as the tumans ate anything that

345

moved. Yet each spare mount carried bows and shafts, pots, food and a hundred other items the men needed for the campaign, even the wicker and felt for gers. Tsubodai had sent him well equipped, at least.

'I think you are right, Ilugei,' Baidur said, weighing his chances. 'They want to protect their precious city, so they cluster around it, waiting for us.' He grinned. 'If they are kind enough to stay in one place, our arrows will speak for us.'

He turned his pony and rode back, ignoring the enemy scouts who had come close while he sat and observed. As one of them darted in, Baidur drew an arrow smoothly, fitting it to his bowstring and loosing in one movement. It was a fine shot and the scout went tumbling. A good omen, he hoped.

Baidur left their shouts and jeers behind him, knowing the scouts would not dare to follow. His mind was already busy. With the stores on the spare horses, he still had almost two million shafts – each a piece of straight birch, well fletched – bundled in quivers of thirty or sixty. Even with such abundance, he had been careful to retrieve and repair as many as he could from the battles. They were perhaps his most precious resource, after the horses themselves. He looked at the sun and nodded. It was still early. He would not waste the day.

King Boleslav, Grand Duke of Krakow, drummed his gauntlet on the leather pommel of his saddle as he watched the vast cloud of dust that marked the movements of the approaching Mongol horde. He sat a massive grey charger, a beast of the breed that could pull a plough through the black earth all day without tiring. Eleven thousand knights stood ready to destroy the invader once and for all. To his left, the French Knights Templar stood ready in their livery of red and white over steel. Boleslav could hear their voices raised in prayer. He had archers by the thousand and, most importantly of all, he had pikemen

346

who could stand against a charge with lances. It was an army to inspire confidence, and he kept his messengers close by, ready to ride to his cousin in Liegnitz with news of the victory. Perhaps when he had saved them all, his family would finally recognise him as the rightful ruler of Poland.

The mother church would still stand in his way, he thought sourly. They preferred the princes of Poland to waste their strength in squabbles and assassinations, leaving the church to grow fat and wealthy. Only the month before, his cousin Henry had sponsored a monastery for the new order of Dominicans, paying for it all in good silver. Boleslav winced at the thought of the benefices and indulgences Henry had earned as a result. It was the talk of the family.

In his silent thoughts, Boleslav offered up a prayer of his own.

'Lord, if I see victory today, I will found a convent in my city. I will set a chalice of gold on the altar of the chapel and I will find a relic to bring pilgrims from a thousand miles. I will have a Mass offered for all those who lose their lives. I give you my oath, Lord, my troth. Allow me your victory and I will have your name sung across Krakow.'

He swallowed drily and reached for a small bottle of water on a thong hanging from his saddle. He hated the waiting and he still feared that the reports of his scouts were true. He knew they were prone to exaggerate, but more than one had come back with tales of a horde twice the size of his fifty thousand, a great ocean of uncountable horses and terrible invaders, carrying bows and lances like the trees of a forest. His bladder made itself felt and Boleslav winced irritably. Let the damned dogs come, he told himself. God would speak and they would learn the strength of his right hand.

Boleslav could see the dark mass of the enemy as they rode closer. They poured across the ground, too many to count, though he did not think it was the vast army his scouts had described. That thought brought the worry that there might be more out of sight. He had only one report from Russia, but it warned they were fiends for trickery, in love with the ambush and the flanking blow. None of that was in evidence as his pikemen held their position. The Mongol warriors were riding straight at his lines as if they intended to gallop through them. Boleslav began to sweat, fearing he had missed something in the battle plans. He saw the Knights Templar ready themselves to counter-charge, safe for the moment behind the ranks of stolid pikemen. Boleslav watched intently as the pikes came down, the butts firmly grounded in the earth. They would stop anything, gut *anyone*, no matter how fast or fierce they were.

The Mongols came in a wide line, no more than fifty deep. As Boleslav stared, they bent bows and released. Thousands of shafts rose in the air above his pikemen and Boleslav knew a moment of horror. They had shields, but they had thrown them down to hold the pikes against a charge.

The sound of arrows striking men clattered across the field, followed by screaming. Hundreds fell and the arrows kept coming. Boleslav counted twelve heartbeats between each colossal strike, though his heart was racing and he could not calm himself. His own archers replied with volleys and he tensed in anticipation, only to see the shafts fall short of the Mongol horsemen. How could they have such a range? His bowmen were good, he was certain, but if they could not reach the enemy, they were useless to him.

Orders snapped up and down the lines as officers tried to respond. Many of the pikemen dropped the massive weapons. Some reached for their shields, while others tried to balance shield and pike together, neither one serving its purpose. Boleslav cursed, looking over their heads to the commander of the Templars. The man was like a dog straining on a leash. They were ready to ride, but by the pikemen were still blocking the Templars' path into the enemy. There could be no smooth manoeuvre as the foot soldiers pulled aside and let the Templars thunder through. Instead, they lay in tangled heaps of men and pikes like thorns, cowering under their shields as the arrows flew and thumped into them.

Boleslav swore, his voice cracking. His messengers looked up, but he had not spoken for them. He had seen armies all his life. He owed his power to the battles he had fought and won, but what he was seeing made a mockery of everything he had learned. The Mongols seemed to have no directing structure. There was no calm centre to order their movements. That would have been something Boleslav could have countered. Yet neither were they a rabble, with each man acting on his own. Instead, they moved and attacked as if a thousand guiding hands were over them, as if each group was completely independent. It was insane, but they shifted and struck like wasps, responding instantly together to any threat.

On one side, a thousand Mongol warriors clipped their bows to their saddles and lifted up lances, turning a sweep along the line into a sudden crash into the shields of the pikemen. Before Boleslav's officers could even react, they were riding clear and unlimbering bows yet again. The pikemen roared in fury and raised their weapons, only to swallow the bitter shafts that came buzzing back at them.

Boleslav gaped in horror as he saw the scene repeated up and down the lines. He felt his heart leap as the Knights Templar struggled through, shouting and kicking to clear the way of wounded men. They would make order from chaos. It was their mission.

Boleslav could not know how many hundreds of his footmen had been killed. There was no respite in the attack, no chance to re-form and assess the enemy tactics. Even as he realised they would not stop, two more waves of arrows came at close range, taking anyone who chose his pike over a shield. The sound of yelling, bawling wounded grew in intensity, but the Templars

349

were on the move, beginning the slow, rhythmic trot that put the righteous fear of God into their enemies. Boleslav clenched his fist as they forced their horses through the last of the dazed pikemen, the heavy mounts increasing their speed in perfect formation. Nothing in the world could resist them.

Boleslav saw the Mongols lose their nerve as the knights met them head-on. A few of the smaller ponies were bowled over, hammered aside by greater weight. The Mongol riders leapt clear of their falling mounts, but they were hacked down by broadswords or trampled under hooves. Boleslav exulted as they began to fall back. The fluid movement of their units seemed to stall, so that they jerked and lost their smoothness. The Mongols snapped arrows at the knights, but the shafts skipped away from the heavy armour or even shattered. Boleslav *felt* the battle turn and shouted aloud, urging them on.

The Templars roared as they struck the Mongol tuman. They were men who had fought in muddy fields as far apart as Jerusalem and Cyprus. They expected the enemy in front of them to give way and they dug in their heels and stretched into a gallop. Their strength was the unstoppable hammer blow, a strike to tear an army in half, to reach the centre and kill a king. The Mongols collapsed, hundreds at a time turning and racing before the knights, the heels of their horses almost within reach of the great swords and heavy lances. The Templar charge pounded on for half a mile or more, driving all before them.

Baidur raised his arm. The minghaans had been watching for his signal, the moment that was his to choose. They snapped orders along the line. Twenty men raised yellow flags high and roared to the jaguns of a hundred warriors. They passed the order down to tens. By eye or by ear, it spread like fire through straw, taking just moments. Out of the chaos came instant order. The jaguns peeled off to the flanks, letting the knights come without resistance. Some still ran ahead to draw them on, but the flanks were thickening as more and more men readied their bows.

The Templars had come far from their foot soldiers and their vicious pikes. Perhaps ten thousand of them had ridden out, a massive force, well used to victory. They had plunged deep into the Mongol tumans, carried by confidence and faith. The French knights stared out through slits in steel at the chaos of the Mongol retreat and they cut hard with their swords at anything within reach. They saw the ranks splitting away to each side of them, but they still drove forward, focused on punching right through the enemy and reaching their leader, whoever he was.

From both sides, thousands of Mongol archers ceased their frightened yelling and placed arrows on the strings of bows. With calm deliberation, they picked their targets, looking down the shafts at the plunging necks of the huge warhorses. From the front, the animals were armoured in steel. The sides of their necks were either bare or covered in flapping cloth.

Baidur dropped his arm. All the yellow flags fell in response, almost as one. The bows thumped, releasing the vast tension of the full draw and sending shafts whirring into the mass of horses streaming past them. The targets were not hard to hit at close range, and in the first blows, horses collapsed in shock and pain, their throats pierced right through. Blood sprayed from their nostrils in great gusts as they screamed. Many of the archers winced, but they took another arrow from the quiver and sent it in.

The knights roared a battle challenge. Those struck only once dug in their heels and tried to wheel out of the storm coming from both sides. Their horses began to shudder, their legs trembling in agony. Hundreds of the mounts crashed down with no warning, trapping or crushing the knights on their backs. They found themselves on the ground, dazed and struggling to rise.

For a time, the Templar charge drove on, regardless of losses. It was no easy task to turn the weight of horses and armour aside, but as the destruction mounted, Baidur heard new orders roared across them. The man who gave them became the instant target of every archer in reach. His horse fell, bristling arrows, and the man himself was sent reeling, his head snapped back in its iron shell by the impact of a shaft. The visor was punched in, so that he was blinded by it. Baidur could see the man wrestling to pull it free as he lay on the ground.

The Templars turned, wheeling right and left into the body of archers flanking them. The charge split along a line, with each man taking the opposite path to the one in front. It was a parade-ground manoeuvre, one the Mongols had never seen before. Baidur was impressed. It brought the knights into hand-to-hand combat with the men who stung them, their one chance to survive the carnage the charge had become. They had lost speed, but their armour was strong and they were still fresh. They used the great reach of the lance points to smash in the ribs of his warriors, then the huge swords rose and fell like cleavers.

The Mongol riders danced their mounts around them. They were smaller and less powerful, but so much faster than the armoured men that they could pick each shot with care. From close enough to hear the knights panting beneath their iron plate, they could send their ponies skipping aside, bend the bow and send a shaft wherever they saw a gap or flesh. The longswords swung over them, or where they had been moments before.

Baidur could hear the guttural laughter of his men and he knew it was partly in relief. The sheer size of the knights and their horses was frightening. It was like a cool breeze on the skin to see them flail. When the knights struck cleanly, each blow was terrible, the wounds mortal. Baidur saw one knight with a ragged tabard of red and white bring his sword down with such force that it cut a warrior's thigh through and gashed the saddle beneath. Even as the warrior died, he grabbed the knight and pulled him down with him in a crash of metal.

The smooth volleys from the flanks had become a melee of yelling men and horses, a thousand individual struggles. Baidur trotted his pony up and down, trying to see how his men were doing. He saw one knight stagger to his feet and pull off a battered helmet, revealing long dark hair, sweat-plastered to his head. Baidur kicked forward and cut down as he rode past, feeling the shock of impact right up his arm.

He held back, reining in his horse tightly as he tried to keep a sense of the battle. He could not join the attack, he knew that. If he fell, the command would drop to Ilugei's shoulders. Baidur stood in his stirrups and surveyed a scene he knew he would never forget. All across a vast field, knights in silver armour fought and struggled against the tumans. Their shields were battered and broken, their swords lay where they fell. Thousands were killed on the ground, held down by warriors while others heaved at a helmet, then jabbed a sword into the gap. Thousands more still stood, unhorsed, bellowing to their companions. There was little fear in them, Baidur saw, but they were wrong. It was a time to be afraid. He was not surprised to see the tail of the charge begin to wheel, turning in a chaotic mass so that they could run back to the foot soldiers around Krakow. He gave new orders and eight minghaans moved to follow them, loosing arrows as the knights pushed their tired horses into a canter. There would not be many left by the time they reached a safe haven behind the pikes.

Boleslav watched in despair as the cream of the nobility were torn apart almost in front of him. He would never have believed the knights could fail against horsemen if he had not seen it with his own eyes. Those arrows! The force and accuracy was staggering. He had never seen anything like it on the battle-field. No one in Poland ever had.

His hopes were raised when he saw the rear turn back to the city. He had not been able to observe the extent of the destruction and his mouth slowly fell open as he realised how few they were, how ragged and battered in comparison to the shining glory of those who had ridden out. The Mongols came with them even then, loosing their infernal shafts with smooth pulls, as if the knights were merely targets to be picked off.

Boleslav sent out a regiment of four thousand pikemen to protect their retreat, forcing the Mongols to stop in their tracks. The shattered remnant of the Knights Templar came trotting in, almost every man dusty and bleeding, wheezing as chest plates pressed too close on their ribs. Boleslav turned in horror as the Mongol tumans came closer. They would use lances at last, he realised. He had lost his cavalry shield and they would ride through to Krakow. He shouted for the pikes to be raised, but there was no charge. Instead, the arrows began again, as if the knights had never ridden out, as if the Mongols had all day to finish the killing.

Boleslav looked at the sun dipping down on the distant hills. An arrow struck his charger without warning, making it buck. Another hammered his shield, pushing it back into his chest with the impact. He felt a sick fear overwhelm him. He could not save Krakow. The knights had been reduced to a shadow and only his peasant foot soldiers remained. He would be hard-pressed to save his own life. He signalled and his heralds blew retreat across the battlefield.

The light was already failing, but the Mongols continued their shooting as the pikemen began to withdraw. The exhausted Templars formed a thin line in the rear, taking arrows on their armour as best they could to prevent the withdrawal becoming a complete rout.

Boleslav moved into a canter. His messengers went with him,

their heads down. Defeat hung on them all, as well as fear. Instead of sending letters of victory, he would be running to his brother Henry, asking for his charity and his pity. He rode numbly, watching the shadows before him. The Mongols had annihilated the French Templars, to that point the greatest fighting force he had ever known. Who could stop them, if not the martial orders? Those knights had slaughtered hordes of Moslem heretics in and around Jerusalem. To see them torn apart in a single day shook his very foundations.

Behind him, the Mongols howled like wolves, hundreds at a time darting in and killing those who wanted nothing more than to retreat. The arrows continued to fall even after the light was poor. Men were dragged off their saddles from behind, tumbling into the arms of men who laughed as they killed them, pushing and shoving each other to get in a kick or a blow.

As full darkness came, Baidur and Ilugei called back their men at last. The city of Krakow stood naked before them and they walked their horses in as the moon rose.

The moonlight was strong, the air clear and cold as the yam rider galloped at full speed along the dusty track. He was weary. It was hard to keep his eyes open and the ache in his lower back had become a jarring pain. A sudden panic gripped him as he lost count of the way stations he had passed that day. Had it been two or three? Karakorum was far behind, but he knew he would have to hand on the bag with its precious contents. He did not know what he had been given, except that it was worth his life. The man from Karakorum had appeared out of the darkness and thrust it into his hands, snapping hoarse orders. He had been galloping even before the man dismounted.

With a jolt, the scout realised he had almost slipped out of the saddle. The warmth of the horse, the rhythm of hooves, the bells that jingled under him, all of them lulled his senses. It would be his second night without sleep with nothing but the track and the horse for company. He counted again in his head. He had passed six of the yam way stations, changing horses at each one. He would have to hand over the bag at the next one, or risk falling on the road.

In the distance, he saw lights. They would have heard his bells, of course. They would be waiting with a horse and spare rider as well as a skin of airag and sweet honey to keep him going. They would need the other rider. He could feel exhaustion washing over him. He was done.

He slowed to a trot as he reached the stone yard in the middle of nowhere, the visible sign of the khan's influence and power. As the yam staff clustered around him, he swung his leg over and nodded to the spare rider, little more than a boy. There had been a verbal message as well as the bag. What was it? Yes, he remembered.

'Kill horses and men if you have to,' he said. 'Ride as fast and far as you can. This is for the hands of Guyuk alone. Repeat my words.'

He listened as the fresh rider said them all again in a rush, overcome with excitement. The bag was passed from hand to hand, a sacred trust, never to be opened until it reach its destination. He saw a stone seat in the yard, some sort of mounting block perhaps. He sank onto it gratefully, watching the lad begin his run before he allowed himself to close his eyes. He had never run so fast or far in his life and he wondered what could possibly be so important.

CHAPTER TWENTY-EIGHT

The funeral pyre of the khan was an immense structure, half as high as the palace tower in the city behind it. It had been constructed quickly, using vast stocks of cedar wood from the cellars of the palace. They had been found there when Ogedai's instructions were read. The khan had prepared for death and every detail of the ceremony had been set out long in advance. There had been other letters in the sealed package Yao Shu had presented to Torogene. The personal one to her had left her weeping. It had been written before Ogedai went on the Chin campaign and it broke her heart to read the brash enthusiasm of her husband's words. He had prepared for death, but no man can truly understand what it means to have the world go on without him, how it is for those who must live without his voice, his smell, his touch. All that was left were the letters and her memories. Karakorum itself would be his tomb, his ashes placed in a vault below the palace, there to rest for eternity.

Temuge stood on the green grass in robes of golden silk

inlaid with blue. His back hurt him all the time and he had to strain to look up at the top of the pyre. He did not weep for his brother's son. Instead, he clasped his hands behind his back and thought deeply about the future as the first flames spread, charring the wood and releasing a cedar sweetness into the air that would carry for many miles with the smoke.

His mind drifted into the past as he stood there, doing his duty and being seen by the thousands watching. His people were not given to huge displays of grief, but there were many red eyes in the crowd of workers that had come out from Karakorum. The city itself lay empty, as if they had never given it life.

A son of Genghis lay in those flames, a son of the brother he had loved and feared, hated and adored. Temuge could barely remember the first days of being hunted, when they were all just children. It was so very long ago, though there were times when he still dreamed of the cold and the aching hunger. An old man's thoughts often wandered back to his youth, but there was little comfort in it. His four brothers had been there then. Temujin, who would choose the vainglorious name of Genghis; Kachiun, Khasar and Bekter. Temuge struggled to remember Bekter's face and could not bring it to mind. His sister Temulun had been there as well, another one torn from life.

Temuge thought of the yam letter Yao Shu had shown him just that morning. His brother Kachiun was dead and he looked inside for a sense of grief, of loss, such as Torogene displayed in her weeping. No, there was nothing. They had grown apart many years before, lost in the difficulties and irritations of life that soured clean relationships. Of the seven who had hidden in a cleft in the ground, only he and Khasar remained as witnesses. Only they could say they had been there from the very beginning. They were both old men and he felt the aches in his bones every day.

358

He looked past the growing brightness of the wooden tower and saw Khasar standing with his head bowed. They had crossed the Chin nation together when they were young, finding Yao Shu when he was just a wandering monk, waiting for his future to come upon him. It was hard to remember ever being that strong and vital. Khasar looked oddly thin, Temuge noticed. His head seemed overlarge as the flesh had sunk away in his face and neck. He did not look well at all. On an impulse, Temuge walked over to him and they nodded to each other, two old men in the sunshine.

'I never thought he'd go before me,' Khasar murmured.

Temuge looked sharply at him and Khasar caught the glance. He shrugged.

'I'm an old man and the lumps on my shoulder are getting bigger. I didn't expect to see the boy die before it was my time, that's all.'

'You should get them cut out, brother,' Temuge said.

Khasar winced. He could no longer wear armour that pressed against the painful spots. Each night it seemed the growths had swelled, like grapes under the skin. He did not mention the ones he had found in his armpits. Just to touch them was painful enough to make him dizzy. The thought of enduring a knife sawing at them was more than he could bear. It was not cowardice, he told himself firmly. The things would go away in time, or kill him; one or the other.

'I was sorry to hear about Kachiun,' Temuge said.

Khasar closed his eyes, stiff with pain.

'He was too old to be on campaign; I told him that,' he replied. 'No pleasure in being right, though. God, I miss him.'

Temuge looked quizzically at his brother. 'You're not becoming one of the Christians now, are you?'

Khasar smiled, a little sadly. 'It's too late for me. I just listen to them talk sometimes. They curse a lot, I've noticed. That heaven of theirs sounds a bit dull, from what I've heard. I asked one of the monks if there would be horses and he said we wouldn't *want* them; can you believe that? I'm not riding one of their angels, I tell you that now.'

Temuge could see his brother was talking to cover the grief he felt over Kachiun. Once more he looked for it in his own heart and found an emptiness. It was troubling.

'I was just thinking of the cleft in the hills, where we all hid,' Temuge said.

Khasar smiled and shook his head.

'Those were hard times,' he replied. 'We survived them, though, like everything else.' He looked at the city behind the furnace that hid the khan's body. 'This place would not exist if it hadn't been for our family.' He sighed to himself. 'It's a strange thing to remember when there was no nation. Perhaps that is enough for one man's lifetime. We have seen some good years, brother, despite our differences.'

Temuge looked away rather than remember his dabbling in the darker arts. For a few years of his youth he had been the chosen apprentice of one who had brought great pain to his family, one whose name was no longer spoken in the nation. Khasar had been almost an enemy for those years, but it was all far away, half-forgotten.

'You should write this down,' Khasar said suddenly. He jerked his head to the funeral pyre. 'Like you did for Genghis. You should make a record of it.'

'I will, brother,' Temuge said. He looked again at Khasar and truly saw the way he had withered. 'You look ill, Khasar. I would let them cut you.'

'Yes, but what do *you* know?' Khasar said, with a sneer.

'I know they can dose you with the black paste so you don't feel the pain.'

'I'm not scared of pain,' Khasar said irritably. Even so, he looked interested and shifted his shoulders with a wince. 'Maybe I will. I can hardly use my right arm on some days.'

360

'You will need it if Chagatai comes to Karakorum,' Temuge said.

Khasar nodded and rubbed his shoulder with his left hand.

'That's one man I'd like to see with his neck broken,' he said. 'I was there when Tolui gave his life, brother. What did we get for it? A few miserable years. If I have to see Chagatai ride through those gates in triumph, I think I'd rather die in my sleep first.'

'He will be here before Guyuk and Tsubodai, that's the only thing we know for certain,' Temuge said sourly. He too had no love for the lout his brother had fathered. There would be no grand libraries under Chagatai's rule, no streets of scholars and great learning. He was as likely to burn the city as anything, just to make a point. In that regard, Chagatai was his father's son. Temuge shuddered slightly and told himself it was just the wind. He knew he should be making plans to remove the most valuable scrolls and books before Chagatai arrived, just until he was certain they would be honoured and kept safe. The very thought of a Chagatai khanate made him sweat. The world did not need another Genghis, he thought. It had barely recovered from the ravages of the last one.

Köten of the Cumans crossed the Danube in a small boat, a wherry with a surly soldier on the oars who made it fairly skim across the dark water. He wrapped himself tightly in his cloak against the cold twilight, lost in thought. He could not resist his fate, it seemed. The king had every right to ask for his men. Hungary had given them sanctuary, and for a time Köten thought he had saved them all. Once the mountains were behind them, he had dared to hope that the Mongol tumans would not run so far west. They never had before. Instead, the Golden Horde had come roaring out of the Carpathians and the place of peace and sanctuary was no refuge at all.

Köten seethed to himself as he saw the shore approach, a dark line of sucking mud that he knew would pull at his boots. He stepped out into shallow water, wincing as his feet sank into the stinking clay. The oarsman grunted something unintelligible and examined his coin closely, a deliberate insult. Köten's hand twitched for his knife, wanting to cut a scar on the man that would remind him of his manners. Reluctantly, he let his hand fall. The man rowed away, staring back at him with a curled lip. At a safe distance, the man shouted something, but Köten ignored him.

It was the same story across the cities of Buda and Pest. His Cuman people had come in good faith, been baptised as their lord ordered and made every attempt to treat the new religion as their own, if only for their survival. They were people who understood that staying alive was worth sacrifice and they had trusted him. None of the Christian priests seemed to think it strange that an entire nation would suddenly feel the urge to welcome Christ into their hearts.

Yet it was not enough for the inhabitants of Bela's cities. From the first days, there had been tales of thefts and murders by his men, rumours and gossip that they were behind every misfortune. A pig couldn't take sick without someone claiming that one of the dark-skinned women had cursed it. Köten spat on the pebbled shore as he trudged along it. The previous month, a local Hungarian girl had accused two Cuman boys of raping her. The riot that followed had been put down with ruthless ferocity by King Bela's soldiers, but the hatred was still there, simmering under the surface. There were few who believed she had been lying. After all, it was just the sort of thing they expected from the filthy nomads in their midst. They were rootless and they could not be trusted, except to steal and kill and foul the clean river.

Köten disliked his hosts almost as much as they apparently hated him and the presence of his people. They could not take up less room than they did, he thought in irritation, seeing the city of tents and shacks huddled along the river. The king had promised them he would build a new city, or perhaps expand two or three of those already there. He had talked of a ghetto for the Cuman people, where they could live safely among their own. Perhaps Bela would have kept his word if the Mongols had not come, though Köten had begun to doubt it.

Somehow the threat of the Mongols had only increased the tension between the local Magyars and his tribe. His people could not walk down a street without someone spitting at them or jostling the women. Every night, there were dead men left in the gutters, their throats slit. No one was ever punished if they were Cuman bodies, but the local judges and soldiers hanged his men in pairs and more if it was one of their own. It was a poor reward for two hundred thousand new Christians. There were times when Köten wondered at a faith that could preach kindness and yet be so cruel to its own.

As he made his way along the shit-strewn shore, the smell made him gag. The wealthy people of Buda had fine drains for their waste. Even the poor quarters in Pest had half-barrels on the corners that the tanners would collect at night. The Cuman tent-people had nothing but the river. They had tried to keep it clean, but there were just too many of them crowded along too short a stretch. Already, there were diseases ripping through his people, families dying with red marks on their skin he had never seen at home. The whole place felt like an enemy camp, but the king had asked for his army and Köten was honour-bound, oath-bound to him. In that one thing, King Bela had judged his man correctly, but as Köten kicked at a stone, he thought there were limits even to his honour. Would he see his people slaughtered for such a poor reward? In all his life, he had never broken his word, not once. At times, when he was starving or sick, it was all he had left to feed his pride.

He made his way into the town of Pest, human excrement and clay making his boots heavy. He had promised his wife he would buy some meat before he came back to her, though he knew the prices would be hiked as soon as they recognised him or heard him speak. He tapped the hilt of his sword as he increased his stride and stood tall. He felt like a dangerous man to insult on that day. No doubt the next day would be different, but for a while he would let in a little of his anger. It kept him warm.

As Köten clambered up a muddy rise that opened onto the line of merchants' stores that formed a street, he heard something crash to the ground nearby. The wind was in his ears and he turned his head to listen. There was a lamp in the front of the butcher's shop, he saw, but the wooden shutters were already coming down over the serving hatch. Köten swore to himself and broke into a run.

'Wait!' he shouted.

He did not notice the men struggling together until they collapsed almost at his feet. Köten drew his sword in reaction, but they were intent on punching and kicking each other. One of them had a knife, but the other had his hand in a tight grip. Köten knew neither of them. His head came up like a hunting dog as more shouting sounded nearby. The voices were angry and he felt an answering anger. Who knew what had happened in his absence? Another rape, or simply the accusation of one against his brothers? While he hesitated, the butcher finally succeeded in heaving his shutters down, shoving a bar through them from the inner side. Köten hammered on the shutters with his fists, but there was no answer. Furious, he turned the corner.

Köten saw the line of men, no, the crowd of men, stalking down the muddy street in the darkness towards him. He jerked back round the corner in two quick steps, but they had seen him outlined against the setting sun. The howl went up instinctively as they saw a frightened figure run from them.

Köten moved as quickly as he could. He had lived long enough to know he was in real danger. Whatever had brought the men out as a mob could end with his head being crushed or his ribs broken in with their boots. He heard their roar of excitement and he ran, heading back towards the dark river. Their boots sounded on the wooden walkway, thumping ever closer.

He slipped, his mired boots skidding on the wet ground. His sword vanished from his hand, falling on mud so soft that it made no sound at all. Someone crashed into him as he rose and then they were on him, taking out their rage on the shadowy stranger who had shown his guilt by running. He struggled, but they kicked and stabbed with short knives, pressing him down into the filthy mud until he was almost part of it, his blood mingling with the blackness.

The men stood clear of the lifeless body on the bank of the river. Some of them clapped others on the back, chuckling at the justice they had meted out. They had not known the name of the broken thing that lay there. In the distance, they heard the shouts of the king's officers and almost as one they turned away and began to disappear into the shadows of the merchants' quarter. The nomads would hear and be afraid. It would be a long time before they walked without fear through the cities of their betters. Many of the men were fathers and they went home to their families, taking the back alleys so that they would not come across the king's soldiers.

The army that assembled in front of the city of Pest was vast. King Bela had spent days in a sort of frenzy as he came to appreciate what it took to field so many men. A soldier could not carry food for more than a few days at most before it slowed him down and made it harder to fight. The baggage train had taken every cart and workhorse in the country and it spread across almost as much land as the massed ranks before the Danube. King Bela's heart filled in his chest as he surveyed the host. More than a hundred thousand men-at-arms, knights and foot soldiers had responded to the bloody swords that he had sent racing the length and breadth of Hungary. His best estimates were of a Mongol army half the size or less than the one he had been told to expect. The king swallowed yellow bile as it surged into his throat. He may have been facing just half the Golden Horde, but the reports coming to him from the north were of destruction beyond belief. There would be no armies coming to his aid from Boleslav or Henry. From everything he had learned, they were hard-pressed to survive the onslaught of the tumans raiding there. Lublin had certainly fallen and there was a single report that Krakow had followed it into flames, though Bela could not see how such a thing was possible. He could only hope that the reports were exaggerated, composed by frightened men. It was certainly not information to share with his officers and allies.

At that thought, he looked to the Teutonic Knights on his right, two thousand of them in their finest battle array. Their horses showed no sign of the mud churned up by the army. They shone in the weak sunlight and blew mist from their nostrils as they pawed the ground. Bela loved warhorses and he knew the knights had the very best bloodlines in the world for their mounts.

Only the left wing caused him to pause in his proud assessment. The Cumans were good horsemen, but they were still seething about the death of Köten in some grubby river brawl. As if such a thing could be laid at the king's feet. They were an impossible people, Bela acknowledged to himself. When the Mongols had been sent back over the mountains, he would have to give more thought to the practicalities of settling so many Cumans. Perhaps they could be bribed to find a new homeland where they would be more welcome and less of a drain on the royal purse.

King Bela cursed under his breath as he saw the Cuman horsemen move out of place in the line. He sent a runner across the field in front of the city with a terse order to hold position. He scratched his chin as he watched the runner's progress. In the distance, he saw the Cuman riders coalesce around the single man, but they did not stop. Bela let his hand fall in growing amazement. He turned in the saddle gesturing to the closest of his knights.

'Ride to the Cumans and *remind* them of their oath of obedience to me. My orders are to stay in position until I give the word.'

The knight dipped his lance in answer and cantered with dignity after the first messenger. By that time, the Cumans had ruined the neat symmetry of the lines, their horses spreading over the field in no obvious formation. Bela sighed to himself. The nomads could barely understand discipline. He tried to remember the name of Köten's son, who was meant to have command over them, but it would not come to mind.

They did not halt for the knight's arrival, though by then they were close enough for Bela to see him holding his arms out. He might as well have tried to stop the tide, for they simply flowed around him, trotting with no urgency. Bela cursed aloud as he saw they were making for his own position. No doubt they wanted to renegotiate some part of their oath, or ask for better food and arms. It was typical of the filthy breed to try and squeeze an advantage from him, as if he were a grubby merchant. Trade was all they understood, he thought savagely. They'd sell their own daughters if there was gold in it.

King Bela glared as the Cuman horsemen rolled out, moving slowly across his army. His messengers were still coming in with the latest reports on the Mongols and he deliberately busied himself with them, showing his contempt. By the time one of his knights cleared his throat and Bela looked up, it was to see Köten's son staring at him. The king struggled again for the younger man's name, but it would not come. There had just been too many details in the previous days for him to remember everything.

'What is so important that you risk the entire formation?' Bela snapped, already red in the face from suppressed irritation.

Köten's son bowed his head so briefly it was almost a jerk.

'My father's oath bound us, King Bela. I am not bound by it,' he said.

'What are you talking about?' Bela demanded. 'Whatever your concern is, this is not the place or the time. Return to your position. Come to me this evening, when we have crossed the Danube. I will see you then.'

King Bela deliberately turned back to his messengers and took another sheaf of vellum to read. He jerked his head up in amazement when the young man spoke again, as if he had not just been given his orders.

'This is not our war, King Bela. That has been made clear to us. I wish you good fortune, but my task now is to shepherd my people out of the way of the Golden Horde.'

Bela's colour deepened and the veins stood out on his pale skin.

'You will return to the lines!' he roared.

Köten's son shook his head. 'Goodbye, your majesty,' he said. 'Christ bless all your many works.'

Bela took a deep breath, suddenly aware that the Cuman horsemen were all staring at him. To a man, they had their hands on swords or bows and their faces were very cold. His thoughts whirled, but they were forty thousand. If he ordered the son killed, they could very well attack his royal guards. It would be a disaster and only the Mongols would benefit. His blue eyes grew still.

'With the enemy in *sight*?' Bela roared. 'I call you oath-breakers!

I call you cowards and heretics!' Bela shouted at Köten's son as he trotted away. Christ, why could he not remember the man's name! His words might as well have been empty air. The king could only froth and rage as the Cumans peeled off in a mass of riders after their leader. They took a path that led around the great army of Hungary and back to the encampment of their people.

'We did not need goatherders in the ranks, your majesty,' Josef Landau said, with distaste. His brother knights growled their affirmation on all sides. The Cumans were still streaming across the main lines and King Bela struggled to master his fraying temper. He forced a smile.

'You are correct, Sir Josef,' he replied. 'We are a hundred thousand strong, even without those . . . goatherders. But when we have triumphed, there will be a reckoning for such a betrayal.'

'I would be pleased to teach the lesson, your majesty,' Josef Landau replied, his expression unpleasant. It was matched or exceeded by Bela's own.

'Very well. Spread the word that *I* sent the Cumans from the field, Sir Josef. I do not want my men dwelling on their betrayal. Let them know that I chose to fight alongside only those of good Hungarian blood. That will raise their spirits. As for the nomads, you will show them the price of their betrayal. They will understand it in those terms, I am sure.' He took a deep breath to calm his anger.

'Now I am weary of standing here listening to the plaintive voices of cowards. Give the order to march.'

CHAPTER TWENTY-NINE

Tsubodai watched the army of King Bela begin to swarm across the river, the bridges black with men and horses. Batu and Jebe sat their mounts and stared out with him, judging the quality of the men they would face. Their horses whickered softly to themselves, munching at the grass. On the plains, spring had come early and it showed green through the last patches of snow. The air was cold still, but the sky was pale blue and the world was bursting with new life.

'They are good enough horsemen,' Jebe said.

Batu shrugged, but Tsubodai chose to answer.

'Too many,' he said softly. 'And that river has too many bridges. Which is why we are going to make them work for it.'

Batu looked up, aware as always that the two men shared an understanding from which he was excluded. It was infuriating and clearly deliberate. He looked away, knowing they could both read his anger all too easily.

All his life he had been forced to scramble for everything

he had achieved. Then the khan had dragged him up, promoting him to command a tuman in his father's name. Batu had been honoured publicly, and instead of his habitual hatred for the world, he had been forced to a new struggle, almost as painful as the first. He had to prove he was *able* to lead, that he had the skills and discipline men like Tsubodai took for granted. In his desire to prove himself, no one could possibly have worked harder or done more. He was young: his energy was almost infinite compared to the old men.

Batu felt torn as he looked at the orlok. One small, weak part of him would have given anything to have Tsubodai clap him on the shoulder and approve, just approve of him as a man and leader. The rest of him hated that weakness with such a passion that it spilled out, making him an angry companion for quieter souls. No doubt his father had looked up to Tsubodai once. No doubt he had trusted him.

It was part of growing-up to crush that sort of need in your-self, Batu knew very well. He would never gain Tsubodai's trust. He would never have his approval. Instead, Batu would rise in the nation, so that when Tsubodai was withered and tooth-less, he would look back and see he had misjudged the young general under his care. He would know then that he had missed the only one who could take the legacy of Genghis and make it golden.

Batu sighed to himself. He was not a fool. Even the fantasy of an old Tsubodai realising his great error was a boy's dream. If he had learned anything in manhood, it was that it didn't matter what other people thought of him – even the ones he respected. In the end, he would patch together a life, with its sorry errors and its triumphs, just as they had. He tried not to listen to the inner need that wanted them to hang on his every word. He was too young for that, even if they and he had been different men.

'Let them get about half their number across the Danube,'

Tsubodai was saying to Jebe. 'They have . . . what? Eighty thousand?'

'More, I think. If they'd hold still, I could be certain.'

'Twice as many horsemen as we have,' Tsubodai said sourly.

'What about the ones who rode away?' Batu asked.

Tsubodai shook his head, looking irritated. He too had wondered why tens of thousands of riders would suddenly break from King Bela's army before the march. It smelled of trickery, and Tsubodai was not one who enjoyed being fooled.

'I don't know. They could be a reserve, or part of some other plan. I don't like the idea of so many soldiers out of sight as we pull back. I'll send a couple of men out to look for them, have them cross further downriver and scout around.'

'You think they are some sort of reserve?' Batu asked, pleased to be part of the conversation.

Tsubodai shrugged dismissively. 'If they don't cross the river, I don't care what they are.'

Ahead of them, King Bela's army trotted and marched across the wide stone bridges of the Danube. They came in clear units, the movements revealing much about their structure and offensive capability, which was why Tsubodai watched with such interest. The different groups linked immediately on the other side, establishing a safe bridgehead in case of attack. Tsubodai shook his head slightly at seeing their formations. King Bela had almost three times as many trained soldiers as he did, if you didn't count the ragged conscripts Tsubodai had brought with him. For three tumans to achieve victory over such a host would take luck and skill and years of experience. The orlok smiled to himself. He had a wealth of those things. More importantly, he had spent almost a month scouting the land around Buda and Pest for the best spot to bring them to battle. It was certainly not on the banks of the Danube, a line of battle so vast and varied that he could not control it. There was only one response to overwhelming numbers: remove their ability to manoeuvre. The largest army in the world became just a few men at a time if they could be squeezed through a narrow pass or across a bridge.

The three generals watched with grim concentration as the army of Hungary formed up on their side of the river. It took an age and Tsubodai noted every detail, pleased that they showed no more discipline than any of the other armies he had encountered. The reports from Baidur and Ilugei were good. There would be no second army coming from the north. In the south, Guyuk and Mongke had razed a strip of land as wide as Hungary itself, throwing back anyone who looked as if they could be a threat. His flanks were secure, as he had planned and hoped they would be. He was ready to drive through the central plains, against its king. Tsubodai rubbed his eyes for a moment. In the future, his people would ride the grass-lands of Hungary and never know he had once stood there, with their future in the balance. He hoped they would throw a drop of airag into the air for him when they drank. It was all a man could ask for, to be remembered occasionally, with all the other spirits who had bled into the land.

King Bela could be seen riding along the lines, exhorting his men. Tsubodai heard hundreds of trumpets sound from the massed ranks, followed by streaming banners raised above their heads on lance-poles. It was an impressive sight, even to men who had seen the armies of the Chin emperor.

Batu watched them in frustration. Presumably Tsubodai would share his plans with him at some point, perhaps when he was expected to risk his life to break that vast host of men and horses. His pride prevented him from asking, but Tsubodai had revealed nothing during day after day of cautious manoeuvring and scout reports. The tumans and conscripts waited patiently with Chulgetei, just two miles back from the river.

Already, the Magyar scouts had spotted the generals leaning on their saddle horns and observing. Batu could see arms pointing at their position and men beginning to ride out towards them.

'Very well, I've seen enough,' Tsubodai said. He turned to Batu. 'The tumans will fall back. Slow retreat. Keep . . . two miles between us. Our footmen will have to run alongside the horses. Pass the word that they can hang on stirrups, or ride the spare mounts if they begin to fall behind and think they can stay in the saddle. The king has foot soldiers. They will not be able to force a battle.'

'Fall back?' Batu said. He kept his face calm. 'Are you going to tell me what you have planned, Orlok Bahadur?'

'Of course!' Tsubodai said with a grin. 'But not today. Today, we retreat from a superior force. It will be good for the men to learn a little humility.'

Sorhatani stood on the walls of Karakorum, looking along their length as the sun rose. For as far as she could see, teams of Chin labourers and warriors were building them higher, adding courses of limestone slabs and lime cement, before slathering more lime over it all in layer after hardening layer. There was no shortage of willing labour and they started early and finished only when it was too dark to see. Everyone with a stake in the city knew that they must expect Chagatai Khan to come. He would not be allowed to enter and there was no doubt then what would follow. His tumans would begin an assault on the walls of their own nation's capital.

Sorhatani sighed to herself in the morning breeze. Walls would not stop him. Ever since Genghis had faced his first city, the tumans had been perfecting catapults and now they had the gritty black powder capable of extraordinary destruction. She did not know if Chagatai's artisans had followed the same paths, but it was likely he knew every detail of the latest cannons and barrel-throwers. To her left, a platform for a field gun was being constructed, a squat tower capable of taking the weight and force of such a powerful weapon as it recoiled.

When he came, Chagatai would not have it all his own way, she had made sure of that. The city would belch fire at him and perhaps a tongue of righteous flame would end the threat before he broke the walls and entered the city.

Almost from habit, Sorhatani counted the days since the khan's death. Twelve. She had closed the yam station in the city as soon as her own message had gone out to Guyuk, but the system was flawed. Another chain of way stations stretched west from Karakorum to Chagatai's khanate, fifteen hundred miles or more. A rider from the city had to reach only one link in the chain and the resources of the precious yam could be used to send Chagatai word of the khan's death. She thought over the distances again in her head. At the best speed, he would not hear for another six days. She had gone over the figures with Yao Shu as they began to fortify the city. Even if Chagatai set out immediately, if he ran to his horse and had his tumans standing by, he could not bring his tumans back for another month after that, more likely two. He would have to follow the yam route around the edge of the Taklamakan desert.

At the best guess, Chagatai khan would arrive in midsummer. Sorhatani shaded her eyes to look at the progress of the workers on the walls, their faces and hands grey with wet lime. By summer, Karakorum would bristle with cannon, on walls wide enough to hold them.

Sorhatani reached down and crumbled a piece of chalky stone in her hands, rubbing it to dust and then slapping her palms together. There was a great deal still to do before then. She and Torogene were holding the empire together with little more than spit and confidence. Until Guyuk brought the tumans home and assumed his father's titles, until the nation gathered to swear an oath to him as khan, Karakorum was vulnerable. They would have to hold the walls for two months, even three. Sorhatani dreaded the thought of seeing a red or black tent raised before Karakorum.

In a strange way, it was Ogedai's triumph that the city had assumed such importance. Genghis might have called the nation to him, somewhere out of sight of the white walls. Sorhatani froze for a moment as she considered it. No, Chagatai did not have his father's imagination, and truly Karakorum had become the symbol of the people's ascendancy. Whoever would be khan had to control the city. She nodded to herself, ordering her thoughts. Chagatai would come. He had to.

She stepped lightly down steps set into the inside of the wall, noting the wide crest that would allow archers to gather and shoot down into an attacking force. At intervals, new wooden roofs sheltered spaces on the wall that would house quivers, water for the men, even fire-pots of iron and clay, filled with black powder. The city Guards were stockpiling food as fast as they could, riding out for hundreds of miles in all directions to commandeer the produce of farms. The markets and livestock pens had been stripped of their animals, the owners left with just Temuge's tokens to be redeemed at a later date. The mood in the city was already one of fear and none of them had dared to protest. Sorhatani knew there were refugees on the roads east, slow trails of families hoping to escape the destruction they saw coming. In her darker moments, she agreed with their conclusions. Yenking had held out against the great khan for a year, but its walls had been massive, the product of generations. Karakorum had never been designed to withstand an attack. That had not been Ogedai's vision of a white city in the wilderness, with the river running by.

She saw Torogene standing with Yao Shu and Alkhun, all of them looking expectantly at her. Nothing went on in the city without passing through their hands. Her heart sank at the thought of another hundred problems and difficulties, yet there was a part that revelled in her new authority. This was how it felt! This was what her husband had known, to have others look to you, and *only* to you. She chuckled at the sudden image of Genghis hearing that his fledgling nation was ruled by two women. She remembered his words, that in the future his people would wear fine clothes and eat spiced meat and forget what they owed to him. She kept her expression serious as she reached Yao Shu and Torogene. She had not yet forgotten that fierce old devil with the yellow eyes, but there were other concerns and Karakorum was in peril. She did not think her right to the ancestral lands would last long once Chagatai became the khan of khans. Her sons would be killed as the new ruler made a clean sweep and put his own people in charge of the nation's armies.

The future depended on stalling Chagatai long enough for Guyuk to come home. There was no other hope, no other plan. Sorhatani smiled at those who waited for her, seeing her own worries etched in their faces. The morning breeze lifted her hair, so that she smoothed it back with one hand.

'To work then,' she said cheerfully. 'What do we have this morning?'

Kisruth cursed the sky father as he galloped, using one hand to feel the graze on his neck. He had never known the road-thieves to be so bold before. He was still sweating with the shock of seeing a man step out into the road from behind a tree and grab at the satchel on his shoulders. Kisruth wrenched his neck back and forth, assessing the stiffness there. They had nearly had him. Well, he would tell old Gurban and let them see what happened then! No one threatened the yam riders.

He could see the ger that marked twenty-five miles of the run and, as he always did, he tried to imagine one of the grand yam stations in Karakorum. He had heard tales from riders passing through, though he sometimes thought they exaggerated, knowing he hung on every word. Their own kitchen, just for the riders. Lamps at all hours and stables of polished oak, with row upon row of horses ready to race across the plains. One day, he would see it and be honoured among them, he told himself. It was a common dream as he rode back and forth between two stations so small and poor that they were barely more than a few gers and a corral. The city riders seemed to bring the glamour of Karakorum with them.

There was nothing like that at his home post. Gurban and a couple of crippled warriors managed it with their wives and they seemed happy enough with so little. Kisruth had dreamed of taking important messages and his heart still thumped at the words he had been given by an exhausted rider. 'Kill horses and men if you have to, but reach Guyuk, the heir. His hands alone.' Kisruth did not know what he carried, but it could only be something important. He looked forward to handing it over formally to his brother and repeating the words to him.

He was irritated to see no one waiting as he came charging across the last stretch. No doubt Gurban was sleeping off the batch of airag his wife had brewed the week before. It was just typical of the old sot that the most important message of their lives should find him sleeping. Kisruth gave the bells a last flick with his hands as he dismounted, but the gers were peaceful apart from the line of smoke from one. Stiffly, he strode across the open yard, yelling for his brother or any of them. Surely they could not all have gone fishing for the day? He had left them only three days before, taking a sheaf of minor messages down the line.

He kicked at the door of the ger and stood in the yard rather than go inside, his letter giving him confidence.

'What is it?' his brother said peevishly from inside. 'Kisruth? Is that you?'

'Am I the one who has been shouting your name? Yes!' Kisruth snapped. 'I have a letter from Karakorum, to go fast. And where do I find you?'

The door opened and his brother came out, rubbing his eyes. There were creases on his face from where he had been sleeping and Kisruth struggled with his temper.

'Well? I'm here, aren't I?' his brother said.

Kisruth shook his head. 'You know what? I'll take it on myself. Tell Gurban there is a family of thieves on the road east. They nearly had me off my horse.'

His brother's eyes cleared at the news, as well they might. No one attacked the yam riders.

'I'll tell him, don't worry. Do you want me to ride on with that bag?' he said. 'I'll go now if it's important.'

Kisruth had already made up his mind and, in truth, he was reluctant to see his part in the excitement end. It had not been hard to decide to go on.

'You go back to your sleep. I'll take it to the next post.' He jerked back as his brother reached for his reins, wheeling the pony in the yard before his brother's temper woke them all. Suddenly Kisruth just wanted to be gone.

'Tell Gurban about the thieves,' he called over his shoulder, kicking his mount into a gallop. It would be almost dark by the time he rode the next section, but they had good men there and they would be ready when they heard his saddle bells. His brother shouted incoherently behind him, but Kisruth was riding once again.

CHAPTER THIRTY

Day after day, the tumans of Tsubodai stayed just out of reach of the Hungarian riders. Batu had lost count of the Hungarian king's attempts to bring them to battle. The foot soldiers on both sides slowed them down, but on the first day away from the Danube river, King Bela had sent twenty thousand horsemen out on the charge. Tsubodai had watched dispassionately as they closed on his rear lines until, with what Batu considered to be infuriating calmness, he ordered volleys of arrows, while the ragged conscripts grabbed saddle horns and let themselves be taken over a fast three miles, opening the gap once more. When the Magyar horsemen pressed too hard, they were met with swarms of dark arrows, shot with terrifying accuracy. The Mongol minghaans had a discipline their adversaries had never seen, able to take position in the teeth of a charge, shoot two volleys and then turn to rejoin the main tumans.

The first day had been the hardest, with repeated lunges and attacks that had to be beaten back. Tsubodai had worked in a frenzy to keep the two armies separate as they marched, until Buda and Pest were lost to view. As the sun set that first night, he had smiled to see the huge walled camp Bela's army built, almost a town in itself. The Magyar host lined sandbags to the height of a man in a vast square on the grasslands. They had carried the weight of them all the way from the Danube. In its way, it explained why they could not run the Mongols down. It confirmed Tsubodai's impression of the king that only he and his most senior officers rested behind the security of the sandbag walls. The rest of his army camped in the open, as unregarded as any of his servants.

The Hungarian king might have expected to eat and sleep well in his command tent, but each night Tsubodai sent men with horns and Chin firecrackers to keep the Hungarian army awake. He wanted the king exhausted and nervous, while Tsubodai himself slept and snored, making his personal guards smile as they watched over his ger.

The following few days were less frantic. King Bela seemed to have accepted he could not make them turn and fight his host. The charges continued, but it was almost as if they were for show and dash, with knights pulling up with brandished swords and insults before triumphantly trotting back to their own lines.

The tumans rode on, retreating mile after slow mile. On broken ground, some of the horses went lame and were quickly killed, though there was never time to butcher them for meat. The foot soldiers running by their saddles were hardened, but even so a few of them picked up injuries. Tsubodai gave orders that anyone who fell behind was to be left with just a sword, but his tumans had worked and fought with the ragged conscripts for a long time. He turned a blind eye as they were heaved up behind warriors, or tied to a saddle on one of the spare mounts.

By the afternoon of the fifth day, they had covered the best part of two hundred miles and Tsubodai had learned everything he needed to know about the enemy he faced. The Sajo river was in front of him and he spent most of the morning giving orders about crossing the sole bridge. His tumans could not risk being trapped against the river and it was no surprise that the Magyar riders began to press more closely over the morning. They knew the local land as well as anyone.

Tsubodai summoned Batu, Jebe and Chulgetei to him as the sun passed the highest point in the sky.

'Jebe, I want your tumans to cross the Sajo river without delay,' he said.

The general frowned. 'If I were the Hungarian king, I'd hit us now, with the river preventing us from manoeuvres. He must know there is only one bridge.'

Tsubodai turned in the saddle, staring out over the thread of the river, just a few miles away. Already, Chulgetei's tuman was being compressed on the banks. They could not stay there, up against the deep river.

'This king has driven us in triumph now for five days. His officers will be congratulating themselves and him. As far as he knows, we will run right to the mountains and be pushed back over them again. I think he will let us go, but if he does not, I will still have twenty thousand ready to show him his error. Go quickly.'

'Your will, orlok,' Jebe said. He dipped his head and rode clear to pass on the order to his tuman.

Batu cleared his throat, suddenly uncomfortable in Tsubodai's presence.

'Is it time to reveal your plans to lowly generals, orlok?' he said. He smiled as he spoke, to take out the sting.

Tsubodai glanced at him. 'The river is the key. We have run and run. They will not expect an attack, not now. They will press us when they see we are beginning to cross, but we will hold

382

them with arrows. By nightfall, I want them on this side and our tumans on the other. It is no more than this king would expect from such easily driven enemies.'

Tsubodai smiled to himself. 'Once we are across the Sajo, I will need the last minghaan to hold that bridge. It is the only weak spot in my preparations, Batu. If that thousand is quickly overwhelmed, they will be on us and the choke-point of the river bridge will have been wasted.'

Batu thought about the bridge, which he had seen on the first crossing, when the tumans came trotting towards Buda and Pest. It was a main road of stone, wide enough for a dozen horses to ride abreast. He could hold it for days against knights, but the Magyar archers would simply use the banks to send shafts in tens of thousands. Even with shields, whoever stood on that bridge would fall eventually. He sighed to himself.

'Is that your task for me, orlok? Another suicidal stand that I should not survive? I just want to be sure I understand your orders.'

To his surprise, Tsubodai chuckled. 'No, not you. I need you tomorrow before dawn. I will leave it up to you whom you send for the task. They cannot retreat under attack, Batu. Be sure they understand that. The Hungarian king must believe we intend to run clear, that we cannot face his host in the field. Holding that bridge will convince him.'

Batu tried to hide his relief as he nodded. In the distance, Jebe's tuman was already on the move, riding as fast as they could through the narrow structure that spanned the river. A seasoned officer, Jebe allowed no delays and Batu could see a growing stain of men and horses on the other side. He heard trumpets behind him and bit his lip as the Hungarian Magyars continued to close the distance.

'This will be bloody, Tsubodai,' he said quietly.

The orlok looked at him, judging his worth with cold eyes.

'We will pay them back for our losses. You have my word.

Now go and choose your men. Make sure they have torches to light the bridge at sunset. I don't want any mistakes, Batu. We have a busy night ahead.'

Temuge paced the corridor outside the healer's rooms. He was pale at the muffled cries he heard, but he could not go back in. The first cut into Khasar's shoulder had released a white liquid that stank so terribly it had been all he could do to keep from vomiting. Khasar had remained silent then, but he had shuddered as the knife sliced deeper into his back, gouging him. The black paste was still thick on his tongue and Temuge thought his brother was hallucinating when he began to call for Genghis. Temuge had left at that point, with his sleeve pressed over his mouth and nose.

The sunlight had darkened in the corridor as he paced, though the city was never quiet now, not even in the palace rooms. Servants trotted past in groups, bearing anything from food to building supplies. Temuge had to stand back when one group came with a huge beam of oak, for what purpose he did not know. His nephew's woman, Sorhatani, had begun preparations for siege almost on the day Ogedai had fallen. Temuge sneered at the thought, wishing for a moment that Genghis could return to slap some sense back into her. The city could not be held, any fool could see that. The best they could hope for was to send an emissary to Chagatai to begin negotiations. The only living son of Genghis was not so powerful that words were useless, Temuge told himself. He had volunteered to begin negotiations, but Sorhatani had only smiled and thanked him for his suggestion before he was dismissed. Temuge seethed afresh at the thought. At the very moment when the nation needed his expertise, he had to deal with a woman who understood nothing. He resumed his pacing, wincing as Khasar cried out, worse than before.

The city needed a strong regent, not Ogedai's widow, who was still so stunned with grief that she looked to Sorhatani for guidance. Temuge thought again of forcing the issue. How many times had he come close to ruling the nation? The spirits had been against him before, but now it felt as if the bones had been thrown into the air. The city was terrified, he could feel it. Surely this was a time when a strong man, a brother to Genghis himself, could seize the reins? He cursed under his breath at the memory of the senior officer, Alkhun. Temuge had tried to sound him out, to gauge his feelings about the two women running Karakorum. The man had known his purpose, Temuge was almost sure. Alkhun had shaken his head. Before Temuge could do more than broach the subject gently, the man had dismissed himself with extraordinary abruptness, almost rudeness. Temuge had been left in a corridor, staring after him.

His thoughts were interrupted as the healer came out, wiping blood and the white filth from his hands. Temuge looked up, but the Chin man shook his head in silence.

'I am sorry. The growths were too deep and there were too many. The general would not have lived much longer. He lost a great deal of blood. I could not hold him here.'

Temuge clenched his fists, suddenly angry. 'What? What are you saying?' he demanded. 'He's *dead*?'

The healer looked at him sadly. 'He knew there were many risks, my lord. I am sorry.'

Temuge shoved past him and went into the room, almost gagging at the stench of sickness there. He jammed his sleeve into his mouth once again as he saw Khasar staring up at the ceiling, his eyes glassy. The exposed chest was a mass of scars, white rope lines of a thousand battles, reaching down to his arms which were thick with them, so that it barely looked like flesh. He saw again how thin Khasar had become, the bones showing clearly under tight skin. It was a relief that the healer had laid him face up. Temuge had no wish to see those purple wounds again, not while the odour filled his lungs. He gagged as he approached his brother's body, but he managed to reach out and close the eyes, pressing hard so that they remained shut.

'Who will look after me now?' Temuge muttered. 'I am the last of us, brother. What did I ever do to deserve such a fate?' To his astonishment, he began to weep, the tears feeling hot against his cheeks.

'Get up, you fool,' he said to the body. 'Just get up and tell me I am weak and pitiful for weeping. Get up, please.' He sensed the healer's presence at the door and spun round.

'My lord, do you want . . .' the man began.

'Get out!' Temuge roared. 'This is not your business!'

The healer vanished from the door, closing it softly behind him.

Temuge turned back to the figure lying on the bed. Somehow the smell had ceased to bother him.

'I am the last of us, Khasar. Bekter and Temujin and Kachiun, Temulun and now you. You are all gone now. I have no one left.' The realisation brought fresh tears and he slumped into a seat. 'I am alone in a city that waits to be destroyed,' he whispered.

For an instant, his eyes brightened with bitter rage. *He* had the right to inherit his brother's line, not some bastard son who had been nothing but a trial to his father. If Temuge had commanded a loyal tuman, he knew Chagatai would not live to take Karakorum. Chagatai would burn all the books in Karakorum's library, without understanding for a moment what treasures lay within. Temuge swallowed his grief and began to think and weigh his options. Sorhatani did not understand the stakes involved. Perhaps the city could be held if it had a man who understood its value, not a woman who had merely inherited her power through no talent of her own.

Tsubodai would hear soon, and he despised Chagatai. The entire army would come east like a storm to defend the capital city. Temuge concentrated harder, weighing his decisions and choices. If the city survived, Guyuk would be grateful.

It felt as if his life had been preparing him for this point, this decision. His family were no more and without them he felt a strange freedom. With the last witnesses gone, his old failures were just ashes, forgotten.

There would be some who chafed under Sorhatani's rule. Yao Shu was certainly one and Temuge thought the chancellor would know of others. It could be done before Chagatai arrived. Sometimes, power could change hands as quickly as a knife thrust. Temuge stood up and looked down at Khasar's body for the last time.

'He will burn the books, brother. Why should I allow that? I was there in the beginning, when death was just a breath away. I promise I will not be afraid now, with your spirit watching me. I was born to power, brother. It is the way the world should be, not the way it has become. I am the last of us, Khasar. This is *my* time now.'

King Bela watched as the camp was set around him, beginning with his own tent. It was a magnificent affair of oiled struts and sturdy canvas against the wind. He could already smell the meal his servants were preparing. Standing at the centre of it all, he felt a surging pride. His army had not needed the Cuman nomads to drive the Mongols back, day after day. Good Magyar steel and courage had been all that was required. It amused him to think he had herded the Mongol shepherds like one of their own flocks. He could regret that he had not driven them harder against the banks of the Sajo river, but they had not checked in their headlong retreat, barely pausing at the bridge before flowing across it. When he shaded his eyes against the setting sun, he could see the enemy tents, strange circular things that dotted the landscape across the river. They had none of the order and quiet efficiency he saw around him, and he relished the thought of the pursuit still to come. He had the blood of kings in his veins and he felt his ancestors crying out to see the invader thrown back, broken and bloody on the mountains they had come from.

He turned as one of Von Thuringen's knights came riding up to him. The Englishman was a rarity among their number, though Henry of Braybrooke was a renowned fighter and deserved his place.

'Sir Henry,' King Bela said in greeting.

The knight dismounted slowly and bowed. He spoke in French, both men fluent in that language.

'My lord, they are attempting to hold the bridge against us. Eight hundred, perhaps a thousand of them have sent their horses back to the others.'

'They would prefer it if we did not cross, eh, Sir Henry?' King Bela chuckled expansively. 'They have felt our breath on their necks for days and they would rather we left them to their retreat.'

'As you say, my lord. But it is the only bridge for a hundred miles or more. We must dislodge them tonight or in the morning.'

Bela thought for a moment. He was in a very good mood.

'When I was a boy, Sir Henry, I would collect limpets from the rocks near Lake Balaton. They would cling to the stones, but with my little knife, I would work them free for the pot! Do you follow me, Sir Henry?'

Bela laughed at his own wit, though the knight only frowned slightly, waiting for orders. The king sighed at such a stolid companion-in-arms. There was little humour in the ranks of knights, with their dour version of Christianity. A waft of roast pork reached them on the air and King Bela clapped his hands together in anticipation, making his decision.

'Send archers, Sir Henry. Let them have a little sport, a touch of target play before sunset. Hit them hard and drive them back over the river. Is that clear enough for you?'

The knight bowed again. Sir Henry of Braybrooke had a boil on his leg that needed lancing and a sore foot that seemed to be rotting in its bandages, for all the unguents and poultices he tried. The meal he would enjoy would be a thin soup and stale bread, with perhaps a little sour wine to force it down his dry throat. He mounted carefully, stiff with his discomforts. He did not enjoy slaughter, though the godless Mongols deserved to be wiped from the face of the good earth. Still, he would follow the king's order, honouring his vow of obedience to the knights.

Henry of Braybrooke passed on the king's command to a regiment of archers, four thousand bowmen under a Hungarian prince he neither liked nor respected. He stayed just long enough to watch them begin their march to the bridge and then went to join the lines for soup and bread, his stomach growling.

Chagatai looked out into bright sunshine. In his right hand he held a yellowed parchment that had travelled more than a thousand miles along the yam stations. It was stained and grubby from its journey, but the brief lines written there made his heart pound. The yam rider who had delivered it still held position with one knee bent, his presence forgotten the moment Chagatai had begun to read. In hastily scrawled Chin characters, the message was one he had both expected and almost dreaded for years. Ogedai had fallen at last.

It changed everything. Chagatai had become the last surviving son of Genghis Khan, the last in the direct line of the nation-maker, the khan of khans. Chagatai could almost hear the old man's voice as he thought through what lay ahead.

It was a time to be ruthless, to snatch the power that had once been promised, that was his by right. Tears sprang to his eyes, partly in memory of his youth. He could be the man his father had wanted him to be at last. Unconsciously, he crumpled the yellow papers.

Tsubodai would stand against him, or at least in favour of Guyuk. The orlok had never been in Chagatai's camp. He would have to be quietly killed, there was no other way. Chagatai nodded to himself, the simple decision opening up other pathways into the days to come. He had stood in the palace of Karakorum with Ogedai and Tsubodai. He had heard his brother talk of Tsubodai's loyalty, but Chagatai knew he could never trust the orlok. There was simply too much history between them and he had seen the promise of death in Tsubodai's hard eyes.

Karakorum was the key to the lock, he was certain. There was no history of direct descent of power, at least not in the tribes of the Mongol nation. The khan had always been chosen from those best suited to lead. It did not matter that Guyuk was Ogedai's eldest son, or that Ogedai favoured him, any more than it had mattered that Ogedai was not the eldest of his brothers. The nation knew no favourites. They would accept whoever held the city. They would follow whoever had the strength and will to take Karakorum. Chagatai smiled to himself. He had many sons to fill those rooms, sons who would make the line of Genghis stretch to the end of history. His imagination filled with a dazzling vision, an empire that would reach from Koryo in the east to the western nations, under just one strong hand. The Chin had never dreamed so far, but the land was vast and it tempted him to try to hold it all.

He heard footsteps behind him as his servant Suntai entered the room. For once, Chagatai had the news before his spymaster. He smiled to see the ugly face flushed, as if he had been running.

390

'It is time, Suntai,' Chagatai said, his eyes bright with tears. 'The khan has fallen and I must gather my tumans.'

His servant glanced at the kneeling yam rider and, after a moment of thought, he copied the position with his head bowed.

'Your will, my lord khan.'

CHAPTER THIRTY-ONE

Guyuk leaned forward in the saddle, balancing a lance as he galloped along a forest path. Ahead of him, he could see the back of a Serbian horseman, risking life and limb at full speed through the woodland paths. Guyuk felt his right arm burn as the weight of the lance pulled at his muscles. He shifted his stance as he rode, rising on the stirrups so that he could soak up the impact in his thighs. The battle was over days before, but he and Mongke still pursued the fleeing forces with their tumans, riding hard and making sure there were so few left alive that they could never support the Hungarian king. Guyuk thought again of the numbers of ethnic Magyars he had found across the borders. Tsubodai had been right to send him south, where so many villages might have answered Bela's call to war. They could no longer do so; his sweep across their lands had seen to that.

Guyuk cursed as he heard a distant horn. He was close enough to the Serb to see his terrified glances behind, but the general took his responsibilities seriously. He lifted the reins from where he had dropped them over the wooden saddle horn and pulled gently with his left hand. His pony steamed in the glade as he came to a halt and watched the terrified Serb rider vanish into the trees. Guyuk made an ironic salute with his lance, then jerked it into the air, catching it along its length and fitting it back into its sleeve by his leg. The horn sounded again, then a third time. He frowned, wondering what Mongke could have found that was so urgent.

As he rode back along the path, he caught glimpses of his men returning with him, coming out of the green gloom and calling to each other, boasting of their personal triumphs. Guyuk saw one of them waving a fistful of gold chains and he smiled at the man's expression, lifted by their simple joy.

When Tsubodai had given him his orders, Guyuk had worried it was some sort of punishment. It had been clear enough that Tsubodai was removing Batu's closest friends. The drive across the south had not promised much in the way of glory. Yet if the recall was the first signal to rejoin Tsubodai, Guyuk knew he would look back on those weeks with intense affection. He and Mongke had worked well together, each man learning to trust the other. Certainly his respect for Mongke had grown over a short time. The man was tireless and competent, and if he did not have Batu's flashes of brilliance, he was always where he was needed. Guyuk remembered his relief only a few days before, when Mongke had routed a force of Serbs that had ambushed two of his minghaans in the hills.

At the edge of the forest there were rocky outcrops and Guyuk picked his way past the broken ground as it merged with grassland. He could already see Mongke's tuman forming up, as well as his own men coming in from all directions and taking their positions. Guyuk kicked his mount into a canter and rode across.

Even from a distance, Guyuk heard the jingle of bells that

meant a yam rider had reached them. His pulse raced with excitement at getting news of any kind. It was too easy to feel isolated away from the main army, as if his battles and raids were the whole world. Guyuk forced himself to relax as he rode. Tsubodai would be calling them back for the final push to the west. Truly the sky father had blessed their enterprise, and he had never once regretted coming so far from the plains of home. Guyuk was young, but he could imagine the years ahead, when all those who had ridden in the great trek would share a special bond. He felt it already, a sense of shared danger, even of brotherhood. Whatever else Tsubodai had intended, the trek had forged bonds between the generals who had ridden with him.

As he rode up to Mongke, Guyuk saw his friend was flushed and angry. Guyuk raised his eyebrows in unspoken question and Mongke shrugged.

'He says he will speak only to you,' he said stiffly.

Guyuk looked in surprise at the young yam rider. He was travel-stained, though that was normal enough. Guyuk saw great patches of sweat on the rider's silk tunic. He wore no armour, but carried a leather satchel on his back that he had to struggle to remove.

'My instructions are to give the message only into the hands of Guyuk, my lord. I meant no offence.' The last comment was directed at Mongke, who glowered at him.

'No doubt Orlok Tsubodai has his reasons,' Guyuk said, accepting the satchel and opening it.

The weary rider looked uncomfortable in the presence of such senior men, but he shook his head.

'My lord, I have not seen Orlok Tsubodai. This message came down the line from Karakorum.'

Guyuk froze in the process of pulling out a single folded parchment. The men watching saw him grow pale as he examined the seal. With a quick snap, he broke the wax and opened

394

the message that had travelled almost five thousand miles to reach his hand.

He bit his lip as he read, his eyes travelling back to the beginning over and over as he tried to take it in. Mongke could not bear the strained silence.

'What is it, Guyuk?' he said.

Guyuk shook his head. 'My father is dead,' he replied, dazed. 'The khan is dead.'

Mongke sat still on his horse for only a moment, then dismounted and knelt on the grass with his head bowed. The men around him followed suit, word spreading among their number until both tumans were kneeling. Guyuk looked over their heads in confusion, still unable to take it in.

'Stand up, general,' he said. 'I will not forget this, but I must return home now. I must go back to Karakorum.'

Mongke rose, showing no emotion. Before Guyuk could stop him, he pressed his forehead against Guyuk's boot in the stirrup.

'Let me take the oath to you,' Mongke said. 'Allow me that honour.'

Guyuk stared at the man looking up at him with such fierce pride in his eyes.

'Very well, general,' he said softly.

'The khan is dead. I offer you salt, milk, horses, gers and blood,' Mongke replied. 'I will follow you, my lord khan. I give you my word and my word is iron.'

Guyuk shuddered slightly as the words were echoed by the kneeling men around them, until they had been said by all. The silence held and Guyuk looked over them, beyond the horizon to a city only he could see.

'It is done, my lord,' Mongke said. 'We are bound to you alone.' He mounted in one leap and began snapping orders to the closest minghaan officers.

Guyuk still held the yellow parchment as if it would burn

him. He heard Mongke ordering the tumans north, to join Tsubodai.

'No, general. I must leave tonight,' Guyuk said. His eyes were glassy, his skin like wax in the sunlight. He barely noticed Mongke bring his horse alongside, or felt the grip as Mongke reached out to touch his shoulder.

'You will need the other tumans now, my friend,' Mongke said. 'You will need all of them.'

Tsubodai crouched in the darkness. He could hear the river running close by. The air was filled with the odour of men and horses: damp cloth, sweat, spiced mutton and manure, all mingling in the night air. He was in a grim mood, having watched a minghaan of warriors slowly cut to pieces as they tried to hold the river bridge on his orders. They had completed their task, so that darkness came without the main Magyar army crossing. King Bela had forced just a thousand heavy horse across in a bridgehead, establishing his position for the morning. They would not sleep, with Mongol campfires all around them. The sacrifice had been worthwhile, Tsubodai thought. King Bela was forced to wait for the morning before he could flood across the bridge and continue his dogged pursuit of the Mongol army.

Wearily, Tsubodai cracked his neck, loosening tired joints. He did not need to motivate his men with a speech or fresh orders. They too had watched the last stand of the minghaan. They had heard the cries of pain and seen the splashes as dying men tumbled into the waters. The Sajo river was running full and fast and they drowned swiftly in their armour, unable to rise to the surface.

The moon was half full, casting its light over the landscape. The river shone like a silver rope, blurred into darkness as the tumans splashed through the shallow ford. This was the key to Tsubodai's plan, the fording place he had scouted on the first crossing out of the mountains. Everything Bela had seen made him believe the Mongols were running. The way they had held the bridge showed its importance to them. Since then, Tsubodai had used the dark hours as the moon rose above the grasslands around the river. It was a gamble, a risk, but he was as tired of running as his men.

Only his ragged conscripts now held the land beyond the river. They sat around a thousand fires in the moonlight, moving from one to another and making it look as if a vast camp had been set. Instead, Tsubodai had led the tumans three miles to the north. On foot, they led their horses across the fording point, out of sight and sound of the enemy. He had left not a single tuman in reserve. If the plan failed now, the Hungarian king would storm across the river at dawn and the ragged levy would be annihilated.

Tsubodai sent whispered orders to hurry the pace. It took hours to get so many men across, especially as they tried to keep quiet. Again and again, he jerked his gaze up to the moon, watching its passage and estimating the time he had left before dawn. King Bela's army was huge. Tsubodai would need the entire day to avenge his losses in full.

The tumans gathered on the other side of the river. The horses were snorting and whinnying to each other, their nostrils blocked by the grubby hands of warriors to muffle the sounds. The men whispered and laughed with each other in the darkness, relishing the shock that would ripple through the army chasing them. For five days they had run. Finally, it was time to stop and hit back.

In the gloom, Tsubodai could see that Batu was grinning as he trotted up for orders. He kept his own face stern.

'Your tuman is to hit the vanguard of their camp, Batu, where their king rests. Catch them asleep and destroy them. If you can reach the sandbag walls, tear them down. Approach as quietly as you can, then let your arrows and swords shout for you.'

'Your will, orlok,' Batu replied. For once, there was no mockery as he spoke the title.

'I will ride with the tumans of Jebe and Chulgetei, to strike against their rear at the same moment. They are certain of our position and they will not expect us tonight. Their walls are worse than useless, for they feel safe within them. I want them in panic, Batu. Everything depends on routing them quickly. Do not forget that they outnumber us still. If they are well led, they could rally and re-form. We will be forced to fight to the last man and the losses will be huge. Do *not* throw away my army, Batu. Do you understand?'

'I will treat them as if they were my own sons,' Batu said.

Tsubodai snorted. 'Ride then. Dawn is close and you must be in position.'

Tsubodai watched as Batu vanished silently into the darkness. There were no signal horns or naccara drums, not with the enemy so close and unsuspecting. Batu's tuman formed up without fuss, setting off at a trot towards the Hungarian camp. The Mongol carts and gers and wounded had remained behind with the conscripts, left to fend for themselves. The tumans were unencumbered, able to ride fast and strike hard, as they preferred.

Tsubodai nodded sharply to himself. He had further to ride than Batu's tuman and time was short. He mounted quickly, feeling his heart beat stronger in his chest. It was rare for him to feel excitement and he showed nothing in his face as he led the last two tumans into the west.

King Bela came awake, starting in his sleep at a crash of sound. He was covered in sweat and rubbed the last wisps of a nightmare from his eyes as he stood. In his blurred thoughts, he could hear the clash and screams of battle and he blinked, becoming aware that the sounds were real. In sudden fear, he stuck his head outside the command tent. It was still dark, but he saw Conrad von Thuringen on his horse, already in full armour. The marshal of the Teutonic Knights did not see Bela as he trotted past, shouting orders Bela could not make out over the tumult. Men were running in all directions, and out beyond the sandbags, he heard battle horns sound in the distance. Bela swallowed drily as he recognised a distant rumble that was growing louder and clearer with every passing moment.

He cursed and turned back to his tent, fumbling for clothes in the darkness. His servants were nowhere to be found and he stumbled over a chair, hissing with pain as he rose. He pulled a pair of heavy trousers from the fallen chair back and yanked them on. It all took precious time. He grabbed the embroidered jacket of his rank, pulling it over his shoulders as he raced out into the night. His horse had been brought and he mounted, needing the height to see.

The first light of dawn had stolen upon them in those moments. The sky to the east was growing pale, and with a shock of horror, Bela could see his ranks boiling in utter chaos. The sandbag walls there had spilled across the grass, worse than useless. His own men were coming through the gap, driven back by the savage riders and arrows slaughtering them outside. He heard Von Thuringen bellow orders to his knights as they rode to shore up the defences there. Desperate hope kindled in him.

The roar of drums began again and the king spun his charger on the spot. The Mongols were somehow behind him. How had they crossed the river? It was impossible, yet the drums rattled and grew.

Stunned, Bela rode through the camp, preferring to move rather than remain still, though his mind was a blank. His

Magyars had breached their own camp boundaries in two places, pouring through them to what felt like safety. He could barely comprehend the losses they must have taken to be falling back in such a way.

As he watched, the holes widened and more and more crammed themselves behind the sandbags. Beyond them, the Mongols still tore into his bewildered men, sending them reeling with arrows and lances. In the growing light, there seemed no end to them and Bela wondered if they had somehow hidden an army until then.

Bela struggled to remain calm as the chaos increased around him. He knew he needed to retake the perimeter, to restore the camp and marshal his men within the walls. From there, he would be able to assess the losses, perhaps even begin a counter-attack. He bawled the order to the messengers and they rode out through the milling horsemen, shouting the words to anyone who could hear: 'Rebuild the walls. Hold the walls.' If it could be done, he might yet save the day from disaster. His officers would make order from the chaos. He would throw the tumans back.

The knights under Josef Landau heard him. They formed up and charged back across the camp in a solid mass. There were Mongols at the walls by then and a hail of arrows buzzed through the camp. In such a crush, there was no need to aim. Bela could hardly believe the losses, but the knights struggled on like men possessed, knowing as he did that the walls were their only salvation. Von Thuringen led a hundred of his own armoured men, the enormous marshal easy to mark with his beard and longsword.

The knights proved their worth to him then, Landau and Von Thuringen shattering the Mongols who had dared to enter the camp, driving them back towards the wide holes in the walls. They fought with righteous rage, and for once the Mongols did not have room to nip and dart past them. Bela watched with his heart in his mouth as the Teutonic Knights blocked one breach with their horses, holding shields against the arrows still pouring through. Landau was struck by something and Bela had a glimpse of his head lolling limp as his horse bolted away. For a moment, the knight struggled, his arms flailing, then he fell into the churned mud almost at Bela's feet. There was blood coming from under his neck plates, though Bela could see no wound. Trapped and suffocating in his armour, Landau died slowly, his body buffeted by those running around and over him.

Unhorsed men yanked and sweated at the sandbags, rebuilding the walls as quickly as they could. The Mongols came again, using their horses to ride right up to the walls and then leaping over them, so that they landed tumbling. One by one, those intruders were killed, taken by the same regiment of archers who had assaulted the bridge the night before. Bela began to breathe more easily as the threat of imminent destruction receded. The walls were repaired, his enemies howling outside them. They had taken grievous losses, though nothing like his own. He thanked God he had built the camp large enough to shelter his men.

King Bela stared at the heaps of dead soldiers and horses piled around the edges. They were thick with shafts, some still twitching. The sun was high and he could not believe the time had passed so quickly since the first alarms.

From the back of his horse, he could see the Mongols were still pressing close to the walls. There was only one true gate and he sent archers to cover it against another attack. He saw Von Thuringen gather the knights there in a column and Bela could only watch as they pulled down their visors and readied lances. At a bellow from Von Thuringen, the gate was pulled open. Almost six hundred kicked their chargers into a gallop and rode out into the storm. Bela thought he would not see them again.

He had the wits to send archers to every wall with full quivers. All around him, the snap of bows began and he breathed faster as he heard guttural yells from outside. The Teutonic Knights were in their element, slicing through the Mongol riders, using weight and speed to cut them down as they roared and screamed outside the sandbag walls. Bela could hardly control his fear. Inside the camp, men and horses roiled in a crush, but a great part of his army had been slaughtered in their sleep. Outside, Bela heard the jeers and whoops of the Mongols suddenly choked off as Von Thuringen battered through them. He felt himself grow cold. He would not escape from this place. They had trapped him and he would die with the rest.

It seemed an age before Von Thuringen came back through the gate. The gleaming column of knights had been reduced to no more than eighty, perhaps a hundred. The men who returned were battered and bloody, many of them reeling in their saddles with arrows sticking out of their armour. The Magyar horsemen were in awe of the knights and many of them dismounted to help them down from the saddle. Von Thuringen's huge beard was stained with rusty blood and he looked like some dark god, his blue eyes furious as they fell on the Hungarian king.

Bela needed guidance and he returned the gaze like a deer staring helplessly at a lion. Through the heaving mass of men, Conrad von Thuringen came riding, the marshal's face as grim as his own.

Batu was panting as he rode up to Tsubodai. The orlok stood by his horse on a ridge of land that stretched across the battlefield, watching the battles he had ordered. Batu had expected the orlok to be furious at the way the attack had gone, but instead Tsubodai smiled to see him. Batu rubbed at a clot of mud sticking to his neck and returned the smile uncertainly.

'Those knights are impressive,' Batu said.

Tsubodai nodded. He had seen the bearded giant throw his men back. The Mongol warriors had been too close, unable to manoeuvre when the knights came charging out. Even so, the sudden attack had been unnerving for its discipline and ferocity. The knights had hacked their way through his men like tireless butchers, closing the gaps in their own ranks as arrows found them and sent them falling to the ground. Each one that fell took two or three warriors with him, grunting and kicking out until he was held and cut.

'There are not so many now,' Tsubodai replied, though the attack had shaken his certainties. He had not dismissed the threat of the knights, but perhaps he had underestimated their strength in the right time and place. That bearded maniac had found the moment, surprising his tuman just as they were howling for victory. Still, only a few knights made it back. When the volleys of arrows began to snap out from the walls, Tsubodai had given the order to retreat out of range. His own warriors had begun to return the shafts, but the deaths were unequal as Bela's archers shot from behind a stable wall of sandbags. For an instant, Tsubodai had considered another charge to break the walls, but the cost would have been too high. He had them inside their own walls, weaker than any Chin fortress. He doubted they had enough water for so many crammed into the camp.

The orlok stared out across the plains with its heaps of bodies, some still crawling. The attacks had smashed the Hungarian army, shattering their overconfidence at last. He was pleased, but he bit his lip as he pondered how to finish the work.

'How long can they hold?' Batu asked suddenly, echoing his thoughts so closely that Tsubodai looked at him in surprise.

'A few days before their water runs out, no more,' he said. 'But they will not wait until then. The question is how many men and horses, how many arrows and lances, they have left. And how many of those cursed knights.'

It was hard to make a good estimate. The grasslands were littered with the dead, but he could not know how many had survived to reach their king. He closed his eyes for a moment, summoning up the image of the land as if he flew above it. His ragged conscripts were still across the river, no doubt staring balefully at the small contingent who had forced the bridge and held the other side. The king's camp lay between Tsubodai and the river, trapped and held in one spot.

Once again, Batu had mirrored his thoughts.

'Let me send a messenger to bring the foot soldiers back across the river,' Batu said.

Tsubodai ignored him. He did not yet know how many of his Mongol warriors had been killed or wounded that morning. If the king had saved even half his army, he would have enough left to force a battle on equal terms, a battle that Tsubodai could only win by throwing his tumans in hard. The precious army he had brought on the great trek would be reduced, battered against an enemy of equal strength and will. It would not do. He thought furiously, opening his eyes to stare at the land around the camp. Slowly he smiled, and this time Batu was not there before him.

'What is it, orlok? Shall I send a messenger across the river ford?'

'Yes. Tell them to slaughter the king's men across the river. We must retake that bridge, Batu. I do not want the king sending men to the river for water.'

Tsubodai tapped his boot on the ridge beneath him. 'When that is done, I will pull my tumans further back, another mile from this point. Thirst will make their decision for them.'

Batu could only look on in confusion as Tsubodai showed his teeth in what might have been a grin.

CHAPTER THIRTY-TWO

Temuge was sweating, though the air was cold in the court-yard of the palace. He could feel the hard length of the knife he had concealed under his robe. There had been no search of the men summoned there that morning, though he had made sure by hiding the weapon so that it chafed his groin and caused him to shift his weight.

In the distance, Temuge could hear hammering, the sound that filled his days. The fortification of Karakorum went on day and night, as it would do until the banners of Chagatai were seen on the horizon. If Sorhatani and Torogene held the city long enough for Guyuk to return, they would be praised above all women. Men would talk of the way they had girded Karakorum for war for generations to come. The name of Temuge, keeper of the khan's libraries, would be forgotten.

He stared coldly at Sorhatani as she addressed the small crowd. Alkhun was there as the senior minghaan of the khan's Guards. Temuge felt the man look strangely at him and ignored him. He breathed deeply of the cold air, thinking, planning, deciding. His brother Genghis had once walked into a khan's ger and cut his throat. Genghis should not have survived it, but he had quieted the man's tribe with words and threats. They had stopped to listen. Temuge burned at the thought that the men and women in the courtyard would stop and listen to him.

He fingered the hilt of the knife under his clothes. There was *no* destiny in life, nothing beyond what a man could take and hold for himself. Temuge had been witness to the bloody birth of a nation. Whether they understood it or not, they owed him their city, their lives, everything. If it had not been for Genghis, the men and women in that cold yard would still be grubby goatherders on the plains, with each tribe at the throat of the next. They were even living longer than the men and women he had known as a boy. Chin and Moslem healers had saved many from illnesses that had once been mortal.

Despite the surging anger, part of him was still terrified of what he planned. Again and again, Temuge let his hands fall open, telling himself the moment had passed: his moment in history. Then the memory of his brothers would surface and he could feel them mocking his indecision. It was just a death, nothing more, certainly nothing to unman him in such a way. He felt sweat trickle down his neck and wiped at it, drawing the gaze of Yao Shu. Their eyes met and Temuge was reminded that he was not alone in his plotting. The chancellor had been more than open with him. The man hid a vicious hatred of Sorhatani that had led Temuge into revealing more of his thoughts and dreams than he had planned.

Sorhatani dismissed the officers of Karakorum to their day's work and began to turn away. Torogene went with her, already discussing some detail.

'A moment, my lady,' Temuge said.

His mouth seemed to work without his volition, spitting

out the words. Sorhatani was in a hurry and barely gestured for him to follow her as she stepped down and walked towards the cloistered hallway back into the palace rooms. It was that casual gesture that firmed his nerve with anger. To have such a woman treat him as a supplicant was enough to bring a flush to his features. He hurried to catch up with the women, taking strength from the presence of Yao Shu falling in with them. He glanced back at the open courtyard as they passed into shadow, frowning as he saw Alkhun was still there, staring after him.

Sorhatani had made a mistake in letting him come so close in the shadows. He reached out and took her arm. She shook off his grip.

'What do you want, Temuge?' she snapped. 'I have a thousand things to do this morning.'

It was not a time for words, but he spoke to cover the moment as he reached for the knife under his deel robe.

'My brother Genghis would not want a woman to rule his lands,' he said.

She stiffened and he brought out the blade. Torogene gasped and took a step away, already panicking. Sorhatani's eyes widened in shock. Temuge grabbed her with his left hand and drew back his arm to drive the dagger into her chest.

He felt his arm gripped with such strength that he stumbled and cried out. Yao Shu held him and the man's eyes were cold with disdain. Temuge yanked at his arm, but he could not free himself. Panic spread through his chest, making his heart flutter.

'No,' he said. Spittle had gathered in two white specks at the corner of his mouth. He could not understand what was happening.

'You were right after all, Yao Shu,' Sorhatani said. She did not look at Temuge, as if he had ceased to matter at all. 'I'm sorry to have doubted you. I just never thought he would truly be so stupid.'

Yao Shu tightened his grip and the dagger fell with a clatter on the stone floor.

'He has always been a weak man,' he replied. He shook Temuge suddenly, making him cry out in fear and astonishment. 'What do you want done with him?'

Sorhatani hesitated and Temuge struggled to find his wits.

'I am the last brother of Genghis,' he said. 'And what are *you*? Who are you to sit in judgement of me? A Chin monk and two women. You have no *right* to judge me.'

'He is no threat,' Yao Shu went on, as if Temuge had not spoken. 'You could banish him from the khanate, send him far away like any wanderer.'

'Yes, send him far away,' Torogene said. She was shaking, Temuge saw.

Temuge felt Sorhatani's gaze on him and he took a long, slow breath, knowing his life hung in her hands.

'No, Torogene,' she said at last. 'Such a thing should be punished. He would not have shown mercy to us.'

She waited while Temuge swore and struggled, allowing Torogene the decision. Torogene shook her head and walked away, her eyes brimming.

'Give him over to Alkhun,' Sorhatani said.

Temuge shouted for help, suddenly desperate as he writhed against the grip that kept him helpless as a child.

'I was there when we found you in the forests, monk!' he spat. 'It was I who brought you back to Genghis. How can you let my nephew's whore rule over you?'

'Tell Alkhun to make it quick,' Sorhatani said. 'I can do that much for him.'

Yao Shu nodded and she walked away, leaving the pair alone. Temuge crumpled as he heard footsteps approach and saw Alkhun come out of the sunlight into the shadowed cloister.

'You heard it?' Yao Shu said.

The minghaan's eyes were furious as he took his own grip

on Temuge's shoulders, feeling the thin bones of an old man through the cloth.

'I heard,' he said. He had a long knife in his hand.

'Damn you both,' Temuge said. 'Damn you both to hell.'

Temuge began to weep as he was dragged back into the sunshine.

By the second day after the night attack, Bela's men had repaired the sandbag walls with broken carts and saddles from dead horses. His archers were on permanent alert, but they were already dry and gasping. There was barely enough water for a single swallow in the morning and evening for each man. The horses were suffering and Bela was desperate. He rested his chin on the rough canvas of a bag, staring out over the Mongol army that had camped nearby. They of course had access to the river and as much water as they could drink.

As he gazed out across the grassland, Bela struggled with despair. He no longer considered the reports from the north to be exaggerated. The Mongol general had far fewer men, but they had routed the superior force in a display of manoeuvre and tactics that made him burn. For the rest of that appalling first day, Bela had expected an all-out assault on the camp, but it had not come. He felt trapped there, crushed in among so many men and horses that they could hardly move. He could not understand why they had not come, unless they took some perverse pleasure in seeing a king die of thirst. They were not even threatening the camp and had moved back far beyond arrow range. Bela could just make out their movements in the distance. It gave a false sense of security to see them so far away. He knew from reports and his own bitter experience that they could move at incredible speed if they wanted.

Von Thuringen left a conversation with his knights to approach. The man had shed his armoured breastplate, revealing scarred arms and a quilted jerkin, stained and filthy. Bela could smell the sweat and blood on him still. The marshal's face was stern and Bela could hardly meet his eyes as Von Thuringen bowed stiffly.

'One of my men thinks he's found a way out of this,' Von Thuringen said.

King Bela blinked. He had been praying for salvation, but the answer to prayers seemed unlikely in the huge bearded man before him, still matted with someone else's blood.

'What is it?' Bela said, standing up and squaring his shoulders under the knight's scrutiny.

'Easier to show you, your majesty,' Von Thuringen replied.

Without another word, he turned and pushed his way through the mass of horses and men. Bela could only follow, his irritation growing.

It was not a long journey, though the king was buffeted among the men and barely avoided being knocked down as a horse reared. He followed Von Thuringen to another section of wall and looked in the direction the marshal pointed.

'See there, three of my men?' Von Thuringen said flatly.

King Bela peered over the wall and saw three knights who had removed their armour, yet still wore the tabards of yellow and back that marked their order. They were standing in full view of the sandbag walls, but Bela saw how the land dipped before rising to the Mongol camp. There was a ridge there that ran west. Hope leapt in him as he considered the possibilities.

'I couldn't risk horses in daylight, but in darkness, every man here could ride out below that ridge. With a bit of luck and if they keep their heads down, the Mongols will find an empty camp tomorrow morning.'

Bela bit his lip, suddenly terrified of leaving the fragile safety of the camp.

'There is no other way?' he asked.

Von Thuringen drew his brows together, so that his eyebrows met.

'Not without a supply of water. Not without a much larger camp and materials for the walls we need. We're crammed so tight in here, we'd be worse than useless if they attacked. Be thankful they haven't yet realised our weakness, your majesty. God has shown us the way, but it is your order to give.'

'Can we not defeat them in battle, Von Thuringen? Surely there is room to form up on the field?'

The marshal of the Teutonic Knights took a breath to control his anger. He was not the one who supposedly knew the lands around the Sajo river. His men could never have predicted a ford just a couple of miles downstream. The blame for the appalling losses was at the feet of the king, not his knights. It was all Von Thuringen could do to remain civil.

'Your majesty, my knights would follow you to death. The rest, well, they are frightened men. Take this chance and let us get away from this damned camp. I will find another place where we can take revenge on the goatherders. Forget the battle, your majesty. A campaign is not lost because of a single bad day.'

King Bela stood, working a ring on his hand round and round. Von Thuringen waited impatiently, but eventually the king nodded.

'Very well. As soon as it's dark enough, we go.'

Von Thuringen turned away, already issuing the orders to the men around him. He would organise the retreat, hoping that no Mongol scout wandered too close to the ridge that night.

As soon as the sun set, Von Thuringen gave the order to leave the camp. The final hours had been spent wrapping cloth around hooves to silence them, though the ground was soft enough. The Teutonic Knights supervised the first men who crept out in darkness and began to walk their mounts beneath the ridge, their hearts pounding at the thought of a shout from the enemy. It did not come and they moved quickly. The knights were the last out of the camp, leaving it abandoned in the moonlight.

Von Thuringen could see the Mongol campfires in the distance and he smiled wearily at the thought of them finding the camp empty in the morning. He had spoken the truth to the king. The losses had been grievous, but there would be other days. Even if he accomplished nothing more than finding a good field for battle, it would offer better odds than dying of thirst behind sandbags.

As the night wore on, Von Thuringen lost track of the mass of men ahead of him. The first miles were an agony of suspense, but once the camp was far behind, the lines stretched out into a long trail of men over many miles as the faster ones outpaced the injured and slow. Even his knights felt it, a feverish desire to put some real distance between them and the Mongol army.

The marshal of the Teutonic Knights ached from the battering he had taken. Von Thuringen knew his flesh would be a colourful mass of bruises under his armour from arrow strikes. There was already blood in his urine. As he rode in the darkness, he considered what he had seen and did not enjoy the conclusions. There was another reason to preserve the Magyar army to fight again. If the reports from the north were true, they were the last army between Hungary and France that had a chance of stopping the Mongol invasion. The very thought appalled him. He had never thought to see such a threat in his lifetime. The nobles of Russia should have torn the enemy to pieces, yet they had failed and seen their cities burn.

King Louis of France would have to be told, Von Thuringen thought sourly. More importantly, the struggle for power between the Pope and the Holy Roman Emperor would have to be put aside. None of them were safe until the true enemy had been destroyed. Von Thuringen shook his head as he urged his charger to a trot again. Somewhere ahead, the king of Hungary rode with his personal guard. Von Thuringen could have wished for a better leader at such a time, but that was the fortune he had been given. He would not fail after a single lost battle. He had suffered through defeats before and always returned to send the souls of his enemies screaming back to hell.

The first light of dawn was showing and Von Thuringen could only guess how far he had come during the night. He was mortally tired and his throat was dry, the supply of water long gone. He knew he should look for a river as soon as there was enough light, to restore some strength to the horses and men. He reached down and patted the neck of his charger at the thought, murmuring words of comfort. If God was with them, the Mongols would not realise they had gone for a morning or longer. He smiled at the thought of them waiting patiently for thirst to drive the Magyars into their arms. It would be a long wait.

The tasks he faced rattled through his head as the light began to turn from silvery grey to gold. The priority was to find a river and drink their fill. The thought of fresh water made him work his lips, clearing them of thick spit.

As the light spread across the land, Von Thuringen saw a dark line on his right hand. At first he thought it was trees, or some outcropping of rock. Then, in a moment, the shadowy forms resolved and he froze, pulling on the reins.

Mongol warriors on horseback lined the path, with bows held ready. Von Thuringen tried to swallow, but his throat was too dry. His gaze swept up and down the lines, seeing the thin trail of men ahead of him. By God, there was not even a herald to blow a warning horn! Only a few of his knights

413

rode nearby and they too reined in, looking back at him in grim realisation.

The world held still for a long time and, in silent prayer, Von Thuringen made his peace, his final penitence. He kissed the ring on his finger with its holy relic for the last time. As he spurred his charger forward and reached for his sword, the arrows began to fly, the first ones keening through the air like screaming children. The Mongols fell upon the thin and broken line of escaping soldiers and the butchery began in earnest.

Baidur and Ilugei returned to Hungary to find Tsubodai resting with his tumans. The mood of triumph was visible in every face they saw and they were greeted with drums and horns. The tumans with Tsubodai knew the part Baidur had played in their own victory and he was cheered as he entered the camp around the Danube.

The cities of Buda and Pest had been sacked over days, then looted carefully of anything that they needed or desired. Baidur trotted through streets of half-burnt houses, seeing stones that had been hot enough to shatter into rubble over the open road. Though King Bela had escaped, the army of Hungary had been slaughtered, almost too many to count. Tsubodai's tallymen had collected sacks of ears and some talked of sixty thousand dead or more. The scouts were already out roaming further west, but for a season, the tumans could pause in the great trek, growing strong and fat on rich meat and stolen wine.

Tsubodai sent riders to Guyuk and Mongke to bring them in. Their flanking rides were ended and he chose to gather them all in one place, ready to push on to the sea.

Batu had seen the riders go out and so he was surprised when one of his men brought him news of tumans coming from the south. It was too early for Tsubodai's orders to have reached Guyuk, but he called to Baidur and they rode out of camp.

They were among the first to recognise the banners of Guyuk's tuman. Batu laughed at the sight and dug in his heels, sending his pony galloping across the open grassland. There were many stories to tell and he anticipated enough drunken evenings to recount them all. As he and Baidur drew closer, neither man noticed the dark expressions on the faces of the returning warriors at first. There was no mood of jubilation in the tumans of Guyuk and Mongke. Guyuk in particular looked as grim as Batu had ever seen him.

'What is it, cousin?' Batu said, his smile fading.

Guyuk turned his head and Batu saw his eyes were red-rimmed and sore-looking.

'The khan is dead,' Guyuk said.

Batu shook his head. 'Your father? How? He was still young.'

Guyuk looked at him from under lowered brows, forcing the words out.

'His heart. I must see Tsubodai now.'

Batu and Baidur fell in at his side. Baidur had paled and he was lost in thought as they rode. He knew his father better than anyone and he was suddenly afraid the men around him had become his enemies.

CHAPTER THIRTY-THREE

Batu stayed with Guyuk, Mongke and Baidur as they entered
the river city of Buda and made their way through the streets
to the palace Tsubodai was using for his base. It was left to their
senior minghaan officers to find lodging and food for the men
in the ransacked city. The four princes rode to the royal palace
and dismounted at the outer gate. They passed the guards
without a challenge. The orlok's officers took one look and chose
discretion rather than the letter of their orders.

For once, Guyuk led the small group, with Batu striding at
his right shoulder. They found Tsubodai in an empty ballroom,
where a huge dining table had been dragged in and piled with
maps and papers. The orlok was deep in conversation with Jebe,
Chulgetei and Ilugei. The other men were nodding as Tsubodai
adjusted coins to show the position of tumans on the landscape. Batu took in the scene at a glance and smiled tightly to
himself. It was a meeting of young and old, and for the first
time, Batu was confident he could predict the outcome.

Tsubodai looked up as the four princes crossed the hall, their steps echoing in the space. He frowned at the sight of their stern expressions and stood back from the table.

'I did not summon you here,' he said. He was looking at Batu, but his gaze snapped over in surprise as Guyuk answered.

'My father is dead, orlok.'

Tsubodai closed his eyes for a moment, his face stiff. He nodded to himself.

'Please sit down,' he said. His authority was so deeply ingrained that all four moved to the chairs around the table, though Batu held back, wanting to keep the impetus they had brought with them. Tsubodai spoke again before anyone else.

'Was it his heart?' he said.

Guyuk took in a breath. 'So you knew then? Yes, it was his heart.'

'He told me, when he told his brother Chagatai,' Tsubodai replied. His eyes fell on Baidur as Guyuk turned in the chair.

'I knew nothing,' Baidur said coldly.

Guyuk turned back, but Tsubodai let his eyes remain on Baidur until the young man was shifting uncomfortably.

Tsubodai had a hundred things he wanted to say, but he controlled himself with an effort of will.

'What are your plans?' he asked Guyuk. The more detached part of him was interested to see how Guyuk would respond. Whatever remnant there was left of his youth had been suddenly strangled. Tsubodai looked at the young prince, understanding the quiet reserve he now saw. There was new weight on Guyuk's shoulders, whether he wanted it or not.

'I am my father's heir,' Guyuk said. 'I must return to Karakorum.'

Once more, Tsubodai looked to Baidur. The orlok grimaced, but the words had to be said.

'Are you aware of the threat from your uncle? He has a claim to the khanate.'

417

Neither man looked directly at Baidur as he flushed.

Guyuk cocked his head slightly in thought and Tsubodai was pleased to see him weigh his response. There was no place for the foolish young man he had been, not any longer.

'The yam rider reached me a month ago. I have had time to consider it,' Guyuk said. 'I will require an oath of allegiance from the tumans here.'

'That will have to wait,' Tsubodai said. 'When we are finished here, you will summon the nation as your father did.'

Baidur shifted again and was ignored. His was an impossible position, but he was growing desperate to speak.

'I can let you have four tumans, leaving me only three,' Tsubodai said. 'You must return in force to secure the khanate. Chagatai cannot put more than two, perhaps three, in the field.' He stared coldly at Baidur. 'It is my recommendation that you have Baidur remain with me, rather than force him to choose between cousin and father.' He dipped his head to Baidur. 'My apologies, general.'

Baidur opened his mouth, but he could not find the words. It was Batu who spoke next, for the first time. Tsubodai's eyes and jaw tightened instantly at his voice, betraying an inner tension.

'You know Chagatai Khan better than any of us, except for Baidur. How do you think he will react when he hears the news?'

Tsubodai did not look at Batu as he replied, keeping his gaze locked on Guyuk. Every word seemed to be dragged out of him.

'If he is rash, he will take his tumans to Karakorum.'

'If he is rash . . . I see,' Batu replied, enjoying the discomfort he saw. 'And what will follow, when Guyuk Khan returns home?'

'Chagatai will either negotiate, or he will fight. No one can know his mind.' Tsubodai clasped his hands on the table and leaned closer to Guyuk. 'Believe me: Chagatai Khan is not the threat you believe.'

It looked as if he might go on, but then Tsubodai clamped his jaw and waited. The decision was not simply a military one. Batu could hardly control the quirking of his lips at seeing Tsubodai at a loss.

Guyuk let the men at the table sweat for a time before he shook his head.

'If you can offer me no more than that as assurance, orlok, I must take the tumans home. All of them.' He glanced at Jebe and Chulgetei, but the older men were not part of the decision. Tsubodai had ultimate authority over the army, but this was not a military problem.

Tsubodai let out a long breath. 'General, I have new maps that show lands that are not even legends to us. The city of Vienna is but a hundred miles further west. The homeland of the Templar knights is beyond it. Italy is to the south. Already, I have scouts in the mountains there, planning the next stage. This has been my life's achievement.' He stopped himself rather than beg, as Guyuk gazed stonily at him.

'I will need all the tumans, Orlok Tsubodai. All.'

'You do not need the ragged conscripts. Leave me but those and two tumans and I will go on.'

Slowly, Guyuk reached out his hand and gripped Tsubodai's shoulder. The gesture was one he would not have dreamed of making a month before.

'How could I leave you behind, Tsubodai? The general of Genghis Khan, at the time I need him most? Come home with me. You know I cannot allow you to stay. You will come back another year, when there is peace.'

Tsubodai stared at Baidur and his pain was visible to all. Baidur looked away rather than see. When the orlok's gaze swept over Batu, his eyes blazed.

'I *am* an old man,' Tsubodai said. 'And I saw the beginning of it all, when Genghis himself was young. I will not come back here again. I have spoken to prisoners. There is nothing

419

between us and the ocean, *nothing*. We have seen their knights, Guyuk, do you understand? They cannot stop us. If we go on, the land is ours to take, sea to sea, for ever. Sea to sea, general. Ours for ten thousand years. Can you imagine such a thing?'

'It is not important,' Guyuk said softly. 'The homeland is where we began. I cannot lose all that for lands here.' He brought his hand back and his voice was steady.

'I will be khan, Orlok Tsubodai. I need you with me.'

Tsubodai slumped slowly in his chair, the energy draining from his face. Even Batu looked uncomfortable at the changes they had wrought in him.

'Very well. I will make them ready to ride home.'

Chagatai stood looking out at the river as the sun came up. The room was bare of furniture, the palace itself empty, beyond a few servants who would clean the rooms. He did not know if he would ever come back there again and he felt a pang of loss at the thought. He heard footsteps approaching and turned to see his servant Suntai enter the room. The man's scarred face was welcome, while Chagatai's heart soared with visions.

'It is time, my lord khan,' Suntai said. His gaze fell to the crumpled parchment in Chagatai's hand, read and reread a thousand times since it had come just days before.

'It is time,' Chagatai echoed. He took a last look at the sun rising, lighting the backs of a flight of geese rising from the still waters. In such a mood, he stared straight at the ball of gold on the horizon, daring it to burn him.

'I can be in Karakorum months ahead of him,' Chagatai said. 'I will take the oath of our people as khan, but there will be war when he returns. Unless I take the example of my beloved brother, Ogedai. What do you think, Suntai? Would Guyuk accept my khanate here in exchange for his life? Come, give me your counsel.'

'He may, my lord. After all, you did.'

Chagatai smiled, at peace with the world for the first time in years.

'Perhaps I would be storing up trouble for the future, or for my son, Baidur. I must think of his life now. By the spirits, if Guyuk would just die in his sleep, my path would be clear! Instead, I have sent him a hostage to my goodwill.'

Suntai knew his master well and he smiled as he came to stand behind him.

'Guyuk may believe so, my lord, even Orlok Tsubodai, but will such a hostage truly stay your hand?'

Chagatai shrugged. 'I have other sons. The prize is too great to turn aside for just one. Baidur will have to fight his own way out. After all, Suntai, I gave him my best warriors for his tuman. They have no equal in the nation. If he falls, I will grieve for him, but his fate is in his own hands, as always.'

Chagatai had not noticed Suntai's soft boots in place of his usual sandals. He did not hear the final step. He felt a sting at his neck and choked in surprise, reaching up to his throat. To his astonishment, there was a terrible wrongness there. As he pulled his hand away, he saw it was covered in blood. He tried to speak, but his voice was lost to him and only creaked through the line that striped his skin.

'It is said that the kirpan dagger is so very sharp that little pain attends a death,' Suntai said. 'I have never had the opportunity to ask. Its name translates as "hand of mercy" for that reason.'

The servant leaned closer as he saw Chagatai's lips move, though a low gargling was the only sound he could make. Suntai stood well back as his master sank to one knee, still clutching his throat.

'The wound is mortal, my lord. Try to be calm. Death is coming swiftly.'

Chagatai's head sank slowly to his chest. His right hand came away bloody and reached for the sword on his hip, but he did not have the strength to draw it beyond the first gleaming line of steel.

'I was told to pass on a message to you, my lord, if there was a chance to do so. I have memorised the words. Can you still hear?'

Suntai watched as Chagatai fell forward in a clatter. Someone shouted nearby and Suntai frowned at the thought of what must come.

'The message is from Ogedai Khan, my lord, to be given at the moment of your death: "This is not vengeance, Chagatai. It is for my son. I am no longer the man who let you live. By my hand striking far, you will *not* be khan."' Suntai sighed. 'I have never been truly your servant, my lord, but you were a fine master. Go with God.'

Chagatai's hands fell limp and his guards came storming into the room, drawing their blades as they saw Suntai kneeling and whispering into the ear of their master. He stood as they rushed towards him, his face peaceful as the swords swung.

On a cold, clear morning, Tsubodai mounted his horse and looked back. There were no clouds and the sky was a perfect blue. Seven tumans were waiting in formation, the best warriors of his nation. Behind them, the baggage and carts stretched for miles. He had taken generals, some of them almost boys, and he had shown them their strengths. Despite his flaws, Guyuk would be a better khan because of what he had learned on the great trek. Baidur would be more of a man than his father before him. Mongke would make his father's soul proud.

Tsubodai sighed. He knew he would never see such an army again. Old age had crept up on him and he was tired. For a time, he had thought he could ride for ever with the young men, the lure of the sea bringing him further from home than he could once have dreamed. When Guyuk had called a halt, it was like a whisper of death in his ears, an ending. He stared into the distance, imagining cities with spires of gold. He knew their names, but he would never see them: Vienna, Paris, Rome.

It was done. He knew he would take arms if Chagatai challenged for Ogedai's khanate. Perhaps he *would* see battle one last time. With the princes, he would take the field in glory and show Chagatai why Tsubodai Bahadur had been the general of Genghis Khan.

The thought lifted him for an instant, enough to raise his hand and drop it. At his back, the Mongol tumans began the journey of five thousand miles that would take them home at last.

EPILOGUE

Xuan looked out of the windows in a long cloister as he walked. Each one revealed a view of Hangzhou, with the river leading out into the bay. He had been moved often since coming into Sung lands, as if they could not think what to do with him. On rare occasions, he was even allowed to sail on the river, and he saw his wives and children twice a year, in strained meetings, with Sung officials watching on all sides.

The cloister ran along the spine of yet another official building. Xuan amused himself by timing his steps so that his left foot hit the stone at the centre of each pool of sunlight. He did not expect great news from the summons. Over the years, he had realised the Sung officials delighted in demonstrating their power over him. For too many times to count, his presence had been demanded in some private office, only to find the official had no connection with the court. On two occasions, the men involved had brought their mistresses or children to observe as they fussed with permissions and the allocation of his small income. The meeting itself was irrelevant. They had just wanted to parade the Chin emperor, the Son of Heaven himself, for their wide-eyed dependents.

Xuan was surprised when the small group of officials did not stop at the usual branching corridors. The apartments of more important men lay beyond, and Xuan controlled the first stirring of excitement as they went further and further still. More than one door was open, as dedicated scholars and bureaucrats laboured inside, peering out at the footsteps they heard. Xuan took a grip on his hopes. They had been dashed too many times to expect his letters to have been answered at last, though he still wrote every day.

Despite his forced calm, he felt his heart beat faster as the bowing servants brought him to the door of the man who administered the examinations for almost all the posts in Hangzhou. Sung Kim had taken the name of the royal house as his own, though Xuan suspected he had been born a commoner. As one who controlled the funds Xuan was given to maintain his small household, Sung Kim had received many of his letters over the years. Not a single one had been answered.

The servants announced him and then stood back with their heads bowed. Xuan walked into the room, pleasantly surprised to see how it opened up before him. The administrator lived in luxury, amidst sculpture and art of better than average taste. Xuan smiled to himself at the thought of complimenting Sung Kim. In such a way, he could force the odious little man to make him a present of whatever he admired, but it was just a spiteful thought. His upbringing would not allow him to be rude, despite his circumstances.

While other servants trotted away to announce his arrival, Xuan wandered from one painting to another, taking care not to linger too long on each. Time was something he had in abundance and he knew Sung Kim would make him wait.

To his intense surprise, Sung Kim himself came out of the

426

inner rooms almost immediately. Xuan inclined his head and accepted an equally brief bow from the other man. He endured the polite observances with his usual restraint, showing no sign of his mounting impatience.

At last, he was guided into the inner rooms and tea was brought for him. Xuan settled himself comfortably, waiting.

'I have extraordinary news, Son of Heaven,' Sung Kim began. He was a very old man, with white hair and wrinkled skin, but his own excitement was visible. Xuan raised an eyebrow as if his heart did not beat harder with every moment. It was all he could do to remain silent.

'The Mongol khan is dead, Son of Heaven,' Sung Kim went on.

Xuan smiled, then chuckled, confounding the older man. 'Is that all?' he said bitterly.

'I thought . . . I must offer my apologies, Son of Heaven. I thought the news would bring you great joy. Does it not signal the end of your time of exile?' Sung Kim shook his head in confusion and tried again. 'Your enemy is dead, your majesty. The khan has fallen.'

'I meant no offence, Sung Kim. I have outlived two Mongol khans and that is indeed welcome news.'

'Then . . . I do not understand. Does it not fill your heart with happiness?'

Xuan sipped the tea, which was excellent.

'You do not know them as I do,' he said. 'They will not mourn the khan. Instead, they will raise one of his sons and they will look for new enemies. One day, Sung Kim, they will come here, to this city. Perhaps I will still be a prisoner here when that time comes. Perhaps I will stare down from these very corridors as they bring their armies to the city walls.'

'Please, Son of Heaven. You are the guest of the emperor, never a prisoner. You must not say such things.'

Xuan grimaced and set his cup down gently.

'A guest can walk away when he pleases. A guest can ride without guards. Let us be honest with one another, Sung Kim.'

'I am sorry, your majesty. I had hoped to bring you joy, not sadness.'

'Be assured, you have done both today. Now, unless you wish to discuss my written requests, I will return to my rooms.'

The administrator bowed his head. 'I cannot grant your desire to see your soldiers, Son of Heaven. Such things are far beyond my small powers.'

Xuan rose from his seat. 'Very well, but when the new khan comes, they will be needed, strong and fit. You will need *every* man then, I think.'

It was Sung Kim's turn to smile. The city of Hangzhou was ancient and powerful. It lay far from the border with the old Chin lands. The idea of an army ever coming close enough to cause concern was amusing.

HISTORICAL NOTE

The third son of Genghis was great khan for just twelve years, from AD 1229 to 1241. At a time when the Mongols were sweeping west into Europe, Ogedai's death would be one of the crucial turning points of history. Western Europe could not have stood against them. The medieval castles there were no more daunting than walled Chin cities, and in the field, the Mongol style of fast-striking tactical warfare would have been practically unstoppable. It is no exaggeration to say the future of the West changed when Ogedai's heart failed.

We know Ogedai was still young and died only fourteen years after his father. We do *not* know why he built Karakorum – the son of a khan who not only despised cities, but who had spent his entire life demonstrating how weak a defence they actually were. Yet Ogedai built a city as the throne of empire. Contemporary descriptions of it do survive – for example the words of a Christian friar, William of Rubruk. The silver tree

429

was historical fact, as was it having shamanist temples, Islamic mosques and at least one Nestorian Christian church.

It is hard to explain why Ogedai would build such a thing at all. One explanation that fits the facts is that he was a little like Cecil Rhodes, a man whose heart pain began as young as sixteen. Before a heart attack finally killed Rhodes at forty-eight, he had built an empire for himself in Africa: a man driven to leave a mark, always knowing that he had little time to do it. Ogedai may well have had the same sense of urgency.

The second question is why he might build a city so influenced by those of the Chin – cities he had often seen burn. There, the influence of Yao Shu can be seen. Though Yao Shu was a real adviser to Ogedai, the character I have rendered is in fact an amalgam of two Chinese Buddhists from the period. I have not yet finished his tale. Worried by the khan's heavy drinking, Yao Shu showed Ogedai how wine corroded an iron bottle. It is also true that Ogedai agreed to halve the number of wine cups he drank each day, only to have cups made that were twice the size. Buddhist advisers brought a sense of Chinese civilisation to the Mongol court, subtly influencing each of the khans. As a result, cities would one day open their gates to Kublai as they never would have to his grandfather.

The Three Games of Men (Naadam) in Mongolia are wrestling, archery and horse racing. The Naadam festival is indeed much older than the time of Genghis, though in previous centuries it was also a chance for tribes to horse-trade, mix bloodlines, gamble and be told the future in divinations. The modern Naadam festival has women taking part in archery and the races, though not wrestling, which is still the men's sole preserve. The description of the archery wall is accurate. Shots are taken from around a hundred paces and archers compete in groups of ten, the smallest unit of Genghis' army. Each archer has four arrows, and rather than judge individual shots, they must hit a certain number of targets to succeed. It is interesting that the archery tradition is one of teams, bearing in mind the martial nature of the sport and the vital role it played in the armies of Genghis Khan.

The horse races of the festival, which take place over three days, are all endurance races. In comparison to the West, endurance was the quality that made the khan's armies mobile and again it is interesting to see how that has remained the pre-eminent quality of equine greatness, rather than a burst of speed from a horse bred and built like a greyhound.

I have taken a small liberty with history in including a foot race. There's no record of it, but it would have been a possibility. I have no doubt other events have come and gone before the current form, just as the modern Olympics used to include a tug-of-war competition from 1900 to 1920, won twice by Britain.

It is sometimes believed that Genghis left a will. If such a document ever existed, it has not survived. If it was an oral will, we do not know if it was given at the point of death, or long before. Some versions of history have Genghis dying almost instantly, while others have him lingering for days after a fall or a wound, where he could easily have arranged his own legacy. Either way, it is generally accepted that it was Genghis Khan's desire to have Chagatai inherit a vast khanate, while Tolui received the Mongol homeland. As the official heir, Ogedai inherited the northern Chin territories and whatever else he could win for himself. I have put that distribution in Ogedai's hands, in part because it would have been his final choice, no matter what his father intended. If Ogedai had executed Chagatai then, the bloodlines of that part of the world would have been very different, down to the present day.

Instead, Chagatai Khan died just a few months after Ogedai in 1242. The exact manner of his death is unknown, though the incredibly fortuitous timing allowed me to write and indeed suspect that he was killed.

The earliest written formula for gunpowder is Chinese, from around 1044. It was certainly used in siege warfare during the period of Ogedai's khanate. Hand-held cannon of the sort I have described have been found dating back to Kublai Khan's period. One of the earliest recorded uses was by the Mongols in the Middle East in 1260, but they certainly went back further than that.

They were the cutting edge of military technology for the period, effectively a hugely powerful hand weapon that fired stones or even a metal ball. Iron vessels filled with gunpowder and lit with a fuse would have made effective shrapnel grenades. We do know the Mongols encountered them first against the Chin and Sung – and were quick to adopt such terrifying weapons. In fact, it was the vast territory covered by Mongol armies that led to the proliferation of such weapons across the land mass.

That said, the formula for Chinese gunpowder was poor in saltpetre, so lacked some of the explosive punch we associate with the material. A rush of flame would have been more common, with batches of the mixture varying enormously between makers, regions and periods.

The extraordinary incident that led to the death of Tolui is from *The Secret History of the Mongols*. On his only campaign in northern China, Ogedai fell ill and 'lost [the use of] mouth and tongue' – a massive stroke, or perhaps grand mal epilepsy.

Mongol shamans and soothsayers made divinations, assuming that the spirits of the Chin were attacking the khan. They asked to be shown the correct sacrifice and, in response, Ogedai spasmed and suffered violent cramps. Using that response, they asked if a kinsman was needed. Ogedai then came round and drank water, asking to be told what had happened.

Prince Tolui did not have to be asked. The man who was father to Kublai and Mongke, both of whom would be khans, willingly gave his life to save his brother.

On the subject of slaughtering horses, I took the opportunity to speak to slaughtermen who had killed many hundreds of elderly horses over the years. In the preparation of kosher or halal meat, the animal needs to remain alive for the heart to pump out the blood. They begin by cutting the throat. The man I spoke to wanted a much faster kill, so he preferred an initial thrust to the heart, then drew the blade across the throat. Between 6 and 10 per cent of a horse's bodyweight will be blood. It's a rough estimate, but in a Mongolian pony, that would be around forty pints of blood.

As the *Secret History* records, Tolui took poison rather than die by the blade, but I changed his ending. The bloody sacrifice of animals was part of the attempt to save Ogedai and the two events seemed to fit together. His son Mongke was certainly present, though no exchange is recorded between them.

A quick note on the subject of distances: By Ogedai's time, a network of way stations had been set up wherever Mongol influence extended. Set 25 miles apart on major roads, they were well furnished. With regular changes of horses, an urgent message could be taken 100 miles in a day, if necessary by the same man. The riders wore belts of bells, so the way stations could hear them coming and have water, food and a fresh mount waiting. A thousand miles in ten days was not just possible, but commonplace. Such lines of communication made the armies of the khans modern in a sense that no other force of the century could manage.

The shaman Mohrol is fictional, though of course the khan would have had diviners and shamans. In Mongolia, it remains the case that an extra finger will mean a child is 'chosen' to be a shaman. They do not hunt or fish and are supported by the tribes to be magic- and medicine-workers as well as keepers of history and tradition. They are men of power still.

The ancient Buddhas of Bamiyan in Afghanistan did exist. One was around 114 feet high, the other 165 feet. They were dynamited by the Islamic Taliban in 2001. There are still legends of a third, 'sleeping Buddha' in the hills there.

Tsubodai's campaign against the west lasted from around 1232 to 1241. Over that time, he encountered Russians, Bulgars and Hungarian Magyars, took Buda and Pest, attacked Poland and modern-day Serbia, and sent scouts as far as northern Italy. In just one winter, over a period of two months, his tumans took twelve walled Russian cities. They had learned the use of catapults, ballistae, even a form of wall-smashing trebuchet in their wars against northern China. Russia had nothing capable of stopping the war machine of the Mongols.

It is true that Tsubodai preferred to campaign in winter and used the frozen rivers as a network of roads through the cities. Like Genghis before him, he and his generals were ruthless with fallen enemies, slaughtering vast populations. His one worry seems to have been the wide battlefront making it easy to flank or encircle his tumans. Time and again, he sent tumans out in sweeps into Poland, Hungary or Bulgaria to clear the way of possible enemies.

The legendary French Knights Templar said at the time that there was no army between Tsubodai and France that could stop him. Yet even the death of Ogedai might not have halted Tsubodai, had he not had the princes of the nation with him. Batu, Jochi's son, was there, as was Guyuk, Ogedai's son. Ogedai's grandson Kaidu was also present. It was he who raided into Poland with Baidur and fought the extraordinary battle of Liegnitz, preventing the Polish armies flanking the main attack against Hungary. I have not used Kaidu as a character here, for fear of the 'Russian novel problem', where every page brings new characters until the reader loses track. I did include Mongke in the campaign – he was there for most of it, including Kiev. Kublai was not present as one of the princes. He remained in Karakorum, studying Buddhism and establishing the Chinese influence that would dominate his adult life.

Jebe too was absent for that campaign, though I have kept him as a minor character. The *Secret History* does not tell his ending, unfortunately. As with Kachiun and Khasar, a once great leader simply slipped from the pages of history and was lost. Early death was common in those days, of course, and they almost certainly met their end through disease or injury, a death so ordinary as to be ignored by chroniclers.

Temuge did make a final, rash attempt to become khan after the death of Ogedai. It was unsuccessful and he was executed.

Interestingly, Sorhatani *was* given her husband's rights and titles on his death. In that one decision, she instantly became the most powerful woman in the khanate – and in the world at that time. Three of her four sons would become khan through her influence and training. She supported Ogedai as khan and was consulted by him as the empire grew and became established. The one time she refused his wishes was when he offered to marry her to his son, Guyuk. She turned the offer down, preferring to concentrate her considerable energies on her sons. History confirms her wisdom in that matter.

When Tsubodai's tumans entered Hungary over the Carpathian mountains, he faced the armies of the Hungarian King Bela IV. That monarch had accepted 200,000 Cuman refugees from Russia, a Turkic people similar to the Mongols in many ways. In exchange for their conversion to Christianity, they were given a brief sanctuary. Their leader Köten was baptised and his daughter married King Bela's son to seal the agreement. In exchange, King Bela was able to field an army of nomadic horsemen in addition to his own forces. He also expected help from the Holy Roman Emperor, Frederick II, who was king of what is now Germany, Italy, Sicily, Cyprus and Jerusalem, or perhaps Pope Gregory IX. However, they were locked in their own struggle for power, with the Pope excommunicating Frederick II and even declaring him the Antichrist. As a result, the king of Hungary was left to resist the Mongol invasion almost without support. He did have forces from Archduke Frederick of Austria, but they withdrew after the death of Köten in a riot. The Cumans also left.

It is true that King Bela sent bloody swords throughout his kingdom to raise the people. There is a record of Batu's missive to the king, demanding that the Russian Cumans and their leader Köten be handed over. Batu's message was stark and simple: 'Word has come to me that you have taken the Cumans, our servants, under your protection. Cease harbouring them, or you will make of me an enemy because of them. They, who have no houses and dwell in tents, will find it easy to escape. But you who dwell in houses within towns – how can you escape me?'

It is interesting to note that the demand was sent in Batu's name. As a senior prince and son to Jochi, the first-born of Genghis, he was in nominal command of the Golden Horde, as they were known. Yet it was Tsubodai who led them strategically and tactically. It was a complex relationship and it came to a head when news of Ogedai's death finally reached them.

Budapest is around four and a half thousand miles west of Karakorum in the same land mass. Tsubodai's extraordinary campaign took the Mongol tumans right across Kazakhstan, Russia to Moscow and Kiev, Romania, Hungary, Poland, Lithuania, Eastern Prussia and Croatia. They were knocking on the door of Austria when Ogedai died. It was in fact the French King Louis IX who fixed a confusing name for the Mongols in European minds. As he prepared his armies to march, he told his wife that his soldiers would send the Tartars to hell, or the Tartars would send them to heaven. He deliberately punned on the Latin word for hell, 'Tartarus', and the erroneous name 'Tartar' stuck for centuries as a result.

I have omitted a detailed description of the battle of Liegnitz, which took place as the climax of Baidur's sweep through Poland. It is the nature of such a sweep that there are many battles, against varied opponents, but there is a limit to how many can be squeezed into a novel, even one about the Mongols. In history, Liegnitz is one of the few really well-known Mongol battles – omitting it is the equivalent of writing about Nelson without mentioning the Nile. For the sake of the plot flow, however, I think it was the right decision. At Liegnitz, Baidur used the feigned retreat, but he added the innovation of tar barrels that sent white smoke across the battlefield. This simple device prevented one half of a Polish army seeing what was happening to the other half. It could easily have been the climax of this book, but the other well-known battle is Sajo river and that was Tsubodai's triumph.

Tsubodai's final recorded battle combined not only a night attack and flanking manoeuvre, not only the masterful use of terrain in the way he made the river work for him, but also the now ancient trick of leaving a path for the enemy to escape, only to fall on him as he does. Tsubodai led three tumans across a ford to the south of the encamped Hungarian armies, sending Batu against the left flank at dawn, while the rest galloped further to hit the Hungarian rear. King Bela was forced to take refuge in his night camp, while the Mongols caused chaos with firecrackers, burning tar in barrels and shooting random arrows. They had gone from the prey to the hunter and made the most of it.

In the midst of the chaos, King Bela's men saw a ridge of ground running west that lay out of sight of the Mongols. He tested the escape route by sending out a small number, watching as they rode to safety. As the day wore on, the king tried to send his entire army from the camp. In their panic, they lost formation and were strung out over miles. It was at that point that Tsubodai's men attacked the column. He had scouted the ground. He knew the ridge and had deliberately left the route open to trap them. Depending on the source, the Mongol tumans slaughtered 40–65,000 of the Hungarian army, ending it as an entity for a generation or more. King Bela escaped the slaughter and fled to Austria. When the Mongols left, he went on to rebuild Hungary from ruins. He is still honoured as one of Hungary's great kings, despite his disastrous encounter with Tsubodai.

In many ways, it was a fitting end to Tsubodai's military career, though of course he did not see it like that. Hungary was in ruins when the news came of Ogedai's death and everything changed.

The brilliant tactical manoeuvres of Liegnitz and the Sajo river were rendered void by the Mongol withdrawal. They are rarely taught outside military schools, in part because they did not lead on to conquest. Politics intruded on Tsubodai's ambitions. If it had not, all history would have changed. There are not many moments in history when the death of a single man changed the entire world. Ogedai's death was one such moment. If he had lived, there would have been no Elizabethan age, no British Empire, no Renaissance, perhaps no Industrial Revolution. In such circumstances, this book could very well have been written in Mongolian or Chinese.